Amanda Cadabra
AND THE RISE OF SUNKEN MADLEY

HOLLY BELL

Other titles by Holly Bell

Amanda Cadabra and The Hidey-Hole Truth
(The Amanda Cadabra Cozy Mysteries Book 1)

Amanda Cadabra and The Cellar of Secrets
(The Amanda Cadabra Cozy Mysteries Book 2)

Amanda Cadabra and The Flawless Plan
(The Amanda Cadabra Cozy Mysteries Book 3)

Other books published by Heypressto

50 Feel-better Films
50 Feel-better Songs: from Film and TV
25 Feel-better Free Downloads

Copyright © Heypressto (2019). All rights reserved.

www.amandacadabra.com

This book is a work of fiction. Any references to real events, people or places are used fictitiously. Other names, characters, places and incidents are products of the author's imagination. Any resemblance to actual events, places or people, living or dead, is entirely coincidental.

www.heypressto.com

Cover art by Daniel Becerril Ureña
Cover concept by Chartreuse at Heypressto

Chartreuse@heypressto.com
HollyBell@amandacadabra.com
Twitter: @holly_b_author

Sign up an stay in touch

Amanda Cadabra
AND THE RISE OF SUNKEN MADLEY

HOLLY BELL

To Alwyn and Philippa

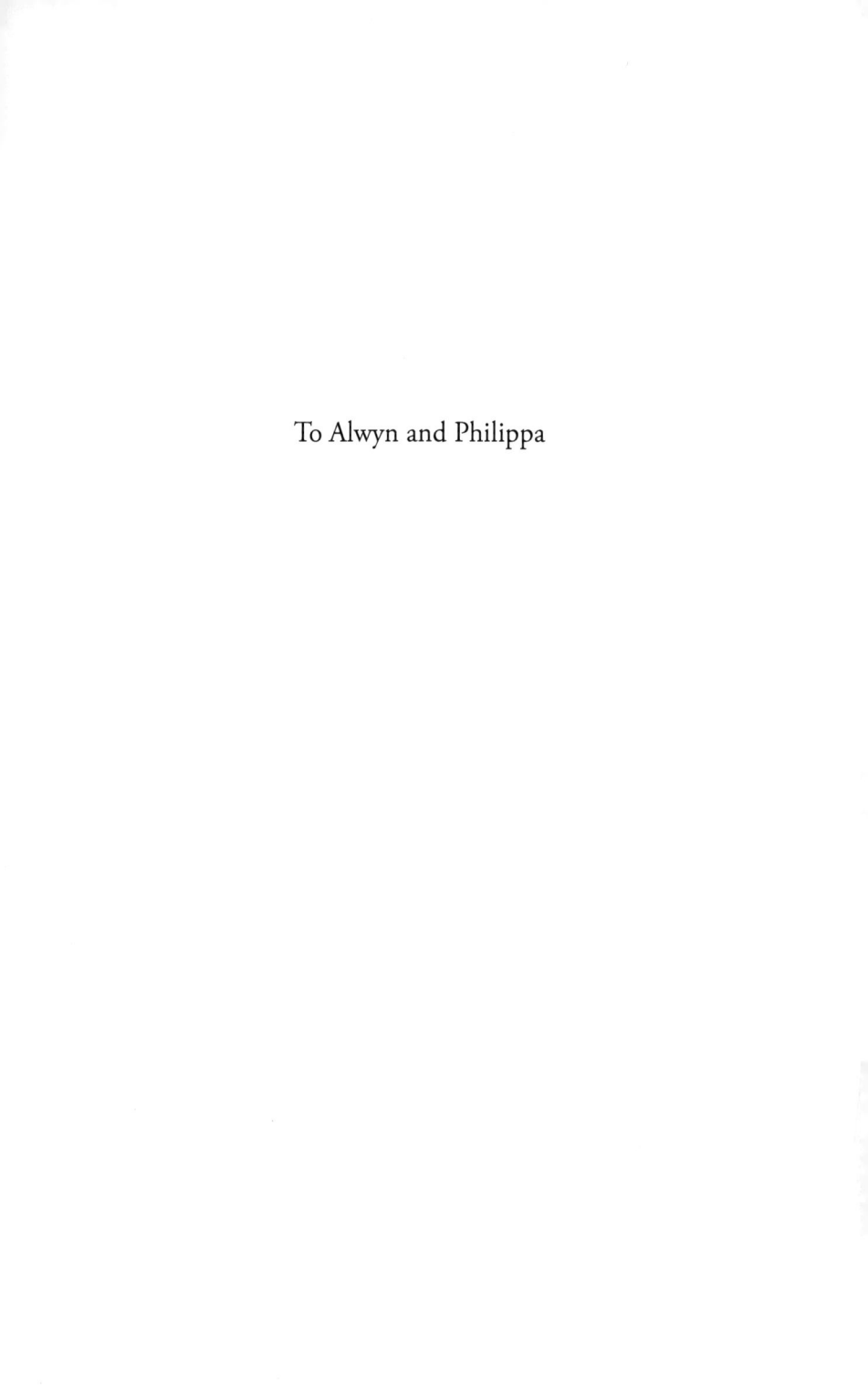

A new day,

a fresh try,

one more start,

and perhaps a bit of magic

waiting somewhere behind the morning.

– J B Priestley

CONTENTS

Map of Sunken Madley & Lost Madley 8
Plan of The Grange 9
Map of Cornwall and S England 10
Introduction 12
Chapter 1 13
Into the Globe
Chapter 2 20
The Big Day is Announced
Chapter 3 28
Inspector Trelawney's Mission
Chapter 4 34
Getting Personal
Chapter 5 41
Spell-power, and Amanda's Wish
Chapter 6 45
Old Times, New Information
Chapter 7 51
Mrs Uberhausfest
Chapter 8 59
The Date is Set
Chapter 9 67
Inertia
Chapter 10 73
Reuters - New Man in the Village
Chapter 11 80
John Bailey-Farrell
Chapter 12 87
The New Ship Inn
Chapter 13 94
The Handover
Chapter 14 104
On the Road to St Austell

Chapter 15 111
Into the Grimoires
Chapter 16 117
Howdunnit
Chapter 17 121
Accessory
Chapter 18 125
A First for Thomas
Chapter 19 129
Why
Chapter 20 134
Thomas in Search of Normal
Chapter 21 139
The Secret of the Trelawneys
Chapter 22 144
The Piano, and The Florist
Chapter 23 *151*
Pipkin Acres
Chapter 24 *159*
The Knitting Circle
Chapter 25 *165*
The Grange
Chapter 26 172
Starburst
Chapter 27 177
Arrivals
Chapter 28 182
Positions
Chapter 29 187
Intangibles
Chapter 30 195
Amanda Receives Attention

Chapter 31	200	*Chapter 47*	306
Thomas Decides		**Case Closing**	
Chapter 32	206	*Chapter 48*	313
The French Connection		**The Ball**	
Chapter 33	211	*Chapter 49*	321
Naomi		**After the Ball**	
Chapter 34	217	*Chapter 50*	328
POAPs		**The Hardest Task**	
Chapter 35	224	*Chapter 51*	335
Miss de Havillande, and Mercury		**Joan and Jim**	
		Chapter 52	340
Chapter 36	233	**An Afternoon Out**	
Lunch, Poison, and Hope		*Chapter 53*	348
Chapter 37	240	**Doubt, and a Chance for Thomas**	
French Conversation, and Miss Armstrong-Witworth		*Chapter 54*	353
		Marram	
Chapter 38	247	*Chapter 55*	359
The Council of Four		**I Am Viola**	
Chapter 39	254	*Chapter 56*	365
Amanda's Last Shot		**Revelations**	
Chapter 40	260	*Chapter 57*	374
They Are Coming		**Naming The Day**	
Chapter 41	269	*Chapter 58*	381
Into Flamgoyne		**A Walk in the Orchard**	
Chapter 42	277	*Chapter 59*	386
The Defence of Sunken Madley		**Nora's Story, and New Questions**	
Chapter 43	281		
Their Finest Hour		*Author's Note*	390
Chapter 44	288	*About the Author*	391
Man Down		*Acknowledgements*	391
		About the Language	393
Chapter 45	295	*Questions for Reading Clubs*	393
Song of the Sea		*Glossary of British English*	394
Chapter 46	300	*Accents and Wicc'Yeth*	401
Claire		*The Last Word ... For Now*	401

The Village of Sunken Madley

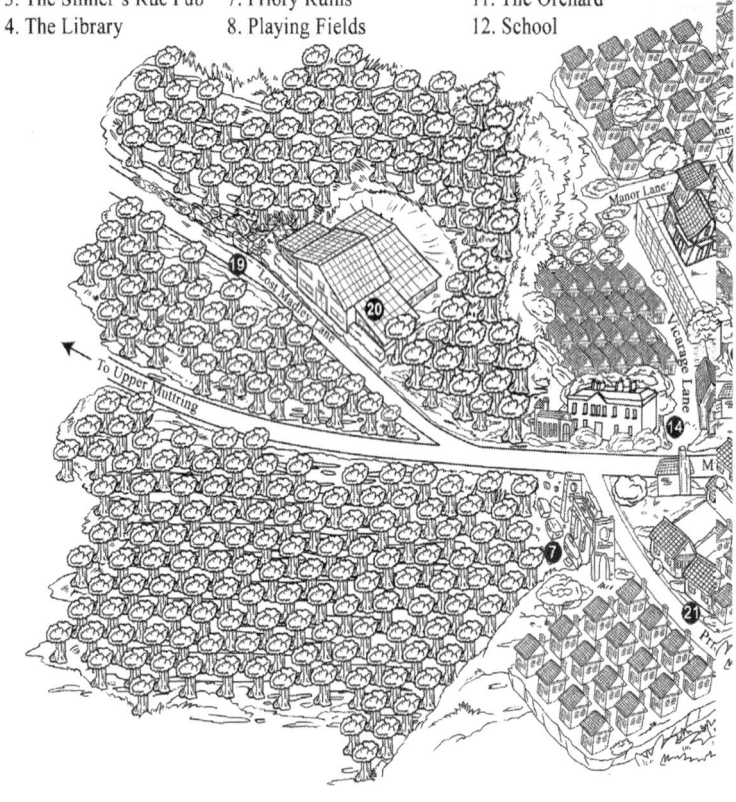

KEY
1. Amanda's House
2. Sunken Madley Manor
3. The Sinner's Rue Pub
4. The Library
5. St Ursula-without-Barnet
6. Medical Centre
7. Priory Ruins
8. Playing Fields
9. The Snout and Trough Pub
10. Post Office/Corner Shop
11. The Orchard
12. School

AND LOST MADLEY

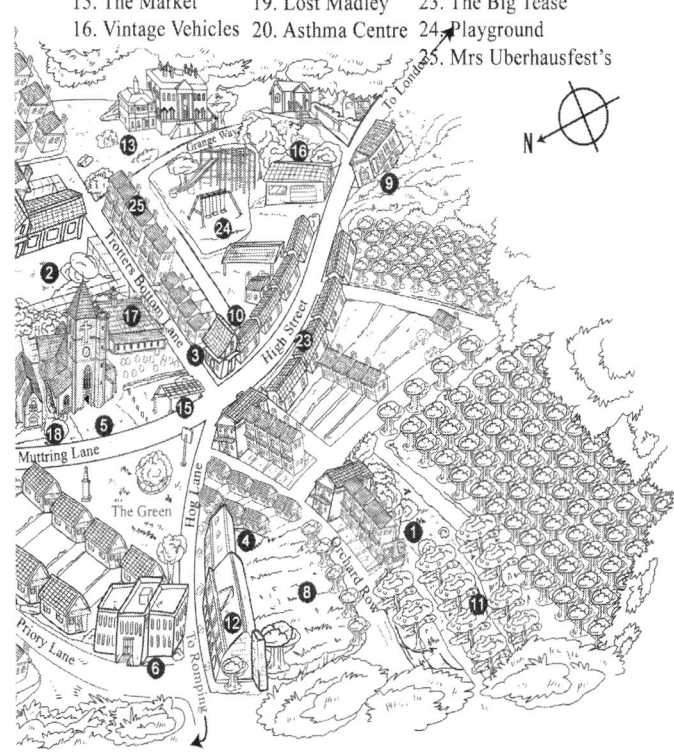

13. The Grange
14. The Elms
15. The Market
16. Vintage Vehicles
17. Church Hall
18. The Rectory
19. Lost Madley
20. Asthma Centre
21. Reisers' House
22. Salon
23. The Big Tease
24. Playground
25. Mrs Uberhausfest's

PLAN of THE GRANGE

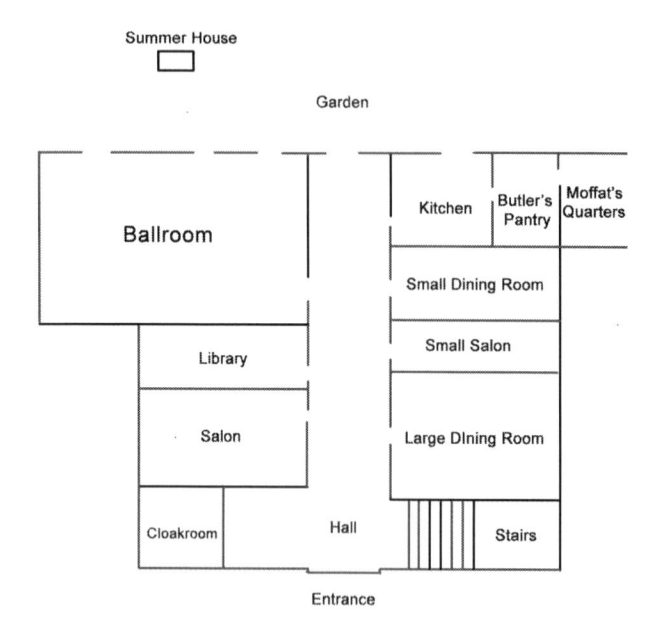

Summer House

Garden

Ballroom		Kitchen	Butler's Pantry	Moffat's Quarters
		Small Dining Room		
	Library	Small Salon		
	Salon	Large Dining Room		
Cloakroom	Hall	Stairs		

Entrance

Grange Way, Sunken Madley

10

KEY

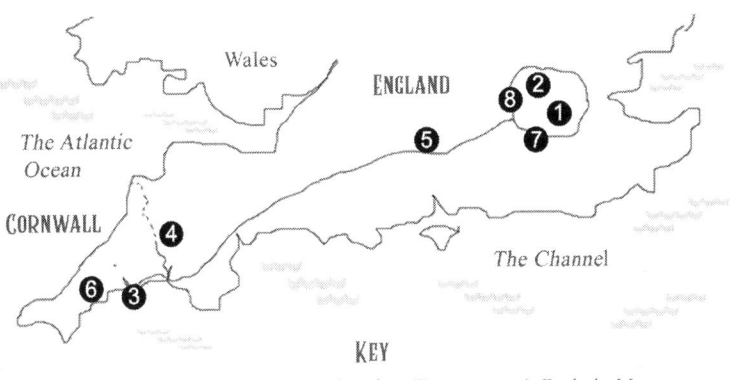

1. London
2. Sunken Madley
3. Parhayle
4. The River Tamar
 & the border
5. M3 Highway
6. Bodmin Moor
7. M25 Orbital Road
8. Heathrow Airport

Map of Cornwall and The South of England

Introduction

Please note that to enhance the reader's experience of Amanda's world, this British-set story, by a British author, uses British English spelling, vocabulary, grammar and usage, and includes local and foreign accents, dialects and a magical language that vary from different versions of English as it is written and spoken in other parts of our wonderful, diverse world.

For your reading pleasure, there is a glossary of British English usage and vocabulary at the end of the book, followed by a note about accents and the magical language, Wicc'yeth.

Chapter 1

INTO THE GLOBE

'It will all be over very quickly. One way or another,' said Aunt Amelia. She stared intently into the glass sphere on the round, lace-covered table.

'Very quickly?' asked Amanda Cadabra, pushing back her mouse-brown hair and glancing up from following the goldfish. Unlike her aunt, it was pretty much all the ball ever showed her.

'An hour only, perhaps.'

'And the villagers? Everyone will see it. If the magical world is supposed to be so secret and the entire Flamgoyne witch-clan descends upon Sunken Madley with fire, brimstone and hurricane, that is going to raise more than a few eyebrows on a whole lot of Normals, assuming that any survive.'

Amelia frowned into the globe 'The village will empty.'

Amanda looked at her in wonderment. 'How come?'

Her aunt shook her head, 'That is not shown to me …. The glass is clouding … I'm sorry, Ammy, that's all.'

'I'll have an hour to somehow repel them — without striking a single blow — but the village will empty?'

'Yes.'

'And I will have to defend it alone? — But no, you said I'd have help.'

'That's what it showed.'

'So just me and my ... helpers ... whoever they will be.' Amanda pondered, doubtfully.

'Rrrrrr,' interjected Tempest, in a marked manner.

'Principal among whom will be Tempest, of course, 'she added for the benefit of the thick, grey ball of grumpy cat, curled up in the most comfortable chair in the room.

Amanda's familiar preened himself.

Not that I'm getting involved, he thought. This is a test for my human. But I'll lend a paw if absolutely necessary. Dear me. The very idea is exhausting. How tiring this species is.

He shut his eyes and went to sleep.

* * * * *

Amanda Cadabra stared at the sky. The thunderous swirl of cloud was racing towards her village of Sunken Madley. She stood at its heart, before the green, opposite The Sinner's Rue, on the old crossroads. She stood, feet planted apart, wand pointing at the ground, ready. Tempest sat by her side.

'How?' she wondered. 'I'm just a furniture restorer. I have asthma and an annoying cat. I should be in my workshop, polishing Mrs Kemp's aunt's commode. How in the world did I come to this ...?'

* * * * *

It was a recurring dream, but the situation was imminent, and the question was both real and pressing. The answer might have been said, and was by Granny, to be that Amanda had brought it on herself.

'If only,' Senara Cadabra had lamented, 'you had not cast that spell. The very one your Aunt Amelia warned you not to perform, if you didn't want to bring the Flamgoynes down upon the village.'

On the other hand, Grandpa, in his light Cornish accent, said that she had had no option.

'When the crunch came, it was a choice between saving herself and the inspector, or sending up a beacon that Sunken Madley was the epicentre of powerful magical activity.'

Former Chief Inspector Hogarth of the Devon and Cornwall police saw it another way: an opportunity to solve a cold case that was over 30 years old.

Aunt Amelia, Amanda's confidante and would-be divination tutor since she was nine years old, not only refrained from repeating I-told-you-so but was both sympathetic and constructive.

It was January, one of their regular Tuesday dinners together. Leaving the tea brewing in the kitchen, Amelia Reading, in deep red velvet splendour, sailed into her sitting room, her long dress wafting behind her, and seated herself.

'Let's see if the crystal will tell us more about the help that will come to you.' Amanda, sitting opposite, could only see, reflected in the glass surface, Amelia's bright brown eyes in a face framed by a chestnut bob. Apart from that, all she ever got was goldfish or a plastic Paris in a snowstorm. This had been the case for more than 20 years. Until now.

Suddenly, Amanda was electrified. 'Wait!' she cried excitedly.

'What?'

'Aunt Amelia. I see something!'

'What, Ammy? What do you see?'

'It's ... a big ... banjo? .... No! Cello. It's a big cello ... it's getting smaller ... a violin? No. Oh.' Her enthusiasm deadened. Amanda looked at Amelia questioningly. 'A viola?'

Her aunt chuckled. 'Ah, well that does happen in divination if you ask the same question twice or more. You get a joke or gibberish. At least this wasn't the latter.'

'The message is the same as the one I got from our conversation about having help to defend the village: find Viola. Except it's not vee-*oh*--la, it's *Vie*-oh-la.'

'It shows you're on the right track, and what a breakthrough for your divination, sweetie!'

Amanda was cheered.

'You're right, Aunt, on both counts. OK. So, what do we know about Viola? She was a friend of Granny's. They met during the war. She was living here back then and told Granny, or "Juliet", as you called her in your story, that she and Grandpa, "Romeo", could have a peaceful life here. Yes? There wasn't any more than that, was there?'

'I'm afraid not.'

'So, at least, the crystal ball confirms that this Viola is still alive. Unless ... she's not a ghost, is she?'

'Was the cello — viola — clear or transparent?'

'Perfectly clear,' answered Amanda.

'Alive then, I'd say.'

'She must be old then .... I've thought of three people that she could be — Ah, the tea must be brewed by now. Shall I go and get it?'

'Oh, use magic to bring it in. It's perfectly all right here,' Amelia assured her. 'I've got this place as psychically secure as Fort Knox.'

Amanda pulled a certain Ikea pencil out of her orange

16

woollen jacket pocket, flipped up the end and extracted a tiny slim wooden shaft topped with a citrine. She leaned across so that she could see into the kitchen, pointed the wand and said,

'*Aereval.*' The tea tray, bearing its load of Devon rose-patterned Wedgwood pot, cups, and bowls containing milk and sugar, two silver spoons and a plate of gingernut biscuits, rose from the worktop beside the kettle.

'*Cumdez,*' instructed Amanda. It glided through the air, along the passage to the sitting room and hovered.

'*Sedaasig.*' The tray lowered itself gently onto the table beside them. Amanda would not usually have bothered with a wand, but there was hot liquid involved, so extra control was needed. Hopeless though she was at divination, this was her special, and exceedingly rare, magical talent: a Cadabra family trait inherited from her grandfather. It enabled her, in spite of asthma that was all too easily agitated by physical exertion, to carry on the family business of furniture restoration, with all of its strenuous activity. Of course, any spell-working had to be conducted out of sight of Normals.

'You were saying, dear,' Amelia reminded her, adding sugar lumps to the teacups. 'Three possibles.'

'Yes,' replied Amanda. '*Mecsge,*' she added. The spoons began stirring. 'There's Mrs Uberhausfest, who distinctly told me that she and Granny had been friends for over 50 years — and you know how fond Granny is of her, invoking her whenever she talks of how, "we both did our bit in the War".' And with her line of work, if anyone could organise a Home Guard, *she* could!'

'And the other two?' enquired Amelia.

'*Sessiblin,*' said Amanda. The spoons stopped stirring. 'The ladies who live at The Grange. Miss Armstrong-Witworth — the one who worked as field agent for the government many years ago, I told you? But I gather she always operated alone, so not an organiser, I'd say — well, she and Granny never seemed very close at all, so, out of the two of them, I'd plump for Miss de Havillande. Both she and Granny are strong-minded, outspoken, *definitely* organisers, and with *Views* on every subject. In fact, I'd often thought they could have been two peas in a pod!'

Amelia laughed. 'I know what you mean.'

'Although,' remarked Amanda suddenly, then stopped to think.

'Yes?' encouraged her aunt.

'Well, what if ... Viola isn't a woman, at all?'

'I think I see where you're going with this, but carry on.'

'Well. Viola isn't from Shakespeare's *Romeo and Juliet*, is she? She's from *Twelfth Night*. She's the sister, cast up on an enemy shore, who, believing her brother to be drowned, takes on the disguise of man and gets a job working for the local count. So what if Viola is a sort of code name, but for a man?'

'Or a woman pretending to be a man?' Amelia hazarded.

'Possibly, but I don't think you could live in Sunken Madley and carry off a disguise like that for the better part of a century.'

'True. What men would be eligible for the role of Viola, then?'

'Well ... old Mr Jackson, but he retired to Eastbourne to live with his son, so I don't think it can be him.'

'Someone at Pipkin Acres Residential Home?' suggested Amelia.

'Possibly .... But ... well ... what about Moffat?'

'The Grange ladies' butler?'

'He's far more than the butler,' Amanda pointed out. 'He's pretty much run the house and estate for them all these years, and no one knows how old he is.'

'That gives you four candidates then: Mrs Uberhausfest, Cynthia de Havillande, Gwendolen Armstrong-Witworth and, er — does anyone know his first name? — Moffat.'

'Yes. And, I gather, Viola will be the means of assembling the rest of the people who will help on the day that the Flamgoynes attack.'

'What's your next move then, Ammy?'

'Well... what I need is a reason to visit Irma Uberhausfest. And soon.'

Fortunately, thanks to stilettos, a spanner and a piano, one was in the making.

Chapter 2

❦

THE BIG DAY IS ANNOUNCED

'They're doing a re-enactment!' announced Ruth excitedly, her brown eyes sparkling behind round lenses.

Amanda had dropped in to the Reisers' to check that the bannister she had stripped and polished was gleaming sufficiently and didn't require an additional coat of wax.

Esta Reiser's young teenage daughter had just returned from school in an unusually enthusiastic mood. She was a fan of Amanda's — whose pinned-up plait, practical for the workshop, Ruth imitated for her own long, much darker brown hair — and not just because she occasionally helped Ruth with her history homework.

'A re-enactment of the Battle of Barnet?' asked Amanda in surprise, following her and, consequently, Tempest, into the kitchen. 'They do that every year. We went, remember?'

'No. The Battle of the Common!'

'Totteridge Common?' Amanda hazarded, casting around for a local Common candidate.

'No, the Battle of Barnet Common,' explained Ruth patiently, taking a tin of salmon out of the cupboard above the work surface.

'The what? When did *that* happen?' Amanda thought she knew her local history well enough for this nugget not to have passed her by.

'Allegedly in the medieval period,' said Ruth, who was something of an expert on those centuries, 'when a local lord was trying to enclose the land and deprive the land*less* of the means to gather food, and to feed their flocks and herds.' She reached into the bread bin and pulled out a slice.

'I thought it was enclosed in the 1700s without any armed protest.'

'No, this was, well, *supposed* to have been, *much* earlier,' Ruth countered confidently, applying a tin opener to the salmon.

'Really? First I've heard of it.'

'Well, me too,' admitted Amanda's young friend, abandoning her stance, 'but Joan says, "What does it matter if it's an excuse for a party?" And there *were* disputes over common land. I expect they'll draw on those. It'll be a sort of play with a historical setting. They might even want some input from people who do actually *know* something about the period,' she ended on a hopeful note, slathering her bread with butter.

'Ah.' Amanda began to see why the prospect of commemorating an entirely apocryphal event was so engaging the attention of her teenage pal. Ruth and her new friend Kieran, the son of Amanda's loyal and able solicitor Erik, were two who did 'actually know'. Acting as consultants to the grownups for a local jamboree could not but have its appeal.

'Yes,' continued Ruth, getting back into her flow, 'and there'll be a free fair with free food, drinks, games and prizes.' She emptied half of the salmon onto her bread and put the tin down on the floor. Tempest gave her a questioning look.

'How generous,' remarked Amanda appreciatively. 'Oh, he doesn't eat out of tins.'

'Oops, pardon me, my lord,' Ruth addressed him, 'I quite forgot.'

'Who's paying for this, I wonder?'

'Oh you'll never guess!' said Ruth, bubbling over, giving a little hop, then picking up the tin and emptying the contents into a china dessert bowl.

Amanda grinned. 'Go on, tell me then.'

'Mr Gibbs! Publicity for his good deeds, especially his pet project of the Marian Gibbs Asthma Research Centre after you-know-what happened there.'

The brand new centre, only months old, was just, up the road in the village's annexe of Little Madley, or Lost Madley, as it became known, in a part of Madley Wood.

'Rrrrrl' said Tempest pointedly. Ruth, in her glee, was still standing with the bowl in her hand.

'Oh sorry, your graciousness. Here you are,' she said, putting it down before him.

'Well, that's extremely kind of him, all the same,' said Amanda.

'The free-everything is only for people who live and work in Sunken Madley. We're VIPs!'

Amanda was impressed. 'How splendid, Ruth. Will you be taking any part in the re-enactment?'

'Certainly not,' said Ruth loftily. 'I'm an historian. I do *not* perform.'

'Of course,' replied Amanda hastily. 'What was I thinking? So, when is The Big Day?'

'To be announced, but soon. Next month I think.'

Later, after a chat with Mrs Reiser, as Amanda drove home with Tempest, seated in regal pose on the back seat, she mulled over Ruth's news. Everyone from Sunken Madley would go, as guests of honour.

'"The village ... will empty",' Amanda recalled aloud Amelia's words. 'That day. *That* will be the day the Flamgoynes will come. The Big Day. In more ways than one .... And I still don't know who Viola is.'

No, marvelled Tempest, she really doesn't. Amazing that such an intellectually challenged species managed to make it so far up the food chain. But then, he expected it wasn't as obvious to the dear little thing as it was to him. Of course, it did help, being omniscient. He licked a silken paw and waited for his human to park the car and open the door for him. There were certain things she *was* good at. Like ... opening doors. Sweet, in her way.

Tempest's favourite door was, of course, to home. Home was 26 Orchard Way, Sunken Madley. The village lay thirteen miles north of The Houses of Parliament and just three to the south of the Hertfordshire county border. Officially, it was now at the edge of Greater London; however, it was formerly within the boundary of the neighbouring home county, and, in spirit, retained its rural flavour.

The cottage, along with the family business of furniture restoration, had been bequeathed to Amanda by her grandparents. Although having, what they described as, 'transitioned to the next plane of existence', they were still frequently in residence, especially on Classic Film Nights. They brought their own food.

Amanda noticed that they were usually absent, except to give her a brief word or two of encouragement, during any crisis or conundrum. This was both somewhat irritating but also a testimony to her capabilities and independence. At least, that's what *they* said.

'What I need,' said Amanda to Tempest, whom she was stroking as he lay flopped over her lap on the sofa, receiving her attentions with imperial nonchalance, 'are three openings:

an excuse to talk to Mrs Uberhausfest, a way in to interview the oldest residents of Pipkin Acres Residential Home, and … a reason to visit the Grange. Not that I don't have an open invitation, but a reason to be there long enough to talk to both ladies and Moffat. Until I get one of those … I'm stuck.'

She looked at her familiar, hoping for inspiration, but he merely turned onto his back and raised his chin. In automatic response, she began gently scratching underneath it. He purred ecstatically, stretching his paws back onto the neighbouring cushion on the sofa. It was pale gold, the colour of wheat. Wheat, thought Amanda. 'Farms.' she murmured. 'Farmers. The Cadabras are farmers, and yet they have defended their lands against the neighbouring witch-clans for hundreds of years. Well, two hundred.'

It was true. Since time immemorial, the great houses of the rival tribes of the Cardiubarns, Amanda's grandmother's family, and the Flamgoynes had glared at one another across the rough terrain of Cornwall's Bodmin Moor and the bleak waters of the Dozmary Pool that had claimed so many hapless lives. And there, to the north of both estates, marched the farmlands of the Cadabras. The Cardiubarns and the Flamgoynes, known in magical circles for unscrupulous use of their powers, had never been able to infringe on the fields and homesteads of the Cadabras, who lived by the tenet 'A Witch does not strike out.'

In the past, before it mattered, Amanda had wondered idly how they had managed to hold their own. Now that she, as the as-yet anonymous defender of her village, was to be called upon, as a Cadabra, to keep to that credo, the urgency of discovering just how they protected themselves was upon her.

'There is one thing I *can* do,' she declared. 'Grandpa, Granny!' At her call, her grandparents appeared and solidified. They were eating toast and marmalade and some oddly-coloured concoction.

'Yes, dear?' said Senara Cadabra.

'All right, *bian*?' asked Perran, who since her birth had affectionately termed Amanda his *bian*, Cornish for 'baby'.

His granddaughter was momentarily distracted from her purpose by the strange, lime-green contents of the pot they had with them.

'What on earth is that?' Amanda asked.

'Greengage jam, love,' Grandpa explained, as they settled themselves in their favourite armchairs opposite Amanda.

'I had no idea you could still get that.'

'Oh, that's one of the great things about existence on this plane. You can get anything you can think of,' Granny replied airily.

'It does need the Cornish double cream with it, though. It's a bit tart,' Grandpa remarked. 'But did you want us for anything special or did you just want company for teatime?'

'No, it's for something in particular. Grandpa, if I am to defeat the Flamgoynes — who just may have inherited their forbearers' ability to wield the weather, as well as all manner of combat spells — without so much as firing a single magical volley, then I need to know how the Cadabras have defended their land all these years.'

'Hm. Well, you know, *bian*,' Grandpa replied thoughtfully, before taking a sip of tea. 'It's best you find out these things for yourself.'

Amanda had expected this and was prepared to counter it. 'Grandpa, it's not like I can take a trip to Bodmin and knock on the Cadabras' door. First of all, you told me long ago that I must never cross the Tamar,' she said, referring to the river that divided Cornwall from Britain. 'Besides which, since you eloped with Granny back in the last century, they've washed their hands of you, haven't they? And presumably, also your descendants, in this case, me.'

'You'll have to find another way then, *bian*. Remember

what I used to tell you when you were a little 'un and your planes used to get stuck up on your cupboards? When you were practicing levitating them around your room?

'And after I'd said, "no magic in the house," tutted Granny indulgently.

'Use your resources,' Amanda repeated, robot-like.

'That's right,' said Grandpa approvingly.

'OK. So ... what connections do I have with Cornwall? Well, there's the inspector. He lives there and ... ah ... of course ... his father! I'll bet his father knows how the Cadabras did it. Even if Uncle Mike doesn't, which I'll *also* bet he does and would probably say the same as you. Yes! I'll ask the inspector.'

'Go on then,' said Grandpa encouragingly. 'Give him a call.'

Amanda felt she would have preferred some privacy, but got out her phone. It would be the first time she'd spoken to him since the New Year's Eve ball where ... well ... there'd been a moment of ... well ... anyway, never mind that, she chided herself. It would also be her first opportunity to thank him for the present he'd arranged Amelia to deliver. Because, of course, it would not have been right for them to have exchanged Christmas gifts, given the professional nature of their relationship.

The inspector had, after all, been investigating the mysterious deaths of her estranged, and singularly unpleasant, parents, their siblings and progeny and whoever else was in that minibus that went over a cliff in Cornwall, when Amanda was only three years old. She herself and her grandparents should have been on that transport too. Only, as Granny had explained to the inspector, and before that to Chief Inspector Michael Hogarth — now 'Uncle Mike' to Amanda — their little granddaughter had been too ill to travel and so the three of them had elected to stay at home.

The possible murder suspects had narrowed down, on

the one hand, to the Flamgoynes — the family of the inspector's maternal grandmother, — and, uncomfortably, on the other, to … Granny. The question was, how had Granny dunnit. An anonymous witness had said that there had been something on the road that she had swerved to avoid, but the van behind her had driven onto. Black ice. On a day that was too warm for it. It suggested magic, only Granny was 300 miles away from the crime scene at the time, in Sunken Madley. If the Flamgoynes were responsible though, how had they known that the Cardiubarns would be travelling *en masse* on that road, on that day?

There was the added complication that the occupants of the minibus had not perished as a result of the collision with the rocks below Shierdrop. Cause of death: unknown. Probate: withheld. Consequently, Amanda could not inherit the Cardiubarn estate, but as the bequest was the last thing she wanted, she didn't see this as a problem. Nevertheless, the inspector's dogged pursuit of the truth of what happened on that day kindled in her a desire to know that, at least, Granny was exonerated. Although Amanda herself was having increasing doubts on that score.

Chapter 3

∽

INSPECTOR TRELAWNEY'S MISSION

Detective Inspector Thomas Trelawney cast his hazel eyes, one final time, over his report on the performance of his station's staff, clicked on File: Save, and sent his screen into restful, if temporary, sleep. He straightened his tall, slim frame from under his desk, neatened his suit jacket on the back of his chair, and walked to the window. A red-faced goldfinch was tucking into the bird feeder hanging from the oak tree in the car park, puddled by the persistent Cornish rain. He raked a hand through his light brown hair, a mannerism of his mother's, and rolled back his white-shirt-clad shoulders.

He looked back at the hand-written notes and papers on his desk. Inspector Trelawney preferred to do his own filing, but it seemed to upset Detective Constable Nancarrow when he forgot to leave that to her. Hogarth, his former boss and mentor and now best friend, would have pointed out, in amusement, that it gave the attractive young constable an excuse to be in the sanctum: Thomas's office, in proximity to the object of her admiration.

Trelawney was blessed with excellent staff, who coped well during his regular weekend absences. The command structure was vague, but even though Hogarth had retired, it seemed that Thomas was still working for him, and *his* assignments took priority. For several Saturdays, he had been pursuing an undercover operation of sorts: attempting to identify a spy in Sunken Madley, who was keeping Miss Cadabra under surveillance, for a purpose as yet unknown. Trelawney's cover was attending ballroom-Latin dance classes, a prospect that he had, at first, regarded with a mixture of horror and bewilderment. However, it had turned out to have its advantages.

It was part of the job, but it was still an apparently social activity that stopped his well-wishers from continually telling him to 'get a life'. He now looked forward to Saturdays. He was actually getting rather adept at the various dance forms, according to his mother, who was giving him private lessons all too willingly. Besides, he had to admit that he and Miss Cadabra were a good team, and he even found himself enjoying her company. Still, it would be nice if she could go five minutes without tripping over a dead body. That last one had been a close call. On which note … his phone rang. The screen declared her name. It was a welcome sight.

'Miss Cadabra, I was just thinking of you.'

'Oh, good. Are you on a break?'

'I am. What can I do for you?'

'Are you planning to have dinner with your father between now and Saturday?'

'Er … I wasn't, but I can ask to invite myself over.'

'That would be most kind. You see, I urgently need some information that I think he may possess.'

'I see. And on what subject do you wish me to pump my revered parent?'

Amanda laughed, as he had intended she should.

'I need to know how the Cadabras have defended their land from the Cardiubarns and the Flamgoynes these past centuries, without raising so much as a wand.'

'Have you asked your grandfather?'

'Yes, and he told me to use my resources.'

'And you think my father might be just that?'

'I'm hoping,' replied Amanda wistfully.

'Then, of course, I shall ask him. Have you tried your "Uncle Mike"?'

'I'm pretty sure he'd say the same as Granny and Grandpa: use your resources to find out for yourself.'

Trelawney thought she was probably right. He'd only had one conversation with Hogarth since his former boss had returned from an impromptu visit to his sister Vera and brother-in-law Harry in Spain.

* * * * *

Fresh from a startling and hazardous experience, Trelawney, after an enthusiastic exchange of greetings, had fairly marched into his best friend's sitting room and plumped himself down in his preferred chair.

'Amanda Cadabra is a witch,' he declared.

Hogarth smiled with kindly amusement at his younger friend.

'And this is a shock to you, is it?'

'Well …,' Thomas uttered hesitantly.

'How could the granddaughter of Senara Cardiubarn and Perran Cadabra be anything else?' asked Hogarth.

'She did everything to hide it,' he half-grumbled. 'But yes, I suspected there was something odd.'

'Felt it in your policeman's boots, no doubt,' Hogarth said good-humouredly.

'Yes ... ' Thomas thought back. 'From that first time: the smell of magic. Even though, I didn't then recognise it for what it was .... That innocent look. I don't know she does it.'

'So, yes, Amanda is a witch. Does that make her a suspect then? A three-year-old of such extraordinary magical powers that she could plot a murder, then could cast a spell from 300 miles away? Now Senara at that tender age — nothing much would surprise me about her capabilities, but even I would draw the line at that.'

'This is serious, Mike,' Thomas insisted.

Hogarth sat down opposite him, forearms on his knees.

'Indeed it is. Amanda Cadabra is possibly a concatenation of the powers of four witch-clans: levitation, divination, spell-weaving and control of the weather. That would make her the most dangerous force to walk this green and pleasant land in many a century. Fortunately, dangerous for them, and not for us. So far, we don't know the extent of what she is. But she is a card we cannot afford openly to play. Perhaps we never shall.'

Trelawney was taken aback by the enormity of the situation. 'I see.'

'Do you understand why I passed this cold case to you? It is no ordinary unsolved mass murder. It goes straight to the heart of the balance of power among the witch-clans. And believe me, Normals have been harmed in the struggle. It is for their sakes that we must hold this in check. Amanda Cadabra is the greatest advantage we most likely shall ever have. Not just her powers, whatever they may turn out to be, but her memories, her deeply buried, forgotten memories. Her memory is the mole within the Cardiubarn camp, just as yours is within the Flamgoyne stronghold.'

'If they have impinged on the lives of Normals,' Thomas responded, 'then there's many a strange case that might be explained.'

'That is my point, Thomas. The Normals have no part

in this struggle; they would be helpless in the face of attack. They deserve to be shielded from it. It is right that they should be. It is just. If you need a cause, my young Galahad, you have it right there. And Amanda Cadabra is our weight in the scales of justice.'

The room was quiet for a beat. Thomas spoke:
'Then, I will serve this cause with my life.'
'Whatever it takes?'
'Whatever it takes.'

* * * * *

Since then, Trelawney's ardour for the cause had cooled somewhat, but he was still willing to be Amanda's agent in approaching his father. He had just three days to do it, before he would see her again on Saturday.

Amanda had not wanted to stress the urgency of her request and put him under pressure, but she approached the day when she would next see him with eager anticipation.

The ballroom-Latin classes were recommencing in their new home, in the function room of the Snout and Trough. Located at the south entrance to the village, it was also known as Sunken Madley's Other Pub, but was rather a gastropub star. Of course, being only decades old, it was a mere new-comer, compared to the venerable Sinner's Rue that traced its pedigree back 400 years to the coaching days.

As the dance classes were in the interest of raising money to rebuild the old church hall, Sandra, proprietor of the Snout and Trough, allowed them free use of it. Her generous and attractive sister Vanessa, a successful physical trainer and competent dancer, acted as instructor, also without charge.

The students were a little rusty after a short break, but

soon got back into the swing of things when Vanessa rebooted with the waltz. Amanda had little time for conversation with Trelawney, as they rotated partners every few minutes.

'Hello, Inspector,' she said, looking at him hopefully as they practiced their chassée.

He grinned. 'Hello, Miss Cadabra, and yes, … I did ask.'

She sighed with relief. 'Tell me afterwards?'

'Of course.'

Following the conclusion of the class, they were to make their way, as was their routine, to 26 Orchard Way, for their weekly consultation. Amanda would brew the tea while Trelawney made up the fire in the sitting-room.

On this occasion, however, their conference was delayed by an unforeseen and unwelcome encounter.

Chapter 4

✑

GETTING PERSONAL

Amanda and Trelawney had descended the stairs from the function room of the Snout and Trough. They were about to exit the pub, when they were hailed by a shriek.

'Thomas, isn't it? Yes, of course, it is! Dear boy!'

'Mrs Guthrie?' he responded politely, to the short, curvaceous woman, with brass-highlighted brown curls, rapidly bearing down upon them.

'*Gertrudina*, please,' she insisted, arriving and laying a heavy hand, decorated with dense floral nail art, upon his arm. 'It makes me feel quite a hundred to be called "Mrs Gurthrie" by my dear Penelope's child.'

'Well, I'm sure you're far from —' Trelawney began courteously.

'Why, you do carry *your* years lightly, dear boy. I remember you when you were a teenager, not that it does my vanity any good to say so, but I'm *constantly* assured that no one would think me more than thirty-five!'

Trelawney wondered briefly who might be giving her such misleading information.

She patted her over-zealously rouged and contoured cheeks that were puffy with filler.

'Ah, I must admit to having had a *teensy*-weensy bit of work done, as they say.' As her skin bore a certain mask-like appearance, he gathered that this was a mastery of understatement. 'But enough about Little Me. What are you doing in this neck of the woods?'

'I am here in the course of my work,' Trelawney replied with deliberate vagueness.

'Oh? But how thrilling. Do tell!'

'I'm afraid I —'

'Oh yes, you were always such a secretive boy. Your mother too, dearest Penny, was always rather reticent on the subject of her darling son. And of course, ' she added gravely, 'understandably, given the Sad Circumstances.'

'Er, quite,' he replied hurriedly, hoping to depress any pretention to further discussion of the subject to which he knew she was referring. But Mrs Guthrie was not to be denied her relish of unfortunate events.

'First that dreadful Perpetua. Well, I always said ... But with an over-aspirational name like *Perpetua*, coming from the Moppe family. Then again, you understand why she hoped to ally herself with yours.'

'Yes, well, that is all water under —'

'And then Patricia,' lamented Mrs Guthrie. 'Who would have known? You seemed so perfect for one another. But then .... *Nature* ....the clock ticking... the alarm going off ....'

'It was all —'

'— a great shock, I'm sure. One can understand a change of heart but ... to set about it the way that she did... behind your back like that! And with the milkman!'

'It wasn't —'

'Oh, the postman.'

'No, it —'

'Oh. I remember now. It was the farmer from next door! Not but what she was very attractive. Well, both she and Perpetua. But *ambitious*, I'd say,' she remarked, wrinkling her nose in distaste. 'Both of them.'

She suddenly seemed to register Amanda.

'What you need,' Mrs Guthrie said confidentially to Thomas, lowering her voice, 'is a nice plain girl, a simple village girl without any airs or big ideas.' She nodded in Amanda's direction.

Good grief! thought Amanda. Does she think I can't hear her?

'I'm sure your dear mother would agree with me. How is she, by the way?'

Trelawney's relief at the change of subject was almost apparent.

'Very well, th—'

'Now *she's* one that doesn't let the grass grow. I saw her at the Royal Academy private view with a very charming *young* man, or was it two?'

'My moth— '

'Not that I begrudge her. She's had a trying life, and I wish her every happiness. You know she found the most delightful piece for my reception room. I've had it redone in ironic kitsch for the spring.'

'Have y—'

'Floribunda was in raptures over it. You know, it's a shame neither Shiraz nor Chardonnay would do for you. But too young and far from simple! Well, I can't stand here gossiping all day. Give my love to darling Penny. Goodbye, Thomas.' She nodded again in Amanda's direction, and tottered off on her 4-inch Gucci platform sandals.

Trelawney and Amanda simultaneously exhaled with

relief at her departure and shock at her stream of tactless indiscretions, before lapsing into suppressed laughter.

'I feel I owe you a treat for subjecting you to that appalling woman,' he said apologetically.

'A client of your mother's, I gather.'

'Indeed, a very long-standing and lucrative one, alas.'

'Why did she start talking about roses and wine in the middle of everything?'

'She wasn't. Floribunda is her daughter, and Shiraz and Chardonnay are her grandchildren.'

'You can't be serious.'

'Oh, I am. With difficulty, granted, but I am.' Amanda was diplomatically silent. Trelawney grinned. 'It's quite alright to express yourself on the subject.'

'No. If they are friends of your mother's, it would be most improper.'

'Friends? I doubt my fond mamma would thank you for thus describing them!'

'Well, clients, then,' said Amanda.

'Indeed.'

* * * * *

Finally, back in the haven of Amanda's cottage, with the fire lit and tea served, Trelawney returned to the encounter.

'I feel I owe you some explanation.'

'None needed, I promise you,' Amanda assured him kindly. 'None of my business.'

'All the same.'

She sensed he wanted to get something off his chest and said gently, 'If you want to tell me.'

Trelawney took a breath and looked into his tea.

'Perpetua was at police college with me and it seemed like an ideal match. It turned out that I was just her starter kit. Patricia also seemed ideal, especially as we agreed that we didn't want a family. Unfortunately, a few years later, her feelings changed about that, and ... she started one with someone else, which came as rather a shock.'

'I gathered something of that from what Mrs Guthrie said. I'm so sorry, Inspector. That must have given you a rather jaundiced view of women.'

'It did,' he agreed, 'for about a week, in both cases, but then I reminded myself that they were only two out of millions in this land. And my mother would never have done anything like that. For all the time that she was married to my father, and I don't think they were ever really happy, she was always honest with him and faithful, regardless of whatever opportunities or temptations that I bet must have come her way, because I always remember her being very pretty and vivacious. I can't imagine my aunt behaving so either. And they are the women that I've known the longest.'

'It does you credit to be so fair about it. Perhaps you were just unlucky,' Amanda suggested.

'Perhaps, but then again I grew up with parents who made a choice of mate that wasn't the best, my mother being a Normal and my father part of a witch-clan, however unwillingly. I suppose it's no surprise that I didn't do too outstandingly in that department either.'

'Well, if it's any comfort, in spite of having a very long and happy marriage before me in my grandparents, I never found anyone to whom I was suited. Just a number of false starts, none of any significant duration. There was one that might have been ... but we both had commitments a long way apart and so chose friendship over romance.'

Trelawney looked up at that. He found himself asking,

'Do you think one day it could ever ....?'

'No,' Amanda answered decidedly. She was surprised by her own certainty. Why was she so sure? But now was not the time to pursue that line of enquiry, she told herself sternly.

This was, by far, the most personal conversation they had ever had. Suddenly, they grew self-conscious, and Amanda relieved the tension by asking,

'So. You asked your father? Oh hold on, I've forgotten to bring the treats.' She hurried off to the kitchen and soon returned with another tray. In addition to gingernuts for her and shortcake for him, was a Victoria sandwich.

'Hello,' Trelawney remarked enthusiastically, the mood suddenly lightened. 'Is this a celebration?'

'Well, a sort of New Year one maybe, but actually, it's a present from Aunt Amelia. Perhaps a consolation prize.'

'For what?'

'Oh I don't know,' she replied ruefully, 'perhaps for having the sole responsibility of defending the village against your remarkably unpleasant family, with no one that I yet know of to help me, and in which we could all go up in green and purple smoke.'

'First, I do wish you refrain from referring to them as my family. I am a Trelawney, not a Flamgoyne,' he reminded her lightly.

'Sorry,' she interjected, with a smile.

'Secondly, if Aunt Amelia says you'll have help you can be sure you will,' Trelawney assured her.

'And third?'

'You've survived two close calls in the last six months. I believe you are made of sterner stuff than anyone imagines. If I were a betting man, I'd place a substantial sum on the chances of your survival.' Amanda was heartened. 'And speaking of the most recent of those close calls, are we going to talk about that, Miss Cadabra?'

Amanda became very still. She had been expecting this

moment and now … the other boot had dropped. She had to say something. Finally she spoke,

'Ah. The elephant in the room, you mean?'

Chapter 5

SPELL-POWER, AND AMANDA'S WISH

Amanda knew he was referring to the spells she had had to resort to, that day they had been in mortal danger. Those very spells had included the fatal cast against a human. She had done it to save him, and now it was bringing the Flamgoyes down upon her village. Not only that, but in doing so she had exposed the magical side of herself that she had kept hidden from him, all this time. He had tactfully refrained from mentioning the matter … until now.

'I suppose there's no point in denying it,' she finally said.

'So you can do spells. It was a relief to find out, you know.'

'Yes, you always suspected, didn't you, that there was something more than meets the eye to us three Cadabras?'

'I did. Am I right in thinking that it is thanks to spells that you are able to perform the work of a furniture restorer?'

Amanda took a deep breath. Secrecy was ingrained

in her. She had always done everything in her power to give the inspector only need-to-know-information. However, she perceived a compromise: she didn't have to tell him, outright, about being a levitant: that she had the rare ability to make objects move by themselves. Admitting to being able to perform a few spells was not such a big step, not when he had already seen the evidence. She exhaled.

'Yes, Inspector.'

'Then I am sure you have been given the training you need to survive the attack on the day the Flamgoynes come.'

'Thank you. I do appreciate the vote of confidence. But it's not enough for *me* to survive; everyone else has to as well. But I'm hoping that you have some information that may facilitate that.'

'Yes, indeed. Well, my father granted my request with his customary warmth ....'

* * * * *

Kytto Trelawney served half of the contents of a Pyrex dish, hot from the oven, onto his son's plate.

'Don't you ever get tired of Shepherd's pie?'

'Not yours, Dad,' replied Thomas, with conviction.

They brought their laden trenchers into the dining room and sat at the table.

'So, how's your Miss Cadabra?' asked Kytto, sprinkling salt onto his crispy cheese-coated mashed potato and savoury mince.

'She's not ...' began his son, before abandoning his automatic response as futile. 'She's pretty much recovered, I think. In fact, she's the reason why I am sampling your cooking, so soon after last time.'

'You're always welcome, son.'

'Thanks, Dad. I know, but you do have a pretty full schedule.'

'Well, we're here now, so ... how can I help?'

'What do you know about the Cadabras?'

Kyt put down his knife and fork. 'Hmm, now there's a question. Farmers of some pedigree with land to the north of our ... I mean, *Flamgoyne* land, and bordering on their neighbours, the Cardiubarns.'

'Yes, that much I know.'

'A witch-clan of good repute.'

'How so?' asked Thomas.

'Well, their credo is "strike not" and "abundance through peace". That certainly gives them the moral high ground over either the Flamgoynes or the Cardiubarns.'

'But the Flamgoynes and the Cardiubarns don't baulk at using force.'

'Well, not openly. They gave up the futility of beating one another over the head with stone wands long ago. They prefer more subtle methods.'

'Like sending one another over cliffs?' suggested Thomas.

'For example.'

'So if the Flamgoynes and the Cardiubarns will use any unscrupulous, not to say homicidal, method to gain ground, how have the Cadabras managed to survive, thrive and hold their land against their neighbouring clans?'

'I have been out of the Flamgoyne loop for almost as many years as you, Thomas, so all I have is old stories. But, based on those, I would say they use repelling, bouncing back, and mirroring spells.'

'Like a bullet ricocheting? It could bounce around and hit the person who fired the gun?'

'Yes, like that.'

'Dad, did you hear any other stories about their methods.'
Kytto shook his head.

* * * * *

'And that's all he could tell you?' asked Amanda.
'I'm afraid so, Miss Cadabra.'
'Still, it's a start. Thank you, Inspector.'
'Any progress with Viola?' Trelawney enquired.
'Only a shortlist, but no real way in to interviewing any of them.'
'With whom would you want to start?'
'I don't know why,' Amanda answered at once, 'but Mrs Uberhausfest. You know? Over-70's party planner? She's been at the dances.'
'Ah, yes.'
'I just wish I had an excuse to really talk to her ….'
By 1.47 in the morning, while Amanda was fast asleep, her wish was coming true

Chapter 6

OLD TIMES, NEW INFORMATION

Trelawney was parking the car outside his mother's house in Crouch End when his phone rang.

'Hello, Yokel' said a familiar voice. 'How's it going?'

'Ross, good to hear from you. All's well, thanks.'

'Yes, I heard you barely made it out of that last debacle relatively unscathed. You do seem to lead an interesting life for someone tucked away in the sticks.'

'I try,' replied Trelawney, with a chuckle.

'Look, I hear you're spending most of your weekends up in the Big Smoke. Though how you're swinging that, I can't imagine. Knowing you, it has to be in the line of duty, and I know better than to enquire too closely. But since you're up, fancy a jar in the old local tonight?'

'Sure. What's the time now? I can see if my mother can bring dinner forward and meet you at say, 8.30?

'Fine by me. Shall we say 8.30 in The Tardis, then? I don't mind waiting if you get a bit delayed,' said Ross cheerfully.

'Great. It'll be good to catch up.'

'See you then.'

Trelawney was pleased. They'd been friends at Hendon Police College. Ross was a straight-up guy, and that resonated with Thomas. They'd led very different lives: Ross, in the rough and tumble of city life, had got in with the wrong crowd as a teenager, and was lucky enough to have been thrown a life-line by a fatherly detective sergeant, who saw the best in the youngster. Ross had been determined to pay it forward one day, and like his mentor, joined the police. His jovial manner belied the earnestness that lay beneath, and his help had been indispensable in the last case with which Trelawney had been involved.

Back at the house in Crouch End, Thomas had dropped off his car and luggage and had had dinner with his mother. He had spent every school holiday here since he was 12 and his parents divorced. Even now, his old room was always ready for him.

Intending to have a couple of drinks, he took a cab and found Ross already at work on a pint of Sonik Screwdriver, one of the craft beers for which the pub was justly famed.

'Greetings, Yokel.' They shook hands and clapped one another on the back. 'You managed to return to civilisation then.'

'Yes, Ross, once I reached tarmac roads. They 'orse tracks be hell-of-a-job,' replied Trelawney, in authentic Cornish brogue. Ross threw his head back with laughter. 'You were always good with accents. What can I get you?'

'Pint of Cloister Bell, thanks.'

Settled with drinks, they chatted about the previous case.

'Something I've been wanting to ask you,' said Ross. 'How on earth did you get out of that place alive?' This was an awkward question, and Trelawney had created a fudge of an answer, just in case.

'Well, you know as a building shifts, all sorts of gaps can open. I was very lucky.'

Ross seemed to accept that and agreed.

'Don't suppose you'd like to let me in on this other business that brings you to these parts, every weekend?'

'Oh it's just a cold case. Cornwall.'

'How cold?'

'Thirty years.'

'That's pretty refrigerated. Do I know it?'

'Van full of people went over a cliff.'

'Wait ... whole family, right?'

'Yes.'

'Each one received a letter on weird paper with odd-coloured ink but no evidence of them was found?'

'Uhuh.'

'But the person responsible was never tracked down?'

'How come you know all about this, Ross?' asked Trelawney, suspiciously.

'Erm ... I think you may have mentioned it,' he attempted casually. Thomas felt that his friend was building up to something, so he let this go. 'So ... any progress.'

'Nope,' Trelawney admitted, and indicated that that was as far as he was prepared to discuss it.

Ross nodded, fell silent and rotated his glass on the coaster. Trelawney, increasingly, had the distinct feeling that there was something specific that Ross wanted to bring up that was not connected to the case. However, he let his friend get to it in his own time. At the end of his second pint, Trelawney having got that round and the snacks, Ross went off for their last refills. He returned, sat down and fidgeted a little. Trelawney waited patiently. Finally, Ross asked with apparent nonchalance,

'Ever see any of the old crowd?'

'From our college days?'

'Well, not all of them were at the college,' said Ross carefully.

'True. No, no, I can't say I do really. We have all gone our separate ways, for the most part.'

'Well ... not all of us ...' Ross paused awkwardly. 'Pete, Naomi and I. We were all very sorry, you know, Thomas, about ....'

Trelawney knew he was referring to Perpetua. 'Thanks. I guess I should have seen it coming. I know you tried to warn me.'

'Yes, well, perhaps we should have tried harder. I mean, *I* should. I just didn't want to cause a rift between us,' Ross explained.

'I know. Thanks for trying. I guess I was dazzled and she just seemed so much the logical choice. Same career, we'd understand about the unsociable hours and ... I couldn't see beyond ....'

'She was very glam,' Ross said, mitigatingly. 'But ....' A hint of mischief entered his voice. 'You do know what we used to call her?'

'Petty, I suppose,' replied Trelawney with a half-smile.

'No.'

'What then?' Now he was curious.

'Tensing!' announced Ross.

'As in "getting uptight"?' asked Trelawney.

'No, wally, as in "Sherpa."'

'Sherpa Tensing? Why?'

'Because it was obvious to the rest of us that she was a climber. You were the best and brightest in our year, Yokel. She thought you'd go far, get noticed. You were the next rung on the ladder.'

'Hm, and Inspector Turnbull was the *next* one up,' added Trelawney.

''Fraid so. Didn't think it would go as far as marriage with you two, old chap,' said Ross, apologetic once more.

'Well, water under the bridge,' Trelawney assured him without rancour. 'It was all over and done with, within the shortest possible time. But yes, I should have listened. You always said I should have asked Naomi out. You were probably right. How is she? Have you kept in touch?'

'Yes, we have, as a matter of fact,' Ross replied slowly 'We bumped into each other on Facebook, would you believe? And met up in here. You know she married, had three children? Well ... it didn't work out, and she's been single for quite a while now. She's Naomi Hollister again.'

'Oh yes?' replied Trelawney with polite interest. They'd been chums, but it was so long ago, he'd practically forgotten all about her.

'She, er ... she asked about you,' said Ross tentatively.

'Ahuh.'

'Wondered if you'd like to give her call sometime.'

Trelawney sat back in his seat in surprise. 'Are you setting me up, Ross?'

'No. Just thought ... you always got on well ... both single now ... she always liked you. I mean, *really* liked you. You have the profession in common. She's done well. Respected medical examiner now.'

'Did she ask you to ...?'

'She just asked to be remembered to you, and to tell you that if you felt like touching base with an old friend, well ... that I should give you her number.' Ross passed a card across the table. Trelawney looked a little doubtful. 'Just take it,' said Ross. 'She's a useful contact. If you ever need an inside track or a second opinion or just another colleague to sound something out with,' he added reasonably.

'Yes.' Trelawney felt comfortable with that. 'Thanks. Yes. OK.' He looked at the rectangle of white pasteboard and then put in into his pocket. 'I expect that's how you "remember" so much about my cold case? Naomi was always a good researcher.'

'OK, got me there. But don't think I'm playing Cupid, Yokel,' insisted Ross on a jauntier note, having fulfilled his commission. 'Only, it might be nice to have some other aspect to your sad, lonely old bachelor life, besides your beloved station desk, don't you think?'

Thomas grinned. 'Of course.'

'And it's been years since Deecey,' Ross added.

'Deecey?'

'Oops. Didn't you know?'

'D.C.? I've never been to Washington,' Thomas replied in confusion.

'Another nickname, I'm afraid,' replied his friend, comically shame-faced.

'Oh?'

'Patricia. It's what we called her: D.C. — Disaster Central. Sorry.'

'That's hardly fair. We were happy while it lasted. At least ... I thought I was .... Actually, in fact, I think all I was really doing was playing out my parents' relationship.'

'Look the last thing I want to do is rake up the past, old chap. Let's think about the future. Wouldn't you like to have ... you know, ... someone to come home to, do stuff with at the weekends, talk to ... I don't know, have fun with before you turn into an old codger muttering about the state of the nation and the youth of today.'

Thomas chuckled. 'I'll think about it.'

Ross changed the subject, entertaining his friend with some anecdotes about his former boss, Detective Inspector Worsfold, whom Thomas had encountered on the last case. Thus they ended the evening on a high note.

The following Monday, Thomas tapped a new contact into his phone, filed the card away in the appropriate box, and Naomi Hollister was, once again, forgotten.

Chapter 7

✑

MRS UBERHAUSFEST

Irma Uberhausfest, after moving with her husband to the UK after the war, had lived a respectable life as an accountant, wife and resident at number 3 Rattling Bridge Row. On his much-regretted demise, having grieved his loss, Irma decided it was time for her to begin a new chapter in her life.

To this end, Irma reinvented herself. She created an elegant, artistic boho style, and, quite by chance, discovered a new career path, leading to the creation of Finely Aged Festivities. By the age of 91 she was the most senior party planner in England, with a long waiting list. Furthermore, both she and her reconditioned VW Beetle — a former police vehicle, with a Porsche engine, in metallic purple — had appeared on the cover of *Hey There Magazine*, the prestigious *Trending Now* as well as *Silver Rogue*.

Her insight into the hidden real tastes of the misleadingly named 'old dears' had proved the foundation of a thriving business. Far from downsizing, as empty nester peers were doing, she had purchased a larger establishment with a sizeable reception room. This she had soundproofed and furnished with air-conditioning, for parties of a more intimate size than her legendary big bashes.

It so happened that, that very Saturday, Irma was arranging a function for Mrs Adela Slott's 77th birthday. In her teens, Adela had been a cabaret dancer at the notorious Room 102 at the members-only Dead Parrot Club, located in a discreet corner of Soho. There she was talent-spotted by impresario Jack Slott, credited with the invention of Tie Die Smiley Car.

Mr Slott had long since taken the road to The Great Beyond. Nevertheless, under the influence of her fifth serving of Irma's signature cocktail, she was persuaded, with becoming reluctance, to demonstrate her terpsichorean skills upon the, fortunately closed, lid of the grand piano. Irma was in the kitchen making up a fresh batch of what she had named A Slow Up Against It Coconut Screwdriver, and by the time she had ascertained that Mrs Slott was wearing stilettos and performing with zest to *Shakin' All Over*, it was too late to save the highly polished case of the instrument.

Consequently, the following lunchtime, Amanda received a phone call.

'Amanda, my *liebschen*.'

'Irma!' she answered with delight.

'Oh, I have bad news and good news.'

'Bad first, please,' Amanda requested.

'Stiletto damage on my grand piano.'

'Again? Oh dear,' sympathised Amanda.

'The good news: only you can save it, and the insurance is paying!'

The latter was hardly news. Mrs Uberhausfest's insurance was high but easily paid for itself at least once a month. However, even better, here was the wished-for opportunity to see if Irma was, in fact, the mysterious Viola.

'Of course, Irma. Shall I come this afternoon?'

'The cleaners are here. The glaziers are coming tomorrow afternoon and the new hall carpet on Tuesday.'

There would be no chance for a private chat with other people around.

'Tomorrow morning?' suggested Amanda. It would be mean postponing retouching an antique Chinese cabinet, but Irma was top priority.

'Ah, you are such a sweet girl to do this for me.'

'It will be my pleasure. How about 9 o' clock?'

'Is good!'

Amanda hung up and rubbed her hands together excitedly.

'Tempest, we're on our way!'

* * * * *

Monday morning dawned, and Amanda arrived promptly at the door of Festival Cottage, Trotters Bottom Lane. The cat sat on the mat, looking up at the trees in a manner expressive of *ennui*.

'I didn't ask you to come,' said Amanda pointedly.

Tempest shrugged. Never let it be said that I was delinquent in my supervision, he thought, with an air of martyrdom.

Mrs Uberhausfest opened the door joyfully, and tossed her purple feather boa over one shoulder.

Come, come my …' — she spotted Tempest — 'my dears. Come, Prinz, I have some shrimp fishballs for you.'

'He's had breakfast,' said Amanda, apparently to the empty air. While Tempest's second meal of the morning was being served, she went into the reception room to inspect the damage to the piano. As she feared, it was so severely chipped that it would have to be sanded and re-polished. Again.

Irma came into the room, and Amanda gave her the news.

'So ... strip, polish, sand. My insurance — you know? — Slite, Trisk & Gayne? They will pay.'

'That's good, but Irma, if I keep doing this, eventually, the wood is going to get too thin to hold together,' explained Amanda.

'So. Then we get a new lid,' replied Irma simply.

'But matching a new lid could be a challenge: getting the right grain, patina, colour, stain, to harmonise with the rest of the wood. I think we should try to save this one if we can.'

'How?' Irma enquired. 'I cannot ask my clients not to express themselves.'

'May I ask what prompted the particular expression that led to this damage?'

'Adela was drinking my Slow Up Against It Coconut Screwdriver cocktails.'

'Ah. How many, I wonder.'

'Oh, only four or five. Some people are sensitive to it.'

'Really? What's in it?'

'Malibu, Rum and Mr Mieting's pear liqueur.'

'Good grief, Irma,' exclaimed Amanda, who'd sampled one of the lady's concoctions, at the end of her last repair visit. 'I'd think five of those would require a call-out of the paramedics.'

'Maybe the double pear liqueur was not such a good thought. It was Dennis's idea. He knows Adela has a sweet tooth.'

'Oh, Dennis was there, was he?' Dennis Hanley-Page, owner of Vintage Vehicles on the other side of the village, even in his 70s was still a dashing man. He had proposed, on various occasions, to both Amanda's Bentley-owning Aunt Amelia and

Irma. As both ladies were well aware that his admiration was principally car-centric, they both graciously declined.

'Of course. He is so good at helping to start the dancing,' replied Irma.

'Yes, well, I digress. I have an idea,' said Amanda.

'Good. I like your ideas. Yes, we do that,' Irma responded, at once.

'I haven't said what it is yet.'

'All right. Say, my dear, say.'

'I could make a cover for the piano lid that would offer some protection. And when it's convenient, I can come and do the strip, sand and polish,' Amanda suggested.

'Good but not yet. The piano tuner comes next week.'

'Mr Spinnetti? That's nice.'

'No, no, his deputy,' returned Irma.

'Oh?'

'Mr Spinnetti is having a new hip.'

'Ah.'

'I remember when I had mine,' Irma reminisced. 'I was just 72. I am so glad I did. Sometimes, I have to encourage the dancing myself. Before the spirits have released the spirit, you know!'

'Er, yes, I think so,' replied Amanda, with an understanding smile. 'So, when will the tuner be coming?'

'I think next Monday.'

'All right. Well, I can take a template now and make up the lid cover, and after the tuner has finished, I can come and make sure it fits properly.'

'This is good,' Irma approved.

'Also, I will need to either make a tent around it here or take it to the workshop. Even so, it's no good doing it while there are workman around who can't help making a lot of dust. The tiniest speck will show up in the polish.'

'You are right, my dear, as always.'

'Thank you, Irma. I have some paper in the car for the template.'

'And then I make you some coffee, and we have some of *Donauwelle*!'

'Have you been baking?' Amanda asked in surprise.

'No,' said Irma, with a laugh and a wave of her hand. 'The nice boys make it for me.'

Amanda guessed she meant the tea shop owners. 'Sandy and Alex at The Big Tease?'

'Of course. Such nice boys. No dairy. You can eat it, my dear.'

'It's a bit early, but I can't resist!' admitted Amanda delightedly. 'I'll get the paper.'

She soon returned with large rolls of thin card, Sellotape and a marker pen.

'I help you,' Irma declared.

'Thank you.' Amanda had rehearsed her opening bid. 'Granny always spoke with great respect of you, Irma.'

'Ah yes, she was a good friend.'

'How did you meet?'

'After the war. I came here.'

'It can't have been easy. There must have been some prejudice.'

'I met my husband during the war, and we wrote letters to each other when he was interned in this country. He became very close with a family here. His family ... they were no more, and so he wanted to stay here, so, after the war I came too. It was ... at times ... not so nice, but now ... you know what? I am a British citizen for a long time. Now, whenever I say I was born in Germany, they say always the same thing: "You must be very efficient!"' Irma chuckled.

'Well, you *are*, Irma. You couldn't be a successful party planner unless you were.'

'But that is my nature. My husband was not so organised.

I have lived many more years here than in Germany, I think in English, I know the films, the books, the plays, the food. Even Mrs Sharma says I make a good Chicken Tikka Masala.'

'You like British literature?'

'Not all, but I like the classics: Jane Austen, Charles Dickens.'

'Shakespeare?' suggested Amanda tentatively.

'Only the funny ones!'

'Not Romeo and Juliet?' Amanda asked.

'No,' said Irma scornfully. 'It is too silly. There were at least four other solutions to their problem. I have no patience with their foolishness.'

Amanda had to admit that she saw Irma's point, but here was her way in. 'Ah, well, what about *Twelfth Night*?'

'Ha. I read the first page, and it was enough,' Irma stated flatly.

'Enough?' asked Amanda.

'That count. He is always complaining because some woman he has only seen, and doesn't even know, won't communicate with him. His problem is he has nothing to do. I shut the book.'

'I know what you mean. But the play is full of wonderful and energetic people ... Viola, for example,' said Amanda, covertly observing Irma's face and switching up her emotional radar.

'Hm, who is she?' Irma asked, with nothing more apparent than polite interest.

'A girl from a country at war with the count's land. She is shipwrecked on his shores and disguises herself as a man so she can get a job with him and provide for herself.'

'She sounds better,' remarked Irma absently. Amanda had finished marking out the template. Irma clapped her hands gently. 'It is done. Come. We have coffee and cake in the kitchen.'

Amanda was unable to revive the subject. Either Irma

was not Viola or was covering her tracks. Faces told Amanda very little, but she had not sensed any strong reaction to her mention of the name, Viola.

She wasn't crossing Mrs Uberhausfest off the list entirely, but for now … she was eager to move on.

Chapter 8

THE DATE IS SET

Thomas Trelawney and former Chief Inspector Michael Hogarth of the Devon and Cornwall police often had dinner together. Hogarth was Thomas's one-time official boss and, seemingly, his current *un*official one, but also his best friend and confidante,

Neither being a keen cook, dinner invariably comprised the sterling efforts of one of their favoured local takeaways or restaurants that provided a delivery service. This evening, for Trelawney, it was that UK traditional staple: Chicken Tikka Masala, and for Hogarth, Lamb Rogan Josh.

Once trays were installed on laps, Hogarth looked across at his young friend and smiled knowingly.

'Go on then, lad, ask.'

Trelawney met his eyes with an answering gleam.

'I was trying to be sociable. Dinner first, questions after.'

Hogarth shook his head, gathered a forkful of lamb, sauce and rice, and replied,

'Unnecessary.'

'Well … Miss Cadabra needs to know how to defend her village without striking a blow. She asked her grandparents, who told her what I thought you would tell me: to use one's resources to follow the trail.'

'And you were her resource,' Hogarth correctly observed, with amusement.

'And you,' countered Trelawney.

'But I expect she thought as you did, about the usefulness of turning to me.'

'Quite. So she asked me to ask my father, and he told me he gathers the Cadabras have used repelling spells to bounce back attacks. Does that tally with what you know, Mike?'

'It does. But I can't tell you what spells or how to cast them. The Cadabras are private people. Oh, they're friendly if you meet them at the local villages, on market days and so on. Seem very normal and down-to-earth folk. But I've never got any further with them than the weather and the progress of the crops. Not that I've tried, especially.'

'Then, Miss Cadabra has only one remaining resource: her grandparents,' said Trelawney.

'How much time do you think she has to work out a defence of the village?'

'According to Aunt Amelia, the attack will come on the day that the village empties. The one day when that will happen, is a local event that seems to be honouring the Sunken Madleyists, in some way.'

'Do we have a date for that?' asked Mike, calmly.

'No. But the word on the street is that it will be within just a few weeks.'

'Hm. Not long,' Mike observed, before taking a sip from the mug of tea on his tray. 'No. Not long at all.'

* * * * *

In the night, the dream came again to Amanda: standing alone at the centre of the village, watching the storm approach. She awoke unrefreshed. The urgency to find Viola was again upon her. Granny and Grandpa continued to be too busy to discuss the matter of the defence spells.

Amanda managed to get herself dressed, for an estimate for an original wooden floor repair, at the new home of Chris Reid, Sunken Madley cricket team's prized spin bowler and dentist. He had recently bought a home of his own, and the arrival of the new fridge had resulted in a gouge in the entrance hall.

Like many of her fellow villagers who had congratulated Chris on this landmark event of the purchase of his first property, Amanda was pleased for him, and she did not want to let him down by cancelling the appointment.

'Oh Tempest, I'm going to get there, but I'm too tired to make breakfast. Let's go to The Big Tease.'

Her familiar required no persuasion. The modernised reincarnation of the former Ye Olde Tea Shoppe that had been run by Miss Hempling, now happily installed with her friends at Pipkin Acres Residential Home, had been provided with a cat-and-dog-friendly corner. Alexander, formerly of The City or possibly construction, and Julian having likewise done rather well in his own career as a hairstylist, had moved back to their childhood village and were creating a small something of a fashionable buzz with their hand-made baked delicacies.

On entering, Tempest took up his position at one of the feline-height tables, inset with shining bowls, and directed an expectant look at Julian, who had advanced to the counter at the sound of the ding from the opening door.

'Hello, Amanda. Sandy! It's our Miss Ammy!'

Alex came out from the kitchen, wiping his hands on a clean cloth, to greet her with a welcoming smile.

'Well, well, now this is an unexpected event, Amanda. Now, isn't Jules? Miss Ammy here for breakfast. What *is* the occasion?'

'Hello, Julian, Alexander. Fatigue, actually, I must admit. Too tired to make my own, I thought I'd visit for breakfast.'

'Oo, well, lucky us, is all I can say,' asserted Alex. 'Jules, give Miss Ammy the breakfast menu. I can do you a special, though, Amanda. What do you fancy? Now you look like —'

'Rrrrowl!'

'Ooo, pardon us, your lordship,' cried Jules, 'I'm sure we didn't see you there.'

This, and the catering standard, were the reasons why Tempest approved of the patisseurs. They provided suitable facilities for the superior species of the village and showed its prime member due deference. That their respectful form of address was intended as anything but seriously never crossed his mind.

'Will tuna be your pleasure this morning?'

Tempest gave a slight but gracious inclination of his noble head, indicating that the suggestion was satisfactory. Within 90 seconds, one of his bowls was filled with Ortiz Bonito Del Norte tinned tuna, garnished with a small peak of cream. The Big Tease remained up there on his endorsed list, only just below Mrs Sharma. No rodent, fox, bird or ill-behaved customer dare approach more than three feet from the threshold of any establishment under his protection.

Amanda was sipping tea, and about to tuck into scrambled eggs on sourdough toast and Marmite, when Ruth and Kieran entered for a pre-school breakfast.

'Hello, you two early birds,' said Julian cheerfully.

'They're not on a date!' came Alex's voice from the kitchen.

'Of course not,' agreed Amanda emphatically.

'Hello, Amanda, Julian, Sandy,' the two young teenagers returned their greetings politely.

It was thanks to Amanda that Kieran, formerly regarded by Ruth as a sports moron, had risen in Ruth's estimation to fellow history buff and firm friend. The two of them had agreed, between planning to attend the same university, five years hence, and what lessons might be learned by the current British government from Gibbons' *Decline and Fall of the Roman Empire*, that they both owned Amanda several favours for bringing them into their present harmonious state.

'Amanda! A date's been set!' said Ruth animatedly.

'For the fictional enactment?'

'That's right,' Kieran confirmed.

'Saturday 9th February, starting at 2 o'clock,' stated Ruth.

Amanda was startled. She'd expected that it would at the *end* of February, reaching towards the, hopefully, better weather that March sometimes brought.

'That soon?'

Ruth noticed her reaction and wondered at it. 'Yes, why not?'

'Well ... I thought battles weren't fought during the winter,' returned Amanda, thinking on her feet.

'The Battle of Nantwich was fought on 28th January,' Kieran contributed deferentially.

Budding historian Ruth's brown eyes turned towards him with a glowing look of admiration, then to Amanda with simple pride in her friend.

'Really? Ah .... Well remembered, Kieran,' Amanda commended him. 'In that case ... but won't it be a muddy affair?' she objected.

'Battles *were* muddy affairs,' Ruth pointed out.

'Yes, well it will probably approximate the Somme by the end of the day,' said Amanda.

'Oh, you know Mr Gibbs,' Kieran chipped in, 'he won't spare any expense; there'll be some sort of flooring in the tents and around the stalls.'

'And macs and umbrellas will be provided,' added Ruth. 'It's going to be at the Quintana Open Space.'

The other side of Barnet to the south, well away from the village, thought Amanda. The teens were expecting her response.

'You're very well-informed,' Amanda observed.

'He came and made and an announcement at the pub,' Ruth explained.

'Mr Gibbs, at The Sinners' Rue,' Kieran offered for clarification.

'Er … you were there?' Amanda asked cautiously.

Ruth gave her a look of strained patience. 'It *is* a family pub, and we're allowed to be served soft drinks.'

'Yes, yes, of course, of course,' came Amanda's hasty reply. 'I didn't mean to imply —'

'It's good that Miss Cadabra is concerned for our well-being,' Kieran said sincerely to Ruth, putting a hand on her blazer-clad arm.

'You're right, Kieran,' Ruth replied, seeing the evident sense in his reminder. She turned to her older friend. 'Thank you, Amanda.'

Just as Amanda was feeling somewhat overwhelmed by the gravitas of the teenagers, the skittering of feet broke the brief sound of silence. It was abruptly followed by a command.

'Churchill! Heel!' ordered a voice in stentorian tones. The stately figure of the village's most venerable and oldest resident paused on the threshold. She made her entrance with an elderly terrier at her feet. Churchill began wisely snuffling into the corner, as far away from Tempest as was caninely possible.

'Good morning, Miss de Havillande,' chorused the breakfasters. Julian hurried out from the kitchen.

'Miss de Havillande! What a pleasure. How may we be of service?'

'Alexander, Julian. Good morning. Ladies and gentlemen ... *I* ... have come to a decision.'

The assembled cast turned their expectant gaze toward the lady.

'This dreadful weather, with its perpetual wind, cold and damp, appears to be wearing down the spirits of the village. Consequently, Miss Armstrong-Witworth, Moffat and I have decided to hold a St Valentine's Day ball, in order to give people's thoughts a happier direction.'

Balls at The Grange were legendary and irregular. There had not been one for at least two years.

'Oo,' cried Alex in delight. 'Do you hear that Jules?' He gave a little clap of his hands.

'You two,' she said to the bakers, 'will kindly liaise with dear Sandra. The Snout and Trough will naturally be very busy at that time, and so any of the load that you can take on will be greatly appreciated.'

'Of course, Miss D.H., it will be our pleasure.'

'Excellent. I knew that I could rely upon you. And so I told dear Sandra. Amanda, it is fortuitous that I should find *you* here. We have also decided to begin the restoration of the ballroom. It has been sadly neglected over the decades. It will be an expensive affair, but a beginning *must* be made. If you would be so good as to visit The Grange, we would like your expert contribution at the council of war upon the creeping dereliction, and when and how you would like to commence a counter-attack.'

It would be a vast undertaking and an exciting one.

Amanda's face lit up. For above all, and of the greatest urgency, it would give her the opportunity she so desperately needed: a chance to see if one of The Grange ladies or Moffat might be her Viola.

Chapter 9

INERTIA

Once the quote for Chris Reid was out of the way, Amanda's outstanding job was the piano lid cover for Mrs Uberhausfest, but there was no hurry for that. The piano tuner wasn't coming yet. Besides, Granny and Grandpa always said she should give Miss de Havillande priority. They now appeared, sitting at the empty chairs at her table to make sure she had not forgotten.

Amanda wished, as always, that her beloved grandparents would refrain from manifesting themselves to her when other people, to whom they were necessarily invisible and inaudible, were present.

'You know what we always say, *bian* about Cynthia,' said Grandpa.

However, this time, Amanda didn't need any encouraging.

'Would later this morning suit you, Miss de Havillande?'
'After you've looked at dear Christopher's floor?'

'Er, you know about that?'

'Well, naturally,' Joan said she had dropped into Iskender's for kebabs for dinner for Jim and herself and found the shop closed for 20 minutes. When Iskender returned, he explained that he had been helping Christopher to move the fridge into the kitchen after the delivery person, having damaged the floor, abandoned it. It was a foregone conclusion that a quote for repair would be required for insurance purposes.'

'Of course,' replied Amanda, wondering why she had asked.

'If you would like to come straight to The Grange afterwards, we can all have tea or lunch together, before we begin.'

* * * * *

'Now,' said Miss de Havillande, 'we will need to prioritise and draw up a reasonable schedule of what might be accomplished before the ball. We will be having the chandelier cleaned and the piano tuned, of course. Dear Neeta has kindly agreed to perform for us.'

Neeta was Amanda's physician of many years' standing. She and her husband Karan were the village general practitioners, as well as providing their skills at the local Barnet Hill hospital. There, especially in her earliest years, Amanda had been a frequent patient.

Both doctors were dedicated healers. However, Neeta was the one who possessed the most detailed experience and history of Amanda's life-threatening respiratory condition. It was Neeta Patel who had recommended the new Asthma Research Centre to her patient. Amanda's attendance there had not, so far, yielded results beyond inducing a relaxed state after each treatment that Amanda was very far from feeling at the moment.

The date of the local, village-emptying Event, and therefore most likely the attack, was set. The clock was ticking. Yet, the grandparents had been elusive, and the list of possible Violas only provisionally reduced, so far, by one.

Although Amanda wished for instant colloquy with her grandparent on the subject, there would be no opportunity until she was back home. She could, at least, do one thing. As soon as Miss de Havillande turned her attention elsewhere, Amanda got out her phone.

* * * * *

Inspector Trelawney was reading through a list of statements, from local shopkeepers regarding shoplifting incidents, that his constable had dropped on his desk with the words,

'I blame the parents.'

It had been going on sporadically for a while, and the local council and the town estate agents had been complaining. They wanted the culprit found and found now, before the outbreak soured the reputation of the area and put off potential property buyers.

Trelawney's new and able Detective Sergeant, Bry Kellow, and Detective Constable Nancarrow had duly visited the merchants bereft of their property, for more detailed statements than they had hitherto supplied. Trelawney had only one left to read, when his phone announced the arrival of a text. He finished the statement, then turned to look at the small screen.

Date set. Saturday 9th February. AC

The inspector's eye's widened a trifle. Only about four weeks? His impulse was to call her. No. Miss Cadabra must be at work, or she wouldn't have just sent a text. He replied:

Viola?
No-

By the end of the day, the imminence of the attack, and the lack of progress on any front, was irking him. He sent a text to another contact:

Mike, dinner tonight? T
Sure. M.

Uncharacteristically, Trelawney left work on time and headed for Hogarth's cottage in the nearby village of Mornan Bay.

Hogarth's private life had been even more of a mystery to his staff and colleagues than any case they encountered in the course of their police investigations. It seemed he lived alone. Whenever Trelawney was there, no one else was in evidence, though that in itself was inconclusive. All that anyone knew was that he often visited his sister Vera, and her husband Harry, in Spain, whence they had emigrated many years ago.

The younger members of the station had speculated that their boss had suffered a disappointment in youth and, thereafter, forsworn all hope of ever again finding True Love. Hogarth had listened to the rumours with his customary good humour and had made no comment, either before or since his retirement. He was always there to lend an ear or enjoy a companionable evening with Thomas. And as far as the latter was concerned, that was all he needed to know.

'Hello there, lad, I'll go and put the kettle on. I'd say sit down, but I can see you're all of a fidget, so come and get the biscuits out.'

'Thanks, Mike.'

Trelawney went and propped the kitchen counter, shortcake and Hobnobs forgotten. 'I had a text from Miss Cadabra saying 9th February for the reenactment. If that's when the Flamgoynes are going to strike, it leaves us barely four weeks,' he said tensely.

'To do what precisely?' came the calm reply, as Mike got out two navy-blue mugs bearing the words 'Keep calm and party with a police officer.'

Trelawney was surprised that Hogarth could even ask the question. 'Why, prepare. That date gives us only four weeks,' he repeated.

Mike picked two teabags out of the caddy and said,

'It gives *Miss Cadabra* only four weeks.'

'But … I want to help.' Thomas was bewildered by his friend's apparent unconcern. The kettle boiled. Mike picked it up and streamed the hot water into the first cup, asking,

'Do you expect to be there?'

'Well … I … there must be *something* I could do.'

Mike filled the second mug.

'This is not your fight, Thomas. This is Amanda Cadabra's and the village's.'

Clearly, Hogarth was telling him to stay out of it.

'But … well, what about you?' Trelawney asked.

'It is not mine either.'

Thomas shook his head in disbelief. 'But we can't just leave her to ….'

Mike put the kettle back on its base and turned to him. 'I can promise you, lad, on that day, you will not be idle.'

'Of course; there's always police work.'

'That is not what I mean, Thomas. If all goes as I believe

it will, you shall be needed. Though not as you think. I see an opportunity opening up. But I want you to see it for yourself. That's how we've always done things, isn't it?'

Trelawney looked thwarted but then sighed with resignation. Hogarth had been his mentor for long enough for Thomas to trust him, even now when he felt impelled to act for action's sake.

'Very well, Mike. But there must be *some*thing I can do. If maybe I could just make progress with this cold case. The van ... the cliff ....'

'You know, Thomas,' Mike said slowly, 'sometimes the answer is right in front of us, lying at our feet, staring us in the face.' His friend looked perplexed. 'And sometimes ...,' Mike continued, 'inspiration comes from ... an unexpected source.'

He let that sink in and then changed the subject to more mundane matters. At the end of the evening, Trelawney, having shrugged into his dark blue coat and scarf, paused with his hand on the door latch. He could not resist asking,

'Don't you fear for Miss Cadabra?'

'Thomas,' said Mike, laying a hand on his friend's shoulder, 'there is never anything to be gained by fearing for someone. The most we can do is to hope for the best. Take heart. If it helps, my instinct tells me that when the hour comes, there will be forces at work other than just the ill-intent of the Flamgoynes and Amanda's lone wand.'

Chapter 10

༄

REUTERS – NEW MAN IN THE VILLAGE

After a careful examination of the ballroom at The Grange, a consideration of the logistics and a lengthy consultation, Amanda drove towards home. She parked the British racing green Vauxhall Astra opposite the corner shop. The vehicle was a legacy from her grandfather and bore the legend Cadabra Restoration and Repairs along each side in gold.

'Staying in the car or coming?' she asked Tempest, enthroned on the back seat.

He looked at the door handle meaningfully.

'Very good, your highness.'

Tempest disregarded the possibility of mockery and accepted the title as his due. Amanda performed her office, and he minced forth onto the pavement, across the road and into the shop.

'Hello Aunty,' Amanda greeted Mrs Nalini Sharma, her one-time babysitter along with Mrs Sharma senior, who had held the little girl spellbound by stories of her life back in India. They had also shared secret sweets that, needless to say, Granny knew about perfectly well, but it made them all the more exciting and delicious.

Nalini's willowy form wafted forth from the back of the shop.

'Hello, Amanda dear, have you recovered properly after your experience, so recently? I hope you are not going back to work too soon.'

'I am much better, thank you and starting slowly.' Which was true in relative terms, she reflected.

'How was the visit to Irma?' asked Mrs Sharma.

'Er, how did you know …?'

'Mr Flote the glazier was in here this morning. And Mr Nottage, who lives across the road, saw the party going into Irma's house on Saturday.'

The villagers' powers of deduction were formidable, and their network of intelligence would have been the envy of Walsingham, Elizabeth I's notorious spymaster. Its HQ was The Corner Shop. Mrs Sharma was its 'M'.

'Of course, Dennis was there too. No doubt, he enjoyed himself,' Nalini added with approval. 'Hmm, Adela's 77th. I expect Irma called you over about the piano.'

'Er … yes …,' replied Amanda. How do they do it? she asked herself. 'Did … have you seen Irma since …?'

'It was a foregone conclusion, my dear. A birthday, celebratory imbibing, a little reliving the glories of the past. I am sure she was very talented in her youth.'

'You know about the cabaret dancing?'

'Her granddaughter was at college with my niece,' Mrs Sharma explained helpfully.

'Ah.'

'M' leaned down below the counter and straightened up, now with a napkin in her hand. It enclosed, as usual, one piece of Orijen Tundra Cat Treats. She passed it to Amanda to be placed before Tempest, asking,

'How can I help you today, my dear?'

Amanda put the delicacy on the floor and handed over a piece of paper.

'I have a list from Irma.'

'Of course, she will have to stay home to receive the repairers and deliveries. It is very good of you to get her shopping for her,' commended Nalini.

'Not at all,' Amanda replied, genuinely.

As she read through the items, Mrs Sharma asked,

'So. Have you met them?'

'Er ... met who, Aunty?'

'The new men.'

Amanda groaned inwardly.

'No,' she replied politely.

'You will. I am not sure about the mother. She seems like a respectable woman, and her references check out. But the son seems, well, a little meek and mild perhaps, but honest and eager to please, and I think a good worker.'

Ding! went the shop door.

'Well now!' announced the newcomer.

'Joan.'

'Nalini. I have to say! Well! Hi Amanda.'

'I was just telling her about the other one,' said Mrs Sharma.

Joan nodded. 'Oh, well, less dazzling, but he could be solid.'

Amanda glanced from one to the other. She wished they wouldn't talk in code. So puzzled was her expression, that Joan was moved to sympathy.

'Oh love, you don't know what we're on about, do you?'

'No. Do I want to?'

'Oo I think *so*. The new florists. They've taken over the

hairdressers that was. Such a shame,' commented Joan shaking her head sorrowfully.

'A great shame,' agreed Nalini, sagely.

'We did think he might do for you, Amanda. Successful, nice-looking, lovely manners, and he did take a shine to you and no mistake.'

'You found someone to take over the shop very quickly then, Aunty,' was Amanda's attempt to divert the matchmaking stream of the conversation.

'It was providence. No sooner had I told the estate agents, than there was an enquiry that very afternoon.'

'A mother and son,' Joan contributed. 'I'm not sure how much of your type *he* is but ...'

Ding! The door opened a crack.

'Churchill! Heel!'

'Hello, Cynthia,' Nalini greeted Miss de Havillande with pleasure.

'Nalini, Joan. Ah, Amanda. Excellent. I trust that you have been informed?'

Good heavens, she thought, have they betrothed me to the florist's son?

'Erm ... informed?'

'That the former salon has been taken over.'

'Yes, Miss de Havillande. Though it really doesn't —'

'The salient point is that there may be a Prospect there for you, however tenuous.'

'I'm really not looking —'

'We know,' replied Miss de Havillande firmly. 'That is why we look *for* you. Especially in view of the ones that never came to anything. Well, of course, one of them came to a —'

'Yes, well no need to dwell on those,' intervened Joan, comfortably.

'The fact is ...'

Ding!

'Ladies.'

He was dapper in greenish-brown tweeds and co-ordinating peaked cap, driving gloves and scarf. Entering Mrs Sharma's domain, the gentleman gallantly swept off his hat, revealing well-cut grey hair.

'Dennis.'

'Hello, Mr Hanley-Page.'

'Ah, Amanda, have you *seen* it?' he asked her, with face aglow.

'It?'

'The chap drives a Lamborghini Miura in metallic green, converted to electric. Smooth as silk, and silent as falling snow,' Dennis of Vintage Vehicles recounted dreamily, lapsing into poetry, his eyes misting over. 'Chap who drives one of those can't be all bad.'

'The florist?' asked Amanda.

'No, no Ryan F—'

Ding!

This heralded the arrival of Sylvia, the lollipop lady, so titled because she carried a circular 'stop' sign on a stick used to halt traffic when the school children were crossing the road.

'He's here!' she cried. 'Right here! Talking to that florist woman. Oo, if I were 30 years younger!'

The company greeted her with interest.

'Afternoon all. If ever I saw a man good enough for our Amanda — oh, there you are, dearie. I was just saying if I were 30 years nearer your age, I'd give —'

'£12.45,' said Mrs Sharma, handing a one-hundred-per-cent recyclable plastic bag over the counter.

'Thank you, Aunty.' Amanda passed her a twenty-pound note, anxious to get her change and make her escape.

'Keep your eyes open for 'im, dearie,' Sylvia encouraged her, with a wink.

'I really don't —' Amanda began in vain.

'The clock is ticking,' Joan pointed out nodding wisely.

'Time and tide wait for no woman,' added Miss de Havillande.

'I know what you're thinking,' said Sylvia, shaking her head.

I doubt it, thought Amanda.

Ding!

'And she would right be cautious,' agreed former headmaster of Sunken Madley School, Gordon French, as he joined the throng in the small space of the corner shop.

'Ladies, Dennis, Amanda, as I am always saying ....'

'Yes, indeed Mr French,' replied Amanda, relieved to have an ally. 'That I ought to be careful of people who are not Village.'

'She's thinking 'e's not all e's cracked up to be,' explained Sylvia.

'Here's your change, dear,' said Mrs Sharma, holding it out across the counter.

'Thank you, Aunty. I really must get back to work.'

'Mind 'ow you go, dearie.'

'Look out for him, love.'

'It's a full moon tonight.'

'Goodbye, everyone!'

Amanda made good her escape to the sounds of Joan, Dennis and Sylvia breaking into the chorus of *By the Light of the Silvery Moon*.

Exhaling with relief, she hurried across the road with her familiar at her side.

'Good grief!' she expostulated to Tempest. She looked thoughtfully across at the Sinner's Rue. She thought longingly of a gin and tonic, in peace, in the quiet corner beyond the double fireplace, and took a few steps towards it.

'No,' Amanda declared aloud. 'I do have an afternoon's work before me.' She spun back resolutely and cannoned into a tall, well-built form, in a camel cashmere coat and cream scarf.

'I'm sor ...,' she began instinctively, looking up the 6-foot-1-inch-form of gentlemanly perfection, and into dark brown, intelligent eyes, aglow with kindly concern.

Chapter 11

༄

JOHN BAILEY-FARRELL

Amanda had thought Jonathan Sheppard, the assistant librarian, the best-looking man she had ever seen, however, there was something of the Old Masters' boyish model about him. But this vision before her, if she had been asked to conjure the most handsome male she could possibly imagine, she could not have done a better job. Dark hair, crisply curling off a high noble brow, a complexion that could have had skin products flying off the shelves ….

'Stop staring! It is rude to stare.' Amanda jumped at the voice in her ear. Granny had appeared, invisible to the man before her, and, having made her injunction, vanished with equal suddenness. Amanda immediately gathered her wits, closed her slackened jaw and repeated herself.

'I'm sorry. I wasn't looking where I was going.'

'That's OK. Neither was I,' he said, with a smile that was the visual equivalent of the taste of sun-ripened peaches on a summer day. Amanda was suddenly acutely aware of her overalls, messy plait, no make-up, and stain under her nails.

'May I introduce myself?' he asked courteously, in well-spoken tones. 'John Bailey-Farrell, I'm a friend of Ryan's — Ryan Ford.'

'Amanda Cadabra,' she replied, taking the warm hand he held out to her.

'Ah, what a pleasure, Miss Cadabra. Ryan has mentioned you.'

The name of the person whom she and Trelawney knew had her under surveillance brought her down to earth somewhat. I'll bet he has, she thought.

'Ah,' replied Amanda noncommittally.

'I'm staying with him at Madley Towers while some work is being done on my house,' John Bailey-Farrell explained.

'I see …. Well, erm, welcome to Sunken Madley,' she replied with a smile.

'Thank you. I've heard so much about your village that I'm looking forward to getting to know my way around, and … hope to have a chance to know some of its residents.'

He said it with such grace, Amanda was disarmed.

'Well, … there's a dance class every Saturday,' she told him. 'You'd be very welcome to come along. You'd meet most of the village notables there.'

'Thank you. I'll be sure to try and make it,' he answered her, sincerely.

'And there's the hub of the village, of course,' Amanda continued.

'The Sinner's Rue?'

'Well, in the evening, yes, but during the day … The Big Tease.'

He laughed melodiously. 'I love that name. But … yes, The Big Tease, Sunken Madley. Ryan told me, and I'm sure I read about it in the Café Society "British Village Guide Top 50" article in *Tattler*.'

'Oh, Julian and Alexander would be delighted to hear that. The proprietors. Very nice people. Actually …,' — Amanda found her lips moving and her voice coming out without the apparent involvement of either her brain or her will — 'would you like me to take you over there and introduce you? I am on a break and could certainly use a cup of tea.'

'That would be wonderful. Please, allow me to treat you,' Farrell offered courteously.

'That's most kind. This way.' They set off toward the café.

'Ryan is occupied this afternoon,' explained Farrell, 'or I am sure he would be doing the rounds with me. He is a good friend and a most considerate host.'

'Of course,' Amanda replied levelly. They arrived at their destination, and he opened the door for her. 'Hello, Julian,' she called.

'Oo, it's our Miss Cadabra back again. And who's this handsome stranger then?'

'This is Mr John Bailey-Farrell.'

'Oo no!' exclaimed Julian.

'Er, yes I am, I do assure you,' Farrell assured him with a charming grin.

'Oh, go *on*! Not *the* Mr John Bailey-Farrell?'

'Yes,' he answered modestly, 'that would be me.'

'Sandy!' cried Julian. Amanda and John looked at one another in slight alarm. 'Come quickly! Mr John Bailey-Farrell is in our tea shop!'

Alexander hurried out, taking off a floury apron decorated with a cartoon of a cook offering a burger to a man at a restaurant table and with the words 'Patty, sir?'

'Hello, Sandy, and Julian,' said Farrell, as they each shook his hand warmly. Amanda looked bewildered. She was useless with faces.

'Oh bless 'er, 'eart, Jules.' Alex turned to her. 'You don't know who this is?'

'Er ....'

'This is the Middlesex cricket team's left-arm bowler!'

'Hold on ... ,' said Amanda, her visit to Lord's cricket ground last summer flashing back. '... not ... Jake?'

'Yes,' Farrell chuckled, 'that's what Ryan calls me.'

'It was your birthday,' she remembered, 'erm, last ....'

'That's right. Ryan told me about you.'

'And you kindly said to invite me.'

'Yes, but unfortunately I didn't get the opportunity to meet you,' said Farrell regretfully. 'I believe you had to leave early.'

'Um ... yes.' Actually, Amanda remembered that she couldn't wait to get away fast enough. 'I'm so sorry I didn't recognise you with your —'

'With 'is clothes on!' chimed in Alex, naughtily.

'In mufti,' she amended with a smile.

'And out of my natural habitat,' Farrell said understandingly. 'I'm sure I look quite ordinary off the field and out of whites.'

'No,' said Amanda, her honestly overcoming any reticence. 'Not ordinary in the least, Mr Bailey-Farrell. Just different.'

'Oh please, *John*, or Jake if you prefer.'

'What can I get you two lovelies?' asked Julian. John looked at Amanda.

'Cappuccino, please.'

'With coconut milk and cream, of *course*. No dairy for our Miss Amanda, what with 'er asthma. But so well she copes. She's a marvel, Mr Bailey–Farrell!'

'*John*.'

'Oo *John*, so proud of 'er we all are. Aren't we, Sandy? Aren't we that proud of our Amanda?'

'That we are, Jules, we are. *Amazin'*, she is. What she can do with a piece of antique furniture, you *would* not believe.'

'You have a furniture restoration business, Miss Cadabra? Ryan told me, and very successful, I understand.'

'*Amanda*, please. Yes, it was my grandfather's. He taught me pretty much everything I know about it.' 'Pretty much' was accurate. Granny had taught her some extra spells.

'Cornish pasties just out the oven. Can I tempt you?' asked Julian.

'Yes, please,' replied Amanda, enthusiastically.

'Two please,' Farrell requested, 'and a latte for me.'

'Sit down, I'll bring it all over.'

'What a welcome,' marvelled Farrell. 'Is everyone in the village so kind?'

'Yes, on the whole. We don't get many outsi— I mean, visitors — so they stand out.'

'Well, I hope I can soon graduate from stranger status.'

'So do I,' she said slowly, gazing at him in a half-daze. Amanda gave herself a little shake. What was she? ... 12? What she should be doing was extracting intel about Ryan. Although Amanda knew he was keeping her under surveillance, she didn't yet know why. Surely it could only be because he was in the pay of the Flamgoynes. However, he surely didn't need money, and he seemed entirely unconnected with them.

'How is Ryan?' she asked

'He's fine. At the nets this afternoon, I think.'

'I imagine he's glad to have your company.'

'Yes, he said so,' agreed Farrell.

'Just him rattling around in that huge mansion.'

'It is pretty sizeable.'

'And not even any live-in staff, I believe,' remarked Amanda.

'He values his privacy, I think.'

'And how are *you* finding The Towers?' enquired Amanda casually.

'It's spectacular, certainly. But yes, I'm used to rather

more … company. I grew up with … well, there were five of us: parents, my sister and brother, and lots of sociable dinners with relations and friends. My mother is a famous cook. There's magic in her food, I always say.'

Amanda's ears pricked up at the word 'magic.' Tempest, curled up on her feet under the table, half-opened one eye.

'I've just acquired my first, very own house,' Farrell told her happily. 'I have to say, that the peace and quiet at the Towers, and that I anticipate in my new place, is growing on me, but I still go home for Sunday lunch whenever I can. Mum says there's nothing makes her happier than having us all round the table.'

'That's nice.' Amanda considered she had learned from him as much as she was likely to, for now. They chatted about food until they had finished their pasties and drinks, at which point she said, 'Well, thank you for the tea. I must get back to the workshop. Why don't you visit The Sinner's Rue? I'm sure they'd be delighted to see you.'

'You're very welcome, and thank you for the suggestion, but I think I'll get back and see if Ryan is planning anything for this evening.'

They left together, and Farrell set off for Madley Towers. Amanda decided she'd like to get a pie and salad for the evening and re-entered The Big Tease.

'Well!' pronounced Alex portentously. Amanda regarded him with a doubtful smile. 'The way he was looking at *you*! Wasn't he, Jules?

'Oo yes.'

Amanda was hopeless at reading facial expressions.

'How was that exactly?' she asked.

'Like all 'is Christmasses 'ad come at once!'

'Oh, surely not,' replied Amanda incredulously. 'He could have any woman he wanted. Models, film stars ….'

'Well, you're a star to us, luvvy!' countered Alex.

As she left the tea shop, Amanda caught sight of her reflection in the window. It made no sense. It simply made no sense. Not that it wasn't nice ... very nice .... He was ... really ... very nice, she ended lamely. Although never left in any doubt by her grandparents that she was loved, Amanda had not been inclined to overrate her level of physical attractiveness. She thought of herself as averagely pretty on a good day but certainly not the equal of Jessica James, the village's home-grown supermodel, or her darling Claire, both of whom she greatly admired.

No ... it made no sense. There could only be one explanation. John Bailey-Farrell must be working with Ryan. Another pair of eyes on her ... and yet ... John seemed so ....

Chapter 12

~

THE NEW SHIP INN

It was, in fact, the oldest pub in the village of Shierdrop, close to where the van incident had occurred. The *Old* Ship Inn has been destroyed in the great fire of 1783, and had risen from the ashes as The *New* Ship Inn. More importantly, it was of insufficient quaintness or smartness to attract the tourists, and consequently where the locals drank. Even more importantly, it was where the venerable seniors raised a glass or two.

Trelawney, brushing off a few drops of rain that had managed to find his shoulders in the short hurry from the car, managed to make a discreet entrance and position himself at the end of the bar. This was separated, by a helpfully obscuring pillar, from the long stretch of oak on which two locals were leaning, with pints at their elbows, whilst deep in meteorological discussion.

'I wouldn't call this *rain*, Ken,' said the taller and portlier of the pair.

'Well, Bran,' replied his shorter and wirier companion,

'not compared with the Great Downpour of 1996.'

'Or the Great Flood of 1958.'

'Piddledowndidda? But only one fatality then. Not like the Great Storm of 1987, see?'

'Though, they say that weren't nothin' compared to the Great Tempest of 1703.'

'I'm glad I weren't around for that, me 'andsome. Not but what I remember what 'appened to my car in the Great Hail of 1968. Covered in little dents, it was, and the insurance trying to tell me as it was a "Act o' God"!' concluded Ken with a snort.

'But you weren't 'avin that, now, was you, Ken?'

'That I wasn't.'

'But you'd be too young to remember the Great Freeze of '54. And 56.'

'You got me there. But don't tell me as you recall The Great Blizzard of 1891!'

That drew a guffaw from his friend.

'People always tellin' me as I don't look my age, mind!'

'No, I weren't around then I'm glad to say.'

'Best not. Four days cut off from they up North!'

'Anyone notice?' The pair collapsed into mirthful cackles revealing Bran's two missing teeth.

''ere, Bran, when you getting your new dentures?'

'Dreckly. I seen them. Just need bit of adjustin'.'

'Nice, are they?' asked Ken politely.

'Proper job.'

At this point, Trelawney decided to make his presence known by ordering a bag of ready salted crisps, in a more noticeable volume that he had asked for his coca-cola.

''Arternoon, me luvver,' said Ken, with a friendly nod.

Bran looked at the stranger with curiosity, then offered, 'Awright?'

'Good afternoon, gentlemen,' Trelawney greeted them.

'And good to be in out of the wind and rain.'

'Not that you can call this rain, lad.'

The inspector intervened before the record played again.

'Yes, you were saying. Your knowledge of the history of weather is impressive.'

'Well, it's been a matter of life and death in my line o' work,' said Ken.

'Oh, yes, of course … at sea.'

At this Bran chortled. 'You thinkin' e' a fisherman and I a farmer, eh, lad?'

'Ah. I'd be wrong, wouldn't I,' smiled Trelawney.

'Don't you judge a book by its cover, see?' advised Ken. Bran jerked a thumb at his chum.

'Pilot.'

Ken nodded. 'They retired me and now I tutors up-and-coming flyers for their theory exams, and I teaches evening classes: technology for seniors.'

Trelawney raised his eyebrows admiringly.

'And you, sir?' he asked Bran.

'I owns Dreckly Bakery. Does gluten-free. I was a baker. Then I retired. My grandson — little un' — turns out to be coeliac, poor mite. I got time on my 'ands. I gets to experimentin', and before I knows it, I got staff and a nice little business going. Keeps me outta trouble, as my missus says!'

Ken guffawed. 'We all wishes!' he said jovially. He looked with interest at Trelawney's crisps. The inspector politely offered the bag.

'What's they?'

'Ready salted.'

'Oh, I likes cheese and onion, myself.'

Trelawney got the attention of the bar staff and ordered some. He looked at Bran.

'I'll 'ave a smokey bacon, thank 'ee, kindly. I'm Bran and 'e's Ken.'

'Hello, I'm Thomas. Thomas Trelawney.'

'Oh ar,' remarked Ken, and Bran gave an approving nod in recognition of a fellow Cornishman. Here, the inspector's name was his passport, and he knew it.

'I'll 'av to go out the back for the smokey bacon. Back dreckly,' said the barman and strolled off.

'From Looe, are you?' Ken asked.

'Parhayle.' This earned Trelawney some more brownie points; being from a small fishing port.

'You don't look like you go out wi' the fleet!' jested Bran.

'Well, certainly not in this suit,' he responded jovially. 'But my grandfather, grandmother, uncles and one of my aunts are fishermen.'

'Ar now ... your granddad .... 'e wouldn't be old *Clemo* Trelawney, would 'e?'

That drew a smile from the inspector.

'He would indeed.'

'Ar. Well now. You tell 'im as Bran Penberth sends 'is best.'

'I shall. Thank you.'

Once the snacks had arrived and the three were munching in companionable silence, the inspector asked casually,

'You've lived here a long time then, I take it?'

'Most of our lives hereabouts,' acknowledged Bran.

'Were you here in 1988?'

''88? Lemme see ... ar, that were a good year. Pubs started openin' all day. New licencin' hours.'

Ken waved a crisp. 'I remember that. Yes, lad, we were in these parts.'

'Do you remember a van full of people going off the cliff just by here?'

'Oh, that.'

Bran shook his head sorrowfully. 'Terrible it were.'

'All them souls.'

'Never solved that one did they, the bobbies?' Ken gestured with his pint. 'What are you? Insurance?'

'No,' said Bran scornfully, at his friend's being so wide of the mark. ''E a copper, anyone can see that.'

'Do you remember anything about that day?' asked Trelawney evasively. The pair considered at length in silence. Finally ….

'Might 'ave rained,' said Ken. '… Or not. I can't remember.'

Bran sipped his beer meditatively. 'That bend in the road ….'

Trelawney let the pause linger then finally prompted, 'Did you see it? The accident?' The baker had clearly been thinking about something else entirely, for the inspector's words recalled him from his reverie with a slight start, only to utter the words.

'Oh, I weren't 'ere. You 'ere, Ken?'

'Me? No.'

'Did you hear any of the locals discuss it?' Trelawney enquired patiently.

'Oh, ar, lotta talk, journalists a-buzzin' around like Christmas, Easter and their birthdays 'ad all come at once. Not often we get big news in these parts.'

'Old Cubert Pollock, 'e done special tours to the site o' the crash for a bit. Wozelike! Takin' advantage of they emmets, eh? Before 'e got stopped, see?'

'Bad taste, they said,' explained Bran.

But this sounded hopeful to Trelawney. 'Was this Cubert there when the accident happened, or was that just what he told the tourists?'

'No,' Ken replied flatly. ''E weren't there.'

Bran nodded. 'Zackly. 'E just read all the papers, see?'

Trelawney knew there was no rushing Cornish people.

Interviewing was a slow and painstaking business at the best of times, but, in the land of his birth, especially so. One of the most used words in these parts was 'dreckly', the Cornish equivalent of 'mañana.' Consequently, he took his time. Rather than asking questions, it was wiser just to get people talking, then hold a net in the stream, hoping to catch a fish in the flow.

'Mind you,' remarked Ken. 'That bend. Not the first to go over there.' A sudden buffet of wind off the sea shook the window nearest them for a moment.

'Ar,' agreed Bran. 'I'llItellywot, my granddad used to say, coach and horses went over in 1834 ....'

'... on the old post road,' Ken took up the thread, 'coming from up North down to the Tamar, to Cremyll passage, then followed the coast to Looe and Falmouth.'

Several fat drops of driven rain banged noisily against the old glass panes. Then into the comparative silence that followed, fell Bran's words: 'They say that bend be 'aunted.'

Ken raised a finger portentously. 'By the ghost of a young man. They do say he was racin' 'is mate from Plymouth to St Austell. Then again ....'

Bran cocked his head to one side, as though considering the story's merits, then added, 'In all fairness, they do say once a year, a carriage is seen appearin' and disappearin' at that bend ...'

Bran looked up at Trelawney, an idea occurring to him. 'P'raps the van driver see it ... if he's one with The Sight. Got spooked and went off the road ....'

'Hmmm. That's a possible explanation,' the inspector acknowledged. The rain had abruptly abated, and a shaft of sunlight pierced the window. He drained his glass. 'Thank you, gentleman. You've been a great help.'

'Any time, lad.'

Trelawney sat in his car, tapping the steering wheel. This was the first he'd ever heard of the tale. It was nowhere in the report; he'd been over the file so many times he knew every word by heart. Could it have been that? There was so much of the supernatural tied up in this case that … was it just possible? Hogarth's words came back to him.

'Sometimes, the answer is … lying at your feet.' Suddenly Trelawney was sure. It wasn't about finding witnesses at all. It was about … the *road* …. It *had* to be all … about … the road ….

Chapter 13

༄

THE HANDOVER

'You're going to have to show 'er, love,' was the gently expressed but firm opinion of another Cornishmen. On another plane of existence.

'I suppose so,' replied Senara, with reluctance and uncharacteristic sheepishness.

'She won't be pleased,' added Perran.

'No,' his wife agreed.

'Of course,' said Perran optimistically, 'she might be too busy to notice. What with 'avin' to find the right spells for the battle.'

Senara brightened a little. 'There's always that chance, I suppose. But knowing our granddaughter, I'd say … '

Perran nodded. '… it's a pretty slim one ….'

* * * * *

Amanda was back home. She looked at her phone, in case there was word from the inspector. Nothing. If he'd got anything from Uncle Mike, he surely would have let her know.

Today was 14th January. She had to assume that the Flamgoynes would attack in three weeks and five days. And her 'resources' were exhausted. Expecting a debate, she went first upstairs, showered and changed, had a sandwich and fed Tempest. She took up a position on the sofa and inhaled.

'Gra...'

The telephone rang. It had to be an old client. They were the ones who had the landline number; the newer ones called Amanda's mobile. She leaned over to the end table and picked up the receiver.

'Hello, Cadabra Restoration and Repairs.'

'Good afternoon,' replied a pleasant, gentle, educated voice. 'Please, may I speak to Mrs Cadabra?'

Odd request for a customer, thought Amanda. Perhaps it was about an unpaid bill or a lost invoice. Granny had handled all the admin.

'I'm afraid Mrs Cadabra is not here. I'm Miss Cadabra, perhaps I can help you?'

'Oh, hello, Miss Cadabra. I hope you will forgive my calling your family like this. Only I was given your number, together with those of all of the others in your village who are clients of Mr Spinnetti.'

'The piano tuner?'

'That's correct. I am Melius Honeywell, and he has bestowed upon me the honour of deputising for him, while he is recovering from an indisposition.'

'Yes, I heard. He's having a hip operation, is that right?'

'It is indeed. We have been friends for many years and, knowing Mr Spinnetti, he will make a swift recovery, and he looks forward to being at your service in six-to-twelve months. In the meantime, I understand that your family has an instrument that Mr Spinnetti usually tunes?'

It was true. There was a small upright piano behind the dining room door that Granny had optimistically thought Amanda might like, one day, to play. She had made a start, but her enthusiasm was short-lived. As she already had Wicc'yeth, spells and carpentry in her curriculum, Granny had not insisted, but sometimes played it herself. She had had it tuned when Mr Spinnetii made his annual visits, however, just in case her granddaughter should change her mind.

Amanda was about to decline Mr Honeywell's services, preoccupied as she was with work and the Flamgoynes. However, it then occurred to her that having the piano tuned would be a pledge of good faith to herself that she would survive to return to, what passed for, normal life for a witch, and perhaps fulfil Granny's wish.

'Yes, we do, that is ... I do, and I would like it tuned.'

'Wonderful. When would suit you?'

'Erm ... let me check my schedule. Just a moment, please .... Could you do Thursday afternoon on 31st? That day is completely clear. I'll just be in the workshop. Will you still be in the area then?'

'Certainly, Miss Cadabra. Shall we say 2 o'clock?'

'Perfect.'

'Let me give you my telephone number, in case you need to rearrange for any reason, or a day becomes free sooner.'

'Thank you, I have paper and pencil.' He read off the digits. 'Thank you. And how much will it cost?'

'The same as Mr Spinnetti charges, naturally.'

'Which is ...?'

'Mr Spinnetti has frozen his prices for long-standing, valued clients such as your family, so it will be just £40.'

Amanda had a vague idea that usually tuners charged quite a bit more.

'That is most kind, Mr Honeywell.'

'My pleasure, Miss Cadabra. I look forward to seeing you at 2 o'clock on Thursday, 31st January.'

'Me too. Thank you.'

There! thought Amanda, that should earn me some brownie points.

'Grandpa. Granny.'

Senara solidified beside her on the sofa, and Perran in his favourite armchair opposite.

'Yes, dear,' said Granny.

'We're here, *bian*.'

They'd shown themselves too immediately, and, unusually, there was no cream tea in progress. Amanda sensed there was something out of the ordinary going on here. It took the wind out of her sails slightly.

'Well, er … here's the thing: I need spells. Defence spells. Not the primer stuff. I need more than a personal-space one. I've got to protect this entire village. I'm going to need a bigger shield. I need repelling spells, armour spells, deflection, and how to raise a sphere of power. Luckily, I'm a spell-weaver. But I'm still going to need guidance.'

'You're not,' Senara said shortly.

'Not what?'

'A spell-weaver.'

Amanda frowned in bewilderment. 'What do you …? Yes, I am; I can do any number of —'

'— No,' Senara felt obliged to cut her granddaughter short. 'That is,' she relented, 'yes, you *can. Can cast*. You have an aptitude for spells. You are, in fact, good at spells. That is *not*, however, the same as being a spell-weaver.'

Amanda looked from one to the other of her grandparents.

'What's the difference?'

'Long ago,' intervened Grandpa calmly, 'there were many witch families, each with a predominant gift, but without the spells to make the most of it. When there was something new and special they wanted to do, they'd come to the spell-weaver. She or he understood the magical power of words. The spell-weaver would create a spell for them.'

Granny took up the thread. 'In time, this power became concentrated in the hands of the Cardiubarn clan. And, inevitably, they began exacting payment. Hence they grew in wealth, power and influence.'

'So they have the magical powers of all the clans!' exclaimed Amanda.

'No,' Senara assured her. 'The spell reaches its full potential only in the hands of someone who has the special power that the spell is intended to manipulate or enhance.'

Amanda was trying to visualise how that would work. Granny smiled slightly and explained.

'I, for example, could use some simple levitation spells for around the house and garden, at need, but I could never do the complicated and delicate tasks that you and your grandfather could, and can, do.'

This was new to Amanda.

'Really?' Granny had used so little magic that Amanda had somehow imagined her power to be infinite.

'Indeed,' Senara said with a nod. She let this sink in and then continued. 'The Cardiubarns, long along, wrote protection spells for the Cadabras. Long before the conflict began.'

'Those spells are linked to levitation because they involve erecting barriers of kinds, you see, Ammy love,' explained Perran.

'So you can teach me these spells, Grandpa? They're not in *Forrag Seothe Macungreanz A Aclowundre*.' This was the Cadabra spellbook, *For the Making of Wonderful Things*, from which Perran had taught her. It was only through the use of levitation that she was able to engage in a profession whose physical demands would otherwise have lethally exacerbated her asthma.

'No, that book is just for woodworking, and no, I never needed big defence spells.'

'Well, they're not in Granny's *Wicc'huldol Galdorwrd Nha Koomwrtdreno: Aon* either,' she protested, turning an anxious face to him. 'So what do I *do*? Grandpa, you have to help me!'

'They *are* written down,' he replied quietly.

'But *where*?'

Granny spoke.

'Come with me, Ammy.'

She led the way up the stairs to the attic. Tempest followed with interest. Amanda was pretty sure of their destination: to where she had stashed Granny's hereditary grimoire, together with her own magical tools, during a day of crisis only weeks before. That was the first time she had become aware of Senara's secret hiding place. It was currently under a stack of suitcases.

'*Aereval*,' said Amanda on entering, gesturing with her right hand, palm up. The luggage rose. She guided it away from the vital area. '*Sedaasig*,' she uttered, and it sank back down in its new landing place.

Granny knelt down and intoned.

'*Agertyn forrag Senara, atdha mina vocleav*.'

A section of the floor acquired hinges as cuts appeared in the boards: a lid. It opened. Granny gave place to Amanda to get out the things she had had to hide in there: her witch's hat, her long wand, the Cadabra spellbook and the Cardiubarn *Wicc'huldol Galdorwrd Nha Koomwrtdreno: Aon*, or, in English, *Witchcraft: Spells and Potions: 1*.

Once Amanda had removed her things, Granny spoke to the floor again:

'*Agertyn forrag Amanda Cadabra, atdha anhe vocleav*.'

She turned to her granddaughter. 'Ammy, repeat after me: '*Agertyn forrag Amanda Cadabra, atdha mina vocleav*.'

'You're passing the voiceprint spell to *me*?' asked her granddaughter.

Senara nodded. To Amanda, it felt like a significant moment. Like her grandmother was recognising her as a grown up. A witch in her own right. Then, before she could get too emotional, it occurred to her that Granny was quite capable of having half a dozen other hiding places in this attic, all still voiceprinted to herself.

However, Amanda responded politely, 'Thank you, Granny,' and repeated, *'Agertyn forrag Amanda Cadabra, atdha mina vocleav.'*

'There,' said Granny. 'It's yours now.'

'But the spell isn't in either of these two books that I have,' Amanda pointed out.

'Er ... no dear ... so ....' Senara cleared her throat. 'You may want to look a little further inside ...'

Amanda, questioningly, looked over her shoulder at Granny. She leaned forward, reached back down into the secret space, and stretched out her hand to the left a few inches more. In the dark depths, her fingers met ... leather. Amanda grasped what felt like the shape of a box and pulled out ... a book: the same size as her primer. Was it a spare copy? She read the title: *Wicc'huldol Galdorwrd Nha Koomwrtdreno*: Dewa.

'Dewa? Book 2' Amanda expostulated. 'You never told me there was a Book 2!'

'Your primer does say "Book 1",' said Senara ingenuously.

'Yes, but ... but, I thought it was all you were able to bring with you when you left home!'

'Hmmm,' replied Granny, brushing an imaginary cobweb off her sleeve.

'Why didn't you *tell* me?' Amanda pressed.

Senara shrugged. 'You didn't ask, dear.'

'Well, *really*, Granny!'

Now, even in the midst of her indignation, Amanda could feel a sort of tug from the hole under the floorboards. She looked at her grandmother, suspiciously.

'Waaaait a minute ...' Amanda leaned forward again, but this time, until her ear was touching the floor, so that she could get her arm down and right along the cavity. There was something else in there .... 'Got it!' She had a fair idea of what it was, even before she pulled it out. Another book. She checked the cover: *Wicc'huldol Galdorwrd Nha Koomwrtdreno: Tre.* Book 3.'

Tempest now made his presence felt by taking up a position about three feet away, swishing his tale and, tapping the floor with a paw.

Amanda looked at Senara. 'Do I have them *all* now?'

'You have everything you need,' replied her grandmother, mistress of evasion.

'That's not an answer, Granny,' said Amanda severely, sounding for a moment just like Senara.

'It's the answer you need right now, Ammy dear,' Senara replied serenely, whilst eyeing Tempest with more than her customary disfavour. 'Would you like to do the honours and close up?'

Amanda looked at the floor: '*Bespredna.*' The hatch shut and, at once, all sign of it vanished. The books were heavy, so Amanda used magic to get them downstairs.

'It's going to take me hours to read all of this,' she pointed out. 'Couldn't you give me some page numbers? Or at least a hint?'

'You're a witch; you have to find the spells that fit you. You'll know them when you see them,' Granny stated calmly. When she reached the bottom of the stairs, she seemed to be walking away.

'You're not going, are you?' Amanda objected.

'Just into the sitting room. It's tea-time. Nice to see you

are maintaining the piano, by the way.'

Amanda smiled to herself, took the volumes into the dining room and began her preliminary scan of Book 2.

The grandparents seated themselves side-by-side on the sofa. Perran spoke to his wife in a low voice, as a cream tea appeared on the coffee table.

'She's going to find it, Senara.'

'Nonsense. You know how single-minded she is. Like a dog with a bone. All she's looking for right now are the spells to defend the village. She'll pass it by.'

'Wishful thinking, I know our Ammy. Pass the jam, will you, love?'

Amanda had a procedure for studying non-fiction: look at the cover, the back cover, the contents page, the last page, all diagrams, skim each chapter, then begin at the beginning.

There was no back cover, or contents page and not all of the spells had illustrations. Furthermore, this was part of a series, but the strategy was the same: get an overview first. By dinnertime, pointed out by Tempest in a manner Amanda was unable to ignore, she had completed this stage. It was half an hour since the grandparents had said good evening and gone.

After her meal, Amanda commenced a detailed study of Book 2. It was years since she had been fluent in Wicc'yeth, the magical language in which the grimoires were written, and had to drag out the exercise books from her childhood and teenage years.

By 1 o'clock in the morning, she had learned a good deal about the Cardiubarns that she would rather not have known. Rubbing her tired eyes, Amanda came to a decision.

'Tempest,' she addressed her somnolent familiar, 'tomorrow I am taking the day off. The piano lid can wait, the extent of the work at The Grange is still contingent on the number of people on the guest list, which the ladies and Moffat still have to finalise. And Chris's floor repair quote won't be back from the insurance company for at least 48 hours.'

He snored softly.

'I'm so glad you concur,' she said to the fur bundle on the seat of the chair to her right, tucked under the tablecloth. 'Bed then.' At this, he opened his eyes, yellow points of light in the shadow. He poked his head out from under the velvet fabric and yawned pointedly, as though she had been inconsiderately keeping him up.

Amanda chuckled, marked where she had got up to in Book 2 and gathered him up in her arms. She got a glass of water, turned off the lights and climbed the stair to bed, with Tempest draped over her shoulder, his head nestling under her hair.

This spell-searching, he reflected long-sufferingly, … it's exh*aus*ting.

Chapter 14

ON THE ROAD TO ST AUSTELL

Detective Inspector Thomas Trelawney stood at the side of the B6244, staring down between the pines at the rocks below. It was a treacherous bend, no doubt, for a car travelling fast when the fog rolled in off the sea, thick and cold enough to turn the roads to an ice-skating rink. However, the local council had been extra vigilant, and at the slightest hint of dangerously low temperatures, overnight, the gritters were out, for this stretch if no one other.

Since the van had gone over the cliff onto the unforgiving crag at its feet, a barrier had been erected. Trees had been planted to break the fall, even if a vehicle should get through the posts lining the road.

Trelawney opened the manila folder he was carrying, and looked at the 30-year-old photographs of the road surface at the time. He was missing something. He had to be missing … something.

There were skid marks … and there was the Rorschachtest-shaped pit in the surface of the tarmac. That must have been the cavity containing the out-of-season black ice that the anonymous driver had reported: the ice she had managed to swerve to avoid but which the van driver behind her had not. Why not?

It had not rained properly the night before the incident, only the sprinkling of a Cornish mist. Even if water had collected in the cavity, surely cars driving over it would have displaced it with their tyres, wouldn't they?

Trelawney turned his head, hearing a car drawing up behind where his was parked, and the driver applying the brake. A comely woman, with mid-brown hair curling up off her shoulders, emerged and walked towards him with a warm smile. A camera was slung over one shoulder, its strap proclaiming a Canon EOS. She was of comfortable proportions and about his mother's age, with much of Penelope Trelawney's youthful glow, and yet … there was something far more restful about her.

'Hi there,' said the newcomer.

An American accent indicated her country of origin. She was the antithesis of the misleadingly stereotypical image of the US tourist. Trelawney found most who wandered by mistake into Parhayle were polite, friendly and in wide-eyed, appreciative awe of all they saw there. Like his colleagues, Trelawney knew it was important to spot and keep an eye on them. They tended to have more faith than was warranted in the traffic's willingness to stop and let them cross the road, when they stepped out into its path. The locals were accustomed to the narrow and winding streets and, in the absence of speed controls, were apt to treat the small town like Le Mans.

'Hello, can I help you?' Trelawney offered politely.

'I hope so. I'm kinda lost. And the GPS isn't doing me any favours.'

'Where are you trying to go?'

'A little place called Porthcadoc?'

'Ah, you won't find that on any map, and we keep the entrance road to that hidden, as a puzzle to entertain visitors,' he said ruefully. 'But perhaps it's gone beyond that point?'

'Not really, but I saw you and thought I could get a hint or two. Though I love driving around this place. I dreamed about it for a long time.'

'You're a visitor to these shores?'

'Sure am. My husband and I always promised ourselves we'd make this trip one day.'

'Is he meeting you at Porthcadoc?'

'He passed last year,' she said with acceptance.

'I'm sorry.'

'No, he's with me in spirit. I'm making this trip for both of us.'

Trelawney nodded. 'That's an impressive piece of kit,' he said, looking at her camera.

'Thank you. It's my pleasure and my business back home. I thought I might get a few great views while I'm here. And that's kinda how we met.'

'Your husband was a photographer too?'

'No. There was an accident on the highway. I stopped and got out to see if I could help, and so did he. I took some photos for the police and insurance, and he gave a report on the road. It's OK, no one was badly hurt, and we ...,' she ended with a smile.

'What did he do, if I may ask?'

'Civil engineer; highways. He was a real smart man.' She tilted her head and looked towards the folder in Trelawney's hands. 'Are those, er, photos of the road? Don't wanna be a nosy American ....'

'Oh, not at all. We do nosy here with a lot less subtlety than the polite interest you have just taken. But yes, I was.'

'I picked up a thing or two about highways during 30

years of marriage. That's the secret you know: not just talking but listening.'

'Yes,' Thomas agreed.

'I don't see a ring on your finger,' she observed gently.

'Er ... no,' he replied.

She tilted her head again, but this time to look up at him.

'But ... there's someone ...' An uncharacteristic tell-tale blush infused his cheeks for a moment. Nodding, she said, 'Ah, OK ... there's something stopping you ....' Trelawney looked at her in surprise. She laughed sympathetically. 'My husband always said I was a little psychic. Runs in the family. ... Yeah ... the thing that's stopping you ... it's something to do with,' — She looked at the photos in his hand — '... this ....'

'Erm ... well ....' He didn't know what to think, let alone say.

'Maybe I can help?' she offered.

Trelawney would never usually have discussed a case with a complete stranger. But there was something about this woman, a warmth, a maternal kindliness — no, he thought, it was more than that. It was almost a feeling of ... no, it couldn't be but ... kinship.

'Well ... a van, er, mini-bus, went over the cliff here about 30 years ago. It was September and not cold. Even so, a witness reported seeing black ice on the road.' He showed her the photographs, one in particular, a closeup. 'See this pit in the road? I think that's the only place it could have formed. You can see how the skid marks come out of it. There was just Cornish mist the night before, and possibly morning dew, and anyway, surely the tyres of the passing cars would have displaced the water.'

The woman peered, first, at the wide shot and then the closeup.

'Hold on. Let me get my macro lens.' She handed the

photos back to him and within a minute returned, put the image on the bonnet of his car and focused her camera on the photo. 'Hmmm.'

'Yes?' asked Trelawney, hopefully.

'Well, ... I'm no expert, and I know nothing about your highways here ... but I have a couple of theories.'

'Please,' he invited her.

'OK, look ... you can see there are tiny runnels, like arteries going from around the pit, branching out the sides? Now, on roads, there's a slope. Sometimes it goes from the crown of the road and sometimes from one side of the road to the other, like on this bend. I would have expected it to slope the other way, but maybe there was something in the ground that prevented that.'

'So that water drains away into the side drains?'

'Yes, but these little channels would have collected water running off on either side of the pocket and sent it in there, rather than down into the drain.'

'Can you see if those channels are naturally occurring or man-made?'

She looked again, adjusting her lens and the distance from the paper.

'I'd say man-made. But please remember that mine's not an expert opinion,' she urged.

'So more water than normal would have had the opportunity to accumulate in that cavity?'

'Theoretically.'

'Right. ... Could someone have found a way to create a water supply that could have fed this puddle?'

Here the woman waited for two cars to pass, then crossed over to the other side of the road and looked down into the ditch. 'Yeah, if I wanted to be doubly sure that it would stay topped up, I'd put a container over here. You could sneak it under the edge of the road surface if you were prepared to dig, or just hide it deep in the ditch itself. Then ... see that line on the photo? It looks like a joint or maybe repair that goes right across the road? It could have covered a tube, running from the reservoir and making sure that the little lake was kept supplied. Like a fishpond. You'd need a pump, I guess but ... I know it's farfetched, but that's my theory, for what it's worth.'

'Interesting.'

'There's one more thing. A deep hole holds water longer than a shallower one. This hole could have been deeper and made to look shallow and ... it could have been sealed to make sure no water drained out of the bottom and sides.'

Trelawney stood looking at the road thoughtfully.

'So ... do you know you whodunit, Detective?' she asked merrily.

'Well, let's say I now have a possible part of the puzzle of *how*dunnit. Thank you, ma'am, your help has been invaluable.'

'You're welcome, — what is it? — Inspector?'

'Is it so obvious?'

She laughed. 'My daughter's a cop. I can spot one a mile off.'

'Well, thank you again. I would like to do something in return. Erm, I can, at least, lead you to your destination. And if you're looking for a spectacular shot, I know of none better than at dawn when the fishing boats go out from the point at Parhayle, with the sun rising in the east.'

'Why thanks. Please lead the way, and — who knows? — maybe I'll see you around.'

She returned to her car, before he could introduce himself or ask her name. He led the way back north-east along the B6244, to what looked like little more than a gap in the hedge. There was the track to the hamlet she sought. He stopped at the side of the road. She drew up next to him with the windows wound down.

'It's right in front of you,' said Trelawney, pointing.

'Thanks, Inspector. And don't worry about your puzzle. You'll solve it. It's just a matter of time. You take care now.' She released the brake, the car moved forward and was turning into the side road.

'Ma'am!' Trelawney suddenly called out on impulse. 'Your family name?'

As she drove away, her voice came back to him on the wind from the sea.

'... Trelawney ....'

With a quick intake of breath, an urge to follow her rose in him. And yet, his rational self, stepping in, pointed out, she had not offered her first name nor invited him to accompany her. He would not want her to feel stalked. But if she was maybe staying around here, he could return another day and perhaps, by chance, find her and talk to her ....

Trelawney returned to the bend in the road. It had long since been resurfaced and now had no story to tell of that fateful day. He looked again at the photographs. Wasn't black ice usually in thin sheets? Maybe it had just been ice? Ice that looked black? Or ... was made to look black? What if, Senara had engineered keeping the hole topped up? What was to stop her coming back after the accident and removing the evidence?

The question was then, did she come back to Cornwall after? How about ... to identify the bodies? After all, who else of the family was left? The Cardiubarn solicitor ... he would have had her contact details, wouldn't he? Because of the child, Amanda, being resident with them. She could have come down, done the identifications, taken away whatever she used to create the black ice, then returned to Sunken Madley.

So far, so good. But Senara Cadabra was not here on the day of the incident. So the questions were: how could the water have been frozen? And at the right time to affect only two cars? Time .... His kinswoman's last words came back to him.

'It's just a matter of ... time ...'

Chapter 15

∽

INTO THE GRIMOIRES

The following morning, Amanda was awake with the sunrise, and her head was too busy for further rest. She was soon up, dressed, breakfasted with Tempest and ready to begin a page-by-page inspection of *Wicc'huldol Galdorwrd Nha Koomwrtdreno: Dewa*, Book 2 of the Cardiubarn grimoires.

Halfway through, she found a useful repelling spell, though only for spell-stings. This was the first attack spell she had seen referenced, although it was clear that, like a gnat bite, it was more irritating than anything else. Still, in a conflict, it could perhaps be distracting.

A few pages later, was an incantation for mazing, a sort of hypnosis to create confusion and disorientation. Ah, here was the form of words and wand action for de-activating it. Amanda was getting near the end of the volume, and had yet to see any of the really serious stuff that she needed. At last, her Wicc'yeth, the magical language of spells, was coming back to her and she was reading more quickly.

'Let's take a break,' Amanda said to Tempest, lounging in a patch of tepid sunlight on the table, 'not that anyone else other than me is actually *working* here,' she added. Tempest gave a sigh, expressive of the demands of his arduous role, providing moral support. They went out to the kitchen, where her familiar had a snack and Amanda topped up her tea and added another gingernut to her little tray.

'Come on then. Next shift!' They returned to the table.

It was on the last page, typically, that she struck gold. Though not quite the kind that she was looking for.

Amanda had, long ago, learned a temperature-control spell. It was useful for creating optimum workshop conditions, making the air warmer or cooler as need be. Also, it was ideal for making air currents under her model planes that she loved to fly around her bedroom. But that was a Book 1 spell. The writing before her, described one that was a notch up from that: how to change water to steam or ... ice.

Amanda excitedly read out the spell to Tempest.

'If there was a puddle on the road that the van was driving on that day, when I was only three, Granny would have had the knowledge to turn it to ice. However ... if she had done that the day *before*, the last time she was in Cornwall before the day of the incident, then cars would have been skidding on it for hours,' continued Amanda, with a perplexed frown. 'And there surely would have been, at least, one report of it at the time. Still ... it *is* a *piece* of the puzzle. Lunch!'

Amanda, revived by a roast beef and mustard sandwich and another cup of tea, and having served a light meal of tinned salmon for her familiar, began Book 3 with zest. Some of the incantations were becoming increasingly unpleasant in their intent, but, on the other hand, she was learning antidotes. She now had found the instructions for anti-panic, anti-amnesia, anti-coma, and crucially anti-firebolt.

She was a third of the way through when, at half-past one, her phone rang.

* * * * *

During the morning, Trelawney was occupied with a meeting at the next station along the coast. Madern Eudy, The Cornish Cornet King, had had a win on the Lands End Lottery, and, to celebrate, had, in spite of the season, been driving his ice cream van around handing out free 99s to all and sundry, as a last hoorah before selling up and moving to Barbados. Unfortunately, this had led to a spate of accidents caused by careless motorists proceeding along the highways and byways with only one hand on the wheel. Meanwhile, the other hand was clutching a cone, filled with whipped ice cream with a Cadbury's Flake shoved in the top. The problem worsened as it began to melt, and more attention was required to prevent drips running down the driver's hand than for the road ahead.

Sergeant Pedrick wanted to have a joint initiative to spread the word that, while eating ice cream while in charge of a moving vehicle was not illegal, *per se*, it did present a certain danger of dereliction of duty to take the necessary care whilst driving. Trelawney was inclined to think that the problem would go away when Mr Eudy did. Which, given the size of his freezer and the rapidity with which he was dispensing his particular form of goodwill, could not be many days, if not hours, hence. Nevertheless, in the cause of good relations and public safety, Trelawney had agreed to meet up with the sergeant.

On the way back to the station, however, Trelawney's mind became busy with the previous day's investigation at the bend in the road. The desire that had been born to impart the new theories to Miss Cadabra, but had been suppressed by the requirements of his current workload, was growing. By a quarter-past one, he could no longer contain it. There was nothing of great urgency on his plate at the station, but what was now occupying his thoughts was a pressing matter. Once back in his office, he reached for his phone.

'Miss Cadabra?'

'Hello, Inspector.'

She sounded pleased to hear from him. Good.

'Are you at home?' he asked her.

'Yes, I am.'

'Can you spare the time for a conference?'

'Of course,' she replied. 'I'm glad you called. I've found something that I think may be important.'

'I have something to share with you too. Right. I'm on my way.'

Trelawney asked the ever-helpful Constable Nancarrow to clear his schedule until tomorrow afternoon. He checked that his overnight bag was in the back of the car and sufficiently stocked, let his mother know that he would be descending on her later, and took the road to London.

* * * * *

Meanwhile, back at 26 Orchard Way, Amanda was still at work. She had found the spell for raising a sphere of power around two people, but that would not be nearly enough. She read on. ... ah, this was better, a sphere with radius seven feet ... and this page explained how to expand it.

'We're nearly there, Tempest! I just need the mirror spell. Tea-break time.'

Recommencing and wanting to cover all of her bases and find any charm that might be useful, Amanda was reading much more carefully now. Consequently, her progress through the volume had slowed significantly. She was getting distracted by hitherto unimagined uses for magic, and pausing wide-eyed to try and take it all in. All at once, her progress was halted entirely.

Unseen by his utterly absorbed human, Tempest had reluctantly emerged from his snug sleeping place on a chair seat under the table cloth. He stepped up onto the table and planted himself squarely on the open page of the book.

'What …! What are you doing?' asked Amanda, shocked by his obstructiveness.

He stared with bored patience into her eyes. Then leaned forward and poked one delicate claw between the pages, about three-quarters of the way through the textblock.

'What?' She put a fingernail in the same place, Tempest moved off and she flipped the big wad of pages over. 'Oh, I see. You're saying I don't need to read all of these?'

He moved over to her side of the tome so he could read it. Or this, he thought — with a paw pad, turning the page — or this one — and the next one — or this one … or any of these. All right, she can start … here.

Amanda picked him up and cuddled him. 'Thank you, Tempest! You've saved me masses of time.'

Well someone had to, her familiar considered, or we'd have been here for weeks!

To celebrate, they had another tea-break. Now, back at the table, Amanda's eyes were on the alert for any words to do with reflection. There were a number of things that Amanda did not readily observe, that were easily noticeable for most other people. But one of the things she was good at seeing … was patterns. That's why it caught her eye. There was *some*thing where there should have been *nothing*. Writing ... where there should have been space. A schoolgirl's hand where there should have been archaic script. It was a disruption. And Amanda had to understand the reason for it.

It was an addendum to the text. It began at the bottom

of a right-hand page. The writing got progressively smaller as it filled the footer, then rose up the margin, into the header, and onto the footer of the next page. Amanda's Wicc'yeth was still a little rusty. She wasn't entirely sure what she was reading. Some of the ingredients were obscure, some utterly unknown to her.

By halfway through the third read-through, Amanda was certain of what it was: a time-delay spell.

Chapter 16

HOWDUNNIT

Amanda, with her hands still on the incriminating page, stared up through the window at the bare fruit trees in the garden. She jumped. The doorbell had rung. She went to open it. There was the inspector. They stood for a moment, looking intently at one another.

'Come in,' she said urgently.

'Thank you.' He entered, and she quickly closed the door. They stopped in the hallway and, in low tones, spoke simultaneously:

'I think I know how she did it.'

Unceremoniously, Amanda took Trelawney's arm and hurried him into the dining-room, where she remembered her manners.

'Sorry inspector. Hello. Would you like some tea?'

'Miss Cadabra, thank you, yes please, presently. But first … I have to tell you —'

'— and *I* have to tell *you* No, sorry, let's sit down. Please go ahead, Inspector. You first.'

'Thank you, Miss Cadabra. You see, the most astonishing thing happened to me. I went to look at the road —' He noticed the three tomes, with their arcane illumination and magical script, on the table before them. 'I say. Those look like ....'

'Yes, spell books. I'm a witch, as you well know, but do go on. You went to look at the road where the incident happened?'

'Yes, and a woman stopped and looked at the photos of the road taken 30 years ago. Her husband was a civil engineer, and, although she insisted that she was no expert, she said it looked to her like there were capillaries cut into the road surface' — He opened his folder and pointed to a spot on the top photograph — 'to channel water into this cavity. Presumably, this is where the lethal ice formed.' Amanda listened attentively as Trelawney related the woman's two other theories. 'Then she said — almost her last words — Time ... it was just a matter of *time*.'

'Yes!' exclaimed Amanda. 'And this,' she said, placing her hands on Books 2 and 3, 'is where *these* come in.'

'What exactly are they?'

'They are the Cardiubarn grimoires. I didn't know until today that they existed. That is, I *did* know about — it's a bit complicated. Never mind about that just now —but I found *this* this morning.' She opened Book 2. 'This spell.' Amanda pointed to it and began reading aloud: '*Forrag* —'

'Sorry,' he interrupted her. 'I — I don't understand the —'

'Oh, no. *I'm* sorry, Inspector. It's a temperature-control spell. She could have filled the hollow in the road with water and then used the temperature-control spell to turn it to ice.'

'But she wasn't there at the time,' objected Trelawney.

'Precisely. So she ....' Amanda stopped and took a breath. 'I should stop saying "she". We both know who I mean.' Trelawney nodded. 'Granny. Granny would have needed *this*.'

Amanda turned to the relevant page in Book 3 and pointed to the handwritten notation. 'This ... is a time-delay spell ... a very difficult one. This is *advanced* magic. And it was spell-woven by a child, a teenager at most.'

'Who?'

'Book 1 has notes in it, written by Granny's ancestor — well, and mine too, I suppose — Jowanet. She was notorious. Some of the spells were so hair-raising that Grandpa erased or sealed them before I was allowed to even *see* the book! But I saw one or two of Jowanet's, and so I know her handwriting, and this *here* is not it. I'm sure it was Granny's.'

They were silent, considering the implications of this. If Senara Cadabra was creating advanced magic as a minor, they could only imagine how powerful she became as an adult. What she might have done ....

All at once, words that Granny had spoken to her, a couple of years before, came back to Amanda. It was just before Senara made her transition to the next plane. Granny had asked if it was all right with Amanda if she moved on. The limitations of what she referred to as her 'old bod' were irking her, but there was something she wanted to say to Amanda first. Her granddaughter remembered it, partly because Granny had seemed somewhat embarrassed. And then Granny had said,

'I have a past. I wasn't always as I am now. I did ... certain ... magically related things that I felt were necessary at the time. Things that may not reflect well on you, I am sorry to say.'

Then Grandpa had said that Granny had turned over a new leaf, when they'd met and never gone back, and then he closed the subject. Were *these*, the dodgy spells in these tomes, the 'certain magically related things?' Amanda's mind flashed to the memories of before she was three, and being shown, by her chilling great-grandmother, the family rogues' gallery with its catalogue of 'regrettable accidents'. This was a euphemism for a list of how each unpleasant member of the clan had sent the, no doubt equally unscrupulous, person above them in the line of inheritance to an early place in the Cardiubarn Hall crypt.

Amanda shook her head, as though to clear her mind of the carnival of Granny's family life, returning to the matter at hand.

'Yes, anyway, so …. This is how it looks like it goes. The day before the incident …'

'Senara Cadabra filled the hole in the road with water and made sure it stayed full by one means or another,' supplied Trelawney.

'Then,' continued Amanda, 'used a time-delay spell with the temperature-control spell, so that the puddle would turn to ice at the right moment, to send the van into a skid and off the road, and down the cliff.'

'Only … how would she have known the precise moment?' posed Trelawney. 'That is now the question.'

'You're right,' agreed Amanda. 'I was so excited … I hadn't got that far.'

'Senara would have needed …,' Trelawney began.

'A diviner,' she finished.

'Most likely … a Flamgoyne.'

They sat, eyes locked.

'Surely not,' Amanda said.

'Who else?' he asked.

It *had* to be.

Chapter 17

ACCESSORY

'Well, now, normally I'd say how nice to get a visit from both of you. And, of course, it still is, but I suspect that the circumstances could have been perhaps a little more …. Still, let us have tea. First things first. I expect you've come straight from Parhale, Thomas.'

'I went to Miss Cadabra's house.'

'Of course, and that's where you've been working things out. Clearly, you have received the books, Ammy. Now sit down, take some deep breaths, my dears.'

Aunt Amelia glided into the kitchen. Trelawney and Amanda waited in silence and did their best to maintain their patience and equanimity.

'She seems to know why we're here,' Amanda said softly to the inspector.

'And isn't in the least bit bothered, apparently,' he remarked.

In record time, the tea was ready, and Amelia returned

bearing a tray with the tea things and two plates of biscuits.

'That was quick, Aunt Amelia.'

'Yes, I knew you were coming.'

'Really?' asked her nephew, in surprise.

'Yes dear, one of the perks of being a diviner,' Amelia said cheerfully. She served the tea and handed gingernuts to Amanda and shortcake to Thomas. 'There. Now. I think I can guess why you're both here. But it never does to assume. So … Thomas?'

'We worked out how Mrs Cadabra must have sent the van over the cliff. She engineered a puddle in the road, at the dangerous bend near Shierdrop on the B6244. Then used a temperature-control spell to turn it to ice, which was operated by a time-delay spell to make it take effect at the right moment.'

'How ingenious,' commented Amelia with polite interest, stirring her tea.

'But,' continued her nephew seriously, 'she would have needed to know *when* that moment would be.'

'And for that, she would have needed a diviner,' added Amanda anxiously.

Aunt Amelia took a breath and looked from one to the other with a smile.

'I have wondered about that for a long time. Senara came to see me shortly before The Day. She said she wasn't sure about going on the trip with the Cardiubarns. She said she was apprehensive about some kind of ambush or sabotage by the Flamgoynes on the way. Senara wanted me to look and see the probable route; the pace of traffic, and what time they would be at the riskiest places on the road.'

Amelia paused, calmly, for a sip of tea. Amanda and Thomas waited with rapt attention. She continued,

'Timing in divination is always a tricky one, but I was on form that day. I could see the A38 on the Devon side of the Tamar would have roadworks, causing drivers to turn off to go through Portsmouth and take the ferry over the river to the A374. A burst pipe at the town of Antony, then would send traffic south, down the coast road and toward that treacherous bend. Yes, it all ebbed and flowed before my eyes like a tidal river. I was able to give her a very close estimate of when the van would pass that particular point. Even if I wasn't spot on, Senara would have had one more card up her sleeve: a tripwire spell. There was a story among the Flamgoynes, which I remember from when I was very young, that it was woven when Senara was only about seven years old and was responsible for the demise of Granbror Flamgoyne.'

'How?' asked Amanda, curiously.

'Senara tailed him to get acquainted with his routine. Once a week, he'd go up to the Trippet Circle on Bodmin Moor to gather a certain mineral from inside the ring. One of the stones fell on him. I did ask her about it years ago. The tripwire spell had gone off when he was in proximity to it. She said that the most difficult thing about the procedure was getting the stone to stand up again before anyone would notice.'

'Good grief,' expostulated Trelawney. 'Didn't you object to her having seen off one of your relations?'

'No. Why? They were all thoroughly ghastly, Except for dear Uncle Elwen,' she added, smiling. 'Always so nice to see him when he pops in — from the next dimension, you understand, just like your grandparents, Amanda, sweetie. But I digress. Frightful Granbror would certainly have gone for Senara, with a shot from his wand, if he'd spotted her first.'

'I suppose so,' agreed Amanda.

'But,' Amelia continued, 'they were far from evenly matched. Jowanet was a dreadful child, but Senara was worse. And yet, even within those depths, was a seed of goodness with which every child is born. The first time she saw Perran Cadabra, it received its first taste of water and light and began to grow. But before then, and not that there weren't things even *she* refused to be involved in, Senara was a born spell-weaver, like Jowanet before her.'

'So you had no idea that she intended to use the information that you had given her to send that bus over the cliff?' asked her nephew, bringing his aunt back to the matter in hand.

'No,' Amelia answered at once. 'I believed that all she was concerned about was the safety of the journey, especially for little Amanda.'

Thomas was reassured. 'And, of course, if you had known you would never have —'

'Would I not?' his aunt interrupted him. 'You don't understand, Thomas. You see, later I learned, and I *did* understand ... why Senara did it. And so you see, if she *had-*told me at the time, why and what she intended to do, I would have still have helped her. Willingly. If I could replay it, I would do it all again.'

Taken aback by her unexpected response, Thomas looked at her earnestly.

'Aunt Amelia, can you reveal to us why she did it?'

'Yes, I could. But that is for Senara Cadabra to tell you.'

'Ah yes, but she's ... well, it's hardly like I can interview her now,' he objected. Amelia looked at him with a glint in her eye and asked,

'Can't you?'

Chapter 18

༄

A FIRST FOR THOMAS

Trelawney stood there with a strong sense of déjà vu. It was almost three years since he had stood on this spot, waiting for the door to be opened, recalling all that his boss Hogarth had told him to expect in the formidable person of Senara Cadabra. She had lived up to her reputation. She had played cat and mouse with him right up to last time they had met. The fact that she was now ... well ... not to put too fine a point on it ... dead, would give her even more of an advantage. She would be expecting him to be uncomfortable. He resolved to do his best to take the interview in his stride. After all, he told himself, he came from magical stock too, and every bit as odious as the Cardiubarns. He had never thought he'd see that as morale-boosting.

Unlike the occasion of his first appointment at number 26 Orchard Row, the door was opened by Amanda.

'Inspector. Don't be nervous. They'll appear solid to you, if you expect them to, remember?'

'I remember, Miss Cadabra. Thank you for arranging this.'

'My pleasure. After you.' She gestured for him to precede her, and he walked into the sitting room.

'Fresh blood,' observed Mrs Cadabra.

Those had been her very words that first time. She was regarding him with amusement. 'Do come in.'

She was sitting just as she had that day: upright on the chintz sofa, her white hair in a victory roll. And there was Perran in the Queen Anne chair he had sat in, when he had come in later, from his workshop.

'Hello, Inspector,' he said reassuringly, with the familiar gentle Cornish burr. 'Just you be comfortable now. Ammy will get the tea, won't you, *bian*?'

She nodded and went off. Trelawney sat down, a trifle gingerly, on the sofa beside Mrs Cadabra.

'It's quite safe, I promise you, Inspector,' Perran added. 'You don't want to go believin' all that nonsense you see in horror films.'

'Indeed,' agreed Mrs Cadabra. 'Thank you for the flowers, by the way.'

'The flowers?' enquired Trelawney. Should I have brought some? Is she being sarcastic, he asked himself.

'On our graves. A very tasteful choice.'

'Oh, ... er ... you're welcome.' No one had ever thanked him for doing that before. He gave his head a little shake. Well, of *course*, they hadn't, he told himself.

'Have some tea and biscuits. You'll feel better,' Mrs Cadabra recommended bracingly.

He looked down the cup and saucer in her hands. 'You, er ...?'

But Senara had already observed his gaze. 'Oh yes, we have tea in our dimension, thank you. A great many other delights besides. Your Great-grandfather Trelawney sends his regards, incidentally. And your Great-uncle Elwen Flamgoyne too, of course. He's over the moon that you are regaining your memory.'

'Oh … ah … how nice … erm ….' Whatever was the correct response in such a situation? Thomas asked himself urgently. 'Please say … I mean, send my regards to them too.'

'You *can* speak to them or call for them, any time you want, you know,' Senara pointed out helpfully. She added a proviso: 'I'm not saying your great-grandfather will necessarily *turn up*. He does like to appear curmudgeonly, but it's all a façade. I am sure you must know that.'

'Erm mm.'

Amanda, re-entering with the tray, came to his rescue.

'Inspector, I've brought them up to speed to a certain extent. Because, you see, just because they're Persons of Another Plane doesn't mean that they know everything. I've told them that we know how Granny did it and how Aunt Amelia unwittingly helped. But now, Granny and Grandpa, what we would both like to know,' Amanda stated with sangfroid, 'is exactly what Granny's *motive* was for sending the entire family over the cliff.'

'Although I would have thought that that would be clear anyone who knew them,' Senara said acidly.

'They were not good people, you understand,' explained Amanda to Trelawney, in a mastery of Olympic-standard understatement. 'I was tiny, but even in my flashbacks I picked up *that* much.'

'Has … have *you* been told what the motive was?' he asked her.

'No, Inspector, Granny thought it would be more efficient to tell us both at once.'

And to greater dramatic effect, thought Thomas knowingly. Senara enjoyed the limelight, and now she had centre stage.

Chapter 19

WHY

Fortified by tea and a biscuit, Trelawney put his cup down in a decided manner and turned to Mrs Cadabra expectantly. She looked him in the eye, and commenced,

'It was about the spellbooks. The ones in the dining-room that Amanda showed you.'

'Yes?'

'They are mine,' she stated with finality. 'They were bequeathed to me by my great-grandmother. It was her opinion that I showed promise in that department and left them to me. *To me*, you understand.'

'I see,' Trelawney replied slowly, not sure how much yet.

'And so, when I elected to elope with Amanda's dear grandfather, I smuggled all that I judged to be of value out of the house. Unfortunately, those grimoires are both heavy and sizeable, and I was only able to remove one: the first volume. I considered that having the basics to hand, I would be able to build on them, if need be. And if I should decide to train a witch in the future, it would serve as a primer. Naturally, I was right,' Senara concluded on a note of triumph.

Amanda nodded. 'You were, Granny,' she said and received a smile and gracious inclination of the head in response. Mrs Cadabra then continued,

'It was not until forty years later that I returned to Cardiubarn Hall, by request, for Amanda's birth. She showed no signs of magical aura and, again by request, which was consonant with my own wishes, I took her home that night and every night. We were summoned, daily at first, then at intervals, for my mother to look for any indications of "talent". The visits were brief.' Mrs Cadabra paused to cut herself a slice of Victoria sandwich. Then she went on.

'Once Amanda could walk, it was required that I leave her for an hour or so with her grandmother, who hoped to kindle some mystical spark within the child. It was during those visits, that I smuggled out the additional volumes you have seen here. Ammy, dear, pass the Inspector the shortcake. I think he could do with another one.'

'Thank you, Mrs Cadabra, I'm fine for the moment.'

'As you wish, Inspector. I would not wish you to be lacking in any comfort while you are under this roof,' she returned grandly. 'To continue. It was when Amanda was around three years of age that the family discovered that the books were missing. We had taken Amanda back to Sunken Madley by then, on a permanent basis. They had, in effect, signed her off. She was a sickly little thing, and far more trouble than any one of them was prepared to take.'

'Their loss, *bian*,' Perran said to Amanda, who smiled at him.

'It was *then*,' emphasised Senara, 'that I received a letter. Asking for the return of the grimoires. I replied, accurately, that they were mine.'

Trelawney reflected that it would be a brave person who would argue with that.

'The *next* letter informed me that they intended to take Amanda back. There was be to no negotiation.' This was the first that either Amanda or Trelawney had heard of this dramatic turn of events. 'Two of them were her legal parents. Perran and I would not have had a case. I knew that ... I knew the life she would have... or lack of it .... I asked for time and that, in return, I would surrender the books. I had to think quickly. I sketched out a plan and consulted Amelia. That's when I arranged for letters to be sent to everyone in the entire clan, dangling the suggestion of a large sum of money before each of them, which they would not be able to resist. And then ... come along,' said Mrs Cadabra to Trelawney with a mocking smile, '... tell me how I did it.'

'First,' Trelawney responded, 'the hollow in the road fed by extra runnels to channel the water in, ... and did you use a pump from a reservoir on the other side of the road?'

'I used a capillary spell. I'll give you that much.'

'I didn't see that in any of the books,' objected Amanda.

'Not everything is in books, dear,' replied her grandmother patiently. 'Inspector?'

'You instructed the family solicitor to send out the letters informing them that transport would arrive on a certain morning, to take them to a destination where they would learn something to their advantage. I assume he was bound by an oath of secrecy?'

'An oath is good. A secrecy spell is so much better.'

'Unless you have faith in a person's integrity,' Trelawney countered.

'That isn't something that was nurtured by the Cardiubarns,' Senara informed him. 'And what was the next step in my assassination plot, Inspector?'

Trelawney could see that she was enjoying this.

'It was Miss Cadabra who discovered that.' Amanda duly took up the narrative.

'Granny, I worked out from the grimoires that you must have set up a time-delay spell on a temperature-control spell, so that the puddle would turn to ice at the right time.'

'Aunt Amelia added a tip-off about a tripwire spell,' said Trelawney. 'I am guessing that you recommended a vehicle hire company to the solicitor, which would have only one suitable multi-occupant carrier.'

'Very good, Inspector,' interpolated Mrs Cadabra admiringly.

'In that way, you could somehow tie in that particular van to the tripwire spell, turning the puddle to ice just before the van hit it.'

'Excellent, you are beginning to get a feel for how magic works.'

'Thus you sent it over the cliff, down onto the rocks, where the impact would kill the occupants.'

'Correct. But it didn't,' she stated unequivocally. 'Because they were already dead.'

'That was the medical examiner's opinion. But how can you be certain?'

'Because,' came the portentous reply, 'I identified the bodies. I know death by magic when I see it.' Suddenly the solemn atmosphere was broken as Senara gave a little chuckle. 'Perran dear, doesn't that sound like a posh box of chocolates!'

He smiled. 'Death By Magic! Oh, I like that. Very artisan.'

'So,' interrupted Trelawney attempting to maintain some gravitas, 'whatever your intention, Mrs Cadabra ... you did not assassinate the Cardiubarns.'

'No,' she replied regretfully. 'I did not. Whatever killed them was not down to me.'

'Who then?' he asked.

Senara picked up her cake fork and cut off a small piece of sponge, cream and jam, 'I have no doubt in my mind. Nor have you, Inspector.' She delivered it to her mouth.

'The Flamgoynes?'

Senara savoured her treat for a few moments, before she replied, 'Precisely. Someone got there first … and no one could be more aggrieved than I.'

Silence followed. It was broken by Perran's kindly voice.

'Speak your mind, Inspector.'

'Ask,' invited Mrs Cadabra.

'How did they do it? And how would they have known that the Cardiubarns would all be together at that spot at that time?'

Mrs Cadabra smiled mischievously, then said with relish:

'Just so.'

Chapter 20

THOMAS IN SEARCH OF NORMAL

After that, Senara chatted about some more of Trelawney's deceased relatives who had asked after him, he finished his tea, declined a third biscuit, and thanked Mr and Mrs Cadabra. Amanda escorted him to his car, where he sighed with relief that the interview was over.

'Well done, Inspector. You held your own very well,' she said encouragingly.

'Thank you. Your grandmother, at least, appeared to enjoy my visit.'

'Oh she did,' agreed Amanda sincerely.

'I'm so pleased,' he responded drily.

'Yes, because if you ever need to talk to her again, she'll look forward to it,' Amanda said reasonably.

'Not that it's like she has so few pleasure in life!'

'No, indeed, they both seem to enjoy themselves prodigiously. Anyway, we're further forward than we were, and that's the main thing. We've had any number of things confirmed.'

'We have. Let's confer again on Saturday.'

'After the class. Yes.'

* * * * *

Trelawney stopped the car once he had cleared the village and phoned his father to ask if it was all right for him to come round to dinner. He had things to tell.

During the four-hour journey home, he scarcely needed his favourite talk radio channel. He was providing the commentary for himself.

'I used to be a rational man with a normal job. I used scientific methods to catch criminals who had broken the law in perfectly recognisable ways, using tangible methods. I used to know that ghosts didn't exist and magic was something made up and believed in only by the feeble-minded and gullible!' He thought about Miss Cadabra, Mr and Mrs Cadabra and his Aunt Amelia. They were all far from weak-minded. In fact, if anything they were among the strongest-minded people he'd ever met. And now …. 'And now look at me.'

He continued his monologue at his father's dining table.' If anything …the truth is, Dad, … yes, the truth is … and I expect that's why I've felt so wound up … is that I feel like a right chump.'

'Why's that, son?' his father asked calmly.

'For *not* believing it.'

'I did try to buffer you against the Flamgoynes, so you really have had no experience with magic since you were a boy.'

'I know, and I thank you, but well … look at Aunt Amelia. It was there all the time. Every time I visited her, which admittedly was not that often but ... all those crystal balls, for goodness sake! And there I was just thinking it was her artwork. And then three years ago, Mike started dropping hints about there being "more things in heaven and earth', and I just wasn't having it. I've fought it every inch of the way, but now I find it's undeniable.'

'Actually,' said Kytto, 'magic is more tangible than you might think. It's just another form of energy, just one that physicists have yet to find ways to quantify, to measure precisely, in ways that would make it ... acceptable. Honestly, son, all you thought is the same as millions of people think, many of them highly intelligent.'

Thomas was heartened. 'Thanks, Dad.'

'Now what is it that you have to tell me?' invited Kytto.

Once Thomas had concluded his narrative, he paused then shook his head.

'I still can't believe I'm talking about this mystical whatnot as though it's nothing out of the ordinary.'

'I'm sorry, son, that your parentage has brought you into all of this. But the interview with the Cadabras does seem to have gone well.'

'Oh, it did. It's just that ... it all seems so *surreal*. You know, I need to clear my head and get away for a while from all of this magical nons—, I mean stuff.'

'Yes, well ... why not go and visit your grandfather? Granddad Trelawney.'

Thomas's face lit up. Of course! Normals. That was what he needed.

'What a brilliant idea, Dad. I think I'll go and do just that.'

'Go now, you'll catch most of them down by the water.'

'I don't want to eat and run,' Thomas said hesitantly.

'Nonsense. Off with you, lad. If you're lucky, your granddad will take you back for some of Gran Flossie's Whortleberry Pie!'

135

The Trelawneys, at least, thought Thomas, heading for the shore, were good, solid, normal folk. Yes, Normals, thank goodness. Down to earth, feet on the ground, well, so to speak, given that they spent more hours at sea than on land. But the point is there's none of that irritating mysticism about them.

His uncle Ned was the first to spot him.

''Ey look, Dad, who's 'ere!'

Clemo Trelawney, bent over his work, looked up under bushy brows, grinned, then straightened up.

'Well, if it isn't the little lad!'

Thomas had wisely changed his shoes for Wellington boots and his coat for something more casual, not that he wanted to rob his uncles of the joy of ribbing him for being a 'city slicker.'

'I'll finish up 'ere, Dad. You take 'un up to the 'ouse. Gran'll be want'n' to feed 'im.'

The family home was a comfortable dwelling within sight of the water. Trelawney was soon enfolded in the loving embrace of his doting step-grandmother. He barely escaped a second dinner, but welcomed the pie.

'I know you couldn't say no to my pie, little Tom,' she said with a wag of her finger. 'Made just the way you likes it.'

'You're the only one that can,' he replied truthfully. 'Oh Granddad, Bran Penberth sends his best.'

Clemo chortled, 'Oh, you been hangin' about wi' that old reprobate? Well, you send 'im mine but tell 'im from me not be leadin' my grandson astray!'

After they'd finished eating and his grandfather had had enough of holding forth on quotas and the cost of replacing machinery in this day and age, he took Thomas out onto the 'deck' at the front of the house.

'You know how your Gran don't like my pipe in the 'ouse,' he reminded his grandson, lighting up. 'Ar, I know I grumbles, but it's a good life ... if you've a taste for it. Your cousin's like you. Graduated now, you know. Doin' a start-up, they calls it, with a friend of 'is. Don't know as I understand all of the ins and outs, but I gives 'im a 'and. You gotta let the young people find their way, and give 'em a 'and where you can. Like your dad wi' 'is 'oliday cottages. He didn't 'ave no real taste for the fishin' ... but your great-granddad always used to say, "With young people you speak your piece and then you 'olds your peace."'

'Good advice, I imagine,' said Thomas.

'Well 'e did with me. When I met your grandmother ... 'ed just 'elped me with getting my own boat, see? It was the best day o' my life.'

'Of course.'

'But ... it made me full o' myself. Started thinkin' as I was cock o' the walk. That's 'ow I caught 'er eye, see? And she turned my 'ead, right enough, 'er being such a grand lady and from that big 'ouse of theirs up on the Moor. Ar ... Flamgoyne. .... Cost me dear, she did. Lucky I kept my boat, but I got well shot of 'er in the end. Still ... got me your dad, sure enough.'

'She didn't challenge you over custody?'

'Nohhh, not she. Said 'e wasn't no true Flamgoyne. ''E wasn't good enough for 'er family or some suchlike. Your dad didn't miss 'er none neither. Ar, your great-granddad let me learn my lesson, and I learned it good. Next time I married, it was your Gran Flossie, and she's been better than a castle full of gold to me.'

'To all of us,' agreed Thomas.

'Oh, she's that fond of your dad and you too.'

Thomas looked out down towards the water, seeing his family's boats moored there. This is just what I needed, he thought. Real things: ropes, nets, winches, engines. The stuff of normality.

Chapter 21

༇

THE SECRET OF THE TRELAWNEYS

'So what brings you down 'ere then, little lad?' asked Granddad shrewdly, as they sat down, Thomas wrapping his coat more tightly around him.

'Needed a bit of grounding myself, I suppose you'd say. Reconnect with my roots.'

Clemo looked at his grandson with a mischievous twinkle. 'Oh, you wantin' to come out on the boats are you, Tom?'

'Not quite *that* much re-connection,' he admitted ruefully. Granddad chuckled.

'I thought not. Might crease one of they Saville Row suits of yours.'

'I can't quite stretch to Saville Row on my policemen's salary.'

'One day you'll 'ave the business, you know. Your dad's, I'm meanin'.'

'I'm in no hurry for that.'

'So what you wantin' to reconnect with, zackly?'

'I suppose I'd like to know more about the family. The Trelawneys.'

'Well now,' said Granddad, taking a suck on his pipe and sending a mist of smoke up. 'There's not much is known about our branch with the E.Y. you know. One, 'e went west across the water, the Atlantic, and the other was a man o' law. We was spelled T.R.E.L.O.R.N.E.Y. long ago.'

That surprised Thomas. 'I didn't know that.'

'But my dad said as we'd always been fishermen. Always been one with the sea ....' He gazed out at it as if lost in thought. Thomas waited, He was interested to see where the narrative would go. Tales of bravery, no doubt, battles with sharks, daring rescues.

'There are legends in the family, you know, Tom. Like I says, we was always at one with the sea. Some others went down, but we always had a special relationship with it. She's a temperamental mistress. Don't take no chances. But the Trelawneys always had a bit o' help n their side.'

'Luck?' suggested Thomas.

'Oh, more 'n that,' smiled Clemo, turning to him with a knowing nod.

'I don't understand, Granddad.'

'Why, they as live there.'

'Where?'

The old man gestured with his pipe. 'In the sea.'

Thomas was mystified.

'Ar. At need, we call,' said Granddad quietly. 'They will only answer a Trelawney, see, lad.'

Whatever did his grandfather mean? Some sort of private rescue service? 'Call what? Whom?' Thomas asked.

'*They.*'

'What do you mean?'

'Long, long ago, long before barons and kings, the

Trelorneys fished the waters. One day, Gwalather Trelorney was out on his own, out beyond the Arlodes Rocks, when a lady come swimmin' up to the side of his boat. He couldn't understand what she said, but she was that pretty and that sweet that from that moment he couldn't be thinkin' of no one but her. He went back again and again, and she would bring the fish to him.'

Clemo paused to enjoy his pipe awhile. He took up his tale again.

'Then, one day, ... a great storm blows up, and he trying to get back to shore, but it swept 'im back out and back out. And he calls for her, and she comes and calms the waters, and pulls his boat home. She tells him if ever he needs her, he must sing a song she teaches him, and she will come. They say he never married, but one day, a baby was found in the boat. They say he adopted it, but some said it was his, born of the sea lady. He'd often take the child out with him, for she could not bear to be away from the sea.'

He nodded toward the water.

'They passed the song down from generation to generation. People say it's just an old sea shanty. But we know that at need, if a Trelawney sing it to the waves, *They* will come to their aid. How come you think no Trelawney never perished in the waves all these generations? We know as we're safe out there.'

'What about Gran Flossie?'

'She's a Trelawney, way back.'

Thomas looked grim. This was the last thing he'd expected or indeed wanted to hear: more magical shenanigans. Nevertheless, the tale had charmed him. And something had resonated.

'Hold on ... Granddad ... do I know this song?'

'Ar lad. I teach it you when you were a *bian*.' Thomas had the vaguest of recollections of a melody. 'Remember, little lad?'

'Start me off, Granddad.'

Clemo's voice, deep as the deep, sang out the first two lines.

'Mar dhown, Vorvoren, ple'th esosta
Neuvya ha kana dha vorgan wre'ta'

Thomas found himself joining in, the Cornish words seeming to form by themselves on his lips.

'Hag yn ow skath vy 'karmav dhiso jy
Gwra yskynna ha kana genev vy.'

'Yes, I remember!

'Mermaid, where so deep you be
You swim and sing your song of the sea
While from my boat I call to thee
Come up, my love, and sing with me.'

Granddad smiled knowingly.

'It's in you, lad. I know you go down to the water's edge to run and swim and think. There's no denying it. You can go and live as far inland as you like, but now and now, you'll have to come back to it. Seawater in your veins, sure as sure.'

'And I thought it was all fishing quotas and maintenance.'

Clemo shook his head.

'There are more things in heaven and earth …'

'…than are dreamt of in your philosophy.'

'That's right, Tom, that's right.'

This wasn't at all what he had been anticipating. It was disconcerting. He needed time to adjust.

'Drink?' his Granddad suggested understandingly.

'I have to drive back,' said Thomas.

'Haley'll drive you home. She's very proud of 'er car, well' van, I should say. It were yer Gran Flossie's. Forgot all about it, she 'ad, until our Haley started learnin' to drive. Then she recalls it's in the old shed. 1962 VW van. Oh, she loved that old thing! You know as yer Gran was a hippie artist?'

'Er, really?'

'Oh yes, and back in the day, she painted the van psychedelic orange and yellows that glow in the dark. Your Gran, last week, she give it a good service and tune up and now it's young Haley's, and oh my! She couldn't be more chuffed, bless 'er. She'll love to show it off to 'er Uncle Tom.'

'That's kind of her. Then … yes, please. …. Granddad … how are you managing to do so well?'

'You got to diversify. Fingers in lots of pies: fish, lobsters, bait, tourist trips and the like.'

'How do you manage to compete with all the other tourist boats?'

'Gotta have a U.S.P., see? Unique Selling Point. What's mine? It's this: if they signs a paper sayin' as they won't never tell, I can show 'em a place only a Trelawney knows.'

'Where's that, Granddad?'

The old fisherman winked, put an arm around his grandson's shoulders and spoke low in his ear,

'I takes 'em where the mermaids go!'

Chapter 22

∽

THE PIANO, AND THE FLORIST

Amanda, wearing her green boiler suit, stood in the small space she had cleared in the workshop. She held her long wand in her left hand and her more powerful mini-wand in her right. Feet planted apart, she seemed to be staring at the empty air, a reflective heat-haze like a dome around her.

'Well done, Ammy,' Granny encouraged her.

'You're doing fine, *bian*,' said Grandpa.

'Now. You just need to expand it.'

Keeping her concentration focussed, Amanda uttered the spellword:

'*Tehti*!'

At once, the dome collapsed, and a number of small brown objects fell from above.

'Oh!' cried Amanda, shielding her head with her arms. It was over in a very short time, and she looked in bewilderment at what lay around her feet. 'What happened?'

Granny sighed. 'The spellword for "grow" is *tehvi,* dear.

The word you used, *tehti*, means ... as you see ... "potato".'

'Oh, dear.'

'You can't neglect your Wicc'yeth for years on end and expect to get new spells right, just like that,' Granny pointed out.

'But I *have* to get this right, and I have so little time! And I *still* l have no idea who ....'

The phone rang.

'Amenda?'

She knew only one person with an Australian accent who knew her name: a staff member from Pipkin Acres Residential Home, who was a particular favourite with the residents.

'Megan?'

'Yeh, Pikin Acres.'

'Is everyone all right?' asked Amanda with concern.

'They're as well as they can be. But I've got a bit of a storm in a teacup. Some of the residents have got upset about something that hippend in the night.'

'Erm, if it was a break-in, maybe that's a case for Sergeant Baker?'

'Nao nao, we don't want to get the police involved. It might have been an inside job.'

'Sorry, what does thi—?'

'Someone keyed the piano, if you'll excuse the ixpression,' Megan explained.

'Scratched it, you mean?' asked Amanda.

'Yeah, the case. Every time some of the residents look at it, they get upset again.'

'Surely the insurance will pay?'

'Oh yeah, it's not the cost; it's them seeing it all damaged.'

'I expect it looks worse than it is.'

'But if you could just pop over and patch it up. Mrs Hodster's promised us all a bit of a concert at the weekend, and the piano turner is coming the day after tomorrow, and they don't want him seeing their pride and joy looking all beaten up.'

Amanda had done enough to hide her enthusiasm. For here was a chance to scout around the residential home for anyone old enough to qualify as Viola.

'Of course. I'll come as soon as I can. Erm ... did you say *Mrs* Hodster?'

'Oh yeah, you came for a chat with Bernie, didn't you? Didn't meet his wife? Glamorous lady, always wears red. Yeah, she's a peach. French. Worked for Interpol, you know.'

'Right, well, I must say hello to her. See you later, Megan.'

She hung up.

'Emergency call-out,' Amanda told her grandparents.

'Hm, the piano,' said Grandpa. 'Hard wax job.'

It was an instrument that had seen better days but was still regularly played.

'And then I'll touch it up with some paint, make it look invisible.'

'You're good at that,' Perran observed. 'Always have been.'

'Piano tuner,' interjected Granny.

'Oh my goodness, yes! I'll have to cancel ... no: postpone.'

Amanda hastily called, feeling rather embarrassed.

'Mr Honeywell? Amanda Cadabra here ... yes, actually, I've had an emergency call-out and was wondering if you could make it tomorrow instead? .... Oh, that's most kind of you ... yes ... thank you. Until tomorrow.'

'There now,' said Perran, 'you're all set. Go and do your repair. Like I was saying, you're good at the wax and paint touch up.'

'Thank you, Grandpa,' Amanda responded absentmindedly. She needed to plan her strategy ....

145

'Right,' she said to Tempest, having loaded her toolbox, wax and paints into the Astra. 'Fancy a wander around the grounds up there?'

He planted himself outside the rear passenger door, and looked at her as though she had been keeping him waiting.

'First,' Amanda said, once they were seated and the engine started, 'Flowers for Mrs Hodster.'

Youfloric, as the new shop in the village styled itself, had yet to put up its permanent sign, but pots, urns, vases and buckets of roses, lilies, and carnations were already appearing inside and out. As Tempest and Amanda approached, a man with a hopeful air, came out to greet them.

He was not unattractive, she had to admit: tall-ish, late thirties, thick dark brown hair, large blue eyes with a gentle intelligence. Amanda was trying to think what he reminded her of but soon ran out of time.

'Hello,' came the florist's welcoming, and not over-confident, greeting that Amanda rather approved. 'I don't think we've had the pleasure before.'

'No indeed, this is my first visit to your shop, and welcome to Sunken Madley.'

'Thank you. I'm Dale, Dale Hilland.'

Amanda put out her hand and gave him her name. He paused in the act of shaking it, as though he hadn't heard correctly. It was the usual response.

'Well,' he said, 'what can we do for you ... Miss ... Cadabra? We haven't opened officially, as you can see, but ....'

Amanda looked at the selection.

'Some red carnations and red roses. Half a dozen of each, please.'

'Lovely choice.' He selected the freshest, added some greenery and a few sprigs of gypsophila, asking, 'May I know the occasion? It helps me select the most appropriate wrapping.'

'A thank-you present for a friend,' Amanda replied.

'Must be a special friend. Red roses ....'

'I see the Victorian significance. I don't know her exactly I but think she likes red, that's all.'

At this, he appeared to be relieved, judging by the sigh and the way his posture seemed to relax. Amanda knew she didn't excel at reading people, so she couldn't be sure.

One minute later, he turned from the table inside the shop and presented her with a bouquet. Its inner wrapping was of self-striped yellow paper, the outer was plain, and all was tied with a piece of red twine. He had contrived something bright and trendy.

'Oh, how clever!' exclaimed Amanda. He smiled.

'So glad you like it. Actually, I'm still experimenting, learning the trade, you know.'

'Well, you have a definite talent for it, Dale. How much do I owe you?'

'We haven't quite worked out our prices yet. £10?'

'That's very reasonable. Thank you.' She gave him a £20 note. Amanda was curious. 'May I ask what it was that you did before? Something else artistic?'

'Travel consultant. Adventure holidays.'

'Oh my word, how exciting.'

He hadn't looked the type, whatever that was .... Amanda tried to visualise him in safari gear or up in the Himalayas. She supposed, actually, under the shirt and apron he was fit enough. So what on earth was he doing selling flowers in Sunken Madley?

'Yes, I ....' His phone rang. He looked at the screen and frowned. 'Miss Cadabra, please excuse me for just a moment.' He went back inside the shop .... She could hear his voice though. He sounded agitated.

'Yes ... oh, dear ... not again ... well ... where are you exactly? ... All ... all right .... Of course ... I'll be right there.'

Dale returned with Amanda's change.

'Is everything all right?' she asked.

'It's just Mother. She's had one of her turns. She suffers with her nerves, you know.'

'Oh dear,' said Amanda, and meant it. For he had immediately sunk in her estimation. In her experience, garnered from an acquaintance with Mrs Varst, now, happily for the village, retired to Brighton, persons who claimed martyrdom to their nerves were as hard as nails and twice as sharp. Dale's readiness to pander to Mother Dear did not recommend him to her as anything other than a trader. Surely an intrepid man of adventure could tell a fake fit a mile off and would tell the person to take a hike.

Dale was now running his hands anxiously over his apron. 'I'd better go and find her. She's walked into Barnet and is in a café called ... Happy Leaf or something?'

'The Leaf Happy Café. Drive south along the high street, and it's on your left about a hundred yards down.'

'I'm so sorry to dash off like this,' he said, hurriedly taking the containers of flowers indoors.

'That's quite all right. Goodbye.'

'Oh, just a moment!' He offered her a yellow rose. 'Please, Miss Cadabra, as a sorry and a thank you for your valued custom.'

'Well ... thank you. Dale.'

Tempest had soon tired of the florist, and now was on the bonnet of the car trying to absorb what little warmth there was to had from the feeble winter sun. He was giving her a look. It said: I saw that.

Hopeless at interpreting the facial expressions of humans, Amanda was never in any doubt about what her familiar was intending to convey. They got into the Astra, and she put the flowers on the seat beside her.

'Don't look at me like that. He was just doing some marketing, that's all.' She drove north through the village.

'Although I must say, I don't know quite what to make of Mr Dale Hilland ....'

Chapter 23

PIPKIN ACRES

Before Amanda could tell reception that she was here to see about the piano, she was intercepted by Miss Hempling, former owner of Ye Olde Tea Shoppe — now The Big Tease.

'Oh, Amanda, dear Megan said you were coming. You haven't seen it, have you, dear?'

'No, I've just arrived. Megan told me about it over the phone. It's probably looks a lot worse than it is.'

'Well, I certainly hope so, for your sake. Probably a perfectly innocent explanation. I do hope you didn't take it seriously.'

Amanda was bemused. 'I know that it means a lot to some people here but I really have no personal attachment to it.'

'Oh, dear, no. I don't mean the *piano*.'

* * * * *

The previous night, as Clemo had assured his grandson, Thomas's 18-year-old niece Haley was, indeed, more than ready to give him a lift home, after he had partaken with his grandfather of a bottle of rum. First, however, Haley asked if she might take a selfie with her handsome uncle. To which he innocently agreed.

Having captured the desired image of the two of them smiling cheerily into the camera, Haley promptly posted it on Facebook, so that a certain young man, who had been delinquent in his attentions of late, might observe that he was not the only fish in the sea.

Duly impressed, her friends had shared it, and by morning, it had flowed into Miss Hempling's Facebook stream, via her great-niece's daughter, Grace, who often visited after school. She felt it her bounden duty to keep her great-great-aunt up to speed with social media, as a preventive against any hint of mental deterioration. Consequently, Miss Hempling had accounts on Facebook, Instagram, Twitter, Tumblr and Snapchat, on all of which she enjoyed being active.

'Hmm,' said Miss Hempling, at half-past seven the following morning, to her boon companions Mr Rhys and Mrs Holdforth. 'Doesn't that looks like the inspector? I'm sure I recognise him from The Big Tease.' She passed her phone around.

'Why yes, look you, I see 'im in the pub, so I'd know 'is face anywhere,' agreed Mr Rhys, whose 60-year absence from the valleys had not lessened his melodious Welsh accent. 'Dear me! Well, how unfortunate.'

Mrs Holdforth squinted over her glasses, then nodded.

'That's the inspector, all right. He was at the Apple Festival. I thought you said he was spending a lot of time with our Amanda.'

'Well, I saw them having lunch in the Snout and Trough,' agreed Miss Hempling, 'and I have to say ...'

'Perhaps it was just official police business,' suggested Mr Rhys.

'Oh, I expect so ....' Miss Hempling shook her head. 'Although ... it looked to me like there was something of a connection there ....'

'Well, it's probably nothing,' said Mrs Holdforth doubtfully. She peered again at the phone screen. 'She looks very young ...'

'Perhaps someone ought to tell Amanda,' said Mr Rhys anxiously.

'No, no,' objected Miss Hempling, 'it wouldn't be right to interfere ....'

* * * * *

Amanda put down her wax and paint boxes and gave Miss Hempling her full attention.

'Amanda dear, you know how fond of you we all are. And how much we have your best interests at heart.'

Oh dear, what's coming next? thought Amanda.

'We wondered ... that is, we thought you should ... if you hadn't already ... seen this.' Miss Hempling displayed the photo on her phone.

'Ah.'

'That's the inspector,' said Miss Hempling unnecessarily.

'Indeed,' Amanda confirmed impersonally.

The young lady was apparently nuzzled up against him. He looked very relaxed. He wasn't wearing a tie. She couldn't remember ever seeing him without one. The top button of his shirt was undone. So that was the inspector off-duty. Amanda wasn't quite sure what she was feeling. The girl could be anyone, after all, she told herself. The daughter of a colleague or indeed a colleague or ... or ... anyway, it was good to see that he had been having some downtime. She handed back the phone with a smile and said,

'Well, that's nice.'

'We thought you should know, dear,' Miss Hempling said gravely.

'It's really none of my business what the inspector does in his time off, and I —'

'Well, I'll send it to you anyway. Just for reference.' Miss Hempling tapped away.

'I really don't —'

'There! You'll have it in your messages now.'

'Er, thank you, Miss Hempling. Have you seen —'

'Hiya, Amenda.'

'Hello, Megan.'

'Oh no, now, Miss Hempling, I thought we agreed you weren't going to bother Amenda with that Facebook nonsense.'

Amanda sighed inwardly and wondered if there was anyone in all of Pipkin Acres who hadn't seen the incriminating photograph. No doubt they were all now holding her as an object of compassion. 'It's all right, Megan. OK, please show me the damage to the piano.'

After working for an hour and a half in what was, predictably, called the Piano Room, Amanda had a welcome interruption. Megan popped in to see if she would like to have tea, as it was now being served to all of the residents in the lounge.

'Thank you. I would.'

'Where would you like to sit?'

'Are the Hodsters here?' Amanda asked.

'Yeah, over by the window.' Megan pointed.

Amanda retrieved the flowers from under the piano and

went over to join the couple. Bernie had been helpful with a mystery, a few weeks ago. She was greeted warmly, and kissed on both cheeks by Mrs Hodster, on being introduced.

'These are for you both. Your husband was very kind to me last time we met, and I gathered that you like red.'

'Oh, it was my pleasure,' insisted Bernie Hodster.

'I love fresh flowers. *Merçi!*'

'You're welcome, Mrs Hodster.'

'*Marielle*. And is there something we can do for *you*?' she asked Amanda shrewdly.

'Well, actually, with the New Year's Ball and Lost Madley and so on, it's revived my interest in the wars, and the last one in particular. I was wondering if there were any of the oldest residents here who might be willing to talk to me.'

'Hm, that is quite a good cover story,' she complimented Amanda impishly. 'No, no, you do not need to tell me what it is you seek. But you know, it is not so easy to talk to all of them. Some of them will not speak to strangers, and others need to be spoken to in certain ways. No, what you need … is the hub of the wheel. There is one person who knows all the oldest residents. Angus MacSpadden. But 'e will not speak to you if you approach 'im. 'E is very select about who 'e will talk to. 'E claims he is an old man and 'as no energy for idle chat with strangers.'

'Could you introduce me?' Amanda asked, hopefully.

'We're newcomers. It wouldn't do no good,' chimed in Bernie Hodster.

'Then what can I do?'

The couple looked at one another and went into conference mode.

'There may be a way,' said Marielle.

Mr Hodster lowered his voice.

'The Knitting Circle.'

'They would never let her in for the Special Nights, and

that is the only time Angus is really 'appy, they say,' Marielle objected.

'Special Nights?' asked Amanda.

'Cards,' said Marielle succinctly.

'Bridge, whist,' Bernie explained reassuringly.

'No. Poker,' his wife returned. 'Double the legal stakes, I hear. Drinking, smoking, everything but dancing girls. Once a month. But there's an age limit.'

'An age limit?' repeated Amanda incredulously. 'What? 105?'

Bernie acknowledged her humour but shook his head. 'No, a lower age limit. You 'ave to be over 68.'

'Why 68?'

'It's 18 plus half a century.'

Amanda sighed. 'OK, so that's ruled out. Unless maybe I could see him afterwards?'

'They sometimes play until 4 in the morning,' warned Bernie.

'Oh.'

'And then I don't know how much sense he'd make. But the ordinary Knitting Circle nights might just serve your purpose. If you're lucky and catch Angus in a good-ish sort of mood.'

'You mean,' asked Amanda, 'I might persuade him to help me talk to anyone who might have been around during the war?'

'P'raps.'

It isn't exactly promising, thought Amanda, but it's the only chance I have.

'So this Knitting Circle ...?'

'They meet once a week,' replied Marielle.

'Do you know how to knit?' asked Bernie.

'Well ... yes ....' Granny and Grandpa had made sure she was, at least, rudimentarily versed in all manner of crafts, but

Grandpa had said knitting in Cornwall was a long tradition and he himself was handy with the needles. He said it was a skill everyone should learn, girl or boy. 'I don't like it, but yes, I do know how. Do they allow non-residents?'

Here Marielle raised her voice a little. 'The Knitting Circle? Yes, but it requires three references from residents.' She spoke quietly again. 'Usually, they are very reluctant to include outsiders, but I believe that you have ... *compassionate* grounds?'

'Do you mean ... can you and Bernie?'

'We are not members, unfortunately.'

Miss Hempling had excellent hearing. 'Did you say The Knitting Circle?' she called out, getting up and coming over to the trio.

'Yes, Miss Hempling,' confirmed Amanda. 'Mr and Mrs Hodster have been so kind as to recommend it to me. They thought it might cheer me up,' she added, with the air of one jilted at the altar.

'Well ... I don't know ... we don't normally ....' Miss Hempling turned and called to her two cronies, who made their way across the room.

'What do you think?' she asked them. 'Amanda wants to join the Knitting Circle. I think she feels the need for some company.'

'Oh, living in that cottage *all alone*,' intoned Mr Rhys.

'Of course, you do, dear,' affirmed Mrs Holdforth, sympathetically.

'You wouldn't be able to come on the Special Nights,' Miss Hempling warned.

'No, not those, naturally not,' agreed Mrs Holdforth. 'A shame, because we do have such jolly times, don't we, Mr Rhys?'

'Oh yes, with a nice tipple or two.'

'And dear Mrs Pondside's sister sends such wonderful

cakes from her herbal shop in Nevada. So very kind. And I always sleep so well afterwards,' said Mrs Holdforth serenely.

'And I never have no aches and pains for two days, look you!' added Mr Rhys, enthusiastically.

'*Non, non*, my friends,' intervened Marielle, 'I think just the ordinary nights would work their ... magic upon our dear little Amanda, restore her spirits, don't you think?'

Suddenly Mrs Holdforth clasped her hands at her bosom. 'Oh Miss Hempling ....' She turned to her friend with a burst of feeling. 'If you say dear Amanda is to be admitted into the warm embrace of our Circle, we'll *second* you! *Won't we, Mr Rhys?*'

'Yes, we will.'

'It's *very* kind of you, all' said Amanda as emotionally as she could. 'It will be a great comfort.'

'That's what friends are for,' insisted Miss Hempling.

'Well, I should be getting back to work now. Thank you *all*.'

Amanda managed to finish the piano before the daylight faded. It wasn't perfect, but it was a great deal better, she reflected. Tempest had toured the grounds then persuaded the staff to get him a snack. And then another one.

'Well, Tempest,' Amanda said, as they walked towards the car, 'time to go home for tea. And I need to remember how to knit!'

Chapter 24

༄

THE KNITTING CIRCLE

It was Saturday. The class made some progress with the cha-cha. Afterwards, Amanda and Trelawney, according to their usual custom, entered the cottage, she to make the tea and the inspector to make up the fire. Seated cosily with mugs and biscuits, Amanda said casually,

'I owe you one.'

'Oh?'

'Thanks to you, on Thursday evening, I shall be infiltrating the notoriously exclusive ... Knitting Circle!'

'How impressive. And what part have I played in this mission?'

With difficulty suppressing a smile, she swiped her phone screen, then passed it across to him.

'Oh no!' he exclaimed ruefully. 'The little wretch. This is all over Sunken Madley, I suppose?'

'After being all over Pipkin Acres, I expect so,' replied Amanda with amusement.

'*This* ...,' he pointed to the screen, 'is my niece, Haley!'

'Ah.'

'There I was thinking how nice that she wanted a selfie with her dear old Uncle Tom and ... well, I haven't been a detective for almost 20 years without being able to deduce her real motive.'

'Which was?'

'Oh, to make some teenage boy jealous, I have no doubt.'

'Ah.'

He stopped and frowned at her. 'Why? .... You didn't think ...?'

'I thought that it wasn't any of my business and so I told Miss Hempling, when she showed it to me,' Amanda stated with careful accuracy. She still wasn't sure *what*-she'd thought, or more especially *felt*. Furthermore, with the van case still open and the attack on the village imminent, now was decidedly *not* the time to go there.

'Even so, I hope that you know me well enough,' Trelawney protested, '... I mean ... she looks about 12 in that photo!'

'She does look youthful, but I can see from the background,' commented Amanda, who had studied the photo in detail, for some reason, 'that you're in a car and she's old enough to be in the driving seat.'

'Yes, Haley's just turned 18 and got her first car. She kindly drove me home after I'd had a drink with my Granddad Trelawney.'

'Ah, hence your tie-lessness,' she smiled.

'Yes, and my shirt top button undone, I see. A shameless state of undress.'

'It's good to see that you are capable of relaxing.'

'It can be done. I had ... an interesting evening with the family. But come on, back to your mission. So this photo had your contacts at Pipkin Acres buzzing round, doing their level best to prevent you from becoming a twenty-first-century Miss Havisham, and locking yourself in your workshop with a mouldering bride-cake, right?'

'Precisely,' she responded, with a twinkle. 'The sympathy vote has got me admitted to the Knitting Circle, which is the only way of meeting Angus MacSpadden He is the contact point for all of the senior seniors, among whom might be my Viola!'

Trelawney nodded understandingly. He knew from long experience in interviewing members of the older generations, that if a senior didn't want to talk there was no way of persuading them. Rather than answer his questions, he had had such individuals pretend to be delusional, demented, asleep and even, in one case, dead.

'Well done, Miss Cadabra. Please do text me a report after the meeting.'

'Willco.'

He grinned.

'How about you?' Amanda asked him.

'I was encouraged by the progress we made on the case. One half of the puzzle is complete. We now know that your grandmother made the attempt to see off the Cardiubarns. Also how and why. What we *don't* know is how they were actually killed. I have to admit, I'm stumped. If I could help you to track down your Viola I would, but meanwhile, I'm catching up with police work at the station and cooperating on an initiative to discourage members of the public from eating ice cream while driving. Oh, the life of a copper!'

*****

On the advice of the Hodsters and Trelawney, Amanda arrived at Pipkin Acres on the night of the Knitting Circle, primed with a bottle of Glenlivet founders reserve single malt, which, she suggested to her hostess, Mr MacSpadden might enjoy.

Miss Hempling led her into the Piano Room, where the Knitters convened, and introduced her to the select group.

'Mr MacSpadden, dear Amanda has brought a little treat for us all, but I know you, especially, find it inspirational.' She left it at his elbow with a glass. It earned Amanda a glance from an icy blue eye and a nod. The Scotsman poured himself a small measure and sampled it judicially. He uttered what might have been a grunt of approval.

The door was closed, the knitters seated themselves and took up their needles. The conversation, lively at first, calmed to a hum, then a companionable hush.

A third of the way down the bottle, Angus MacSpadden spoke for the first time.

Amanda started with surprise.

'Ah used to say as Ah din'a hold wi' wimmen knittin'… but Ah come rrrround to it. For Ah'll not have it said as Angus is stuck in his auld ways.'

Amanda had no idea how to respond to this.

'Now who would say such thing,' said Miss Hempling comfortably.

'I'm sure I wouldn't,' agreed Mr Rhys. 'I'm sure the same thing would have been thought in my family about all sorts of things. Now the ladies do it all, and why not, I say? Good luck to 'em.'

'Why thank you, Ms Rhys,' said Mrs Holdforth.

The company fell silent once more. Click, click, click-a-click, click.

Her mind racing, Amanda did her best to pay attention

to her stitches and appear absorbed in her craft. But the clock was ticking. She had to try.

'Are there many people here who remember that far back, do you think, Mr Rhys?'

'As far back as what, would that be, dear?'

'Well ... as far back as the War, say?'

'Oh yes, a few. Not many mind.'

'Would you say the same, Mr MacSpadden?' she asked tentatively.

'Hrrrm,' was his only reply.

The sound of the needles held sway once more. Time passed. Amanda had no idea how to proceed. No more had been said. Angus was two thirds of the way done the bottle. The clock ... struck ... 10. The Circle members were putting their knitting in their kit bags, winding up balls of wool, picking up cups of tea, and rising from their armchairs. Angus remained enthroned, counting his stitches. Amanda lingered, pretending to look for something down beside the seat cushion of her armchair.

'Coming, Amanda?' Miss Hempling called, looking back over her shoulder.

'Just getting my things together. It's all right, I'll see myself out. Thank you, Miss Hempling.'

'All right, dear. Night night.'

Gradually all of the others left. Amanda took a final look back at Mr MacSpadden. She saw him beckon.

'Come here, lassie.'

Amanda went to him and sat down in the vacant chair beside him. He spoke in a voice that had lost much of its rough edge.

'Ma Mary ... she was Sunken Madleyist born and bred.'

Amanda remembered that they'd spent a lot of time away, in Brazil, Africa and the Middle East, and his wife, Mary, had died 20 years ago while they were abroad.

'My grandparents told me, sir.'

'Ay well, ... she'd want me to give ye this.' He held out his hand for hers, then pressed something small, round and smooth into her palm. It was black tourmaline, carved with a simple design of four quadrants, linked in a continuous line: the shield knot. The druid symbol of protection. He closed her fingers over it and looked into her eyes.

'T'is fer *the day* .... Ay, ye ken what I mean.'

Amanda nodded. She felt he knew exactly what she was going to say next. She asked. One word:

'Viola?'

'The one ye seek ye'll not find within these walls. More Ah canna say.'

Amanda nodded. 'Thank you, sir, for telling me, and for the shield.'

'Ay, weel. Thanks fer the dram. Away wi' ye noo.'

Amanda went to the door.

'Lassie,' he called, in something more like his customary tone.

'Mr MacSpadden?'

'Be sure ye bring it back.'

She smiled. 'Yes, sir.'

As Amanda drove home, she reflected on Angus MacSpadden's final words. He was sure she'd live to return the talisman. Or at least his Mary was — someone on the same plane as Granny and Grandpa, who were pretty well-informed.

The future wasn't set in stone, as Aunt Amelia always said, but perhaps, in this little piece sitting snugly in her pocket was, at least, her first glimmer of hope.

Chapter 25

∾

THE GRANGE

'Well done with the foxtrot today,' Trelawney commended Amanda, as she brought the tea tray in. The fire was taking a bit of persuading to catch.

'Thank you. That heel turn is fiendish.'

'You managed it at least twice.'

'I think it looks absurd,' Amanda stated baldly.

'Then, when we dance socially, let's not do it,' suggested Trelawney, with the spirit of rebellion.

An answering sparkle lit her eyes. 'Yes, Inspector, let's not!'

'So, now we've decided that, tell me ... the infiltration was a success?'

'Yes and no,' Amanda replied. 'It didn't turn up Viola, but it did eliminate anyone living at the Acres.'

'And it got you some sort of magical tool?'

'Only on loan,' she reminded him humorously.

'Ah yes, so your text said. Still, it's progress, which is more than I've made in the last week. Viola is the more urgent matter, though, than the mystery of what killed the Cardiubarns.'

'Then again, Inspector, what if they're linked?'

'Viola and the forthcoming attack on Sunken Madley?'

'No, the forthcoming attack on Sunken Madley and the Cardiubarn murders.'

'It's possible,' Trelawney admitted.

'I have only two weeks now.'

'I've been thinking the same thing. How are the, er ... defence spells coming?'

'Better. I haven't rained any more potatoes on my head!'

He laughed. 'Thank you for sharing that with me ... I mean, more about your spell-working capabilities.'

Amanda looked at him out of the corners of her eyes. 'You always wondered, didn't you?'

'How you did your work with severe asthma? Yes.'

'But yes, the spells are progressing. The thing is, that I have nowhere I can practice them, on the grand scale of defending this whole place. And with not yet having found Viola, I do feel so ... unprepared.' She looked a little lost.

'I understand. I wish there were something I could do on the day but ... Mike said a lot of cryptic stuff abut this being your battle and my being needed elsewhere, but not how. So we're both rather in the dark.'

'I guess all we can do is trust that somehow it will become clear ...,' Amanda said doubtfully.

'And in time ....'

* * * * *

Bang! Amanda arrived at The Grange, to the sound of gunfire. Bang! Crash! Clatter, clatter, smash! Squawk! Flutter, flutter, flutter.

As she drove into the driveway, a stout woman of middle years, above medium height, dressed in plus fours and tweeds, looked over her shoulder, lowered her shotgun, and waved. Amanda parked and got out of the car, reassured by the gesture.

'Hello there! You must be Amanda, what!' cried the woman, heartily.

'That's right. Er ...'

'Hilary. Call me Hillers, everyone does.'

'Erm, hello, Hillers,' Amanda offered uncertainly.

'Niece.'

'No, just a friend, I'm here to —'

'No, not you: me. Cynthia's my aunt, don't y' know.'

'Of course.' Amanda smiled, now enlightened.

'Other half is in the library, I expect, getting that old gramophone to work. Humpy.'

'Oh dear,' replied Amanda, imagining Hiller's spouse had some issue with the curvature of his spine.

'No, no, not Quasimodo,' chortled Hillers. 'Just what we call him. Humphrey.'

'Ahhh, I see. What exactly ... erm?'

Hillers followed the line of Amanda's gaze to the firearm in her hands.

'Ah, this? Perfectly legal, licensed 'n all. They keep telling me to get something modern, but I say, if the old Cogswell and Harrison was good enough for Grandmother, it's good enough for me, what! Pigeons.'

'I beg your pardon? Ah yes, I see. I know The Grange has had a problem for years. I suppose it's time for drastic measures,' replied Amanda.

'Oh, I'm not shootin' to kill. Need to scare 'em before the loft people come to mend the roof, where they've been gettin' in and roostin', y'see. No point knockin' em' orf. Vermin, Can't eat them. Father always used to say: can't put it in the pot, shoot it not. Probably his last words.'

'Oh?'

'Fell orf a mountain in Greece. Went up in search of the roc,' Hillers explained matter-of-factly.

'Rock?' asked Amanda, in confusion.

'R.O.C.'

'The mythical bird?'

'That's right.' Amanda was having doubts as to the mental stability of Hiller's deceased parent.

'Oh, I know what you're thinkin', Hillers uttered perceptively. 'Nutty as a fruitcake. That's not what they said when he brought back actual photographs of the, so-called legendary, gilly-gilly warbler from south Patagonia.' She looked at Amanda in triumph. 'Never published, of course, but that's politics for you. Well, let's get y'r gear out of the car!' she said, breaking her shotgun over her arm for safety.

'Thank you, there's no need,' Amanda protested politely.

'Nonsense,' returned Hillers bracingly. 'Cynthia says you're not too hale and hearty. You're a rare commodity, Amanda. Only furniture restorer for miles around. We must look after you!'

Amanda thanked her and opened the boot. Hillers took out all but one small toolbox, tucking a container under each arm and picking up one in each hand, with apparently no effort.

'Thank you!' said Amanda, collecting the remaining box and closing the boot.

Hillers led the way into the 'small dining room', that was larger than Amanda's sitting room and kitchen put together. It had been set aside for her use as a temporary workshop.

'Put it all down here, all right, is it?' asked Hillers.

'Yes, that's fine, thank you.'

Amanda had become aware of a loud, tinny strain of sound coming from the library.

'Best get back to the firing range, what!' With that,

Hillers strode off, calling 'Humpy! Amanda's here!'

'Good show, old girl!' came the reply, as the tinny noise got louder with the opening of the library door.

'Oh, Amanda!' Hillers alerted her. 'Your delivery's here!'

An amiably smiling face appeared around the door of the dining room. 'Hello, I'm Humpy,' said a tall thin man with a stalk of a neck, supporting a head with thinning hair.

'Hello, er, Humpy.'

'Want a hand?'

'No, that's all right, thank you.'

'You don't mind the music, do you?' Humpy asked anxiously. 'Jelly Roll Morton: *Black Bottom Stomp*. Found the record with the gramophone in the attic.'

'No, it's fine, really,' Amanda said politely.

'Where d'you want it, Miss Cadabra?' Two burly young men were carrying in a large mirror with curved edges.

'Oh, here on the table, please. The frame is ready, just lay it face down .... Yes .... Ah ... that's going to need a bit of adjustment ... yes ... that's great. Thank you both.'

'No trouble. All paid up. See you later!'

Humpy looked intently at the frame. 'Bit big here, bit small there and there and there, it seems to me.'

'Yes, that's my first job of the day. It'll be fine.'

'Good show. Well, just say the word, and Hillers and Moffat and m'self'll be ready and willing to lift it into place for you on the ballroom wall.'

'That's most kind. I was wondering how we'd do that, but Miss de Havillande assured me there'd be help.'

'Oh yes, Hillers could probably do it by herself. County champion: shotput, y' know.'

'Really?'

A musical note, bending at the end, sounded. It was being repeated over and over and was coming from the ballroom. Amanda looked at Humpy, questioningly.

'Tuner, last-minute appointment, only time he could come,' he explained.

'Oh, I —'

'— But Cynthia said you'd be working in here all day, except for when we put the mirror in place in there.'

'Yes, yes, of course.'

'Door's closed so the sound shouldn't bother you.'

Amanda wondered if Humpy was being ironic, given the cacophony being created by the pigeon-scaring.

A roar from the garden made Amanda jump. It was followed by an explosion.

'What on earth!'

Miss de Havillande entered.

'Ah Amanda dear, punctual as always, and I see that the mirror has been delivered. Splendid. You've met Hillers and Humpy, of course. Dear Gwendolen would be here to greet you, but she and Moffat are busy in the butler's pantry cleaning the silver for the buffet.' Amanda was glancing anxiously in the direction of the garden. 'Don't mind Mundly. He's got his pride and joy out for the lawn.'

'Isn't February a bit early?'

'For the party. Any excuse, though. It's older than he is, but he's at his happiest when he's out with his mower.'

'Is it steam-powered?'

Miss de Havillande laughed. 'Wouldn't surprise me. The engine's not quite tickety-boo, so don't mind if it lets rip every now and then.'

A series of yaps and yelps was being emitted from upstairs.

'Oh, dear. Churchill. I expect Sir Tempest has accompanied you here,' Miss de Havillande speculated.

'I'm afraid so. I did tell him not to harry poor Churchill,' Amanda replied, regretfully.

'I'll go and calm him down. Let me leave you to it, dear.'

The bell sounded.

'Oh, that'll be the florist. I'm giving them the job for the party, but one of them's keen to see the gardens to get inspiration for a theme for the ball.'

Miss de Havillande hurried off. Amanda wondered which of the two florists had arrived. Hopefully, not the mother. She went to close the door just in case, as Tempest, having sufficiently agitated the Grange's hapless terrier, slipped in. He took up a seat on a pile of clean rags and Holland covers, indignant at the hullaballoo. Amanda put on her blue vinyl gloves, saying,

'I didn't *ask* you to come. You could have stayed at home on your nice comfy sofa in peace and quiet'. He turned his head, assuming a pose of noble long-suffering. Clearly, he was doomed, Cassandra-like, to be unappreciated, in his case for his companionship. Amanda laughed. 'Just so, *Saint* Tempest.'

Gratified by her respectful mode of address, he looked smug, then burrowed under the pile. Amanda set to work. It was long and painstaking, but she was making progress when, again, the doorbell sounded.

Chapter 26

❧

STARBURST

Hillers put her head around the dining room door. 'Chappy here with flowers for you, Amanda.'

'Flowers? I thought the florist was in the garden.'

'Says he's come to offer some chairs from The Towers for the party and hoped to see *you* while he was here.'

'Oh good grief,' replied Amanda exasperated by what she imagined was Ryan's timing of offering a floral tribute. 'Please thank him and just ask him to leave them. I'm right in the middle of something.'

'Right-oh.' Hillers shut the door.

Presently, the sound of gunshots and falling tiles recommenced. Mundly was having more luck with his mower engine, as the roar started up with only intermittent explosions. *The Black Bottom Stomp* was continuing to delight Humpy. The donggggg donggggggg of the piano-tuning went on. The racket was clearly irritating Churchill, whose piercing bark was providing the treble to the bass of the mover and the percussion of Hiller's shotgun. Amanda sighed and resolutely fixed the earbuds for her iPod player into place and turned up her current favourite album, *Reggae Massive*, to full volume.

And that was why it didn't register at first.

It was just another loud noise, out beyond the orbit of her music. Except ... this one had seemed to shake the ground beneath her feet. She frowned, waiting for it to be repeated .... She'd never been good with directions from which sounds came. Maybe Hillers had brought the chimney down! They might need help. She pulled out her earphones and went to the door ... but the shooting, the engine, *The Black Bottom Stomp* and the barking continued.

Now she was in the hall and could concentrate on the existing sounds, she became aware that one was missing. Nothing from the ballroom. Her witch's sixth sense had been activated. Perhaps the tuner was resting or inspecting something, but .... She knocked politely.

No response.

Amanda turned the handle and pushed. The door seemed to be stuck. She had to give it three or four shoves with her shoulder before it loosened and opened.

She stood round-eyed upon the threshold. Only the tuner's legs were visible beyond the piano stool. The rest of him was enveloped in a vast glittering hat, the outside of which had fractured and scattered into a hundred diamonds. They had skated across the floor, radiating out from the glistening globe that was the ballroom's grandest chandelier.

A shadow seemed to emerge from the wreck, and then another. She stepped forward, but abruptly turned her head to the right, as something out of the corner of her eye caught her attention: the semi-transparent image of a little child, coming out from under a console table by the wall behind the door. She was staring toward the piano. Amanda heard a faint voice calling,

'Dolly! Dolly!'

Amanda's head whipped back as a figure rose from behind the splintered and broken instrument. He looked straight at her, smiled, bowed and vanished, together with all of the other apparitions.

She gathered her wits for the first order of business. It wasn't a pleasant task, but she had, at least, done it before. Amanda hurried forward and sought the wrist of the piano tuner. There was, as she had expected, no pulse. Only a miracle could have saved him from the impact of a ton of wrought iron and glass, collapsing upon him from above.

Being the person who finds the body never looks good. Few knew that as well as Amanda. She needed to use the few precious moments, before someone else arrived or she must raise the alarm, to gather all of the information she could from the crime scene.

First, why had the chandelier fallen?

She stretched up to look at the top of it. There was an aged, once-golden rope hooked on the centre. It trailed off along the ground on the opposite side of the piano. The end was frayed, broken. With her eyes, Amanda followed the line of it to a large iron cleat in the wall opposite the door, on the right of the great ornate fireplace. As quickly as possible, she made her way across the room, picking her way amongst the crystals that had come free of their mooring links. The other end of the rope was securely wound in place but, dangling from the cleat, the frayed edge was clear to see.

What a disastrous accident! And yet, it seemed unlike Moffat to have allowed such a vital piece of equipment to have decayed to this fatal point. Of course, Miss de Havillande had said that the ballroom had long been in need of restoration. Something here, though, didn't feel right.

There was no more time. Amanda made her way to the door and called out,

'Miss de Havillande! Miss Armstrong-Witworth, Moffat! Come quickly! There's been an accident!'

Humpy was closest and emerged from the library.

'What's up?'

Amanda beckoned him. 'Come in here.'

He peered into the ballroom. 'Good lords and ladies! So that was what the noise was about.'

'You did hear it then?'

'Yes, but just thought it was ... you know ... Hillers!'

The shooting had stopped. Hilary arrived next, still carrying her rifle. Humpy ushered her into the disaster area, and she took stock while he hastened out to the kitchen and garden, in search of Miss de Havillande.

The study door opened cautiously, revealing the handsome face of John Bailey-Farrell.

'*John?*'

'Amanda. Is everything all right? Mrs, er ... Hillers told me to stay in there and wait ... then I heard a crash and felt the ground move, but I thought ....'

'Yes, so did I, at first.'

As the needle on the gramophone reached the edge of the record of *The Black Bottom Stomp*, the inappropriately jaunty music ceased. Moffat was coming into the hall from the direction of the kitchen. He was shortly followed by Miss Armstrong-Witworth. She hurried forward.

'Amanda, dear. You look as white as a sheet. Whatever has happened?'

'In the ballroom, Miss Armstrong-Witworth. There's been a terrible accident.'

The roar from the garden stopped. Only Churchill's yelps filled the air.

'Churchill!' shouted Miss de Havillande, coming into the hall from the back of the house with Dale. Now, finally, quiet fell. They all joined her niece in the ballroom, looking around in astonishment.

'Is he dead?' asked Hillers, with blunt curiosity.

'Yes,' replied Amanda. 'I felt his wrist. No pulse. Miss de Havillande, shall I call Sergeant Baker?'

'Yes, do.'

Amanda got out her phone from her boiler suit pocket and dialled.

'Detective Sergeant Baker? ... Yes, it is. I have Miss de Havillande of The Grange here for you. There's been an accident.'

Chapter 27

༄

ARRIVALS

As it wasn't a life-threatening situation and the ballroom had been designated as off-limits, it was some time before the police arrived. However, Amanda was on the lookout, and she was waiting at the door when Detective Sergeant Baker of Barnet Hill Station arrived.

'Ah, Miss Cadabra, and, of course, ... there's a -*body*.' He sighed. '*Again*.'

'Hello, Sergeant Baker. I'm sorry. I just seem to keep being in the wrong place at the wrong time.'

'Of course, miss.'

Amanda recognised the dark-haired young woman coming up behind the sergeant.

'Oh, hello, Constable Nikolaides. Nice to see you again.'

'Miss Cadabra, you too.'

'Care to direct us to the scene of the accident?' asked Baker, with ironic nonchalance.

'Yes, of course, Sergeant. It's along the hall to the left, just here.'

'Where is everyone?'

'Erm, around the place, but Miss de Havillande has asked everyone to remain within the bounds of the property, and to be ready to gather in the drawing-room on your say-so. Shall I let them all know that you're here?'

'If you would be so good, Miss Cadabra.'

Constable Nikolaides produced gloves and shoe covers. As she and Baker put them on, she said,

'Please keep everyone out of the ballroom. The rest of the team will be here soon. Once you've got everyone together, let them know I'll be in to take their statements.'

'Yes, Constable,' Amanda replied. 'And I'll be ready to let your people in when they get here. Oh, and Miss de Havillande said to tell you that if you want to interview people separately, then the library is at your disposal.'

'Thank you, miss.'

'What's wrong with this door?' asked Baker, trying to enter the ballroom.

'Oh, it sticks, you have to give it a few shoves.'

'Ah, I see. Thanks.' Baker and Nikolaides disappeared inside.

Amanda toured the property, locating everyone, in the kitchen, the main dining room or the garden, in spite of the cold weather. Then she returned to the front of the house to watch for the next arrivals. The medical examiner turned up, had a look at the piano tuner's legs, then said there was nothing more she could do until they moved the chandelier. Amanda took her to the kitchen and left her with tea and biscuits, while she went to see if the last two team members were in sight.

She was almost at the front door, when the bell rang, startling her. Amanda opened it quickly.

'Oh!' she said in surprise, before remembering her

manners. 'Er, Inspector, hello ....You here?'

'As you see, Miss Cadabra, and hello. Yes, earlier than we expected.'

'Indeed. Erm?'

'I've been seconded. By the Met. As I know this village so *very* well.'

'Did you come by helicopter?' Amanda enquired curiously.

'No, I was on my way up a day early and was redirected here at the eleventh hour — more like fifty-ninth minute.' It was a comparatively quiet Friday, and the previous Tuesday, Hogarth had told him he was looking tired, and should give himself an extra day off and make it a long weekend.

'Well, I'm pleased to see you.' she said sincerely, with a smile.

'Thank you, Miss Cadabra. Did you find the bod....but, of course, you did.'

'Yes, I've already apologised for that to Sergeant Baker. Miss de Havillande is corralling everyone in the drawing-room, by the way.'

'All right. Before I go any further, briefly, what happened?'

'I was in the small dining room when I heard a crash in the ballroom. I came into the ballroom and saw the chandelier on top of the piano tuner.'

'Dead?'

'Yes. I felt his wrist. And no, I didn't otherwise touch anything.'

'Good.'

'I called Miss de Havillande, Miss Armstrong-Witworth and Moffat. And everyone else, hearing me, one by one, turned up, and then I phoned Sergeant Baker.'

'How many people were in the house and grounds at the time of the incident?'

'Eight, that I know of, Inspector.'

The ballroom door opened.

'Sir?'

Trelawney turned and shook hands. 'Sergeant. I've been seconded.'

'They told me. Glad to have you along on our little jaunt, sir.'

'Thank you, Baker. Have you brought your excellent Constable ... ah, Nikolaides, good.'

'Hello, sir.'

'Well, now,' said Trelawney, 'since the gang's all here, where are we?'

'The medical examiner has had an initial look at what's on show,' answered Baker, 'and flash and dabs will be here shortly.'

'Sorry?' queried Amanda.

'It's what we call the photographer and forensics, miss,' Baker explained kindly.

'Ah, I see. The medical examiner is actually in the kitchen, as she can't do any more until the chandelier is removed.'

'Right-oh, well, Sergeant, Constable, let me gown up and have a gander. I will see you later, Miss Cadabra.'

Presently, the Scene of Crime Officer and the photographer turned up and did their jobs. Nikolaides went off to take statements. Baker and Trelawney found nothing except the frayed rope, to indicate what had led to the piano tuner meeting his end. Finally, they lifted the chandelier up and off the body, and the medical examiner came back in. Like most of those in her profession, she did not like to be rushed.

'Well?' asked Baker unwisely, after only a few minutes.

'My initial estimate is that the man was killed by a falling chandelier,' she replied drily. The detectives duly retired to another part of the room and awaited her further comments.

However, in Trelawney and Baker's view, death by falling chandelier was enough. The only question for them was, was it accidental?

Chapter 28

POSITIONS

It was dark outside by the time Trelawney and Amanda were both back at the cottage, fire lit and tea served.

'All right, Miss Cadabra. Time to tell me all the bits that aren't in here.' He waved her statement. 'I hope that by now, I have earned your confidence sufficiently for ....'

'Of course, Inspector.' Amanda proceeded to relate the events she had experienced, since the moment of her arrival at The Grange, up until the time of the phone call to Sergeant Baker.

At the end of the narrative, Trelawney raised his eyebrows and exhaled audibly. 'What a lot of apparitions. Never mind. Let's start with tangibles. Where, as far as you recall, was everyone, at the time that you felt the crash? Top-down, start with Miss de Havillande, please.'

'As I told you,' Amanda began, 'soon after I arrived, the doorbell rang, and Miss de Havillande said it was the florist, who had asked to see the grounds to get inspiration for the arrangements for the ball. That's the new florist in the village. They've taken over what was the salon. A mother and son. I didn't know which of the two it was ,until after the accident and everyone came running.'

'I see.'

'That was why I closed the door of the small dining-room where I was working. I hadn't gained a favourable impression of the mother and anyway, wanted to continue working undisturbed.'

'So after that, between the time that you shut the door of the room where you were working, and the first other person arrived on the scene, you saw no one?' queried Trelawney.

'That's correct,' Amanda acknowledged. 'I heard sounds, though. In fact, it was so noisy it was distracting, and that's why I put my earphones in. The only person who I could really be sure of was Hillers. I could still hear the gunfire even with the music playing, and anyone passing the house would have been able to see her out at the front, I would have thought.'

'Thank you. Where, in your opinion, was each person as the time of the accident?'

'Miss de Havillande was with the florist in the grounds. Miss Armstrong-Witworth was, Miss de Havillande had said, "in the butler's pantry with Moffat cleaning the silver." Hillers was outside scaring the pigeons. Her husband Humpy, Humphrey that is, was in the library, listening to the gramophone. Loudly. And the gardener was mowing the lawn.' Amanda silently counted. 'That's only six ... oh, and John Bailey-Farrell was in the small salon, where he said Hillers had asked him to wait. I don't know why she had done that. When she said he wanted to see me, I had told her to send him on his way. I thought, actually, it was Ryan who had called.'

'Mr Farrell had come to see you?'

'No, he'd come to offer to bring chairs from Madley Towers for the party, and he'd brought some flowers, just in case I was there.'

'Odd to bring flowers on the off-chance,' remarked Trelawney.

'Well, then, I suppose he must have been pretty sure of finding me there. Maybe he heard that I was starting work today.'

'Yes, starting a project like this on a Friday ...?'

'I wouldn't have normally. The glaziers had said that they couldn't have the replacement mirror ready until Monday, but then they rang yesterday and said they could deliver it today. And with the party being only just over three weeks away and so much to do, I accepted.'

'But somehow he knew about this last-minute change?'

'I suppose so .... Bush telegraph?'

'All right. So you looked at the rope that had held up the chandelier?'

'Yes, and it was definitely frayed to breaking point.'

'So you concluded that what had happened was an accident?'

'Well ... yes,' Amanda replied slowly.

'There was doubt in your mind?'

'It just seems so unlike Moffat to let something like that ... I mean, I know that Miss de Havillande said that the ballroom had been neglected ... I just had this feeling that something wasn't right.'

'Let's assume for a moment that somehow someone deliberately caused the chandelier to fall. Who would you consider might have a motive?' Trelawney asked levelly.

'For killing an innocent piano tuner? No one!'

'What if it was intended to fall on someone else?'

'Well, if I were to go the *cui bono* route, maybe Hillers or Humpy, to inherit The Grange. But as far as I know, they stand to inherit anyway. Maybe if they needed money quickly, and the intended target was Miss de Havillande .... That's the best I can think of. John is new to the village, and everyone else was with someone at the time.'

'Not quite.'

'Oh?'

'Although Moffat and Miss Armstrong-Witworth were together, Miss de Havillande says that she left the florist ....'

'Dale Hilland.'

'Thank you. She left Dale Hilland in the grounds while she came back to get the key to the summer house.'

'So then it's only Moffat and Miss Armstrong-Witworth who have alibis?'

'So it would seem.' The inspector wrote in his notebook. Amanda waited until he was ready to begin again. 'So you were closest and responded first?'

'Yes.'

'In what order do you remember people coming into the hall?'

'Let's see ... Humpy first, then Hillers, then John, then Moffat followed by Miss Armstrong-Witworth, and then Miss de Havillande and the gardener, Mundly. Then Dale or maybe he came before Mundly. I'd say I was the closest ... but if someone had been outside near the *ballroom windows* then, I suppose, technically they might have been closer. But if the florist and Miss de Havillande were near the *Summer House*, then yes, I was closest. And yes, I know it never looks good to be the person who finds the body. But it wasn't me who did it. I mean, I hadn't even met him. We'd only spoken on the phone, and he sounded perfectly nice.'

'Ah, tell me about that, if you would, Miss Cadabra.'

'Well ... actually ... in a way ... I think it may be my fault that he's dead,' Amanda said contritely.

The inspector looked at her in surprise.

'Oh, not that I mean that I dropped the chandelier on him!'

'That hadn't crossed my mind. Do go on though, please.'

'He called and said he was deputising for Mr Spinnetti, who usually comes round once a year and tunes all of the pianos in the village: the organ at the church, the piano at The Elms, the one at the school, Ruth's, Erik's, Jim and Sylvia's, the pub's, the Manor's and so on. Mr Spinnetti had given him the list of all our phone numbers, and he was calling round to see who would like it done.'

'I see.'

Amanda explained why she had chosen, after all, to have her piano tuned.

'Good positive thinking,' approved Trelawney. 'So you made an appointment?'

'That's right, for yesterday at 2 o'clock. Only, I had an emergency call-out, so I postponed it until today. But then, the glazier called and said they could deliver ahead of schedule and this big job ... it just seemed ... more important ... well, more *immediate*, I suppose. And I called and cancelled, and Mr Honeywell must have offered the appointment to The Grange instead. So you see, Inspector, if I hadn't cancelled, Mr Honeywell would never have been under that chandelier when the old rope finally gave way, under a hundred years of strain or whatever and released its load upon the poor man.'

Trelawney spoke reassuringly. 'I really don't think you can be blamed for Mr Honeywell's being in the wrong place at the wrong time. Any more than you can be blamed for the same thing and therefore finding the body, either on this or previous occasions. Wouldn't you agree, Miss Cadabra?'

'Seen in that light ... well ... yes, I suppose you're right, Inspector. Thank you.'

'My pleasure.'

'But I can, at least, do my best to help you find out whether or not it really was an accident.'

'Yes, and to that end, perhaps you would like to tell me *all* that you saw when you entered the ballroom.'

Chapter 29

∽

INTANGIBLES

Amanda got up and paced. She halted and stared out of the window at the dark sky.

'I don't need this. I *really* don't need this. Not now. Not when your clan is about to descend on my village in all their sinister force.'

'I do wish you would refrain from referring to them as my clan,' remarked the inspector, as a by-the-way

'Sorry yes, you're a Trelawney. I know. Your grandmother's clan then.

'Better. I'd prefer not to be linked to them at all,' he said with a wry smile.

'You can't help who you were born. Very well. The Flamgoynes. The Flamgoynes are coming. How and when I don't know. And, still, I don't know who Viola is, or of anyone who will help me at the hour ... except Tempest.'

'Well, he has been homicidally helpful in the past,' the inspector pointed out.

'Don't remind me. I have to avoid *his* methods. I'm a Cadabra.'

Trelawney nodded. 'And Cadabras do not strike out at others. Yes. But come, Miss Cadabra, perhaps we can, at least, make some progress with the new puzzle we have before us. Now ... what have you left out of your statement? Off the record.'

'Definitely off the record?'

'Yes, but if it helps, Sergeant Baker said it was possible that, when you found the body, you may have also been "sensing things". Like you did last time.'

Amanda lightened up at that. 'All right, yes, I did.' She related what she had seen.

'Good,' said Trelawney when she had finished. 'So let's unpack this like we would any other evidence. Starting from the first thing, or things, you saw.'

'The two figures that sort of rose or moved out from the chandelier.'

'Human figures?'

'Yes,' Amanda confirmed.

'Male or female?'

'Let me see ... it was all so vague, but I think one was in evening dress and the other ... just jacket and trousers.'

'Like a suit?' suggested Trelawney.

'It was all rather grey but ... no, the jacket was sort of speckly.'

'Like a tweed weave?'

'Yes.'

'With plain trousers?'

'Yes. So, both male most likely. And my sense was ... yes, *male*, come to think of it.'

'Good. Then we come to the child.'

'Yes, I'd say she was about three years old. I didn't look at her for very long because I was almost immediately distracted by the man sort of rising from behind the piano.'

'Floating, do you mean?'

'No, more like someone who had been sitting down and was standing up. And then he smiled and put his ... let's see ... his *right* hand on his chest, and gave a little bow, and then a sort of Gallic shrug and then ... they all vanished.'

'You say Gallic ...?'

'Yes, now why? ...I feel he was French. Yes. Actually, he was the clearest of all of the figures. He was wearing ....' Amanda looked into the middle distance, replaying in her mind what she had seen. 'A white shirt with a collar that stood up, and a necktie, erm, cravat ... and a light waistcoat and a dark coat.'

'Victorian?'

Amanda shook her head. 'No ... earlier ... Regency. Yes.'

'So a Frenchman from the Regency period,' Trelawney summarised.

'Maybe the Napoleonic? An *émigré*?'

'Anything else?'

'No ... as I say, he shrugged ... oh, and then looked down at his clothes, brushed himself off, and then disappeared.'

Trelawney nodded, then moved on. 'The little girl?'

'She was wearing a dress, I think, but ... I hardly saw her. I just had this impression of a very little child behind the door, staring at the piano with big, round, solemn eyes. And her little mouth in an O. Wait! There was one more thing: the word "dolly"; someone was calling it out. Maybe another child looking for her toy? And that really is all I remember.'

'Right, well, Miss Cadabra ... can you do what you did before on the last case? Go and summon them?'

Amanda smiled. 'You don't summon people from other planes,' she said patiently. 'That's just in fiction. It doesn't work and just puts people's backs up. Unless you mean that Darkside stuff that Granny told me you only try if you're just plain silly.'

He was curious. 'Silly? Why? It always looks deadly serious in horror films.'

'"Silly" because it always bounces back, in one form or another.'

'Bounces back?'

'If you go and invoke something to help you harm someone else, it will always end up harming you worse, in some way, or someone close to you,' Amanda explained. 'It's counterproductive.'

'Right,' Trelawney said uncomfortably.

'What's wrong, Inspector?' she asked gently.

'It's just that you're so matter-of-fact about it all.'

Amanda nodded understandingly. 'Well, I have been in training since I was six. So I suppose it all seems perfectly ordinary to me.'

'Yes, I see that. Anyway ....'

'Anyway, you don't go around giving orders to people on other planes. It's just not considered any more polite than on this one. You ask, request them to appear.'

'OK, so can you do that?' he asked.

'Yes .... It's just that Grandpa said that this case would be even more complicated than the last. That, in fact, we might not solve it at all,' Amanda added.

'Thank you. That bodes well for my career.'

'Well, he only said *might*. And I'll do everything I can to help.'

'So you'll go back and try?'

'Of course,' she said willingly.

'Good.'

'But it may not be that simple,' Amanda warned him.

'Why not? I'll come along if you need a man on the job,' Trelawney offered. She chuckled at his reference to the occasion when she had, reluctantly, had to request his assistance.

'Good, but ... sometimes, what you're seeing is not a ghost or person-of-another-plane, as they prefer to be called.'

'You're telling me that 'ghost' is non-PC!' exclaimed the inspector.

'Correct.'

'Fine. Right. I wouldn't want to give offence.'

'It's just that ghosts have rather a bad press ... you know, in fiction. Many, according to my grandparents, regard the word "ghost" as a pejorative term.'

'I see,' said Trelawney, feeling out of his depths again.

'And then there are the ones that are "owning" it, but they use a more trendy spelling,' Amanda went on.

'Seriously?' Thomas asked incredulously.

'Yes: G.O.S.T.E.'

'How do you know all of this?'

'Grandpa reads the "Modern Spirit" column in *The Daily Hereafter*.'

Trelawney was getting that head-spinning, surreal feeling that overtook him whenever he got too close to this strange mystical world, which was still unfamiliar to him. After all, he had staunchly denied its very existence for the past three decades.

'But never mind that now,' said Amanda, sensing his extreme unease. 'Have another shortcake,' she urged him.

'Yes, I could rather do with something for the shock,' agreed Trelawney, half-joking. 'But you were saying that it may not be that simple. That, sometimes what you're seeing is not a gh — person-of-another-plane?'

'That's right. Sometimes it's just a recording. When something of extreme emotion happens to someone, sometimes it can get imprinted on something nearby. It could be a wall or piece of furniture or jewellery or something else. If you're the sort of person who is open to it, it will play back for you. ... I wonder ....' Amanda looked at him speculatively. 'Well, you have already seen and talked to two actual persons from another plane. Would you like to try? Then you'd see how a recording works for yourself.'

'In for a penny in for a pound,' Trelawney responded gamely.

'Then I'll be right back.'

Amanda left him to his shortcake biscuit and, shortly, returned with a blue fabric-covered box.

'Should we switch off the lights or something?' Trelawney asked.

'It's not a séance, Inspector,' she assured him kindly. 'You'd be able to see it in broad daylight.'

She knelt by his chair and opened the box. Inside was a Swiss silver watch, larger than a wristwatch face, with a loop attached to the top

'Relax and pick it up,' Amanda invited him.

Seeing it was an antique, he took it carefully from its white satin cushion and, balancing it on his palm, looked down at it. His face softened.

'It feels ...,' he began.

Then *she* was there. There was the identical watch pinned to her long white apron, which she wore over an ankle-length blue dress. Upon the apron was a red cross that proclaimed the nurse. Dark curly hair was visible under the white cap.

She was bending over a woman in a wrought-iron-framed bed, with white sheets and blankets, and putting a tiny baby into the woman's arms as she spoke.

'Well done, Madame Durand, a healthy baby boy!' The nurse looked down at the watch. 'Time of birth 4.05.' Her face was lit with joy and tenderness. It seemed to illuminate the space around her.

The scene vanished as abruptly as it had appeared. Trelawney smiled and shook his head.

'Was that *real*?'

'Do you mean, were you seeing something that actually happened? Oh yes. Mrs Fosstly from the village asked me to clean it. It's rather a family treasure. Not because it's worth a great deal of money, but because it belonged to a great-great-aunt, who was in the Red Cross during the First World War. She was in France and saw so many dreadful things, so much suffering. But one night, one of the women in a nearby house had a cross birth — you know? Where the baby is lying at the wrong angle? —The owner of this nurse's watch went to help, and it all ended happily. It was an oasis in the desert of her usual work, I imagine. I think it gave her almost as much joy as the mother. The story and the watch have been passed down.'

'I understand,' Trelawney replied. 'The emotion of the moment was so strong that it imprinted itself onto the watch, then?'

'Correct. Well done, Inspector. You're getting the hang of all this.'

'Thank you, Miss Cadabra. But getting back to the crime scene ....'

'Yes, you see, if any of the things I saw when I entered the ballroom are recordings, I won't be about to talk to them, only observe.'

'It may still help,' he insisted.

'But also ...,' Amanda began.

'There's more?'

'Yes, you see even if they are POAPs —'

'Popes?'

'P.O.A.P.s: persons-of—'

'— another plane. I get it.'

'Even if they are around, not all of them just prattle on; sometimes you have to know what it is you want to ask them. It has to be relevant to their experience,' said Amanda.

'And we don't know what that was,' Trelawney agreed.

'Exactly. We need background information. But I can ask Miss de Havillande and Mrs Pagely at the library. I'll see what I can find out. Everyone knows that I'm interested in local history, so it won't look odd. I'll be your man on the esoteric inside.'

'Shouldn't that be *person* on the esoteric inside?' he asked, with a twinkle.

'Indeed, Inspector.'

He checked his watch. 'I should be going.'

'I will still be working at the house tomorrow morning,' Amanda told him.

'So shall I. There may be something we've missed.'

She was silent while he put on his coat, then asked tentatively,

'Inspector … where do I stand … officially?'

'Miss Cadabra, … you found the body, and you don't have an alibi.'

Chapter 30

ଚ୬

AMANDA RECEIVES ATTENTION

By lunchtime, Amanda had got the mirror fitted snugly in the frame, ready to go into its panel in the ballroom. The inspector had had another look at the crime scene and had asked Moffat some more questions about the room.

The next time she and Trelawney were to see one another was at the dance class. The following week's was cancelled because of the re-enactment-fair-Sunken-Madley-VIP-Day and the likely day of the Flamgoyne attack. As Amanda got ready, she couldn't help wondering if this would be the last class she would survive to attend. That was until Granny turned up.

'I do hope you're not allowing any self-indulgently pessimistic thoughts — unless it's about the fate of the Flamgoynes, of course. You can be as pessimistic about that as you please. Certainly, that would be in the Cardiubarn tradition!' she added humorously.

'Of course, Granny. You're right. I must assume the

best possible outcome for next Saturday.'

'Excellent. ... Are you sure you want to wear that for today's dance class?' asked the fashion police. 'You always seem to wear the same thing: an orange dress.'

'No, Granny, sometimes I wear an orange *skirt* and top, and yes, I am sure. Thank you.'

Once she was at the function room of the Snout and Trough, Amanda had no time to think about the following weekend. John Bailey-Farrell approached and engaged her in conversation. It seemed innocuous, asking her about what to expect from the class. What standard would he need to meet? How long had she been dancing? In the interval, he asked if she would be so kind as to practice with him. He claimed he needed all he could get.

Miss de Havillande appeared at Trelawney's elbow, observing the line of his inscrutable gaze.

'Our new neighbour seems delighted with dear Amanda, does he not, Inspector?' she observed casually.

Trelawney was startled out of his reverie. 'Sorry? Oh, yes, quite. And therein shows excellent good taste,' he added, recovering himself.

'I could not agree with you more,' Miss de Havillande returned. 'By the way, Inspector, may I say how grateful I am that you are bringing your expertise to the sad matter of the ballroom accident.'

'I am happy to be of service in getting to the bottom of it. I am fortunate to be working with such a dedicated team.'

'Indeed.'

After the class, Amanda found Farrell's bag was next to hers, and, while they changed their shoes and got their coats on, he asked, what other kinds of dancing did she like, and what was her taste in music.

Back at the cottage, the inspector noticed two vases of flowers on the kitchen counter: one red, one white.

'Miss Cadabra, may I ask, would those blooms in there be the same ones brought to The Grange for you by John Bailey-Farrell, on the morning of the accident?'

'Yes,' she answered readily. 'I separated them into red and white because I don't like mixed colours,' she explained, imagining that this must be Trelawney's query.

'Hmm .... He seemed to, er ... be taking a great interest in you.'

'Doesn't he?' she agreed intently. 'It makes no sense.'

'I beg your pardon?'

'Look at him. He's drop-dead gorgeous; he's highly intelligent, he's kind, he's gentle, strong, courteous, funny, confident but modest, successful ... I mean, what more could any girl want?'

Trelawney found that, for some reason, Amanda's observations were provoking some entirely unreasonable emotions.

'So ....' she went on.

'So?'

'What's he doing paying so much attention to *me*?'

'Well ... your modesty does you credit, Miss Cadabra, but —'

'What if he's working with Ryan? He said he's going to call me. He might even ask me out. I hope he does. I need to get him to talk. You know? While I've got him relaxed and off his guard.'

Trelawney was on the verge of asking how exactly she was planning to do that, then suppressed the enquiry, on the grounds that it was none of his business. And he wasn't sure if he wanted to know or not.

'Hm,' he managed.

'So? Have you turned up anything else about the chandelier business?'

'I asked Moffat, tactfully, about the state of the rope. He

said that that room was usually shut up and not at all maintained. It hadn't been used for parties for a while but, naturally, the chandelier, rope and cleat, would have been inspected prior to the ball. He said that, for reasons of management and economy, a number of rooms at the establishment were not in use, although they were checked periodically for any structural deterioration: damp in particular. Furthermore, the rope had stood the test of time from since before he took up management of The Grange, and there would have been no reason to assume that it would not be good for a few more decades, and was there anything else with which he could assist the inspector.'

'Dear me.'

'I asked him if he had known that the tuner was going to be visiting. He said that it was something of a last-minute appointment, arranged with Miss de Havillande, who unfortunately had not thought it necessary to inform Moffat of the matter.'

'Did you ask Miss de Havillande about it?'

'Yes, she said that Moffat had quite enough to do without worrying about that, and she was perfectly capable of admitting and paying the tuner herself.'

'He can hardly be accused of criminal negligence then.'

'I agree. I asked Miss de Havillande if the tuner expressed any concerns regarding the relative positions of the piano and the chandelier, and she said that he had not.'

'Well, he couldn't have missed that it was hanging there. It's the most prominent feature of the ballroom.'

'Quite. Have you had a chance to do any research on The Grange, Miss Cadabra?'

'Not yet, but hopefully tomorrow.'

'Keep me posted, if you will.'

'Of course.'

'I'll make a move now. Thank you for the tea, as always.'

Trelawney was walking along the hallway when he

stopped, turned and asked Amanda,

'John Bailey-Farrell ... are you quite sure about ...?'

'What, Inspector?' she asked curiously.

He paused, shook his head and finally said, 'Never mind. I will see you on Monday, most likely.'

'Yes. Goodnight, Inspector.'

She waved him off then shut the door, with a slight frown, and looked down at Tempest who had followed her into the hall with thoughts of dinner.

'I wonder what he was going to say? Do you think he's worried about my leading John up the garden path? Or maybe he thinks John might be dangerous .... No, most likely the former. That's rather nice, don't you think? Sort of brotherly.'

She walked past him towards the kitchen. Tempest stared after her in disbelief. His human was definitely, in many regards, one of the brighter of her intellectually challenged species. How could she, when it came to reading certain people, be so ... utterly clueless?

Chapter 31

THOMAS DECIDES

Driving back to his mother's house, Thomas wondered if he was feeling a twinge of ... no, certainly not, he had no right and besides their relationship was purely professional, that is ... of course .... He felt an irrational urge to ... he suddenly remembered that card he'd put away. Maybe he would give Naomi Hollister a call, after all. Why not? Good grief! he chided himself. What am I? 16? He realised he'd been jarred into a frame of mind, in which one did not make the wisest decisions. Besides, the way she'd spoken about Farrell had not been in the least bit starry-eyed. Matter-of fact, rather. But then she was usually matter-of-fact.

Trelawney, through years of practice and experience, was well able to conceal his emotional state. Of course, he was better at this when he himself knew what that was. But in professional circumstances, he was known amongst the criminal fraternity of his area for his ability to conceal the extent to which he credited the veracity of their statements. His face and manner conveyed, at all times, the emotion most suited to the encouragement of information and, indeed, confidences.

To the lady who had been tapping away on her laptop, now observing Trelawney from her sofa — with its view of the hall — noting the manner in which he discarded his coat and shoes, he was an open book. Then again, she was his mother. There was no mistaking that: the same hazel eyes with the same intelligent humour in them. Her hair was fairer than his light brown, but they had the same mannerism of raking their fingers through it when perplexed.

Penelope Trelawney knew better than to ask her son, point-blank, what was amiss.

'Hello, darling, tea's in the pot,' she called out.

'Pot? Special occasion?'

'A grateful client gave me an up-market packet of lapsang souchong.' She nodded at the Fair Trade, wooden table before her. 'Be a dear and freshen my cup, would you? And help yourself. Shortcake in the tin on the counter.'

A few minutes later, settled on the sofa beside his mother, Thomas feigned interest in what she was doing for a while, then asked casually if she followed the cricket.

'Of course, I follow the cricket, as you know perfectly well. What else does a lonely old woman have to do?' she asked roguishly.

There was that phrase again, 'lonely old', the words Ross had used, thought Thomas. Although no two words could more ill describe his vibrant, youthful maternal parent. She always seemed to have half a dozen men at her beck and call, at least one of them, her disapproving son recalled, younger than he was. Amanda had pointed out the error of this way of thinking, insisting that it was ageist and he was only saying that because she was his mother.

'But there's nothing on at the moment.' Penelope was pointing out. 'The season's not starting for another three months. Why?'

'Oh, just wondered how closely you were following Middlesex, these days.'

'They're the local team so it wouldn't be surprising. Why? Is this about Ryan Ford, up in your Sunken Madley? You said they'd asked you to join the local 11 as a reserve, if you felt the urge, as an honorary villager. Why? Is he on your policeman's radar for match-fixing or something?'

'Certainly not! No. He's got another team member staying with him. John Bailey-Farrell.'

Penelope stopped typing and looked at him. 'Oooo.'

'What do you mean, "Oooo"?' asked her son, disapprovingly.

'I mean "Oooo" as in lucky Sunken Madley, entertaining the gorgeous Mr F.'

'Yes, well,' he replied a trifle shortly. This got Penelope's attention. It was not like her stoical son to be bothered by another man's charms. This began to interest her intensely. 'What do you know about him? I mean, you're on the gossip circuit. What's the word on the street?'

'He's an excellent left-arm bowler,' replied Penelope, provokingly.

'That's not what I mean, Ma-*maa*, and you know it,' he replied with a grin, and sipped his tea.

'Hmn ... *well*, he came to the gallery,' she announced with mock swagger.

'Really? I'm impressed.'

'So I should hope. It was to buy something special for his mother's 60th birthday,' Penelope explained.

'And your impression of him?'

'He seemed like a nice guy. We chatted about last season and a particularly spectacular match in which he distinguished himself. He praised his teammates rather than taking all the glory. Modest, mentioned his mother in glowing terms. Didn't dis his ex after the breakup — you know?'

Thomas shook his head.

'That rising film star ... what's her name? Oh, she played Strontium 90 in that superhero film ... I know: Fyah Stahta! That's just her stage name, you know, darling. She's really called Janice Rodd.'

'Ah. So he's single then?'

'Oh yes, only number 9 in *Hey There Magazine's* top 10 most eligible UK bachelors but he's definitely up there. Anyway, as I say, after the breakup, he still spoke about her respectfully. And he seemed to me to be in the game for the love of the sport, rather than the financial opportunities. You know, he refused a very lucrative sponsorship deal with Sugar-Hi, that new drink from Dyie & Beaties. A man of principle, I'd say. And of course, he is unquestionably supremely attractive. Shallow of me, I know, but I have to say that it was the first thing I noticed about him.'

'Thinking "if only I were 30 years younger", no doubt.'

Penelope laughed teasingly.

'Oh no, believe me, if the lush Mr Farrell had asked me out, I would have had no reservations whatsoever about accepting. I promise you, the age difference would weigh with me not at all. But is your interest in Farrell professional? Has he done something illegal?'

'He's a witness in the case I've been seconded to.'

'Ah, and he is dancing attendance on your chief witness in your cold case, and you think he may be some sort of threat?' She had been deliberately ambiguous and watched with some fond amusement as he her son took the bait.

'Of course not! You know perfectly well that my relationship with ... her ... is purely professional.'

'But darling, whatever do you mean? I was only enquiring as to any concerns you might have regarding her safely.' replied his mother ingenuously.

'Oh. Yes, quite. Well, strangers turning up in a small

village like Sunken Madley ... and immediately becoming involved in an incident ...'

'But John Bailey-Farrell seems to be perfectly harmless. Of course, that's all *I* know, and it could all be a mask for an absolute cad who is secretly supplying M16s to the children of Sunken Madley School.'

Thomas chuckled and relaxed. 'Sorry to have been spiky, Ma. The truth is that when I met up with Ross —'

'Yes, it was nice to see that you were capable of having an actual night out,' she interjected happily.

'Quite. But he said one or two things that, I suppose, ruffled my feathers a little.'

'Like, "get a life while there's still sand in hourglass"? You poor old thing,' Penelope said, patting his knee consolingly.

He laughed. 'Something like that. Actually, he suggested that I get back in touch with Naomi.'

Penelope remembered her as a tall, thin, blue-eyed, brunette. Short hair, rueful grin. A sweet, bright girl who seemed like one of the boys. 'Why not? You were all pals together, weren't you?'

'Yes ... only ... it turns out that she ... well ....'

'... felt a bit more than friendship for you?' Penelope suggested helpfully.

'Yes, I ... I had no idea. Anyway, she's single now and asked Ross to just pass her contact details to me in case ....'

'... you wanted to reconnect?'

'Yes.'

His mother knew that Thomas wanted to know what she thought of the idea without having to actually ask. Penelope got to the crux of the matter.

'Why do you want to?'

'That's just it. If I make the call, I want it to be for the right reasons. At first ... well, something happened today that ... got me thinking about that side of my life and I suddenly thought

I'd call Naomi. And then I felt I was reacting irrationally and I cooled down. But then, when I kept thinking about the idea, I started to get this ... gut feeling ... that it was the right thing to do. But the two impulses may have got muddled up.'

'Trust your instinct, Thomas, regardless of the other knee jerk reaction. I honestly don't see that there's any harm in it. A drink and a chat for old time's sake, and if that's all it turns out to be, I'm sure there would be no hard feelings.'

He chuckled. 'It's just a drink, not a binding marital contract, you mean?'

'Precisely.'

'Hm.'

'Go on, pop upstairs and give her a call. I'll start the dinner.'

Chapter 32

෴

THE FRENCH CONNECTION

The following morning, with only six days to go until The Event, Amanda's most intense desire was to attempt to interview The Grange Ladies and Moffat, in the hope of discovering the elusive Viola. However, that would have to wait until tomorrow, when she would legitimately be there for work.

Meanwhile, there was the history of The Grange to be researched. The inspector has assured her that she would get some time alone back in the ballroom, to learn what she could from whomever or whatever she could manage to persuade to appear.

Sunken Madley library was the best place to start. Whatever Amanda found out there would be general rather than personal to Miss de Havillande's family. Furthermore, it would provide her with knowledge that would show she had a genuine interest. Amanda hoped that this would encourage the sharing of inside information by Miss de Havillande. That was the theory, anyway.

* * * * *

It was lunchtime, and Trelawney was back at his mother's, after re-interviewing John Bailey-Farrell. As Penelope had remarked, he seemed a perfectly decent sort of chap.

Farrell said that, on Friday, he'd arrived at The Grange, been shown into the small salon by Hillary and asked to wait. He had stayed there until Amanda had raised the alarm. New to the village, he didn't know anyone there well at all. He hadn't even met the Grange ladies before.

'You had brought flowers for Miss Cadabra?' asked Trelawney.

'Yes, that's right,' Farrell replied with a smile.

'You expected to see her at The Grange?'

'Yes, you see, I had gone into The Corner Shop ....'

Ah, that explains everything, thought Trelawney, as the inevitable narrative followed.

'As I had an errand on behalf of Ryan, to offer the use of chairs for the party, it seemed like an opportunity. Miss Cadabra and I actually bumped into one another practically outside the florists. She seems like a very pleasant young lady and was most helpful and welcoming. I wanted to say thank you.'

'That was thoughtful,' replied Trelawney.

It was all perfectly reasonable and above board. At Trelawney's invitation, Farrell had provided an outsider's perspective of the people at The Grange. However, he seemed the sort of person disposed to think well of his fellow humans and could not imagine any of them being, in any way, connected with foul play.

Trelawney had just removed his coat and greeted his

mother, when his phone rang.

'Inspector.'

'Miss Cadabra.'

'I've got something!'

'Just a moment.' He went upstairs to his room, closed the door and sat at the desk with pad and pencil. 'Fire away.'

'So. I went to the library, and Mrs Pagely gave me the one book that mentions The Grange. It was in the context of houses that were originally silos, granaries. There was the long spiel about how it was built, rebuilt, damaged, repaired, destroyed by fire, flood and sword, rebuilt, expanded, remodelled and so on, until the way it is now. *But*, because of the Frenchman, in his costume from what I thought was the Regency period, I was particularly interested in that era.'

* * * * *

'Well, dear,' had said Mrs Pagely, a motherly woman with whom Amanda was rather a favourite. 'The Grange would have been the country seat of a gentleman.'

The librarian took the opportunity, offered by an ebb of customers and the presence of her library assistant, Jonathan, at the counter, to sit down beside Amanda at one of the reader's tables.

'He and his family,' she continued, 'would most likely have stayed in London during the Season and the Little Season, and retired to The Grange for the rest of the year. They may have had guests to help entertain them during the summer and winter months.'

'What sort of guests, Mrs Pagely?'

'Family, friends, fashionable people of note — that was always good for the householder's reputations. And yes, … just a moment, stay here, I'll be right back!'

Mrs Pagely, the light of pursuit in her eyes, left, and soon returned to the table with a cloth-bound, red book.

'Here, dear: *French Leave – Émigrés in London* by Honor Broadferry. The Grange guests would likely have included at least one of these. You know *émigrés* were particularly popular, bringing fresh culture, fashions, literature, and outlook to London.'

'During the Revolution? French aristocrats?' Amanda suggested.

'And the Napoleonic era too. Not just titled people either. But yes. Between, ooh ... 1789 and 1815 many French came here, to London specifically.'

'But they could have been invited to country houses, off-season?'

'Very likely,' Mrs Pagely confirmed.

* * * * *

'So, you see Inspector, I think that's why the Frenchman was there. I mean, in the house.'

'That makes sense.'

'Now, the next step depends entirely on whether or not he's a recording. And I don't think he *is*,' said Amanda.

'Why not?'

'Because he was the only apparition who looked straight at me,' she explained enthusiastically. 'Now, I know that that doesn't necessarily mean he's *not* a recording, because I could have been standing in exactly the same spot as a person he was talking to at the time, but ... I didn't tell you this ... but there was a ghost at the Asthma Centre building site.'

'That's right. You *didn't*,' Trelawney commented with feeling.

'Well, please don't be put out, Inspector. You wouldn't have been at all comfortable with that information at the time.'

'Fair enough,' he conceded.

'Well, the only people who could see *that* ghost were me and ... and one other person, because we were both of the same profession as the ghost. There was a link, you see.'

'And your link with the Frenchman?'

'The Cadabras! Remember I told you how we got our name? The Frenchman who came to Cornwall, the mix up at immigration? Aristide Cadabra was an *emigré*!'

'Of course. So out of kinship, you think that the Frenchman at the piano may be prepared to help you?' suggested Trelawney.

'It's possible. This is all rather speculative. I'll know more when I get back into the ballroom.'

'All right. Good progress. It's a lead. Not the sort I'm used to, but a lead,' he added lightly. 'How about tomorrow morning? I'll arrange for everyone to be quiet and out of the way. OK?'

'Thank you, Inspector. I'll take Tempest in with me, if I may?'

'Like anyone could keep him out,' replied Trelawney drily.

Chapter 33

෬

NAOMI

Thomas had made the call and was in luck. Naomi was free the next day, Sunday evening. He had felt better for having done something decisive. But then the night had brought strange dreams of the sea, his grandfather ... and a faraway song.

* * * * *

Coffee had become dinner, and they quickly resumed the familiarity of their friendship, exchanging news and shared views. Trelawney had forgotten how easy it was to be with Naomi. She didn't seem to have changed that much at all. The conversation inevitably turned to work. She asked about the last two cases he'd worked on, up in Sunken Madley, so far from his Cornish base. He gave her the party-line and only touched on the cold case.

'Miss Cadabra sounds like quite an exceptional young woman. Certainly doesn't panic in a crisis. Redoubtable,' observed Naomi.

'Yes. Yes, she is,' he agreed.

'You spend a lot of time there, I gather.'

'Yes, what with the last cases and, well, I keep hoping Miss Cadabra will remember something crucial from the day of the murder, when her family went over our dear old Cornish cliff. Something that could lead to the solving of the case,' Trelawney explained.

'Of course. That long ago, I suppose you're lucky to have any witnesses at all.'

'Quite. Thanks for listening to it all, Naomi. It's a pleasure to be able to talk shop with someone who doesn't mind.'

She responded warmly, 'Far from it.'

'Look ... would you like to do this again, sometime ...?'

Naomi suddenly gave her attention to her nearly empty cup and tapped the handle gently. Finally, she met his eyes with the rueful smile that he and Penelope remembered.

'Did you know,' she asked, 'I had the most almighty crush on you, back in the day?'

'I didn't .... That is, Ross did say you liked me ... I didn't realise.'

'One day, you came walking in my direction, carrying a bunch of red roses. I thought my ship had come in. That, finally, I was going to be the One. Then you walked straight past me, and, when I turned, there you were ... with Tensing — I mean — Perpetua.'

Thomas was mortified. 'I'm so sorry, Naomi! I really had no idea.'

She shook her head, smiling. 'Oh, don't be. I was really quite comical, now I come to think of it. The point is if you had asked me out on a second ... meet-up, 20 years ago, I would have said "yes" without a moment's hesitation.'

'But now?'

'I think there's someone standing behind me. Someone different. But someone that you can't walk up to.'

'Sorry?' Trelawney had an idea of what she meant but wasn't entirely sure.

'Let me put it another way, Thomas. You remember how you used to talk about when you were growing up, and you'd visit your family and stand on the beach, waiting for their fishing boats to come in?'

'Yes.'

'Well, I think you're standing on the beach now, waiting for the wind to blow a certain bark southerly.'

'It's a purely —'

'— yes, yes, "professional relationship",' Naomi agreed understandingly, 'because it *has* to be while you're on this cold case. And you're *right*, and it must be. But ... perhaps,' she added with a playful glimmer, 'I can do something, for old time's sake, to bring that bark in a little sooner.'

He looked at her enquiringly.

'When we were much younger,' Naomi said frankly, 'I thought about you lot of the time. Perhaps out of that old habit, when Ross said you might give me call, I thought I'd take an interest in your current project. I gave someone I'd worked with a call and offered a second opinion on the medical examiner's report.'

Trelawney's eyebrows rose. 'You don't mean Chief Inspector Hogarth?'

'Yes, I worked with him on a case once, and we got on well. He sent me a copy of the file and the report.'

'And?' he asked.

'They didn't die from injuries incurred in the crash. That means they were already dead when they hit the rocks,' Naomi recapped.

'That's right.'

'I think you should look at some kind of poisonous agent. I'd say gas. In that confined space inside the minivan, something released would be effective.'

'I thought toxic gas leaves markers in the bloodstream and so on, and none were found,' Trelawney objected.

Naomi lowered her voice. 'What I am about to say is strictly off the record. Just because we don't know of one that leaves no trace, doesn't mean one doesn't exist, Thomas. I wasn't in Cornwall long, and it's a fascinating and dazzlingly beautiful place, but I came across ... things that can't be explained by the rational approach. And I can't begin to say how uneasy that made me. All I'm saying is, *gas*. That's where I'd be looking, if I were you.'

Trelawney pondered. 'It seems like our killer made a belt-and-braces approach: the skiddable substance on the road in the path of the van, and the poisonous airborne agent inside. Or there were separate attempts by two killers.'

'Well, that's your department, Inspector Trelawney,' Naomi said with a smile, collecting her bag. She stood up, and he followed suit as she took her jacket from the back of her chair. 'Thanks for dinner. It was good to catch up.'

'You're welcome.'

She came around the table to him, and made a remark that surprised him.

'We wouldn't have worked, you know.'

'No?"

Naomi followed up with the last thing he expected to hear.

'No. There was always something ... slightly esoteric about you, however hard you tried to squash it down. And I'm ... just too normal.'

He wondered if he looked as bewildered as he felt.

'Good luck,' she said. 'With everything.' Naomi gave

him a peck on the cheek, turned and left. He watched her walk jauntily towards the door and let it swing back behind her.

In mild shock, Trelawney sat down. His head was buzzing with two very new thoughts: Me? Esoteric? And ... *gas*. The second soon swamped the first. How could gas have been introduced into that space? Nothing was found in the wreck of the van. No gas bottle, nothing of that nature. What could have released it that the occupants wouldn't have noticed?

He murmured to himself, 'I think something is starting to make sense .... I need to conduct another interview ....'

Trelawney grabbed his coat and hurried out to the car. It was half-past eleven at night. She might not be awake. Still, he could send a text. If she were asleep, her phone would be switched off, but she'd see it in the morning.

Amanda was yawning with Tempest on the sofa over the last 15 minutes of *Whisky Galore!* — the original — when the message dinged.

'My word. Whatever can the inspector want at this time of night?'

She dialled him back.

'Inspector? Is everything all right?'

'Good evening, Miss Cadabra, please excuse the late hour, and yes, everything is more than all right; I've got a new lead.'

Amanda sat up. 'You have?' she enquired intently.

'Indeed: on what could have killed the occupants of the van.'

'Yes?' She was now wide awake.

'I've just met up with an old friend who is a medical examiner. She gave me an off-the-record second opinion on the report from the accident. She said to look for an untraceable poison gas.'

'Ah! Are you thinking what I'm thinking?' Amanda asked him eagerly.

'I believe so. And that we're looking at either one perpetrator who used dual methods of dispatching your Cardiubarn family, or two perpetrators, each using a *different* method, unbeknownst to one another.'

'Yes! So what's the next step?'

'I would like you, Miss Cadabra, to set up another interview for me,' Trelawney asked hopefully.

'Ah … with …?'

'Yes.'

Chapter 34

༄

POAPS

The inspector was as good as his word. Amanda pretty much had the place to herself. Hillers and Humpy had gone to find some replacement tiles, for one of the bathrooms upstairs, the Misses de Havillande and Armstrong-Witworth had taken Churchill for a walk, and Moffat was about his own business in his domain.

'I'll leave you to it then, Miss Cadabra. I'll be in the small salon, AKA the Situation Room.'

'Thank you, Inspector.'

Amanda, boiler-suited as she had been on the day the chandelier fell, went back into the small dining room and closed the door. The mirror in its frame still occupied the table, and her equipment was around her, as it had been on Friday.

'Right,' she said to Tempest, who actually paid attention, albeit in a languid manner. 'I was standing here, at the end of the dining table, facing towards the back of the house, iPod earphones in. Then,' Amanda continued, pointing in the direction from which each sound had come, in turn, 'bang, clatter from Hiller's shooting at the front of the house: 5 o'clock ... *Black Bottom Stomp* from the gramophone, back left: 8 o'clock, roar from the lawnmower at the gardens at 12 o'clock, dog barking sort of upstairs at 1 o'clock. My song playing then ... crash ... must have been at 3 o'clock. Take out earphones, walk to door, and go into hall.'

She suited the action to the word.

'Listen to noises: one missing. Knock on ballroom door. No response. Hand on handle. Door stuck.' And it still appeared to be. 'Push, shove, shove, open, walk in and ....'

The tweed coat man was not in evidence. Nor was the Frenchman. The pianist in evening dress, though, was now much clearer to see, without the chandelier in its fallen position. He was seated at the instrument, facing the French windows that gave onto the garden. Suddenly he looked up and to the left, as though he had heard a noise. Perhaps from outside or in the room above? Amanda thought. He looked towards the door. What was she picking up from him? ... Nervousness ... anxiety .... No. More! *Fear*. He began to play, seeming still to be trying to listen out over the notes. A loud passage in the music followed, then ... he vanished. Amanda was reasonably confident that what she had just witnessed was a recording. The man's fear had bound the scene to the piano, and it had ended when ... well, he didn't know what hit him.

She had to make sure, though. Amanda went out and repeated her procedure. The scene recommenced.

'Sir? Sir, can you hear me?' she asked. But the man moved as before and played on unheeding until ... the end.

'A recording then,' Amanda said to Tempest, who was now grooming a leg, bored with a puzzle he had immediately solved. 'This must be from when the chandelier fell before. But when was *that*?'

She had not even looked behind the door for the little

girl, wanting to concentrate on one apparition at a time.

'All right. Once more with feeling. This time, I'm going to notice exactly what he's wearing. It should help us to work out what decade this happened in.'

Amanda exited and re-entered, got herself into the right spot, then listed aloud to her familiar: 'White tie, wingtip shirt, white waistcoat, tailcoat, cufflinks, black shoes, black trousers, with a stripe down the side, I think. That's all I can see. If I try to move any closer, I'll lose it. So much for him, then. Good grief, men wear the same rig today, sometimes, so his clothes aren't all that much help.'

Tempest had started on the other leg and gave no indication that he was listening. Regardless, Amanda continued,

'Could he have been performing? I didn't sense or see an audience. And surely if there had been lots of people present, someone would have written or talked about it, and it would be known. And why was he scared? Could he have just been dressed for dinner? This is rather a grand house. When did people stop doing that, I wonder? Moffat or the ladies would know. I wonder if the inspector would be able to date the man's costume?' Tempest turned his head in the direction of the small salon and then looked at her, communicating not to expect much from that human.

'He *might* be able to help. I know you think we're all as thick as two short planks, but we'll just have to muddle along with what we've got.'

'Muddle' is right, thought Tempest, watching a chaffinch that had landed on the terrace outside the French windows.

Amanda went and knocked on the situation room door.

'Come in.'

'OK, Inspector. Here it is: Frenchman and Tweed Man are no-shows, but I saw the evening dress pianist a lot more clearly. The only thing is I can't tell what period his outfit is. Could you come and have a look, please?'

Trelawney was anything but keen. 'Would I be able to see it?'

'You saw the Red Cross nurse,' Amanda pointed out, encouragingly, 'so I don't see why not. You'd just need to stand exactly where I tell you.'

He had not been expecting this. Instead, he had assumed that Amanda would do all the ghostie stuff and just bring back a nice report for him. Trelawney took a deep breath and stood up, a testament to the courage that had enabled him to break up a faceoff between Terence 'Trigger-happy' Jenkins and Benny 'the Barrel' Hines, in the notorious and noisome alley behind the Gin Palace Gambling shop. He'd been given a commendation for that. Trelawney doubted he'd get one for what he was about to do.

'Very well. I'm game if you are.'

He followed Amanda into the hall and to the ballroom door that she'd left ajar. She came round to his left and took his arm.

'I'll walk you in, and just tell me when you can see it. Relax, like you did with the watch, and enjoy the show,' she invited, him with a smile. 'Ready?'

'Ready.'

Amanda manoeuvred him in and, after a slight adjustment, there it was. He saw what she had seen. The abrupt finish took him aback a little. However, at once, she led the inspector out of the room, to avoid seeing the child yet, or at all, if possible. She rightly assumed that two apparitions at once was bound to unsettle even the most resilient mind unused to such things, and she needed his concentration.

'There, that wasn't so bad, was it? You've got the hang of it now,' she said hearteningly.

'Thank you, Miss Cadabra. I'm not sure if it's something I'll ever get used to.'

'You did fine with Granny and Grandpa.'

'I'm glad you think so. Have you arranged ...?'

'Yes, tomorrow lunchtime. At 1 o'clock. Will that be all right for you?'

'It will. Thank you.'

On the way back to the situation room, Amanda went to the dining room to pick up a flask of tea for them to share.

'Well?' she asked presently. 'What period is this pianist from?'

'Ah ... the fact is that men still wear white tie to this day.'

'When exactly?'

'A formal wedding or Ascot perhaps.'

'Was there anything at all about his getup that was anachronistic, in any way?' Amanda enquired.

'Hm ... possibly the shoulders were more padded than today, but from the angle of view it would be hard to say for sure,' he replied uncertainly.

'Did anyone here mention a similar accident in the past?'

The inspector was definite. 'No, not at all.'

'Have you asked?'

'Yes, Miss Cadabra,' Trelawney replied patiently. 'No one was forthcoming with any information concerning a history of accidents with that light-fitting.'

'So ... can we assume it was outside living memory? Or when Miss de Havillande was too small to remember?'

'That would be reasonable .... Let me see ... white tie and tails was most popular in the 1920s and 30s, I believe.'

'In a country house? But yes,' Amanda answered her own question, 'I think people did still dress for dinner then.'

'It would seem reasonable to suppose that they would have done so, in such an establishment as this.'

'So the man could have dressed for dinner, come down early and gone to play the piano?' suggested Amanda.

220

'Possibly. He was clearly uneasy. Expecting or fearing a threat. Why and from whom? It turned out to be justified, regardless.'

'I think the fear is the emotion that caused the imprint on the piano. The recording ended with the fear ...'

'... when the chandelier ....'

'Exactly.'

'Hm,' uttered the inspector thoughtfully, then recapped. 'So far then, what we have is a link, via the chandelier, to a past fall onto a man, also at the piano, who was also killed. We know he was afraid at the time. That, so far, is all we can say for certain. The rest is speculation.'

'It is. Right, I'll go back in and watch the rerun of the little girl,' said Amanda keenly.

'And I'll be here at my nice, normal, present-day desk, with all sources of illumination at a safe distance,' said the inspector with a contented smile.

'You do that! Back soon. Coming Tempest?'

Her familiar roused himself wearily and accompanied his human back to the ballroom. It took four or five goes, but finally, Amanda got into the right place and took the correct step forward, to where she'd begun to see the child. Sure enough, there she was, coming out from under the table and standing staring.

The little girl had fair, side-parted hair with a ribbon the same white as her dress, which had a little collar and came to above her knees. As for accessories, she had a white cardigan, ankle socks and shoes. She couldn't have been more than four years old. Then came the voice:

'Dolly! Dolly!'

The child looked to her right, towards the French windows, moved in that direction and then faded.

Amanda stood and thought. She uttered two words:

'Shirley Temple.' She hurried back to Trelawney.

'Inspector, please, could you Google Shirley Temple 1930s images.'

'Of course.'

She leaned over his shoulder to see the computer screen. '... Yes! That's like the little girl. Check 1940s, please, just in case .... No, quite different. So what if ...?'

'The child and the man were from the same time.'

'She must have been staring at the chandelier falling on him,' said Amanda.

'That would put him in the 1930s too, then. The dress code would fit that.'

'But no one said there was a chandelier accident in the 1930s. You'd think it would be legendary, wouldn't you?' asked Amanda. 'Unless it was hushed up.'

'Rather embarrassing, I suppose,' Trelawney said practically. She nodded. 'This does support, to some extent,' he continued, 'the idea that what happened on Friday was an accident. Yes, if the thing does have a habit of breaking free of its fastenings and plummeting earthward.'

'I wonder if there are any journals where people might have noted it privately,' she wondered.

'It's worth asking Miss de Havillande,' he concurred.

Amanda went quiet.

'You know what was strange, Inspector?'

'What?'

'What I picked up from that little girl was not fear or being horrified but ... astonishment ... more like what she was seeing was the last thing she expected. Deeply felt surprise. And that was the emotion that imprinted on .... must be the console table. What *was* it that so surprised her?'

Chapter 35

༄

MISS DE HAVILLANDE, AND MERCURY

Four days to go, thought Amanda.

Yesterday, the ladies had not come home until the afternoon and then were polite but too busy to chat. This morning, however, she was actually sought out by one of them.

'Miss de Havillande.'

'Ah Amanda, did the second mirror arrive yesterday?'

'Yes, and they kindly moved the first one off the table. The inspector is hopeful that I'll be able to put them up at the end of the week, or early next week.'

'Splendid. One would not wish to minimise the gravity of the accident, but the sooner we can get in there and clean and polish, the better.'

'Of course. ... I wondered if you remember what the ballroom looked like when you were a very little child.'

'I can't say I have many memories of that time. I don't suppose many people do.'

'Did your parents talk about it? What life was like then,

who came to their parties? How it was?'

'Our parents were not the most communicative when it came to their children. Not that they were cold, but my mother was what, these days, is known as "a party girl". She was perfectly charming when she was ... available. But my sister and I were far from neglected, there was always at least one aunt or uncle on hand to take care of us, and at times nannies coming and going. I dare say we enjoyed rather more freedom than many of our peers.'

'Did you ever ... put on theatricals? That was rather popular at the time, wasn't it?'

'Was it? I dare say you are right. In my teens, now, I seem to remember we dabbled.'

'Shakespeare?'

'No ... Oscar Wilde. Always a favourite.'

'You just *read* Shakespeare?'

'Yes, at school, of course, where it was ritually slaughtered by being appallingly read aloud, in class, by bored and distracted students.'

'Did you have a favourite?'

'-*Henry V*. Frightfully rousing.'

'Comedies? ... *Twelfth Night*?'

'Not that I recall. Well, I must get on, my dear. I must see the inspector about the piano. The insurance people need to see it. If it can't be repaired in time for the party, we must hire one for the evening, but, if so, I need to know if we can remove it.'

'Of course. I did see it, Miss de Havillande, and it *may* be possible to patch it up in time. One front leg buckled but the other is still whole. Some of the keys and action will need replacing, but the iron frame took some of the weight and minimised the damage. The case is badly scratched, and the lid will need to be replaced. I couldn't see the strings, but they're pretty strong. Oh ... it may seem tactless to mention this.'

'Do go on, dear.'

'It will need to be tuned, close to the day.'

'Understood.'

'But if I concentrate on the piano, there are other things that will have to be left,' Amanda cautioned.

'Just get those mirrors up, repair the rat hole in the wainscot, and we'll just give it a good clean.'

'Also there are places on the floor that need attention or dancers may catch their feet in them,' Amanda warned

'I will leave it to your discretion, dear. We have more than a whole week.'

'Er ... yes,' said Amanda, with Saturday looming. 'I think it's best if you find someone who can, if necessary, supply a grand piano, if need be.'

'I have already done so.'

'That's good. I'm going to take a lunch hour, if that's all right.'

'You know there is no need for you to ask such things. You organise your own schedule. With plenty of breaks and no late nights here, mind. I will not have you wearing yourself to the bone over a mere party.'

'Thank you, Miss de Havillande. Is Miss Armstrong-Wit—'

'I'm afraid she's spending time on the telephone today, chasing up the RSVPs. We really need some sort of number to give The Big Tease and Sandra.'

With that, Cynthia surged forth to engage with the inspector, and Amanda was left to her work. So, Miss de Havillande was another name provisionally crossed off the Viola list. She still had Moffat and Gwendolen to sound out. Of course, there was always the possibility, it now occurred to her, that Viola did not *want* to be known. What then? How would *she*, or he, know that Amanda needed her help? On the other hand, perhaps Viola *did* know and was working behind the scenes.

'It seems unlikely, Tempest, and yet... while I can't get further with finding Viola ... all I can do is ... hope ....'

* * * * *

Mike. Urgent. Need to see you this evening. On my way back from Cornwall now T
I'll be waiting. M

Trelawney ran up the stairs to his room, crammed what he needed into his overnight bag and hurried back down, calling,
'Mum?'
She was out.

Mum, have to go back to Cornwall. Should be back tomorrow Tx

Sixty seconds later, Trelawney was starting his car.
He'd be hitting rush hour traffic, but he couldn't justify using the siren. He was impatient, but he had time. Yes, there was still time. At least ... for this.
Hogarth had insisted that Trelawney sit down, have a cup of tea and take some deep breaths.
'Yes, having flown to me like winged Mercury, I can see that you have something of considerable import to impart, Thomas. But, unless it is imperative that do so immediately, then it will be better for both of us if you have the clearest possible head when we discuss it.'
Trelawney had to accept that. Once the tray was before them and they were sipping comfortably, Mike said,
'So, first, tell me about the progress of The Mysterious

Case of The Grange Chandelier. Accident or malice aforethought? If the latter, any suspects?'

'It certainly could have been accidental. They seem like a perfectly amiable bunch of people. The niece and husband, charmingly known as Hillers and Humpy, do seem like something out of a PG Wodehouse novel, but Miss de Havillande, Miss Armstrong-Witworth and Moffat all assure me that they really are like that. Farrell, the cricketer, is a thoroughly nice chap, Mundly the gardener seems to live in a happy little world of his own, and even the florist seems a good sort. He's led a fascinating life, wouldn't mind having a drink with him some time and hearing about his adventures.'

'An interesting man?'

'Yes, as long as you keep him off the subject of his mother and her nerves.'

'What does Amanda say about him?'

Trelawney had asked her ....

* * * * *

'Dale Hilland doesn't make sense,' she stated emphatically.

'Really?'

'That's what I think of him. He doesn't add up. There he was, an independent man having an exciting life, being an expert, loving what he does, travelling the world, then he gives all that up to help Mommy Dearest open a flower shop. She's clearly fit as a fiddle and manipulative as the Marquis de Sade. Why didn't he just tell her to take a hike?'

'People do *do* these things.' Amanda looked at Trelawney with extreme scepticism. He felt bound to attempt clarification. 'For example, what if your mother had sent you a letter, claiming to be deeply repentant and desperate to make it all up to you. What would you do?'

'Burnt it,' replied Amanda at once, as though the question were inexplicable.

'You wouldn't respond?'

'Are you serious?' she asked levelly.

Actually, he thought, she had a point.

'All right, all right, bad example ... er ... there must be someone somewhere to whom you have felt some attachment, who isn't the nicest person, that you would respond to if they called for your help,' Trelawney persisted.

Amanda gave it some thought. Looking up at the ceiling as though in search of such an individual. The answer came back unequivocally:

'No.'

'No one at all?'

'No one,' Amanda confirmed. 'All of the people for whom I feel an attachment are nice.'

Trelawney could see he was getting nowhere.

'Very well, Miss Cadabra, but in the course of police work we *do* come across hundreds, if not thousands, of different people who do have emotional ties of a nature that, clearly, is inexplicable to you, but are nevertheless legal.'

'So you're saying, he could have just given up his wonderful life for the love of his mother?'

'He could. I am not saying there might not be another explanation,' the inspector admitted

'Of an even more sinister nature?'

'Yes,' he concurred

'You mean if she has a hold over him? Could she be blackmailing him? Maybe Hilland was guiding a millionaire through the Andes when they found Aztec gold, and he pushed the rich guy off the mountain so he could stash the treasure for himself and then claimed the client got lost in the mist?'

Amanda suggested excitedly. 'And somehow his mother knows?'

'While your remarkable breadth of imagination does you every credit, Miss Cadabra, that's not quite what I had in mind. But a very mild version of that, possibly. However, coming back down to earth, it does seem that Miss de Havillande was either *with* him or *between* him and the house, at the time of the accident.'

'Ah.'

* * * * *

Hogarth threw back his head and laughed.

'What a source of refreshment that girl is!'

'Oh, but she sees everything in black and white,' protested Trelawney, 'and we know that there are multiple shades of grey in between.'

'Not for Amanda,' observed Mike.

Thomas began to object. 'But that's thinking like a chil—'

'— and that's what dear old Dr Bertil Bergstrom has said about her, since he first met her: "Nine. Alvays nine!"' said Mike with a grin, imitating his Swedish friend's accent, affectionately.

'Years old, you mean?'

'Yes, and he said it was her great gift: ever young.'

'Miss Cadabra has led a very sheltered life, I suppose,' remarked Trelawney.

'Not ... entirely,' Hogarth countered.

'Really?'

'Only since her grandparents brought her to Sunken Madley.'

'Well, that's what I mean. She was three ... then again ...' Trelawney recalled the flashbacks Amanda had told him about, from when she was very young indeed: memories of those strange afternoons with her eerie great-grandmother, powerful matriarch of the Cardiubarns.

'Exactly, Thomas.' Hogarth had grown strangely solemn, staring into the fire, glowing in the grate. 'There is something I've been working on for a long time. And a piece of that particular puzzle is in Amanda's memory ... buried deep .... ' Suddenly Mike shook off his sombre mood and looked up with a smile. 'So, to get back to the list of impossible suspects …?'

'Yes ...,' Thomas was looking at his friend curiously, then switched his attention to the question. 'Add in Moffat and The Grange ladies, who couldn't be more harmless, and that concludes the line-up.'

'Have you told Miss Cadabra about Honeywell?'

'No. I didn't think it would be right to discuss details of the case to that degree.'

'Well, you have *carte blanche*. Oh, come now, Thomas, you don't really think Miss Cadabra caused the accident, do you? What? Do you imagine that she nipped across the hall, cast a fraying spell on the rope and brought the chandelier down on the piano tuner, for the sheer fun of it?'

'Of course not,' Trelawney said, with a slight smile.

'So is it that you still don't completely trust her, or are you just being conscientious?'

'I do trust her. After all, she saved my life. At great cost to herself and her village. I suppose, in the midst of this magical melée that has infused itself into my life, I am trying to keep a grasp on things that are *rea*l to me like ... regulations.'

'I understand. But I have authority to grant you permission to share whatever might be useful with Miss Cadabra.'

'All right. I'll tell her about Honeywell.'

'And now,' said Mike, clapping his hand onto the arm of his chair, 'that we have got that out of the way ....The real news. Go ahead.'

'Well, Naomi got in touch with me, as you know ....'

'... And I sent over the documents. So how did the meet up go?'

'Fruitfully. Oh, not on a romantic level. No, Naomi has a theory about what killed the Cardiubarns: a substance released into the air inside the van, namely, toxic gas. She hinted at the possibility of an untraceable one.'

'Aha!'

'Yes, ... the mysterious notes.'

Chapter 36

༒

LUNCH, POISON, AND HOPE

Trelawney timed the pressing of the bell to the precise second: 1 o'clock on the dot.

Amanda opened the door.

'Hello, Inspector, I hope you haven't eaten. I've got the same lunch as my grandparents. I thought sharing a meal might help.'

'Ah,' said Trelawney, whose appetite had been dulled by the prospect of another session with Mrs Cadabra, who was intimidating regardless of what plane of existence she was on. 'How thoughtful.'

He entered the sitting room and found the couple, looking more solid than ever, seated this time in the armchairs and enjoying a luncheon of cheese and ham flan, Scotch eggs, coronation chicken, salad, and, inevitably, tea.

'Good afternoon, Mrs Cadabra, Mr Cadabra.'

Amanda had provided a similar selection, courtesy of Alex and Sandy of The Big Tease, set out on the table before the sofa, where she invited Trelawney to join her.

'Inspector,' said Senara, 'what a pleasure it is to see you back again so soon.' She dabbed her lips delicately with her napkin.

'Thank you for the invitation to lunch,' he returned, even though it had come from Amanda.

'I do believe that you have made some progress with your investigation.'

'Yes, as you may be aware, I received a tip-off, by way of a suggestion, that the Cardiubarns met their end through inhaling a noxious gas, released in the confined space of the van. I further suspect that the source of this was letters that they received, inviting them on the journey.'

'Very good, Inspector,' Mrs Cadabra congratulated him. 'I have always appreciated your keen mind. Yes, indeed. I was suspicious when our letters arrived. Naturally, I could not communicate this to you before, you understand. But because I had arranged for the little outing through a third party, I was expecting ordinary, typed, plain A4 sheets. There would be no reason for the communication to be hand-written on hand-made paper, for my purposes.'

Mrs Cadabra spooned a helping of coronation chicken onto her plate. Trelawney knew better than to rush her. She continued,

'I suspected that what I was looking at was arcane parchment and potion ink. It could only be from one source and, given that, it had to be dangerous. I was careful to put each of the letters, one to Perran and one to myself, back in the envelopes at once. I burned them in the open air, at the earliest possible opportunity.'

'So that was how they "disappeared"?' asked Trelawney.
'Quite.'

'That was news to me, Inspector,' added Perran. 'Although I thought, when I opened mine that it did look odd.

And it did give me reservations about accepting the invitation. Of course, I didn't have the experience with the Flamgoynes that Senara had. I don't blame her for getting rid of my letter. Of course, she couldn't tell me without explaining what she'd been up to!' he said, looking at his wife fondly and shaking his head.

'Indeed, my dear husband knew nothing about it. But I could see that the parchment was imbued with certain substances. The combined odours and appearance of that and the purple-black ink was suggestive of a poison charm. Of course, it would need a catalyst. No use in going off in the hands of the recipients. Just one fatality would have warned the other Cardiubarns off. No, the plan was clearly to take advantage of them all being together in the same place.'

'So the poison letters had to be set to go off, as it were, like a bomb?'

'Indeed, set to dissolve during the van ride. The arrangement that I had had put in place, was to collect the Cardiubarns from along the B3213, off the Devon Expressway, at villages such as Bittaford, Ivybridge and Moorhaven. Being told to arrive at different times, they would not see one another on the way. They would have assumed they were going on up onto Dartmoor. One by one, they would have been picked up until they were all in the van, by the time they reached the crucial bend.'

'I can see that you put a great deal of thought into your preparations,' remarked Trelawney.

'You are too kind, Inspector,' she said, ironically accepting it as a compliment. 'But to continue, the Flamgoyne caster may even have used the same tripwire spell as I did, but further up the road. That would have released the poison, fatally neutralising all of the Cardiubarns, including the driver, and the van would crash on the bend, making it look like an accident.'

'And you are *sure* this was the work of the Flamgoynes?'

'I cannot be a hundred per cent certain. There is only one way to establish their guilt beyond all doubt. However, I suspect that if any Flamgoyne hand was in this, it was that of Gronetta Flamgoyne.'

'Lady Flamgoyne?' asked Trelawney.

'Yes, she, and only possibly, her brother. There is no other she would trust, and not even him, if she could operate alone. The paper used is exceedingly complicated to make, and the same applies to the ink. They both require special ingredients, made or gathered at a certain hour by a certain moon. And she would never have thrown either away or revealed their existence or whereabouts to another soul. If she had to involve her brother, she will have told him that any remnants, not used for the notes, had been destroyed. If she did this deed, the evidence is to be found within the walls of Flamgoyne.'

'Thank you, Mrs Cadabra.'

'Yes, thank you, Granny.' Amanda turned to Trelawney. 'Inspector, you haven't eaten anything. Let me, at least, get you some tea.'

'Thank you.'

Amanda went out to the kitchen, and Trelawney, lowering his voice, said,

'Mr and Mrs Cadabra, you must know that Miss Cadabra has been extremely anxious regarding what is approaching, on Saturday. Especially, in view of the fact that she has, so far, been unable to identify this Viola, who I understand is the sole means of assembling any assistance that might be available. Is there any reassurance that you can give Miss Cadabra?'

Senara put down her teacup and gave Trelawney her full attention.

'Amanda has been trained by her grandfather and myself. That is all that I can say. Just because we are, what so many like indelicately to term, "dead", does not mean that we are prescient. Pray, do not confuse the two, Inspector.'

'But you're saying that Miss Cadabra stands a chance?'

'A chance? Certainly. If she did not, we would have advised her to prepare to surrender. But we have done no such thing. Inspector, be stout of heart; there is always hope. Who knows what Amanda may be capable of, in the hour of greatest need? Who knows who may come to her aid?'

Her tone was so encouraging that it carried him with her. Mrs Cadabra leaned forward a little and looked at Trelawney intently. She asked, 'Do you not understand why they are attacking Sunken Madley, Inspector? It is because they *fear* it. There are powers here ... that no one yet understands.'

'T'is true, Inspector,' said Perran. 'The ground is old, and the water runs deep. Ancient feet have trod here, ancient magic wrought here. They are right to fear.'

His words rang in the air.

'Thank you, Mr Cadabra, Mrs Cadabra.' Thomas felt immeasurably heartened. The kettle boiled and, soon after, Amanda appeared with the tea and sensed the atmosphere.

'What have you all been talking about? The room is alive with portentousness!'

'Your grandparents have been suggesting that the playing field on Saturday may be more even than it presently appears.'

'Good. Although at the moment I'm very far from seeing how.'

* * * * *

'So, you understand why I was so eager to see you,' said Trelawney.

'I do indeed,' agreed Mike. 'Well, the course is clear.'

'Yes, we must get into Flamgoyne.'

'Not *we*,' Mike corrected him. '-*You*.'

Thomas was taken aback. 'Why not you, too?'

'There'll be a security spell on that place. Only a Flamgoyne will be able to enter, without setting off a whole raft of alarms. That would bring the clan back, tyres screeching, to defend the castle. You can bet the Cardiubarns would have the same at The Hall. No, it's not a matter of throwing a couple of steaks to the dogs and knocking out the guards. I can't come with you.'

'But ... it's decades since I was inside there,' Trelawney protested. 'I don't remember the layout of the place at all. It would take me more hours to search it than I could possibly have.'

'Then you must take someone who *does*-remember the layout of the place,' said Hogarth calmly.

'... My father?'

'Why not?' Trelawney thought this over. 'It's not like the Flamgoynes did him any favours, is it, Thomas?'

'True,' he admitted. They had torn apart his father's marriage, kept him under their thumb, and threatened his wife and son. Indeed ... and if ... *what if* they did not return from their assault on Sunken Madley? What if, by some wild train of events, they were wiped out? If there were no more Flamgoynes, would there be a chance that his parents could ...?

But there was no time to think about that now. Infiltrating Flamgoyne was all that mattered.

'Yes. I think my father will help. I'd best see him face-to-face.'

'Quite,' approved Hogarth. 'Best not to risk giving away sensitive information in messages or phone calls. Let me know if he agrees. If Kytto Trelawney says he is in, then I am calling a Council of Four, a briefing in London, tomorrow.

You, your father and I will be there.'

'Why London?' asked Thomas.

'Because,' replied Hogarth, 'that is where the fourth is.'

Chapter 37

FRENCH CONVERSATION, AND MISS ARMSTRONG-WITWORTH

As The Council of Four could not be arranged before two days hence, Thomas returned to London. Mike had explained that if the members changed their plans abruptly, it might draw attention to their movements.

Amanda was glad to see Trelawney. In the privacy of the situation room, he related what had passed between him and her 'Uncle Mike.'

'Who is the fourth in this mysterious-sounding Council of Four?' she asked.

'I think it's a Dr Bertil? From Sweden? A friend of yours, I gather. Secrecy is vital at this stage, it seems, and understandably. I'll get a text telling me where to go just before 2 o'clock tomorrow afternoon. So have you made any progress on the Viola front?'

'Miss de Havillande didn't respond when I mentioned *Twelfth Night*. But I'm starting to wonder whether my Viola test is a valid one.'

'What other test can you apply?' he asked.

'That's just the thing. I can't think of anything else apart from mentioning the Shakespeare play and seeing what reaction I get. I'll just have to keep going. There is one other area where I may be able to move forward, though.'

'Yes?' Trelawney enquired hopefully. 'Oh, before you tell me, did you have a chance to ask Miss de Havillande if any members of the family kept a journal, before she was born or while she was a young child?'

'Unfortunately not. I will ask at the next opportunity,' Amanda offered.

'Or I shall. But I interrupted you. You were about to give me some good news.'

'Our chandelier case. Maybe I can get the Frenchman to talk to me. After all, if he let me see him before, because I share a French heritage, maybe he'll let me see him again. I wish my French were better.'

'It's worth a try. I'll have to release the ballroom soon, you know. And I expect once people are traipsing in and out, it'll disturb the vibes, or whatever?'

'Quite possibly. So you're saying that if I'm going to attempt this interview, I'd better do it soon?'

'Yes, Miss Cadabra.'

'Oh, dear. Everything is urgent: this interview with the Frenchman, talking to Moffat and Miss Armstrong-Witworth, and getting the ballroom ready for the party!'

'You've every right to feel overwhelmed,' Trelawney said, understandingly. 'How is the second mirror coming along?'

'Nearly done. I could take a break *now* and go to the ballroom. Only, I'm hardly dressed for 1800. Mind you, he did seem to acknowledge me before.'

'Ye-es,' replied the inspector, slowly.

'What do you mean: "Ye-es"?'

'Well ... in your boiler suit and hair up, is it possible that he thought you were ... a boy?'

'Hm. I suppose so. Well, I don't mind if he thinks I'm a boy as long as he talks to me. I shall go and prepare myself, and then go in. I'll let you know how it turns out.'

With that, Amanda returned to the small dining room and conferred with Tempest.

'Right, you heard. I'm going to have a go.'

Her familiar looked her up and down.

'What do you mean, dressed like that? Yes, dressed like this. If he doesn't like it then I'll come back in a long gown, all right? Now ... I need to relax ... get into the frame of mind .... What do I want to ask? ... How did the chandelier fall? Yes, that's the question. Right. Let's do this.'

Amanda entered the ballroom and positioned herself.

'*M'sieur? M'sieur? Milor', êtes-vous içi? Je voudrais parler avec vous un peu, s'il vous plaît.*'

'Aha,' said the Frenchman, appearing to be leaning on the far side of the piano. 'It is ze leetle boy of the French ancestor.'

'Oh, you speak English,' Amanda observed with relief. 'Thank you, sir.'

'The alternative is to endure the ravage of my native tongue,' explained the Frenchman, laying a hand to his heart, with a pained expression. 'Although your accent is quite good. With practice, it could become almost ... bearable.'

'Er, ... *merçi*. Sir, may I ask you a question?'

'*Certainement*,' he replied graciously.

'Did you see how the chandelier came to fall?'

'Upon me? At the time, *non*. But afterwards, I could see the frayed rope. Unfortunate, but *c'est la vie*. Or in my case, *c'est le mort*,' he remarked with a mocking smile.

'I'm sorry to hear that,' condoled Amanda, 'What about

in the case of the other two gentlemen?'

'Ohoho,' he cried, waggling a playful finger. 'That is *your* puzzle, is it not?'

'Yes, sir, especially that case which occurred in my own time, that is, most recently. Any assistance you could give me would be of great value.'

He laughed. 'As to that, I have no doubt. I will tell you this much: everything you need to help you solve your case ... is in zis room.'

Amanda waited for more. It didn't come. 'Is that all you can tell me, sir?'

'*Non*. It is not all that I *can* tell you. But it is all that I am *going* to tell you,' he replied mischievously. '*Bon chance, mon ami* ....' And with that, he faded and was gone.

Amanda gave a sigh of irritation. 'I didn't even get his name,' she uttered to Tempest, who was lounging on the console table, outdoing the Frenchman in insouciance.

'Let's go and report to the inspector.' Her familiar declined to move. He was perfectly comfortable where he was, thank you very much, and to have to listen to two humans bumbling around, and helplessly missing what was a perfectly obvious solution to the case, was more than his patience was equal to, at this precise moment.

'That's all he would say?' asked Trelawney, after hearing her report.

'Yes,' Amanda confirmed. 'Everything we need to help us solve the case is in the ballroom.'

'Which we've already been over with a fine-tooth comb. Well, clearly we're missing something. I think I'll take a stroll around the house again, recap where everyone said they were at the time of the accident.'

'Right-oh, Inspector, I'll get back to work.'

However, no sooner had Trelawney set off on his tour, and Amanda had found the right chisel she wanted, than a voice was heard as the door opened.

'Amanda, dear?' There was the very person she wanted to see, coming in with a tea-tray.

'Miss Armstrong-Witworth! How nice.'

'*Gwendolen*, dear. I'm sure you could do with a break, and I've hardly even had time to say hello, since you started work here. I am sorry.'

'I quite understand, Gwendolen.'

'So how are you getting along?'

'I should finish fitting the second mirror snugly into the frame today.'

'That's wonderful.'

'Actually, Gwendolen, as I'm working on a restoration project, I was hoping to get some insight into what the ballroom was like in yesteryear. Miss de Havillande has no memories of it from when she was a little child, and I was wondering if you knew of any journals, diaries, notebooks anyone kept from around, and before, that time. Something that might be in The Grange library, perhaps?'

'Not that I know of. And I have to say, that I, as the indoor type, have always taken more of an interest in the collection than Cynthia. You're welcome to look, my dear, but I strongly doubt that you will find anything helpful.'

'Ah. Well .... You don't recall Miss de Havillande or anyone else ever mentioning a previous accident with the chandelier, do you? One that might have caused a fatality?'

'I would have thought that sort of event would have made it into a history book in Sunken Madley library. People surely would have been talking about it, for miles around, for years. Probably made people wary of coming to the ballroom, even.'

'That's what I thought, Gwendolen. But Mrs Pagely couldn't find anything like that. I thought that even if it was hushed up, someone living here at the time may have written about it in their journal.'

'You'd have thought so, wouldn't you? Well, please, do feel free to browse the shelves, dear. You never know.'

'Thank you, Gwendolen. Although I doubt I'll have time before the party. Is it all right if the inspector has a look?'

'Of course. Anything we can do to assist.'

There was a knock at the door.

It was Trelawney. He was surprised to see that Amanda had company.

'Ah, Miss Armstrong-Witworth. Miss Cadabra. I'm leaving now to pursue enquiries elsewhere. I expect I shall see you both tomorrow.'

'Indeed,' Gwendolen replied warmly.

Amanda met his eyes. 'All the best with your ... further investigations.'

'Thank you, Miss Cadabra. Good afternoon, ladies.' The door closed, and he was gone.

Amanda quickly picked up the thread of the conversation with Miss Armstrong-Witworth.

'Perhaps you can help me to get a picture of what life was like in the big houses, here, back in the day? You seem to have had a very happy childhood, as you've told me, with your parents and all of their Russian friends visiting, and music and parties'.

'Oh yes,' Miss Armstrong-Witworth agreed.

'Did you ever put on theatricals, perhaps of Russian plays?'

'Indeed. Chekov was a great favourite.'

'I can imagine. What about English ones?' Amanda enquired casually. 'Shakespeare, for example.'

Miss Armstrong-Witworth paused, then shook her head. 'Not that I recall.'

'Most people just *read* Shakespeare, I suppose,' hazarded Amanda.

'And went to the theatre too, to see his plays,' added Miss Armstrong-Witworth.

'Of course. Did you have a favourite?'

'Play? Oh yes, I always rather liked *The Merry Wives of Windsor*. So droll! And poor old Falstaff. I became rather fond of him in *Henry IV-Part I*. A flawed character but not irredeemable, I like to think.'

'I like the comedies too,' said Amanda, seizing the opening. 'Especially *Twelfth Night*.'

'Ah, yes. The one with the tiresome count. Yes, well, I must return to my to-do list. I must make sure that everything needed for cleaning and polishing the ballroom is ready. We may be able to get in there on Friday. Wouldn't that be splendid? So nice to see you, Amanda, dear.'

'You too, Gwendolen. Thank you for popping in, and for the tea.'

With a smile, Miss Armstrong-Witworth left the room.

'Well!' Amanda said to Tempest, who was taking an interest in the cream pot for the scones that had been provided. 'It looks like we're only left with Moffat now. How on earth am I to find an excuse to go and talk to *him*?'

Chapter 38

THE COUNCIL OF FOUR

'It's not often I have the pleasure of three handsome men walking into my sitting room,' said the lady, who was hugging her brother.

'It's been too long, Amelia.'

'Not my fault. I can hardly come and visit you, Kyt.'

'True.'

'I hope I get one of those,' interrupted Mike.

'Of course, you do, darling, hugs all round.'

'Me too, Aunt Amelia?'

'Naturally.'

'Right, Mike and Thomas, make yourselves comfortable, Kyt ....'

'Yes, I shall come and help my little sister in the kitchen.' And off they went.

'I was surprised by your text,' Trelawney said to Hogarth.

'Oh, why? You were expecting it, weren't you?'

'Yes, but not its content.' Mike looked at him in amusement. 'I was expecting the rendezvous to be at a hotel or something, with the Dr Bertil you mentioned.'

'I heard that!' called Amelia, over the sound of crockery clattering. She popped her head around the door. 'Expecting the old boy network, were you? Shame on you,' she teased him. 'That a nephew of mine ....'

'Honestly, Aunt, it was only because Mike *mentioned-* the doctor.'

Hogarth smiled, enjoying himself.

'I wondered what you'd do with that crumb.'

Amelia tutted and shook a finger at Mike. 'Laying a snare for my nephew's feet, were you? Naughty boy!'

Thomas protested, 'It's just that you made it sound all so grand: The Council of Four ....'

'You're just digging yourself in deeper,' came his father's voice, laughing over the sound of water pouring into the pot.

Amelia and Kyt returned from the kitchen bearing the tea and cake trays.

'We were the Council of Three, but now you have been graciously admitted,' she said to her nephew.

'And I am most humbly and sincerely honoured, and I apologise for not knowing better than to assume that any magical council could, possibly, be complete without your skill and wisdom,' replied Thomas with aplomb.

'Well done, lad,' cried Mike, applauding.

Amelia graciously inclined her head.

'You are forgiven. Now ... boys ... serious matters call for serious cake.'

'Battenberg!' Mike exclaimed.

'Victoria sandwich,' Thomas noticed appreciatively.

'And fairy cakes,' added Kyt, helping his sister distribute cups, plates, napkins, and cake forks.

'And plenty of both sorts of cream,' said Amelia.

'How grand!' remarked her nephew.

'This is a grand occasion,' declared his aunt, taking her place at the round table. Mike and Kyt nodded. The mood grew more serious. The sky had been overcast, but now the clouds seemed to lower, and the room greyed. She brought candles to the table and added their light to that of the fire.

'Go on, Thomas,' said Mike. 'You have the floor.'

While the other three ate and drank, Trelawney told his aunt about the poison gas, the notes, and Senara's confidence that the lethally magical paper and ink were to be found within the fastness of Flamgoyne.

After he had finished, Amelia sat silent, eyes half-closed. Finally, she looked up and spoke.

'Yes ... my sense is that they are there. All right.' She reached for the notebook and pen on the table and wrote, pausing, every now and then, to think. Finally, she tore off the sheet and slid it across the table to between her brother and nephew. 'Here's a list of possible locations within Flamgoyne where they may be. You must remember that my information is not up to date. I left when I was 16, thanks to Uncle Elwen, and I've taken care not to link with them through cards, ball, tea leaves or anything else.'

'Wisely so,' said Kyt.

'As for any of the staff I knew, I expect all, or most, will be deceased ... for one reason or another. She won't leave it empty, though. Not Mother.' She noticed her nephew's querying expression.

'Are you ...?'

'Yes, Thomas, I am your father's half-sister. After our mother was divorced from your Grandfather Trelawney, she married a scion of the Flamgoyne clan and had me and one other son. My Uncle Elwen was shrewd enough to play the fool and pretend to be useless at magic. I learned from him and kept up the pretence, until I was old enough to make my escape. I was found by Viola and put in contact with your grandparents. As for my younger brother, he was loyal to our mother. How much talent he has or how powerful he has become, I could not say.'

'Thank you, Aunt Amelia, for explaining that.'

'Now, you, Thomas, Kyt, you will have but one chance, our one cast of the dice.'

'On the day of the attack on Sunken Madley?'

'Yes. I will look into the globe for you. But remember we are not fortune-tellers, Thomas. We see only probabilities, possibilities, opportunities.'

Her brother and nephew nodded.

Amelia rose and brought her largest crystal sphere to the table, saying,

'This is not my favourite, but it's the one that gives the best magnification, and for this, even the details may be important.' It was like a giant marble with swirls of white and silver within. The flickering candlelight reflected in its surface. Amelia sat down before the great sphere, placed her hands either side and waited.

'Here it comes … Flamgoyne … I see the portal open, crows come forth ... the gates are flung wide ... they move out onto the road like a single-width column of ants .... Now I see ... the south of England ... yes ... markers in the shape of crows, dotted out in a line between the edge of the Moor and ... Sunken Madley. ... The glass is clouding ... just green mist .... It is gone.' She sat back. 'That is all.'

'It makes sense,' said Hogarth. 'They'll have to maintain their connection with Bodmin Moor, with Cornwall, Flamgoyne in particular, so they will have to leave members of the clan stationed at different points along the way.'

'To conduct the power, as it were?' asked Thomas hesitantly.

'That's the idea.'

'So after the conflict,' said Amelia, 'however it ends, the Flamgoyne who will be stationed at the edge of the Moor will likely return first and therefore soonest. Only during the actual attack on Sunken Madley, can you be sure of being relatively undisturbed in your search.'

Thomas nodded. 'Understood.'

'I have seen the length of time of the battle: one hour. From about half-past two, on Saturday afternoon. Their power will be stretched so far outside their own land, they will hurl all they have at the village, in that short time.'

'It's a four-hour journey by the fastest route to London ....,' Thomas began.

'They will use magic, most likely, and find ways to travel faster,' Amelia forestalled him. 'They could use blanking spells on speed cameras, maze any traffic officials who see them, there are all kinds of ways they could use. I would count on three hours at the most for your search. No more.'

Kyt pulled out a map and pointed to a small road.

'Very well. I suggest we park here up this lane, and wait until they go. Will you be able to see when they leave, Amelia?'

'Yes. I'll text you both: the word "nest". That will mean it's empty.'

'Meanwhile,' added Hogarth, putting down his teacup, 'I will draw off their heavies. I know they employ Normals, or at least semi-Normals, for muscle that will be useless in a magical attack. Gronetta may consider leaving them at Flamgoyne. I've seen a couple of their thugs hanging around near my house, in the past. I'll go down to the shore, send up a very minor spell and kite them along the edge of the water, until I get to my friend Ken's brother's boat. I'll take it out to within sight, and get them to drive along, until I'm ready to duck away and disappear.'

'Good. Thanks, Mike,' said Thomas.

'What will you do,' asked Amelia, 'if the Flamgoyne staff find and challenge you, brother?'

'At the moment, my plan is to hope they don't!' Kyt replied ruefully.' But if they do, then I will say that we were summoned for the assault and arrived late.' His son nodded.

'OK, that's the party line then.'

'You do know that the servants are Flamgoynes, don't you, Thomas?' said Kyt.

'They are? But why? Surely the clan can afford ....'

'It's about who your grandmother will trust. None but blood.'

'Family motto,' Amelia chimed in. 'It can mean more than one thing too!'

'Good grief, so it is. Suddenly I remember that.'

'The servants are scions of the house,' Kyt continued, 'connexions rather than direct descendants, with no or little power. They are trained for service.'

'But that's servitude!' Thomas protested.

'Indeed. But they are also trained to be pathologically loyal. And who knows what enchantments are placed upon them.'

Thomas was appalled. 'I had no idea. How many of them are there?'

'Hard to say. Few offspring are born to the clan. I remember Bersie, the housekeeper, Pasco the butler, Edern — Eddie — he must be in his late 20's now, at least.'

'OK. I'll be on the alert for any of them,' responded Thomas. 'We must be as fast and efficient as possible. Find the paper and ink, anything else is a bonus. Out before any of them returns, leaving nothing to indicate we have been there. We'll be wearing gloves. No DNA traces, if we can possibly help it.'

'Got it,' acknowledged Kyt.

Thomas looked at Amelia's list. 'Right. Dad, once we're in, I suggest you take the study and the library. They're the most obvious places. I'll take Lady Flamgoyne's rooms — that's bedchamber, dressing room, drawing-room and study — and the tower room, then I'll come back down to join you.'

'Thanks, son. You are the one with the searching experience. This will be my first!'

'And last, I hope,' replied Thomas. He turned to his aunt. 'What of Miss Cadabra? Is there anything you can see that could help her?'

'I have tried, Thomas. But all that has been given to me is the length of time of the attack, and that she will have help when the time comes, through Viola.'

He looked around the table.

'But she .... Is there *nothing* more any of *us* can do?'

Hogarth put a hand on his shoulder.

'Only to make the most of the time her defence of the village will give us.'

'I am sorry I couldn't see any more for Amanda,' said Amelia, 'but know that I will be watching you both, as much as the ball will show me. I wish I had been shown more to assist you inside Flamgoyne, too.'

'That's all right, Aunt. I think we're as prepared as we can be.'

'In that case, Thomas, Kyt, all I can say is ... good hunting.'

Chapter 39

AMANDA'S LAST SHOT

Amanda had slept but fitfully. The dream had come again. The thunderous swirl of cloud was racing towards Sunken Madley. She stood before the green, on the old crossroads, feet planted apart, wand pointing at the ground, ready. Tempest sat by her side.

'How?' How in the world did I come to this ...?'

She woke up to see daylight filling the V in the curtains. One more day. One more day in which to find Viola.

'Yes,' Amanda said resolutely, swinging her legs out of bed and dislodging Tempest. 'I *still* have one more day.'

At The Grange, the inspector allowed her to go into the ballroom and remove some parquet flooring tiles, which needed repairing, and take them back to the small dining-room. While she worked, Amanda thought about how she might find Moffat. He was the last on her list of potential Violas, and she was determined to interview him, ever so subtly, of course.

By 11 o'clock he had not appeared, and neither had the

ladies. Noticing the time, Amanda had an idea. She hid her flask and went off in the direction of the kitchen. There was no one in sight, so she called,

'Moffat! Moffat?'

It had always seemed disrespectful to her, to address by their surname, someone who was so much older than herself: especially someone who had the grand bearing of an archduke, at the very least. She had once added the title 'Mr', and he had calmly, but firmly, corrected her.

'Moffat?'

'Yes, Miss Cadabra,' said a voice behind her.

'Oh, Moffat, there you are. I am sorry to disturb you, but I wondered if I might have some tea.'

'Of course, miss. I will see to it at once.'

'Thank you. Please, may I stay while you do so? I wanted to ask you something.'

'Certainly, miss. How may I be of assistance?'

Amanda gave him her story about wanting to get a picture of the ballroom in its heyday and gradually worked round to amateur theatricals, arriving at Shakespeare and *Twelfth Night*.

'Yes, of course,' Moffat responded, 'it is a play of particular interest, given the plot-line about a manager of a great house.'

'Malvolio?'

'Indeed, miss.'

'I actually found the way he was treated rather disturbing. I have to admit, it's the part of the story I like the least,' remarked Amanda.

'Your sympathy does you credit, miss.'

'Thank you, Moffat. What did you think of the other storyline? Involving Viola, the count, and her brother Sebastian.'

'I did find the mistaken identity somewhat fantastical, miss, but it is, of course, a popular plot device in comedy. Your tea is ready. Shall I serve it in the small dining room?'

'Oh. Yes, thank you, Moffat.' He carried it through in silence. The conversation felt at an end. Having placed the tray on a side table, he asked.

'Will there be anything else, miss?'

'I do have one question. I hope that you will not consider it too personal.'

He raised his eyebrows, questioningly.

'The Grange used to have a big estate, didn't it? Owning land around here, is that right?'

'That is correct, miss.'

'Do you remember that?'

'I had the privilege of being born on the estate, miss. My father was estate manager.'

'So you automatically followed in his footsteps?'

'It was my choice, miss. I went to college and studied buildings and estate management.'

'Really?'

'Yes, I took my degree at the Feald Institute.'

'I'm impressed. A prestigious college. And you returned here?'

'Indeed, miss.'

'So you're not the butler, at all?'

'I manage the affairs for the ladies relating to both the house, and holdings, and ensure the comfort and well-being of Miss de Havillande and Miss Armstrong-Witworth. However, it is simpler for others to think of me in that more familiar role of "butler".'

'Thank you for clarifying that, Moffat. I have always said that you are far more than a butler.'

'Thank you, miss. Will that be all?'

'Yes, Moffat. You have been most kind.'

'Not at all, miss.' With that, he returned kitchen-ward.

So ... even if he did know of some history with the

chandelier, if all word of it had been suppressed, he certainly wasn't going to spill the beans. And he hadn't taken the Viola bait either.

* * * * *

'So that's what the Council was about?' said Amanda, as she sat with Trelawney in the seclusion of the small salon.

'Yes. And Amelia said to remind you that around 2.30 is the most likely time for the Flamgoynes' arrival.'

'OK. I'll be ready. Wand-in-hand and all that,' she said, trying to sound confident. 'Should be high noon.' He smiled. 'I spoke to Moffat, by the way. No joy. He didn't own up to being Viola, nor did he supply any information regarding the history of the ballroom and the chandelier.'

'Well done for trying. Viola may appear at the eleventh hour. Perhaps that's his or her plan. I'm going back to Cornwall, this afternoon. Now, in fact.'

'Of course ....' This would be their last conversation before ... or would it just be their last conversation? Amanda put the thought aside. 'Listen, I doubt I will be able to hold them in Sunken Madley for you for any longer than —'

'Don't worry about my father and me,' Trelawney urged her. 'We'll make the best use of whatever time we have.'

'Do you think there'll be staff inside Flamgoyne?'

'Aunt Amelia thinks so.'

'Look,' Amanda said earnestly, if you're challenged by a wand-bearer, don't take any more chances than you would with someone who was armed with a gun, OK?'

'Understood.'

'Good .... You know,' she said thoughtfully, 'in many ways, you're the ideal person for this.'

'Thank you. Not sure how to take that, but thank you.' They both managed a smile.

Trelawney remembered something important.

'Aunt Amelia or I will call or text you once we see that the Flamgoynes are on their way. The codeword is "nest", as in "empty."'

'"Nest." Got it.'

'Well ....' They fell quiet. Thomas thought of something reassuring to say:

'Aunt Amelia will be watching us both.'

'Good ....'

He stood up and put on his coat. Amanda got to her feet. What they both wanted to tell one another was, 'If I don't see you again, I want you to know that ....'

What they said, instead, was ....

'Well, Inspector.'

'Well, Miss Cadabra.'

They shook hands.

'Good luck.'

'Good luck.'

She came with him to the door. He wanted to say something more, *any*thing more. He saw Tempest at Amanda's feet.

'Well, at least you'll have the Duke of Darkness there at your side,' he managed.

Amanda looked down and picked him up saying 'Oh oo is not da Duke of Darkness, iz oo?' She cuddled him. 'Oo is Ammy's ickle minky muffin, isn't oo? Tempest leaned back in her arms like a big furry baby, all four paws in the air. She nuzzled his tummy with her nose, while he turned his head and stared at the inspector with one eye.

Never before had Trelawney seen, in so small a radius, such a condensed concentration of what was purely ... smug.

As he drove home to collect his overnight bag, he

remembered that Hogarth had told him the Cadabras would get under his skin. He reflected that Mike had omitted to mention that, one day, that cat of Amanda's would get inside his head! Thomas could have sworn he heard a low purring voice say,

'She likes me better than you.'

Chapter 40

❧

THEY ARE COMING

Amanda sat in the sitting room with her coat on the settee beside her, her mini-wand in the pocket. Her hat and long wand were at her side. Tempest sat on the window-sill, checking the sky, which was sunshine-filled and clear blue. Bags of salt were piled in the hall. She had memorised her spells, practised whatever she could, and now ... it seemed that somehow, alone, she must soon face her clan's foes.

'Now, now,' said a voice beside her. Amanda was slightly startled even though she was used to her grandparents' occasionally abrupt appearances. Granny was sitting on her left. 'This is no time for sinking into despondency. You were promised help and help you shall have. Viola —'

'Granny. I don't even know who Viola *is*, let alone the identity of anyone else who could possibly come to my aid, at the eleventh hour. And this is *beyond* the eleventh hour. I have just seen the last stragglers driving or walking out of the village.'

'You've got us, *bian*,' said Grandpa encouragingly.

'Can you ...?'

'No. Remember, the dead cannot harm the living, and they cannot help the living unless asked, but that still doesn't include harming the living. Moral support. That's all we can do.'

'That is to say, Ammy, dear,' Granny interjected, 'all that it is *agreed* we should do.'

'We could do more ...,' Grandpa clarified.

'But this is your hour, and the hour of Sunken Madley, win or lose.'

'But you'll come through, *bian*. I believe in you.'

'Thank you, Grandpa.'

'And your Granny does too. Don't you, Senara?' he prompted his wife.

'You are well prepared, dear,' said Granny noncommittally. Amanda looked at her doubtfully. Perran came and sat beside his granddaughter.

'Now, Ammy, when you go out there, there are two things to remember: first, you're a Cadabra, and you know our mottos .... '

Amanda nodded. '"A witch does not strike out" and "abundance through peace".'

'That's right. Second, you can't beat the Cardiubarns at their own game, so whatever happens, look to the defence of the village. However tempted you might be to do anything else, Ammy, *look to the defence of the village*. Then you have surprise on your side. They don't know what you are, they don't understand the Cadabra mind or integrity or love. They won't be expecting what you plan to do. Remember, Aunt Amelia said they will pour all of their power into one short hour. You only have to hold out for that long. It may seem the longest hour of your life, but I have faith in you.'

Amanda nodded and managed a smile.

Grandpa stood up and looked to the south.

'Ah, that's the last of them. The Normals are out of the village. Just one or two. Indoors though.'

'Where's Ryan Ford?' Amanda asked anxiously.

'Hmmm ... in his house.'

'What's he doing, Grandpa?'

'I can't tell you, love.'

'You don't know?'

'I know. I just can't tell you.'

'Oh, good grief!' exclaimed Amanda. Her phone rang. DI Trelawney, said the screen.

'Miss Cadabra?'

'Inspector.'

'Nest.'

'Right. Thank you.'

'Good luck, Miss Cadabra.'

'Good hunting, Inspector.'

She got up and put on her coat.

'They're coming,' she said shortly to her grandparents.

'We know,' Senara pointed out matter-of-factly.

'Ready?' asked Grandpa.

'Yes.'

'Off we go then,' said her grandmother briskly, with a hint of jauntiness in her tone that Amanda found entirely inappropriate.

'Granny, this isn't a trip to the seaside.'

'No, indeed, my dear,' she agreed emphatically.

'It'll be exciting though,' said Grandpa encouragingly.

'I could die out there!' Amanda objected.

'Well, you'll be with us, then. It'll be nice to see more of you, *bian*. Look on the bright side.'

Amanda rolled her eyes. 'Oh, I give up. Tempest?' But he was already leading the way to the door. However, before they reached it, the bell rang.

Her best friend was standing on the mat. She was smiling.

'Hello, Claire?'

'Ammy. There's something you should see'.

'Er ....'

Claire had her car engine running.

'Come on. I'm driving you and, um ...,' she added, seeing Tempest, 'you. Let's just get these salt bags outside the door.'

Claire drove them to the south entrance to Sunken Madley, of which the Snout and Trough formed one pillar. There, on either side of the road, Iskender was hanging blue eyes of protection. Ruth was on her knees with chalk, drawing a complicated-looking star on the ground.

'Hello, Amanda,' they greeted her, cheerily.

'We've done the other gates into the village,' said Ruth.

'This is the last one. We were just waiting for everyone to leave,' Iskender explained.

'Er … thank you, Ruth, Iskender .... But how do you ... did you know?'

'Viola told us,' replied Ruth.

'Who ...?' began Amanda.

'We'd better go,' urged Claire. 'Let them get on.'

'Of course.'

Claire drove them back to the middle of the village. Amanda got out of the car. Tempest stayed close. Claire went to park. Neeta and Karan Patel were carrying a large sheet of plywood onto the green. Amanda went over to look. It was a mandala in different colours.

Her doctor looked up. 'For protection my, dear.'

'You *know* about ...?'

'Of course,' Neeta replied, gently.

'Viola told us,' explained Karan.

Chris Reid came past, saying,

'I'm going to put this in the middle of the green.'

'What is it, Chris?' Amanda asked.

'It's a talisman I made from things in the ground here and bark from the trees. My version of some Caribbean magic. Gran learned the old ways in Jamaica, before she came here. When Viola told me, Gran and I Skyped,' he explained, as though this was all the most natural thing in the world. And of course, thought Amanda, from one point of view, it is.

'Well ... thank you, Chris,' she uttered, amazed. 'I had no idea ....'

At that moment, Kieran came rushing up, looking flushed.

'Hi, Amanda. It's done!'

'Hello, Kieran. What's done?'

'The salt ring. Ashlyn and I —'

'Ashlyn? What, the captain of our cricket team?'

'Yes, why not?' asked Kieran.

'But ... he barely knows me.'

Ashlyn was jogging towards her.

'Hello, Amanda. Kieran and I have been running the boundary, laying it down. The salt.'

'Thank you, Ashlyn. Of course, it's not going to do the fields any good.'

'Oh, it's all right,' Kieran assured her, 'we used bin liners, wherever we could.'

'It doesn't have to be in actual contact with the earth,' said Mr Sharma, joining them. He and Mrs Sharma had supplied the bin bags. The runners handed over what they had left.

Amanda became aware of other villagers. They were all approaching her now. She looked around in bewilderment, and was moved beyond measure: Joan and Jim, Sylvia and her husband, Mr French and Irene James, Miss Hempling, the doctors' eldest son Dilip, his wife, even little Amir, looking solemn but bright-eyed.

Ruth pointed. 'Oh look, here's Miss de Havillande

coming now.'

Viola, thought Amanda.

Cynthia was driving up, in the range rover, with Moffat and Miss Armstrong-Witworth. The three of them disembarked with an air of purpose.

Amanda didn't know what to say. 'But ... but ... all of you ...?'

'You don't think we'd abandon you and our village in the moment of truth, do you?' asked Miss de Havillande spiritedly.

'Well ... I ....'

'As soon as Viola told us, we started getting ready,' Miss Hempling related to Amanda.

'We all want to help,' Dennis Hanley-Page urged.

'We don't have any great gifts,' was Moffat's rider.

'Not like you,' said Miss Armstrong-Witworth.

'But we each have something,' added Mrs Sharma.

'Something small,' explained Irene James.

'Even if it's only good-will,' chimed in Gordon French.

'We can help,' insisted Jane the Rector.

'Sunken Madley is our home,' stated Mrs Pagely.

'Where we're not freaks,' uttered Jonathan.

'We can be ourselves.' That was from Jim, Joan's husband.

'Talk to each other,' his wife sang out.

'We stand our ground with you,' declared Henry 'The Colonel'.

'Come what may,' called Alexander.

'That's right,' seconded Julian.

'Your Home Guard is assembled,' intoned Miss de Havillande.

'Yes, Captain Cadabra,' said Ashlyn.

'Tell us what you want us to do,' encouraged Miss Armstrong-Witworth.

Amanda's eyes were filling with tears.

'Now now,' said Granny, at her elbow. 'This is no time for sentimentality.'

'Your Granny's right,' agreed Irma.

Amanda was astonished. 'You can *see* her?'

'Some of us. The ones with The Sight,' explained Irma.

'Right ....'

Amanda blinked away her tears, sniffed resolutely and turned to the task in hand. 'The ordinary salt is the outer ring. Now we need to lay down the *Epsom* salts.'

'Yes, where do you want it?' asked Chris.

'Make an inner ring, just around here, enclosing this space by the pub: the green, the pond, the crossroads. Go up to the front of the buildings, so you can stand inside the ring and at least have some shelter.'

'And the pink salt will go around you,' added Joan. 'We know.'

Ruth, Kieran, Iskender, and Chris, softly speaking words of protection, were already pouring the curving line of the Epsom salts.

In a few minutes, they were all standing within the ring. Amanda kept looking up at the sky. It was beginning to darken in the west.

Kieran and Ruth were laying down the pink salt ring around her. She waited until they were finished, then spoke.

'Right. Does anyone here know about raising the sphere?'

'Of Power?' asked Sylvia.

'Yes,' replied Amanda.

Sylvia nodded. 'A bit.'

Priya, Dilip Patel's wife, spoke up gently. 'I've helped to do it, in the past.'

'Viola has told us all the theory, at least,' said Joe Mazurek, the milkman,' so we've all brought what we need.'

'Good. Well, we're going to make one, and go one better. We're going to raise a *mirror* sphere. It needs to go under the ground, as well as above us, because we don't know what the enemy may try.'

They nodded. Amanda had never spoken in public before. But there was too much urgency, too much at stake, for nerves now.

'All I know is that this will be over, one way or another in about an hour. We don't have to hold the sphere for long, but it may *seem* long, and we don't know what we will have to hold it against.'

Nods again.

'Now, has everyone got something that will help them to focus?'

'Yes,' the villagers chorused, and stones, crystals, bundles of herbs, jewellery, boxes, candles, bowls and other objects, came out of bags and pockets.

'Please form a circle. Look at your neighbours to your left and right. You need to know and remember who is beside you. Make sure you're next to people you really like, people you know and are the most fond of. We can't afford any weak bonds here.'

There was some shuffling rearranging.

'Thank you. Now when I say the word, focus on the object in your hands. See it glow. Don't force anything. Allow the glow to spread up your hands and arms, and throughout your body. See it spread out to the sides. Until it joins with your neighbours.'

The sky in the west was now a deeper grey.

'Ready?'

'Yes,' came the murmurs of assent.

'Now ... focus.'

Amanda waited. She had no idea if this was going to work. These weren't witch-clan witches. They were half-witch-half Normals and full Normals. But magic is in all things, she reminded herself. They can do it.

The horizon was filling with threatening clouds. Amanda could see they were like thick, bulging rings, dark weather systems dividing the lowering rack.

Tempest was by her feet, looking up. There was no need to say it, but Amanda did anyway:

'They are coming.'

Chapter 41

∽

INTO FLAMGOYNE

Amelia had sat at her table, a pot of tea under a tea cosy, a cup and saucer, sugar and milk beside her. It was going to be an intense vigil. She watched the crystal ball before her. The clock, in the kitchen, ticked off the seconds.

It showed her the gates of Flamgoyne. Linking to it, as their reluctant kith and kin, was a risk. She had surrounded herself with every instrument of protection and concealment at her command. Amelia had long ago departed and changed her name. The clan had no idea where she had gone. Thanks to a bequest from her and Kytto's uncle, they had both broken free: she utterly, Kytto less so, but still ….

Suddenly, there was a change in the depths of the glass. The portal was opening. There they were, like the flock of crows, the unkindness of ravens she had seen and always thought of them. The matriarch, Lady Gronetta Flamgoyne, was scorning any offer of aid to descend the steps, as her open-top jeep appeared at the bottom of the flight. Two more jeeps, in green, and other vehicles, drew up. Yes! Flamgoyne was emptying.

Amelia sent a text.

Nest

Sitting in Thomas's car, tucked up a farm track off the road to Flamgoyne, both Trelawneys saw the message.

They nodded to one another. Thomas made the call to Amanda, drove the mile to the entrance of the great house and parked out of sight.

They got out of the car and approached the gates.

'Now to see how Flamgoyne we are,' commented Thomas.

But the spell knew its own, and the gates obediently swung open before the father and son.

Thomas had equipped them both with skeleton keys, torches, and back up torches. Because, as he told his father, in moments of high-tension and emergencies of a dangerous nature, torches invariably fail.

They ascended the black marble steps. The doors needed keys and a Flamgoyne wielding them.

'I've got this,' said Kytto.

They entered cautiously, listening for movement first.

'All clear,' confirmed Thomas softly. 'Right, phones on vibrate only. Alert one another if we find anything. Start in the study. I'll go up and start in Grandmother's room. Then to the tower.'

'You remember the way?'

'You told me: second floor, right-hand end of the passageway, a door, probably locked, spiral steps within.'

Thomas took the stairs as silently as possible, and Kyt opened the door to the study. He worked methodically through the desk and the secretaire, through each cubbyhole and drawer, but drew a blank. Kyt had begun checking the bookshelves, when he heard a sound in the hall. He cracked open the door to see a tall, thin young man with a shock of light brown hair, coming stealthily down the grand staircase. He carried a rucksack on his back and a holdall in his hand.

'Eddie!' Kytto whispered, as loudly as he dared.

'Mr Trelawney, sir!' the boy responded just as quietly, but with greater urgency. 'You must let me go, sir! Please, don't try to stop me.'

'Where are you going, Eddie?'

'I'm getting out of here. This is my chance. I've done the last of their dirty work. Though I'd rather scrub their floor then be part of ....'

'I understand, Eddie. Of course, I won't stop you. But where will you go?'

'As far from here as I can get. Get myself an education, make a proper Normal life for myself.'

'Why didn't you go before?' asked Kyt.

'Spells. Held me here, pulled me back. But now, their attention and their power are needed elsewhere. I could feel it.'

'All right. Well, once you're over the Tamar, they'll have no hold on you.'

'I know. Bersie's already gone, but I think Pasco might still be here somewhere,' Eddie warned.

'OK.' Kytto pulled a wad of notes from his wallet. 'Here. I wish it were more, but it will see you safe over the border and help you set up wherever you go.'

'Thank you, sir. I'll replay you one day.'

'If you wish. But don't settle North,' Kyt advised him.

'Why not? I was going to head for Durham. They have a good university up there.'

Kyt shook his head. 'If ever they look for you, they will look north. Take a train in that direction, then double back to the east or south coast. What do you want to study?'

'With all of this divination, I thought … statistics, probability,' Eddie answered with a half-smile.

'Then go to Canterbury. Kent university.'

'All right, sir.'

'Let me know when you're settled. Here.' Kyt took out a business card and scribbled on the back.' He was aware of the time and how exposed he was out here in the hall. But Eddie was the best shortcut to their objective, if Kyt could win his trust. 'Once you're clear of the estate, call this number. It's a cab service. Tell them you're on an errand for me. Get you to Plymouth station. Take the first train over the border.'

'I will. Thank you, sir. I always knew you weren't like them. Young master Thomas too.'

'You remember him?'

'Just about. I'd better go now, sir. If there's anything I can ever do for you ….'

'There is Eddie,' said Kyt. 'Do you ever remember seeing some special paper, thick, and sort of see-through, and some purple-black ink?'

'Oh, yes, sir. I saw the ink one day when I was cleaning. The master was proper angry I hadn't knocked. He told me to turn my back, but I see in the glass of the cabinet where he put it. It's in the study, in the secretaire. Open with the key, if you can find it. Left-hand drawer, there's a switch inside opens part of the desk surface. There's a drawer underneath it. The bottle's in there.'

'Eddie, thank you! How about the paper?'

'I don't know about any special paper. Paper would be in the study, or the library down here, or mistress's study. Sorry I can't help more.'

'You've done enough. If you need more funds, let me know.'

'Thank you, sir, but I'll be fine. Working in this house, I can turn my hand to any job. I don't mind skivvying, I promise you, sir.'

'Good luck, son.'

Meanwhile, Thomas, upstairs in Gronetta Flamgoyne's domain, had conducted a search that was swift but thorough. He drew a blank in room after room. Closing her study door behind him, he hurried along the hall. All the while, Thomas was listening. The drugget muffled his footfall. He caught the sound of hushed voices below.

Cautiously, he descended a few stairs and looked over the bannister. His father was in conversation with a young man. He seemed to have things in hand. Thomas went back up to the end of the passage on the second floor. There it was: the door to the tower. He got it unlocked, slipped inside and began the ascent up the steep steps.

As he climbed, the way grew in surreal familiarity. His hand on the thick cord, hooked at intervals to the winding wall, appeared smaller. The door at the top was strangely bound, and yet he knew it. Again, he had recourse to his skeleton keys. They admitted him to a circular room. In spite of the urgency, Thomas was drawn, not to any of the furniture within but to the window. There he stood, looking out.

The afternoon light was changed by memory to a vision of night. Half moonlight shone upon the tower of Cardiubarn Hall. Its distance away seemed closer, as if through a celestial telescope. There was a light in the black shadow of the stonework.

Suddenly, it was as is if the moon shook, and the sky lurched. He blinked hard. Had he imagined it? He felt his father's hands on his 9-year old shoulders.

'Well, son. This night is born your intended. If you both show the promise for which these two houses hope ....'

Young Thomas considered his father's words. Intended? Thomas had no intentions. He had hopes. The same as always: of ending each visit here and never coming back. But now ....

The vision was gone. Thomas's mind was whirling.

There was only one Cardiubarn born when he was nine years old. He reeled at the thought. He shook his head as though to free his mind of what he had just remembered. I must not be distracted, he told himself, and searched the room.

His pocket buzzed.

Found ink.

Trelawney hurried to the ground floor, where he found his father beckoning him into the study.

'Well done.'

'I had help,' said Kyt. 'Invested a few minutes in the fleeing Eddie, and he came through for us. He's a good lad. I think I may have made a friend for us.'

'Good.' Thomas examined the ink. 'Right … paper?'

'Eddie said he didn't know.'

They began a new search of the room. Thomas, kneeling on the carpet and checking low shelves and under the furniture, asked,

'Do you remember us both being in the East Tower, one night, looking over at The Hall? I had a flashback when I was up there, just now.'

'I do, yes,' said Kyt, looking between the books.

'A child was born that night, who you said was my intended. Who was she?'

Kyt stopped. 'I think you know, son.'

Thomas stood up, and they looked across the room at one another.

'Amanda Cardiubarn?'

'Yes,' Kyt confirmed. 'It was hoped that you would combine the magical traits of both houses, and your child ….'

'Good grief. The witch-clans' W.M.D., for whoever got their hands on it. No wonder I was so vital. No wonder they constantly watched me and asked … can he?'

Kytto let the room go quiet … He sensed his son was remembering. There was perhaps so little time and yet … it was a gamble ….

'The library,' Thomas murmured. Trancelike, he walked out of the study. Kyt followed him, mutely. Thomas pushed open the library door …. 'Bored … I'm bored, always bored here … they're all talking, murmuring, muttering … I feel my cheeks burning …. They keep glancing back at me. I have to get away … I come into the library …. I want to sketch. There's a pencil on the desk … but paper … I need paper …. I'm opening …' — Thomas went to the desk — 'this drawer … and this one and inside … under this folder and these big envelopes is ….' And there it was: a shallow pile of strangely transparent yet thick paper. He returned to the present and looked at his father. 'Not hidden. Of course. Why hide it? It's useless without the ink ….'

'Looks like you've found it, son.'

'Yes. Next, we have to try the ink and paper together. But in the open air, for safety. What's the quickest way to the outside?'

'The kitchen garden. But Pasco is most likely on that side of the house.'

Thomas was looking through the desk. He found a fountain pen with an ink sac.

'I'll need to wash this out in the kitchen then fill it from the bottle.'

'Any servants could be hanging around there,' warned Kyt.

'We'll have to risk it. If this ink-paper combo is the wrong one, we have to keep searching.'

The kitchen was clear. Thomas went to the sink, emptied the sac and ran it under the tap, while his father got the door to the garden open. They went outside, and Thomas knelt on the grass. He put a sheet of the paper before him, dipped the pen in the ink Kyt held out for him, then wrote the alphabet. They both retreated … and watched. A faint haze began to rise from the paper. Kyt found some thyme growing by the house. He tossed it onto the page. It curled, greyed and withered, all life drained from the leaves and stem. Kyt went back inside and found a box of matches. He lit a corner of the sheet. It went up in a short fierce blaze of purple. The two men kicked the ashes into the ground, out of sight. It was done. Success.

A sharp voice came from the kitchen.

'Put that bottle down, Master Kytto.'

There in the doorway, glaring at them from under beetling brows, wand in hand, stood the aged but still formidable form of Pasco Flamgoyne.

Chapter 42

~

THE DEFENCE OF SUNKEN MADLEY

Amanda's faith in the villagers, standing in a circle around her, was justified. They had each brought something on which to focus. The attack was imminent. The western horizon was a rim of boiling gunmetal grey. And yet ….

It was strange how time slowed in such a moment of direst peril. Amanda saw, as though magnified, the objects in her neighbours' hands. Most were candles or crystals, but some … it was unexpected what people most cherished under test. Not things of high monetary value for the most part. There was Dennis, holding his mother's empty jewellery box. Amanda had replaced the hinge. He had told her it was for his sister … but even so … there it was in *his* hands. There was Joan and Jim, each holding one of a pair of their daughter's baby shoes. The left one had lost an ornament and Amanda had been able to match it up. Among the villager's treasures, she recognised a grandfather's pipe, a sister's cameo brooch, a candle in a Wedgwood holder — she had repaired them all… a photograph

… an old knitted scarf … there was so much love here that she could feel it emanating, as though from a hundred candles.

If we are to go down, thought Amanda, it will be not in vengeance but in love. And if that is to be our only victory this day, then so let it be. *But* … we have not yet begun, and the Flamgoynes are about to learn *what* they are to contend with.

Time regathered its speed, and Amanda observed, as the villagers focussed each on their cherished item, a warm light shining through the fingers of each pair of hands.

'Let it spread through you,' she said. It was remarkable. They were *actually* doing it. 'Good! Now let it join …' But they seem to accomplish it instinctively. There was now a ring of golden softness running from villager to villager. Amanda's face lit in the first smile of that day. She stood, facing one after another, feeling her connection with each of them, as if she were the hub of a wheel.

'Next, let it spread down into the earth beneath your feet and the air above your head.' The curving sheet expanded. Down … and up. 'Now you're all going to meet in the middle at the zenith, the top of the dome and the nadir, the lowest point under the ground.'

She gathered the energy, pointing her wand below and above. There was a thump as the sphere sealed.

'Well done.'

The wind was rising. The sunshine and clear blue in the western half of the sky was utterly compromised. The cloud canopy in the distance was now clear to see, separated into small weather systems. They looked like the tops of tornados, each wielded by a separate Flamgoyne, Amanda guessed. She could just make out seven in total. Not long now. She must keep her attention fixed on the task.

'Let the sphere expand back behind you.' It moved out. At least the villagers were all inside now, even if they could not manage the next bit. 'Now, let the outer edge of the glow grow solid and reflective, like you're inside a one-way mirror ball.'

Some found it easier than others, some parts were coming and going, now mirror, now glow. The Flamgoynes were getting closer, but Amanda could not afford to panic, or, more importantly, to panic her helpers.

'Those of you finding it easier, please help the person next to you.' Ah yes, that was working better. It was firming up. ... They'd got it. 'This is your sole task: together, hold the sphere.'

Granny now spoke in Amanda's ear. 'You'll have to repel each spell as the Flamgoynes fire it or they will cut through.'

'But how will my counter-spells get through the sphere without disrupting it?'

'They'll be coming from the inside. Inside to out, you can do,' Granny assured her.

'OK. How will I know which spell they're going to fire?'

'You won't until they fire it.'

'I'll have seconds to recognise and counter it!' Amanda protested.

'If you're lucky.'

All at once, she recognised the dream.

She was standing at the heart of the village with the thunderous swirl of cloud racing towards it,

She stood, wand pointed at the ground. But she did not stand alone.

The eyes of Tempest, crouched beside her, glittered virulent yellow, his tongue shooting out and licking his lips in anticipation. Amanda Cadabra glared into the oncoming storm.

'I swear,' she said quietly. 'You shall not take my village. You'll have to come through me first.'

The cloud systems, iron grey, were now approaching firing range. Electricity was building, colours forming. She had done her homework. Amanda repeated under her breath:

'Red. That a spell-burn. The counter-spell is *dyscwen*, quench. Grey is maze: *klyr* clear. Orange harm: *saya* heal. Purple forget: *erkova* remember. Yellow fear: *colek* courage. Black cut: *selya* seal. blue trance: *fynad*e wake, white sting: *ismel* salve.'

Suddenly, lightning darts shot forth. Amanda began blocking with one wand, then both. At first only in front, they started coming from multiple directions, then faster. She had to counter them above, left, right, up down.*Dyscwen, saya, sely, klyr, erkova, ismel, colek, ismel, fynad*e.

The closer the weather systems came, the faster the attack spells.

But the mirror was holding.

The Flamgoynes were keeping their distance, hovering just inside firing range, testing the enemy's defences, expecting a counter-attack and confused at meeting none.

On the road to the north, the houses there were silent, their occupants off at the fair or enchanted. The Flamgoynes had saturated the area with mazing spells. It had, at least, drained some of their power.

Now with growing confidence that the village would not strike at them, they intensified their volley. It was faster than Amanda could repel, and some were now hitting the mirror.

One thing the Flamgoynes had not bargained for: unexpected ricochets of their own spells were hitting the attacking casters. Some of the clan had stings, one or two couldn't remember who they were or why they were there. One, on whom a fear spell had rebounded, was overcome by panic and ran off into the bushes. As each main caster fell away, their whirlwind vortex disappeared and could not be re-evoked.

But each spell that hit the mirror weakened it. Thinning patches were appearing. And cracks.

Chapter 43

∽

THEIR FINEST HOUR

Amanda's hat, her magical amplifier, was at her feet — Grandpa had said to hold it in reserve — next to Tempest, his gaze flickering across the sky.

More Flamgoyne casters were down. But what would give way first? The enemy or the villagers' sphere? Darts were getting through. Dilip was stung but barely wavered. And yet, minor though the hurt was, it kindled a spark of wrath within Amanda that took her unawares. She uttered between clenched teeth:

'How dare you touch my people!' The thought fanned her anger, calling forth the worst of the Cardiubarn within. Her eyes lit, blazing with rage. Catching sight of the veriest edge of Gronetta Flamgoyne's jeep, far up the approach road to Sunken Madley, Amanda, bent on revenge, surged forward. Tempest, racing beside her, contrived to get under her feet, as she heard:

'A witch does not cast in anger.'
'A witch does not strike out.'

'A witch does not take revenge.'
'Look to the defence of the village!'

The words sounded in her head, as though taught, repeated, inculcated, for this moment. Amanda, arrested, gasped. She looked up. In those few seconds of lapsed guard, spell after spell had rained down upon the sphere. She ran back, blocking the hailing darts.

A mazing spell got though. Kieran was looking bewildered and stepped forward. Amanda had to break off her defence to counter it. He quickly recalled his purpose and stepped back. It was distracting. She was missing more and more shots. Fighting against the wind, and with the penetrating spells, the circle was wavering, the sphere was fracturing ....

This was more than one witch repel. The Cadabras had been many. She was one. The villagers, for all their love and loyalty and determination, were no match for a witch-clan bent upon annihilation of any rival power, especially one for good. They could not hold the sphere for much longer.

In that moment, she heard a little voice. A child's voice. Was it hers? Her inner self? It was singing. Its pure high notes were sounding over the noise of the spell impacts.

'Anda litt-el beah.'

The Appel Song! — The old song of the orchard, the song that celebrated the saga of St Ursula: the young girl who had saved the village so many hundreds of years ago.

Other voices were taking up the chorus,

'Our foes will ever flee in fear
When Ap-pel sprits do appear
To lend a hand and find a way
To save us as they did that day.
The Orchards rare
They are still there

Praise Ursula and the li-ttle bear.'

They began the first verse. Amanda saw, rising around the village, wavering, semi-transparent forms of green. They reached from the earth upwards, swaying branch-like arms, in emeralds, limes, olives, jade, moss, pine, chartreuse, towering ethereally. The orchard! The Ap-pel — Apple — spirits! They had to be.

Is this what really happened, she asked herself in wonderment, on the day the village was threatened so long ago? Was it the orchard spirits that saved it?

If Amanda had been able to see up the road, she would have witnessed the eyes of the remaining Flamgoynes widening in fear. All but one of the vortices had gone.

The villagers continued to sing. Now Amanda could understand why there were 43 verses. The enchantment, the call, the defences had to hold: outhold the attack.

Gronetta, Lady Flamgoyne, standing up on the back of her jeep, was cursing her fleeing family,

'You lily-livered cowards! Come back here!' she shrieked. The deadly spells they had been firing had rebounded. Two of the men lay inert far behind her, struck down in the act of flight.

Gronetta alone wielded the storm now. She lashed her wand upwards, lips stretched back in a grimace of implacability, iron-grey hair tightly bunned, her long black clothes flying in the gale of her own making.

Lightning was flinging from the cloud-rack down at the village below, as Lady Flamgoyne began building the power for her culminating blow. Tiles were flying off roofs, Fences were being blown down. The chimney of the Sinner's Rue was rent in two. The sign swung wildly. But still, the villagers held their ground, singing as loudly as they could over the rising gale, holding their glow.

But Amanda knew, even with the orchard spirits, and all their will, and every ounce of spell-power she possessed, against the coming bolt, the defence would not be enough. She had to think fast.

What can I do? A witch does not strike out. A witch defends, heals… cures. Wait … what if she saw that storm as a sickness? What if she could take the cure … to its heart? Take what? A crystal — a healing stone. What was the most potent defender — protector — that she had? Instinctively, Amanda put her hand into her pocket. What was this …? She drew out a stone of black tourmaline carved with … the shield knot!

Angus's — no, Mary MacSpadden's — talisman. What had he said? 'For *the day*!' What day if not this? Yes, but down here it had little effect. And yet … if she could get it up there — into the centre of the storm … But how? She had never levitated anything nearly so high …. Her mind flashed back to her teenage years … in her bedroom … Grandpa telling her about the project ….

'Everyone move forward a step!' Amanda called out. 'Tighten the circle. Ruth, Kieran! Step out. Come here, please.' They rushed up to her. She did her best to keep the counter-spells coming as she talked.' Get my house keys out of my left-hand pocket, Ruth. I need you to run like the wind to my cottage.' Ruth fished them out. 'You'll be outside the sphere, so you'll have to dodge the spells. I don't want to have to answer to your parents.'

'We can do it, Amanda.'

'All right. Ruth, you know my house. In my bedroom, right of the window, third shelf up, model plane, Spitfire — the one with the canopy that opens and closes over the cockpit. Get it. *Fast* as you can. Go!' Ruth was off like a shot.

'Kieran. Do relay. Go to halfway down Orchard Way. When Ruth runs to you, take the plane and sprint to me like you're running for Olympic gold, OK?'

'Sure!'

Amanda turned her full attention back to the onslaught, quenching the spells that got through, joining in the chorus of the song when she could.

The vortex was almost directly above them now, firing shafts down upon the zenith of the dome, breaking it open. She heard the sound of rapid footfall on the road behind her. Now, if ever. was the moment: Amanda Cadabra the Witch picked up her black, wide-brimmed, pointed hat of office, handed down through generations of Cadabras, set it on her head and drew the string tightly under her chin. Here was Kieran handing her the plane.

'Thank you! You and Ruth, back into the circle.'

Amanda put Mary MacSpadden's dark, shining talisman into the model Spitfire's cockpit and shut the canopy.

'*Aereval!*' she cried and launched the plane of Britain's finest hour from her palm. Up to 10 feet it was swift and easy; at 20 to 30 feet it was still soaring. Not too steeply, she told herself, or the cockpit canopy could slide backwards, and the tourmaline fall out. This was a payload that had to be flown all the way home.

The storm, now right overhead, whirled black as night, gathering its force for the great strike.

Amanda reached up with both her wands.

'*Aereval!*'

The Spitfire reached one hundred feet, two hundred, three, four … five, five hundred and fifty ….

The vortex itself was descending, but still, she was at her limit. Suddenly Ruth was at her side.

'Get back!' Amanda called out over the wind.

'No! I can help!' Ruth put her arm around Amanda's waist and stretched her own hand skywards. 'Up!'

The aeroplane was closing with its target. It was surely only feet away. The small object, unnoticed, was escaping direct fire. But the sphere was opening, ruptured beyond all hope of repair in time. Electricity was circling around the ring of cloud, faster and faster, flashing every colour of hostile spell, gathering, amassing ....

All at once, Amanda felt Tempest's warmth around her right leg. A surge of power infused her body. Two small arms wrapped themselves around her left leg. There came the high-pitched shout:

'Up! Up! Ammeee, up!'

The plane rose, closing with the maw of the storm, penetrating its depths. Malice and anti-malice, harm and healing, met in an almighty explosion, flying outward from the epicentre of the stone, in a violent dispersal of dark force.

But not before the parting shot was released. Amanda saw it coming. Heading down towards the empty roof of the sphere.

'*Dyscwen*!' she cried, then threw herself over the children before it hit her, bursting upon her shoulders in a flare of light. She slumped ... inert. Ruth took the weight of her collapsed form, and Amir wriggled out from under her protective embrace.

The storm was gone, the rack flying apart, the sun shining forth. The villagers abandoned their circle, running forward to their fallen captain. Neeta Patel was there first, lowering Amanda carefully to the ground. Karan Patel was dashing to the medical centre.

'Oh my!' exclaimed Joan. 'We must get her to the hospital.'

'No ordinary medicine can help this,' said Neeta. She looked up at Mrs Sharma. 'Nalini. You know what's needed?' She nodded and hurried off.

'We'll get what we have,' offered Miss de Havillande.

'We'll bring it to the cottage,' added Miss Armstrong-Witworth.

'I know what you need too,' put in Jane, the rector.

'Thank you all,' said Neeta. 'It may help, but it may not be enough.'

She looked down at Amanda's blanched face and closed eyes. 'Not nearly enough. Not for this.'

Chapter 44

༄

MAN DOWN

'What are you about, Master Kytto? You are Master Thomas, I warrant. You've grown.' Pasco Flamgoyne kept his wand pointing at the stone flags of the kitchen floor.

'Good afternoon, Pasco,' Kyt replied calmly.

'I'll thank you to put that bottle down, sir.'

Kyt spoke slowly. 'Pasco, you don't know what this is.'

'Do I not? Only I knew where it was hid,' said the old retainer with pride.

'You've used it?' Kyt was careful to keep any hint of accusation out of his voice.

'Not I,' replied Flamgoyne forcefully. 'I'll fetch and carry for them in this house and about, but such deeds will I not do, nor shall any man speak that I have, or will.'

'I believe you, Pasco.'

'But true Flamgoyne and servant of this house, am I. I will let none steal from it. Not even its own.'

Thomas's phone dinged! He put up his hand where it

could be seen and slowly moved it towards his pocket.

Pasco raised his wand.

'I am not armed,' Thomas assured him.

The man nodded.

Thomas checked the screen. It was from Hogarth:

Amanda down. Get to her asap or you may not be in time. Use the siren. M

'I have to go,' he said.

Kyt looked at Flamgoyne. 'Pasco, let Master Thomas leave. This is between us.'

'He leaves the paper,' ordered the man.

'Yes. Put it down, Thomas.'

He would have to trust his father to get out of this with the evidence. Something told him that Kyt would do better with his son out of the way. He clearly had a relationship with the man and some vestige of authority. Thomas, as only the young master, had been careful to remain quiet. He placed the sheaf of sheets on the kitchen table.

'That's right, son. I'll be fine here with Pasco. We are just going to have a chat. Pasco, I have no wand. There is no need for yours.'

Kytto Trelawney, still holding the retainer's gaze, quietly spoke two words:

'Thomas. Go.'

Pasco lowered his wand and stood aside. Thomas hurried to the door, sprinted to the car, threw himself into the driver's seat and floored the accelerator.

In time? 'May not be in time'? For what? To help her? Or to say goodbye? It was unthinkable. He'd never get the chance to say … to tell her …. No. It was no help to anyone to think that way. He just had to concentrate. Get to the end of the track. He plugged in the siren and slammed it onto the roof.

He would be in time. He *had* to be in time.

* * * * *

Dr Karan Patel drove the ambulance up to the knot of people around Amanda. Ruth ran up with the house keys. Karan and Chris Reid got Amanda onto the gurney, Tempest stepped on beside her, and they got it up into the back of the vehicle. Neeta Patel got in with her and accepted the keys.

'Thank you, Ruth.'

'Shall Kieran and I run to the Grange and collect everything from there?'

'Yes, good.'

They drove to the cottage and took Amanda inside. Neeta went upstairs and ran the bath. Karan thanked Reid and sent him off to help with the salt removal. They got Amanda's singed coat off, and opened the top of her dress so they could look at her all-too-pink shoulders.

'Spell sting: bad one. But this, at least, we can treat,' pronounced Neeta.

The teenagers arrived with bags and bundles of herbs.

'Forridge leaves, pottlecap and verigan seeds,' said Ruth.

Kieran held up his collection. 'I've got brage, narby stems and dried mickleberries.'

Karan nodded.' Good. Take them upstairs to the bathroom.'

Sylvia and Nalini arrived. They looked at Amanda's shoulders. 'Hmm. All right, that's do-able.' They went off to the kitchen, and there followed the sound of the gas lighting, chopping, crushing, chanting.

'You two keep an eye on the bathwater now,' Neeta said to the teenagers.

'Yes, Doctor.'

Jane arrived. 'Yortle root?'

'Oh yes, please,' called Nalini from the kitchen.

'In the paste you're making or in the bath?'

'Both please, Rector, if you have enough.'

Ruth came down the stairs with a warm, wet flannel for Dr Patel, who gently wiped Amanda's face with it. They watched her anxiously, but Amanda made no movement.

'Merly weed,' said Joan coming in. 'It's a bit raw but ....'

'Raw's best,' Nalini assured her.

Once the paste was ready, Neeta and Nalini spread it carefully on Amanda's skin. The effect was immediate. They watched with satisfaction as, within two minutes, the hue of her shoulders had returned to normal. At least, the impact site of the spell blow was healed.

'We need to get the bath ready,' said Nalini. The women took turns to stay with Amanda, while they each visited the water to throw in the ingredients that, together, they hoped would bring her back from wherever she was wandering. Finally, Neeta nodded.

'Good. Let's get her upstairs.'

Chris Reid, who had been returned to be on call for any errand, was standing just outside the door, and now offered,

'I can carry Amanda, no problem.'

Claire came in. 'I can help.'

Neeta nodded. 'Thank you, Chris. Please wait in the kitchen for a minute.' Nalini, Neeta and Claire, who knew Amanda best, got her down to her underwear and wrapped her back up again in towels. They called Chris in. He put his arms under her knees and shoulders and began to lift.

'Oh, she's not as light as she looks! I mean ... er ... light as a feather, Doctor.' He got Amanda upstairs and supported her on the edge of the bath. There the ladies took over. 'I'll go back and help with the salt removal, shall I?' Chris suggested.

'Unless you need me?'

'We can manage, thank you, Chris.'

They unwrapped Amanda and lowered her into the bath. They washed her, singing, chanting, talking to her gently.

'Come back, Amanda,' said Mrs Sharma. 'Come back to Aunty now. Time to wake up. There's a good girl.'

'Come on Ammy, we've got a new film to watch. You don't want to miss it,' Claire urged.

But there was no response. They got Amanda dried and into bed. One by one, they attempted calling her back into consciousness.

Joan tried. 'Amanda, I've got post for you. Wake up and answer the door, dear.'

Next Miss Armstrong-Witworth: 'Amanda dear, I've got a cream tea ready for us, but you need to wake up.'

Miss de Havillande tried her hearty approach. 'Come now, Amanda, buck up there, Can't be lying about in bed all day, y'know!'

'Please, wake up Amanda,' entreated Ruth. 'I need help with my history homework.'

Senara and Perran stood in the corner by the sink. They looked at one another and said nothing.

Amanda lay still. The bath, the herbs, the combined healing efforts of every person in the village who had any kind of skill of that ilk, had been for naught. Nalini, Claire, Joan and the doctors conferred.

Neeta was honest. 'Her pulse is slowing, I sense she is getting further and further away from us. We are losing her.'

'The inspector is on his way, Viola told me,' said Joan, hopefully.

'From so far away. I doubt he'll be in time. And even if he is, what can he do?'

Meanwhile, outside, Ruth was scrubbing away the pentacle at the south gate where the villagers would return first. Iskender had removed the eyes of protection from there and was working his way from entrance to entrance. Chris picked up his talisman from the middle of the green, Dilip and his wife had carried away the mandala board. All hands, not at the cottage, were on deck to remove any remaining salt.

At the fair, the villagers had seen the storm over Sunken Madley. However, there had been such bright sunshine above them that it was difficult to make out what was going on. The main thing was that it wasn't raining where they were. Anyone who thought of going home was quickly diverted by Esta, Erik, Sandra or Vanessa. These four had volunteered to keep anyone who had left the village, outside it, by offering to buy them a pint or a scone or engaging them in one of the attractions.

The quartet watched the sky and, when it cleared, finally were able to abandon their efforts. The damage to roofs, chimneys and fences would be easy to put down to the freak weather. Having tidied up, the Sunken Madley defenders were doing their best to present every appearance of normality. They exclaimed to the home-comers about the storm and its depredations and distracted them with thoughts of afternoon tea and supper. When alone, they looked anxiously towards the witch's cottage. From whence came no news that was good news.

Trelawney, having raced the 300 miles from The West, slowed to a respectable speed on the approach road, drove with apparent calm to number 26 Orchard Way, and parked. The door was open. As would be expected by the Normals after one of Amanda's asthma attacks, Dr Patel was there. She heard his car, looked out of the window and hurried downstairs to meet him.

'You got here more quickly than I expected.'
'Siren,' he said succinctly.
'Well, emergency this is. She is nearly gone.'
'How was she injured?' he asked.

'Superficially,' Neeta replied. 'That is healed, but she is … somewhere … somewhere no one has been able to reach her. We cannot get her back.'

'What can I do?'

'I don't know. But something. Or Viola would not have sent for you,' Neeta pointed out.

'Viola? The call came from my —'

'There must be something you can do. Something you *know*,' insisted Neeta.

'What? What kind of thing?' asked Trelawney, at a loss.

'Magic,' said the doctor.

'I – I don't know any … magic.'

Neeta put a kindly hand on his arm. She spoke gently, reassuringly.

'It's in your head somewhere. You just have to look in the right place. But there isn't much time. Come on up. I'll be back down here if you need me.'

Chapter 45

SONG OF THE SEA

ADr Patel led Thomas upstairs.

'Go in.' She closed the door behind him, leaving him alone with the form of Amanda. He had never seen her so still. Animated, yes, exasperated, thoughtful, intent, attentive, but never like this.

He wracked his brain for any memory of Flamgoyne magic that he might have heard or seen, or somehow picked up, in his years of being taken to visit the family. Any scrap, *any*thing at all.

But there was nothing.

He must be looking in the wrong place. Maybe it was simpler than that.

Trelawney had been successful once before, recalling her from a comatose state. But Thomas knew that this was far, far deeper. Still, it was worth trying what he had said before:

'Miss Cadabra ….'

* * * * *

Dr Patel heard his feet on the stairs coming down to her.
'Any luck?' she asked
Thomas shook his head.
'Can you tell me anything about … when she's been like this in the past? There must be something.'
Neeta thought. 'One thing I do remember. She used to say that it was like being under the sea ….'

* * * * *

Amanda had been here before, and she had always liked it, The deeper she sank, the warmer it felt: quite the opposite of the real sea. It was more and more comfortably dark, so much easier to sleep … drowsier and drowsier … it was getting easier and easier to give herself over to rest, to sweet oblivion after utter exhaustion.

* * * * *

At that last word of Dr Patel's, something had clicked in Thomas's mind. He had raced up the stairs before re-entering Amanda's room, quietly.
'The sea …,' he said softly.'… of course. This much magic, I, a Trelawney, do have.'

* * * * *

The quiet, rocking motion of the waves was soothing. Soon she would be there, deeply and utterly fast asleep, dreamlessly. Floating down into the depths of the shadows, she heard a faint sound .... Music? Singing ....

'Mar dhown, Vorvoren ple'th esosta.'

The sound was enchanting ... but so faint. She wanted to hear more. But the place she was in was so warm, and she was so sleepy ... and yet ... she wanted to hear it more than she wanted to sleep .... She could always listen and *then* sleep. She swam up a little way, and the voice grew clearer.
'Neuvya ha kana dha vorgan wre'ta.'
There was something irresistible about the melody ... or was it the words? She could only just make them out.
'Hag y now skath vy 'karmav dhiso jy.'
She paddled her feet a little. It was magnetic. She rose, up and up through the waves, lighter and lighter. The Voice. She knew that voice, didn't she? Yes,... whose was it? Must get closer ... closer.
'Gwra yskynna ha kana genev vy.'
It was a voice she .... She broke the surface.

* * * * *

The colour was returning to Amanda's cheeks, her breathing was deepening. All at once her lashes moved, eyelids fluttered, her eyes opened. Thomas stopped singing.

'Ama ... Miss Cadabra. You're back.' He let out a breath of relief, but spoke calmly. 'We've all been so worried.'

She looked at him hazily.

'I was in the sea,' she murmured.

'I know,' Thomas said, smiling.

Recognition dawned in her expression.

'Inspector.'

'Yes.'

'You're holding my hand,' she noticed sleepily.

'Am I?' He looked down. 'How irregular. Do you mind?'

It was her turn to smile.

'Not at all. You must be very relieved not to have lost your chief witness.'

'I'm glad to see that neither you nor your sense of humour has been lost.' He let go of her hand and touched her shoulder. 'I'll go and get Dr Patel; she's downstairs.'

'You were singing ...,' Amanda said vaguely.

'Yes.'

'You have a nice voice.'

'Do I? Thank you, Miss Cadabra.'

'I had to come back when I heard it. How strange ... don't you think?'

Thomas thought of the magic of the Trelawneys, and the flashback he had had in the top tower of Flamgoyne.

'Actually ... not really.'

Her head was clearing a little.

'You ... here ... did you get into ...?'

'Yes, my father and I got into Flamgoyne.'

'Did you find ...?'

'Yes.'

'And you got it out, and you got me out,' she said, suddenly drowsy, her eyes beginning to close again. 'Out of the sea. You must be a witch.'

'Possibly. But one thing I am certain of: we owe my granddad a bottle of the best rum we can find.'

At that, she opened her eyes again.

'I hope you're going to explain that remark, Inspector.'

'I shall,' he promised. 'Later.'

Chapter 46

༄

CLAIRE

After that, the villagers took it in shifts to be at the cottage. Aunt Amelia visited too, but mostly it was Claire who stayed there. Granny and Grandpa were never far away. Tempest was curled up like a round, furry, grey cushion at her feet. He left only for brief visits to his particular place in the neighbour's garden and made it clear, to whomsoever was in attendance, that he required his meals to be served in his and his human's room.

The first time Amanda saw her grandparents since the attack, it was through a drowsy haze. But she knew it was them. They sat down on the bed either side of her.

'Well done, *bian*, I was sure you could do it,' Grandpa told her.

'You excelled yourself, Ammy dear. We are very proud of you indeed,' added Granny.

'Hmmm,' Amanda sighed with a smile. A memory was coming back to her. Her face grew troubled. 'Oh … but

Grandpa … I almost lost it … I got so ….'

'… but you stopped yourself in time. You remembered didn't you?'

'Everything we'd taught you,' said Senara.

'Tempest …,' Amanda murmured, her expression softening, once more, '… it was Tempest.'

'He just *helped*,' Grandpa insisted.

'That's what he's there for,' commented Granny, condescendingly

Her granddaughter's familiar, on the end of the bed, lifted his head and glared at Senara in affronted indignation. Well, thank *you*! he communicated to her, witheringly. So glad to have been of *service* to a member of the under-species.

* * * * *

Amanda slept a good deal for the first 48 hours, until she remembered that the St Valentine's Day Ball was now only two days away.

'I'm getting up!' she announced, as Claire brought up the tea tray.

'Are you, now? Well, I'd recommend a move to the sofa.'

'I want a shower.' Amanda stood up and, promptly, her knees gave way, and sat her back down on the bed.

'How about a bath?' Claire suggested.

'Good idea,' she responded, laughing.

Downstairs, clean, dressed and on the sofa, she asked Claire,

'Don't you have to work?'

'Taking a break before the next project. The film's in post-production anyway.'

'Is *Blockbuster II* going to make you famous?'

'Notorious, more like! As long as it makes me lots of lovely lolly to pay off my mortgage, I will stoutly bear the shame of my association with this travesty of film-making,' replied Claire with lively stoicism.

Amanda chuckled.

'Thank you for helping with … you know ….'

'The least I could do. Besides, I'm *Village*. This is my home.'

'I had no idea you were —' Amanda began.

'Not entirely a Normal?'

'You know what a Normal is?'

'I do,' answered Claire brightly.

'So …. all this time … why did you never say?'

'Well, you live in the witch's cottage but no one, including me, was ever entirely certain about you, whether you were or weren't, or just *how* witchy you were. Also, that's how we function: we each know two or three like us and not the others. No one knew who everyone was except for Viola.'

'Who *is* Viola, Claire?'

'You don't know?'

Amanda shook her head. 'No.'

Claire turned down the corners of her mouth, comically. 'Then, I can't tell you. Sorry.'

Amanda had to accept that. 'Well, at least, tell me what your gift is.'

'Nothing like you can do. Just an old … *family* trick. Not all it's cracked up to be, mind, and really not at all useful,' said Claire.

'What?'

'Don't you know?' she teased 'And you an historian! Tut tut, Ammy.'

'Erm …?'

'My *sur*name!' Claire hinted broadly.

'Ruggieri?'

'Yes ... think ....'

'Um.' Amanda was searching her memory. Claire came to the rescue:

'Ruggieri. Cosimo Ruggieri, said to be a sorcerer and ... alchemist.'

'What? Oh my word, yes!' Amanda stared in amazement at her friend. 'You're an *al*chemist?

'I can't spin straw into gold, Rumpelstiltskin-style, if that's what you're thinking. I can affect certain minerals but not in a useful way. That's the thing with all us not-quite-Normals. Our gifts, as you call them, just drew unpleasant attention, laid us open to exploitation by the unscrupulous, and the reaction of the fearful and ignorant. And then the attendant strain of always having to pretend to be normal. That's why we either moved ourselves here, or parents brought their children here. It's the only place in the UK where we are protected by charter. When people move here, they sign a document, whether it's a lease or whatever, that they will abide by it.'

'What does the charter say?' asked Amanda curiously.

'Well, I don't know exactly,' admitted Claire. 'I can't read the peculiar language, but Viola said that it says the village vows to protect the inhabitants of the witch's cottage and all magical folk, and all folk of magical something-or-other, within its boundaries.'

'How do Normals react when they read that?'

'Oh, very few bother looking it up,' Claire told her.

'But the few who do?'

'They soon give up, seeing as it's in spell language or something. There's a Latin or even an English translation. Only you have to write away for it, to some obscure place that never answers. So there you go.'

Amanda was fascinated by these revelations. 'So ... how did *you* come to be here?'

'We-ell. One day, at a dinner, I was playing with a spoon and ... I bent it. I did it with more than one. I was as shocked as everyone else. I managed to convince all the folks there that it was just a party trick and I couldn't do it again. But then ....'

'Yes?' Amanda prompted.

'I found I *could*. I could change the shape of all sorts of things. But... it was the last sort of attention I wanted. I had to become very careful that I never did it by accident. My then-partner didn't like it at all. It made a bad situation between us worse. My family, of course, were supportive, naturally, and told me about the Ruggieri "talent" that I hadn't needed to know about before. But ... eventually, I knew I would either have to go and live back in Italy with my them in their village, which is like Sunken Madley. Or, if I wanted to stay in the UK, find somewhere *like* their village, where I could have respite and have times where I could be myself and bend a spoon or two, if I felt like it or just by accident.'

'I see ... how come ... you couldn't let your guard down ... when we were together?'

'As I say, I wasn't sure about you,' explained Claire.

'So how did you find this place?'

'Viola,' answered Claire simply. 'I met Viola, and the rest is history.'

'Wow. Just like Granny and Grandpa .... But you're not going to tell me who Viola is?'

'Ammy, if you're meant to know you will find out. Now ... ,' she said, changing the subject, 'that you're downstairs ... Movie Night?'

'Yes, but you must help me to start moving around. I'm *not* missing the St Valentine's Ball, even if I can have only *one* dance!'

'And I bet I know who with,' said Claire saucily.

'What on earth do you mean?' Amanda asked suspiciously.

'Well, I heard he saved your life, it's the least you can do,' countered Claire with spurious innocence.

Chapter 47

CASE CLOSING

Miss de Havillande phoned to say that Amanda was not to give the ballroom work another thought, until she was quite recovered; it was all in hand. Everyone in the village who knew her, was determined that Amanda should rest and recuperate before the ball without any stress. Trelawney was of the same mind.

'You have to tell her,' Hogarth said patiently, on the phone to Thomas.

'She'll only drag herself from her bed and come over here to The Grange, insisting she can get one of those apparition things to talk.'

'Not if you go and explain the situation, calmly, in person. You do have another week. But CI Maxwell is being perfectly reasonable. You don't have anything concrete, or otherwise, to suggest that the chandelier falling was anything other than an accident. And Baker and Nikolaides are needed elsewhere.'

'You're both right, of course. Look, could you ask him to give me a few more days? Let Baker and Nikolaides go. Just me.'

'Fair enough. I reckon I can swing that. But I think you'll find it's more than "just you" if I know Amanda ....'

* * * * *

It was Tuesday, and Claire and Amanda were looking at prospective dresses for the St Valentine's Day Ball.

'I know I'm cutting it fine. Only two days to go. And I really have no idea what I want. Why can't I just wear something I've already got?'

'Because I will not permit it,' Claire replied grandly. 'This is a victory celebration for those of us in the know, and you *shall* go to the ball in something new!'

'It's very kind of you.'

'And no skimping, Ammy. Money is no object.'

'But you want to pay off your mortgage —'

'If it weren't for you I wouldn't be *alive* to pay it off so ....' The doorbell rang.

Claire answered it and, presently, ushered in a guest.

'A visitor for you, Ammy,' she announced ceremoniously. 'I'll go and make some tea, then do some gardening,' she added ludicrously. 'Inspector, come in.'

'Hello, Miss Cadabra. How are you feeling?'

'Oh, very much better, thank you. How kind of you to call. Do sit down.'

Claire had made herself scarce.

'Thank you.'

'Have you come to give me some news, at last, of the Flamgoynes? I have been rationed to funny films and fluffy animal videos. No one has told me much about anything.'

'I can relate,' replied Trelawney, 'that the police found a string of fatalities between here and Bodmin Moor. Lady Flamgoyne, her son and brother are ... no more. In fact, it appears that all of the Flamgoynes are deceased, comatose, amnesiac or fled, including any mercenaries in their employ. Actually, they found Lady Flamgoyne, er, ... literally, smouldering. Rather like the Wicked Witch of the East.'

'Any shoes?' asked Amanda impishly.

'No ruby slippers have been reported,' replied Trelawney, dead-pan.

'Too bad,' sighed Amanda. 'So what have the police made of it all?'

'Weather, is the official line. The Flamgoynes were found in a line, between here and just the Cornish side of the Tamar. As though they'd formed a sort of bucket chain. The storm came from the Moor. I doubt they'll find a better explanation than that. It did do property damage along the way, and plenty of people saw the lightning.'

'I see.'

'By the way,' Trelawney added. 'Mike and my father assure me, all of the fatalities and casualties incurred by the Flamgoynes were the result of rebounded spells that they themselves cast.'

'I guess it just goes to show: what goes around comes around,' remarked Amanda.

'Just so.'

'Does Flamgoyne now stand empty?'

'Of that, I'm not sure. My father was vague on that point.'

'You got the evidence out though?'

'To be precise, my father did.'

'Did you face any opposition?' asked Amanda curiously.

'We did, in fact, but I believe he dealt with it ably.'

'Oh?'

Trelawney frowned. 'I must admit that on that point too, he has been vague.'

'I expect you'll get him to tell you eventually,' she opined confidently.

He cleared his throat. 'There was a matter I wanted to mention to you.'

'Oh? In connection with …?'

'The Grange case.'

Amanda's eyes it up 'Ah! New evidence.'

'That's just it. No, and what we have is insufficient to make a case for anything other than accidental death. The Chief Inspector, Maxwell ….'

'Oh, yes, I remember him.'

'He thinks we should wrap it up. Soon.'

'What!' exclaimed Amanda, sitting bolt upright. 'But ….'

'Yes, I thought you might react that way …'

'Let me back into the ballroom,' she pleaded. 'There must be something we're missing.'

'I promise you, that I have gone over it and the statements, the forensic and medical reports repeatedly, and found nothing.'

'Wait … there must be a way to get more out of the Frenchman. When I approached him —'

'Ah,' said Trelawney abruptly. A light had come on in his brain. He was silent. Amanda waited tensely. 'Miss Cadabra … perhaps it is not a question of *when* you approached him … but *how*.'

'You mean, I spoke first to him in French, and he thought it was dreadful?'

'No-o …. One thing that I learned from our last, er … case is that persons in the past reacted to different genders differently ….'

'Aha, you mean, the Frenchman thought I was a boy? And so ….'

'You might want a try a more … feminine approach, Miss Cadabra.'

'I think it's definitely worth a try, Inspector. The only thing is … if I get into costume … and there are now people swarming all over the house prepping for the party … and Miss de Havillande wants me to stay away and rest … how on earth am I to get the 10 minutes in there alone, which is surely the minimum I'll need?'

'Well, there's only one occasion on which you can legitimately be there.'

'The ball. But alone …. Of course, the Grange ladies were at the defence of the village, so they either have gifts or are supporters. Maybe I could tell them there is a … someone on another dimension in the ballroom, that will talk only to me and *only* if I am alone, and to ask for just a little time after the ball is over.'

'What time does it finish?' asked Trelawney.

'Midnight. It's a weekday, so people will have to get up for work and school the next day …. Yes, I think I can convince one or both ladies to indulge me, given the events of Saturday. But I'd have to see them in person.'

'As it relates to the case, *I* will ask them to see you, and I shall *take* you to The Grange. Just for a short visit. I'll bring you straight back.'

'Yes, it's better to talk to them there. Please ask them now, if you will. I'll get ready.'

Trelawney made the call.

'They wanted to come and see you' said Trelawney, as he drove Amanda towards the big house, 'but I convinced them it was better for you to drop in and then leave when you were tired. I told them I'd be chauffeuring you.'

'That makes a change,' Amanda said with a twinkle. He picked up the reference to their last case and grinned.

*****

'You see,' explained Amanda, as the four of them sat in the small salon, 'before Inspector Trelawney closes the case, he and I would just like to give me one last chance to see if there's anything, of a more mystical nature, that I might be able to pick up. Given that it's a ballroom, after a ball would be exactly the right atmosphere in which to see what I can sense. I'll just need 10 minutes after the last guest leaves.'

'Well, I'm not quite sure that I understand, Amanda, dear,' replied Miss de Havillande, 'but I don't see why we shouldn't allow it.' She turned to her companion. 'Do you, Gwendolen, dear?'

'I don't see why not. I'm sure Moffat and the helpers and staff could wait for such a short time, before clearing up. Or indeed, wait until the following morning. And think what a relief to bring the whole sad business to a close, knowing that we did our duty to make sure that there was no foul play, having thoroughly explored *every* avenue,' said Miss-Armstrong-Witworth ardently.

'Yes, you shall have your 10 minutes, Amanda,' confirmed Miss de Havillande. 'However, we shall set aside a chamber upstairs for you to rest, during the evening. You are not to exhaust yourself in our cause.'

'Thank you, Miss de Havillande, that is most kind of you.'

'Now run along home, Amanda. Inspector …?'

'Yes. Miss Cadabra, shall we go?'

In the car, Trelawney commented, 'So you decided not to mention *all* of the apparitions in the ballroom.'

'I thought it might unsettle them. After all, they'd have

to live with it, wouldn't they? And I didn't want to get into a long explanation, about recordings and all of the people from different time periods, and why the Frenchman would talk to me, and the boiler suit and so on.'

'I'm sure you are right.'

Trelawney delivered Amanda back to the sofa and Claire's tender care.

'Right,' declared Amanda to her friend. 'Project Regency Dress!'

Chapter 48

༄

THE BALL

'You're not the only one who can work magic!' Claire had said. She had been as good as her word. She had ordered a high-waisted, floor-length gown for Amanda that suited her and her purposes to a T.

'Can't I see a picture of it?'

'It's a surprise, darling! You'll love it. Best of all ... it's orange. Well, sort of.'

'Really?'

Thursday dawned, and Claire made sure that Amanda was well rested. She did Amanda's makeup, hot-rollered her hair, piled it up and let a few curls escape artlessly around her face.

Finally ... the gown. It was of gold chiffon over an under-dress of orange satin. The bodice was formed by two broad, beaded bands coming over the shoulders, forming short sleeves, then crossing into a V-neck and sweeping down diagonally and around her body to create a high waist. It struck just the right note between modern and period. Amanda stared at her reflection, open-mouthed.

'Why, Miss Cadabra! You're beautiful!' said Claire playfully. '*He* is going to be blown away.'

Amanda blushed. 'I assure you, the Inspec—'

'I meant your Frenchman, the apparition,' replied Claire innocently.

'Oh. Yes, well … I suppose that's the idea,' Amanda agreed.

* * * * *

Hogarth was glad to hear from Trelawney.

'It sounds like you are handling things well,' he said into the phone.

'You were right to advise me to speak to Miss Cadabra in person,' Trelawney replied.

'You're going to the ball.'

Trelawney, in spite of his own inclinations, replied hesitantly, 'I'm not sure if it's necessary. It's not exactly in the line of duty and Miss Ruggieri is taking care of Miss Cadabra, who can tell me the next day if she found out anything new.'

'It wasn't a question, my dear Thomas.'

'Oh. A directive. Then, of course, I shall attend. Come to think of it, I do want to see if Ryan Ford will turn up. I really don't understand why he wasn't involved in the action, on Saturday. If he has been spying for the Flamgoynes, you'd expect him to have made some effort to assist them on the day of the attack.'

'Do you know anything of what happened to him?'

'Miss Cadabra said that he was nowhere to be seen. It simply makes no sense. If he turns up at the ball, I'll get a chance to have a chat with him. On an informal basis.'

'Quite right. And you can't be part of the dancing scene up there without attending the socials. So do your duty, young man.'

Thomas chuckled.

'Yes, sir.'

* * * * *

Although the ball was from 8 o'clock, Claire did not bring Amanda until 9. The Grange ladies had reserved seats for them, so there was no need to come any earlier to ensure somewhere to sit.

Tempest consented to accompany them and, on arrival, regally ascended the staircase, in search of the alluring Natasha. This feline was Miss Armstrong-Witworth's Nevskaya Maskaradnaya, a cream, long-haired female with a light brown head and tail.

He had been attempting to court her, at intervals, for some time. She fascinated him, as much with her eyes of sapphire blue, as by alternate feigned acceptance of his tentative advances and … unmistakable rejections. He had once brought her a live mouse as a gift. Natasha had treated him to an icy stare and let the creature scamper off unharmed.

Tonight, Tempest considered he would have three hours in which woo her, before his carriage would be at the door. Natasha was looking forward to teasing him for three hours before *showing* him the door. He knew that. She knew that he knew. And he knew that she knew he knew. The outcome was to be seen ….

The ballroom was already filling up, the villagers wanting to make the most of the evening and the excellent and plentiful buffet. Although many of them had put in a working day, they had all made an effort to honour the occasion. The invitations had said 'black tie'.

'It encourages the gentlemen to do their best, you know,' Miss de Havillande had explained.

Penelope made sure that Thomas always had a dinner jacket in his wardrobe at her house, in case she needed to press him into service as her escort, at one of her work-related functions. Amanda spotted him talking to the Patels. She had seen him before in evening dress. Tonight, she thought, it suited him even better than last time. He was laughing. She rightly guessed that Karan was sharing a new coroner joke with him.

'There's Chris and Ashlyn looking divine,' commented Claire. 'And look at Iskender! I say, … we need to get our chaps out in evening dress more often, darling.'

'The ladies are looking very well, too,' Amanda remarked.

'Yes, I think young Ruth is, one day, going to surprise herself by turning into a swan. That will certainly come as no surprise to Kieran,' Claire observed shrewdly, affectionately regarding the pair with their heads together over an obscure volume of medieval history, which Jonathan had unearthed from the library's peculiar stacks for them.

Dr Patel came over with a glass of lemonade for Amanda and sat down beside her.

'Don't worry, I haven't come to fuss, my dear.'

'I'm much better, Doctor, really. And if I get tired, I will go and rest upstairs.'

'Good. The dancing is about to begin. Don't overdo it.'

However, Amanda had already planned to sit most of it out. Vanessa, as the village ballroom-Latin class teacher, had been asked to lead a half-hour taster of basic steps, so that everyone could join in the dancing if they wished. Amanda was happy to sit quietly and keep watch for the one person she was waiting for.

Claire was asked to dance, and Amanda was happy to be left in peaceful solitude. Trelawney took the opportunity to come over.

'Good evening, Miss Cadabra.'

'Good evening, Inspector.'

'May I say that your appearance this evening is such as must surely have the desired effect, later on.'

She twinkled up at him. 'You are too kind. Please, don't confuse me with Mata Hari, however.'

'An exotic dance would be surplus to requirements. Just be your charming self, and that will easily be enough,' he replied gallantly. Amanda invited him to sit down.

'No sign of Ryan yet, unless he's elsewhere in the house?'

'Not that I've seen,' agreed Trelawney. 'He may be intending to be fashionably late.'

'I didn't want to ask The Grange ladies if he had R.S.V.P.'d. That would look odd coming from me. But you could legitimately enquire. After all, you're practically cricketing buddies.'

'Not quite. Miss Cadabra. I have only been invited to try out at the nets for reserve.'

'Still. I think you'd get away with it.'

'Then, I shall. How are you? I suspect you are flagging a little.'

'Oh dear, am I looking jaded?'

'Not in the least, but you have had only a few days in which to recover.'

'Well, you're quite right. I shall go and rest soon.'

'I think it would be advisable.' He smiled. 'After all, I cannot have you collapsing on the job. You need to be fresh for action.'

She laughed. 'Yes, *sir*.'

It was hard to rest, and not to think about her one

chance, and perhaps a slim one at that, to try and get the goods out of the one witness to the chandelier incident. By the time Amanda returned to the ballroom at 11 o'clock, Ryan was in evidence, and Trelawney was in, apparently, relaxed and jovial conversation with him.

Everyone who was going to turn up was now present. From the members of the Home Guard, Amanda received knowing smiles, looks, handshakes, a brief touch on her shoulder or arm, a whispered 'thank you', She experienced a sense of connection with each one that she had never been able to have, had thought she never *would* have.

Trelawney came over with a fresh glass of lemonade for her and sat with her for a while.

'You look happy,' he noticed with pleasure.

'Oh, I am. Look at them all, all of these people, all of the people of whom I am the fondest, Joan, Jim, the Sharmas, the Patels, darling Claire, Sylvia, Mrs Pagely, Gwendolen, Miss de Havillande, Dennis, all of these and more who stood by me, on that day. And, best of all, who now know and accept the truth of what I really am: a witch. At last, I can have a freedom I never dreamed of having. With them, I can be myself for the first time. I think … yes, this is the best night of my life!'

'I'm glad for you, Miss Cadabra. I can hardly imagine what it's been like for you, hiding all these years.'

'In many ways, it had become second nature, and of course, from the majority of the villagers I still must keep up my guard, but now with these few, "these happy few", from now on it will be different.' Amanda turned to Trelawney. 'Any luck with Ryan?'

'Yes, we had a brief chat. I asked if his property was damaged during the storm. He said that it was just a few tiles blown off the roof, and it was a miracle, but he slept right through it. He said he must have been exhausted, from the last season and training too hard.'

'Really? .... Curious.'

'I'm inclined to agree.'

'What about John Bailey-Farrell?'

'He only arrived about fifteen minutes ago. I didn't want to appear to be ambushing him. But I think he's settled in now. I'll go and see if I can get him to talk about Saturday and if he corroborates Ryan's story. I will see you presently for a dance, I hope, Miss Cadabra.'

'You shall,' she promised him.

Vanessa and Bill MacNair, who was manager of the Asthma Centre up the road in Little Madley, had worked together to create a mixture of classical and modern music from various decades. Amanda was saving herself for a late waltz. The clock ticked on. She sat and tried to rehearse, in her mind, for the dozenth time, how the conversation with the Frenchman might go. He was really quite unpredictable.

Vanessa went over to the inspector and whispered something in his ear. He smiled and walked over to Amanda. Trelawney held out his hand, and the next song began.

'This is our dance, I believe,' he said.

Suddenly, paying attention to the music, she recognised the opening bars of the waltz version of *Roses of Picardy*. It had a special significance for them both. With a gleam, she took his hand and rose.

'Indeed, it is. I think you arranged this?'

'I did,' Trelawney readily confessed.

'Well, it was a most happy thought.'

The remaining minutes of the ball passed until midnight chimed. Many had already gone home. Trelawney took it upon himself, subtly, to encourage the stragglers out of the door, helping them to find coats or any property from which they had become temporarily separated. Finally, the staff, acting on orders, retired. Trelawney promised Claire to take Amanda home, and she had left. The Grange ladies had said goodnight and gone up to bed. Trelawney came back to the ballroom to find Amanda alone.

'All gone?' she asked.

'All gone. As you see, there's nothing left in the room for anyone to come back for.'

'Thank you.'

'Are you ready, Miss Cadabra?'

She stood up resolutely, and smoothed her gown.

'Yes.'

Chapter 49

༄

AFTER THE BALL

Amanda stood alone in the ballroom. The damaged piano had been removed to the large dining room for temporary storage and a hired one brought in. Unfortunately, Neeta had performed while Amanda had been resting so that she had missed it. Afterwards, the instrument had been wheeled to beside a wall, out of the way of the dancers. Last thing, Trelawney had solicited the aid of Ashlyn and Chris to move it back to underneath where the chandelier had hung.

She looked around to check that the setting was suited to her hoped-for interview with the Frenchman. There was the console table behind the door, and a piano in the crucial spot. Although chairs and tables were up against the far walls, with dishes and plates on them, it would, probably, still be sufficiently similar to the way the room had looked, on the day her distant kinsman had manifested himself to her.

Amanda patted her curls into place, straightened her dress on her shoulders and moved to near the piano.

'*M'sieur? Mi'lord?* Are you there?'

His manner of appearing reminded Amanda of the Cheshire Cat, but in reverse. His permanent ironic smile came into view first, then the rest of the head with its tied back hair, the white stand-up collar, snowy cravat, and waistcoat under an elegantly cut coat. He was tapping the lid of the piano with a well-manicured hand.

'*Bonsoir, mademoiselle.* I come, as you see, at your command.'

'Thank you, *m'sieur*'

'Have you enjoyed your ball?'

'I have,' she answered, surprised he had witnessed it. 'You were present?'

'I am present for whatever affords me amusement, *mademoiselle.*'

'That is fortunate, sir. I am hoping that you may have observed certain *other* occasions ....'

'Ah, you sound like the little French boy who was here ....'

'Er ... my brother, sir?'

'You must be twins. He is, no doubt, protective of his lovely sister.'

'Well, thank you for the compliment. I gathered that you understand that I — we ... are engaged in seeking the solution to a puzzle ... regarding the chandelier.'

'Yes, I told 'im, as you must surely be aware, the answer lies within this room.'

'I wonder if I might prevail upon you, *m'sieur*, to be a little more ... *explicit*?'

The Frenchman sighed. 'How far have you got?' he asked.

'The evidence that the chandelier fell, was clear from the body and the damage to the piano. The rope that secured it to the wall was frayed to the point where it gave way under the strain of the chandelier's weight. There was another occasion when the chandelier fell. Another man was seated in the same place. He was anxious, fearful. A child was hiding under the console table there. She came out from under it, stood staring at what had happed to the man at the piano, then, on hearing a voice calling "Dolly", she ran towards the French windows.'

'Your problem is,' he stated with exaggerated patience, 'that you are making an assumption.'

'Concerning?'

'The child.'

'That she is from the same time as the man at the piano, wearing evening dress?' queried Amanda.

'*Non, non*, in that you are correct.'

'Then what?'

'Repeat,' he instructed, 'if you please, what she did.'

'She came out from under the table and stared in astonishment at the fallen chandelier.'

'Ha!' cried the Frenchman.

'What?'

'Are you *sure*?' he asked, looking keenly at her.

'That she was astonished?'

'Not that. That is correct,' he confirmed, with a wave of his hand.

Amanda thought.

'She *wasn't* staring at the chandelier? At something else? But she was definitely looking in that direction. It was hard to tell; I can only see her from one angle.'

'Very well,' he said tolerantly. 'I will help you. Go and stand near the table. I will cause the recording to begin and then you, *mademoiselle*, follow carefully the line of her gaze.'

Amanda hurried into place.

The Frenchman raised his hands as though to conduct an orchestra.

'Commence!' he uttered. At once, the little girl appeared,

came out from her hiding place and stood up. Amanda knelt beside her, looked carefully at the child's eyes and positioned her face parallel to the little one's. Amanda took a quick indrawn breath.

Once the recording ended, she stood up, pointing.

'She wasn't looking *at* the piano. She was looking *past* it!'

'*Très bien*,' approved the Frenchman.

'Yes ... oh, how could I have been so slow! It's obvious. I've seen this before. Why didn't it occur to me? I suppose because it all looks so much more. It wasn't the chandelier's fall onto the man and the piano that made her so surprised. It was what *else* she saw, *who* else she saw.'

The Frenchman applauded. Amanda looked at him.

'It was murder. She saw who did it and how! But ... how does that link to what happened here recently? .... Unless .... ahhh! Thank you, m'sieur.'

'Not at all, *mademoiselle*. I believe I have now given you all of the assistance you require, for you and the so charming inspector to advance your case. With your permission, I shall leave you now.'

'Yes, yes, of course. Thank you again.'

'One more thing, *mademoiselle*.' He gave her a glinting smile. 'You look so much better in a gown.' With that, he melted into the ether.

Amanda chuckled and shook her head. She should have known better than to think she could deceive him. She hurried into the hall, and, seeing it empty, opened the door to the small salon. Trelawney was waiting for her. He looked up at her entrance with a question in his eyes.

She nodded excitedly. 'I have more information.' She sat down and related all that had passed in the ballroom. At the end of her narrative, Trelawney asked,

'So, what was it that the child was looking at in such

astonishment, that you feel you should have realised, Miss Cadabra?'

'Ah. Well. Yes … now I come to a more difficult part … something I didn't tell you ….'

'About?' he asked her, gently.

'About another house … one that you have visited … that I have worked in … that had … the same thing that this house has ….'

'Please, do go on. I promise that the wrath of the law will not descend upon you. This is strictly off the record.'

'Well, … the ballroom has a panel, that is, a hidden door. On the left of the fireplace. You wouldn't know, because the mirrors and paintings look like just framed decorations within larger frames, which are made from beading to look like big panels. Only, one of those framed paintings is, in fact, a door to a space within. I am certain that what the little girl saw was that hidden door opening. I think she recognised the person who cut, or just released, the rope that dropped the chandelier onto the piano-playing man. That's what so astonished her. It would be like a magic door, but someone she knew was coming out of it. A meeting between the real and magical worlds, you see?'

'I do. Er, this other house, you mentioned. I believe I know the one to which you are referring. Is it possible that you would like to share some more details concerning that hidden door?'

'Not at this juncture, Inspector,' Amanda replied, thinking, or at any other!

'Very well.'

'But getting back to the panel in the ballroom,' she then went on, 'what if that child is still alive? She was a witness to that murder back then. What if someone connected with that event wanted to silence her, using the same device? But instead of *her* being at the piano, it was Mr Honeywell. And what if the child was Miss de Havillande? Wouldn't that mean that her life is in danger? That person might try again.'

'That's quite a theory, Miss Cadabra .... There's something else *I* should tell *you*. I have been given permission to share this information with you.'

In spite of fatigue, Amanda was all attention.

'Oh, please do,' she urged him.

'We made enquires and located Mr Spinnetti, at a convalescent home in Bournemouth. He confirmed that his friend, Melius Honeywell, had kindly offered, by telephone, to take over his piano-tuning visits until Mr Spinnetti was recovered. He was unable to supply us with a photograph of Mr Honeywell, but the description seemed to match. He was able to give us a telephone number, however, and a general address, through which we located Honeywell's well-appointed ground-floor flat in Islington. Fortunately, there is a family living next door, blessed with a creative 10-year-old daughter who had just acquired her first mobile phone ....'

'I have the feeling that this narrative is about to take a most interesting turn.'

'Would you be more comfortable back at your cottage, Miss Cadabra?' Trelawney asked solicitously.

'I certainly would, Inspector, but you can't stop now! A 10-year-old-daughter with a new phone ...?'

'Eager to try out its various features, she took some impromptu photographs, including some covertly captured images of Mr Honeywell in his garden.'

'Aha!'

'When we showed these to Miss de Havillande, she insisted that this was *not* the man who had come to tune the piano. A visit to the morgue confirmed the very same.'

'So? Who was the man who was killed? And, what happened to the real Mr Honeywell? I hope he has not been discovered poisoned and stashed in a trunk bound for Timbuktu.'

'While your breadth of imagination does you credit, Miss Cadabra, I am happy to report that Honeywell met with no such fate. Two days ago, the neighbour reported that he had returned to his flat.'

'From where?' asked Amanda eagerly.

'It transpired that he had received a letter notifying him that, when he had purchased a particular item, he had automatically been entered into a competition and had won. The prize was a four-week, all-expenses-paid stay at the Hotel Remota in Chile, remarkable not only for the luxuriousness of the accommodations and beauty of the surroundings but for the complete absence of communication with the outside world.'

'I say! So we have a case of identity theft.'

'We do,' Trelawney confirmed.

'But by whom and to what end?'

'That is, as yet, unclear.'

'Maybe, the pretend Mr Honeywell was in fear of his life, like the 1930s man, and had stolen the real Mr Honeywell's identity in order to hide?'

'But how does that involve the hidden door? Your Frenchman seemed to think that it was of primary importance.'

'Ye-es,' Amanda agreed thoughtfully. 'What *if* ... the pretend Honeywell was the assassin bent on silencing Miss de Havillande? But someone from his shady world got to him first?'

'Someone who doesn't want her silenced, you mean? Who maybe wants her to testify ... or just wants her alive as insurance? It's possible. Well, members of my team are working through the available databases, seeking a match to the man in the morgue. Currently, as we think that he was the intended target, there is no threat to Miss de Havillande.'

'Have you said anything to her about any of this?'

'No, I would not wish to alarm her unnecessarily. Well ... I don't think we can make any more progress tonight. It's late, and I think I must take you home now, or I shall have Miss Ruggieri telling me off for exhausting you.'

'Yes. Thank you, Inspector. And thank you for telling me about Mr Honeywell. This has all been immensely exciting.'

They returned to the hall, and Trelawney went off to get their coats. At that moment, perfectly timed, Tempest descended the staircase with imperial dignity.

'Oh, hello,' said Amanda cheerily. 'Been upstairs visiting Natasha, have you? So how did it go?'

Tempest looked up and glared stonily at her, then, turning his shoulder, walked toward the door in a manner redolent of,

'Don't. Ask. Just *don't* ... ask.'

Chapter 50

❧

THE HARDEST TASK

Claire had waited for Amanda's return. Seeing Trelawney's car draw up to drop her off, she came to help Amanda 'decompress', as she put it, and get to bed. Soon, curled up in pyjamas, dressing gown and with a gin and tonic in her hand, she told Claire about the Frenchman, although she had to keep the Honeywell matter to herself.

'Fascinating!' exclaimed Claire. 'My head will be buzzing, but you had better turn in soon.'

'Why?' asked Amanda, thinking she could easily sleep in the next day.

'Because … from tomorrow …,' Claire said gently, 'they're going to start coming.'

'Who?'

'Everyone … the members of the Home Guard.'

'Well, that's very kind.'

'It's not just that they want to see that you're getting better and to thank you for what you did,' Claire explained slowly, 'but to ask you to do something.'

'Oh?'

'Something that you're not going to want to do, but that they need you to do for them.'

Amanda looked at her, troubled.

'You see,' Claire began, 'we semi-magical folk — and our supporters — our secrecy, privacy, safety, has always depended on our not knowing about each other and what our gifts could be. That was why it was so hard for Ryan to gain any information.'

'You know about Ryan?' asked Amanda in surprise.

'Yes. Viola warned me.'

'Just you?'

'I live next door to The Witch. I get special privileges.'

Amanda grinned. 'It is also my privilege to have my dear friend right next door.'

'Thank you, darling. But to carry on …. Our secrecy and so on depends on not knowing, and, because Viola gathered us for the defence of the village, we do now all know about all of one another and you …. And we don't want that to continue ….'

'And so?' asked Amanda, uncertainly.

'We need you to place a forgetting spell on each of us. We need you to reset us to the level of knowledge we had, before we signed up for the Home Guard.'

'But … surely not you too, Claire?'

'Me too, Ammy.'

'But ... but, I'll be alone again,' protested Amanda

'You've never been alone. You've had us all watching over you, ever since you were brought here as a baby. Well, not *me*, of course, but people like The Grange folk, and Mrs Uberhausfest and Old Mr Jackson who had this house before me, and the Sharmas, Patels, Gordon French, Sylvia, you name them. You don't need to be known as magical, to be loved,

Ammy. Besides which, if you are meant to know who it is, then you'll still have Viola, just like we all do.'

Amanda was stunned. Last night had meant so much to her. She had been surrounded by people who were, in some way, like her, and knew and accepted her for the witch she was .... But she loved them, she had loved them before she knew and they knew, and she would love still them when they ceased to know.

She nodded resignedly but resolutely. 'Of course. I'll have to ask Granny to help me with the precise wording of the spells. That's not a skill I possess. All right, Claire. Please, tell them to give me until lunchtime. Then I'll be ready.'

'Good. Thank you, Ammy, darling.'

'Just one thing. Could you be one of the last, please?'

'Of course, love.'

'Claire.'

'Yes?'

'They do all still want to remember that there are spirits of the orchard, don't they?

'Of course. After all, it's public knowledge. It's all right there in the song:

> *Our foes will ever flee in fear*
> *When Ap-pel spirits do appear ...*"'

Amanda finished,

> *'"To lend a hand and find a way*
> *To save us as they did that day."*

And so they did. They bought us time without which .... Yes. They saved us.'

Amanda slept the sleep of the exhausted. Claire made her a late brunch, and she got up, showered and dressed.

'I need to consult Granny about this spell,' she said.

'I'll be home next door, if you need me, darling,' said Claire, kissing her cheek. And off she went.

Granny and Grandpa appeared at their granddaughter's call.

'Now Ammy, dear, you are not to get all maudlin and melancholy about this,' Senara told her bracingly. 'This is just one of the services that a witch can be called upon to perform, regardless of her own preferences in the matter. You must simply stiffen the sinews and cast the spells to the best of your ability.'

'Yes, Granny,' replied Amanda, seeing the good sense in this and feeling stouter of heart.

'Now … you had better write this down. It's going to be complicated.'

Grandpa contributed suggestions and, after an hour, the spell was woven, and Amanda prepared.

The villagers decided to give Amanda a little more recovery time. Consequently, she had an interval, after Granny and Grandpa had gone off 'to a luncheon party', for reflection.

She tactfully kept off the subject of Tempest's lack of romantic progress the previous evening, as she stroked her familiar, who was slumped across her lap, indicating that he was utterly drained.

'You know, Tempest, I should go and do something nice for the Appel Spirits. I wonder what they would like? Hm. I expect something will occur to me.'

Dressed and ready, but with no visitors, she became restless. Amanda was used to being able to potter. She rarely had to spend so much time on the sofa, and she was getting bored with what she regarded as accomplishing nothing. She started to notice outstanding jobs. Aimlessly, Amanda wandered into the hall. There she spotted the table to the right of the front door, piled high with post. This consisted of flyers and letters that had not been deemed sufficiently important to make it to the dining room or desk for processing, but neither of adequate junk-worthiness to be put straight into the recycling bin.

Here was a sitting-down task that she could legitimately undertake. Amanda bundled everything from the surface of the hall table onto a tray and took it back to the sofa.

And that was when she found it.

Hugh was one of the Huf-Haus team that had come from Germany to build the new Asthma Centre, only last year. He had turned out to be a kindred spirit in more than one way. They had felt a deep connection and it might have become something more. But he had had to go back, and she had had to stay, and they had agreed to be friends. After his return to his homeland, Hugh had sent a gift to Amanda that had arrived at a busy moment and been left on the hall table. Soon, it had become buried under post, leaflets and might-be-interesting and must-look-at-that-sometime.

And now here it was, rediscovered. Whatever could it be? She tried to guess by feel, like she had always done with Christmas and birthday presents. A rectangular ... box, maybe? Perhaps chocolates? That would be nice.

'I just hope that they haven't gone off,' she remarked to Tempest.

Finally, she opened the parcel, then the box inside. There, lying on a black velvet cushion ... was a wooden set of panpipes. With it was a card that just said,

Dear Amanda, take this for a walk. Your friend, Hugh

A walk? Where? She remembered that they had walked in the orchard. Yes, that had been a very ... illuminating walk. She'd strolled there since, and had never had the same experience as when she'd been there with Hugh. However, even though the old orchard was right next door, she wasn't quite up to a walk today.

Instead, Amanda began playing with the flute, the rest of the paperwork set aside. For some reason, the tune in her head was the Appel Song. After some experimenting and consulting the how-to-play-your-flute guide that was thoughtfully included, she managed the first few notes.

Suddenly, she remembered remorsefully that she had never thanked Hugh! His family were woodcarvers, and he must have made this himself! Great skies above! Amanda hastily got out her laptop and sent him a Facebook message, a text message and an email.

She soon received a jovial text in reply. Hugh was amused at her remorse and reassured her that he had known all along she would get round to it one day.

Have you taken it for a walk yet?
Not yet, I'm recuperating after a bit of overexertion. I will try tomorrow
Let me know how it goes

That last was followed by a laughing emoji.

Smiling, Amanda put the phone aside. And the doorbell rang. The Home Guard had begun presenting itself for demob.

Over the next two days, Amanda slept, ate and cast. After the first couple of times, seeing that forgetting what had past didn't really affect the villagers that much, she felt better about helping them, in the way that they wanted. And some had things they wanted to say, while they still remembered. One or two, in particular, were especially enlightening ....

Chapter 51

∾

JOAN AND JIM

Joan and Jim came into the cottage, fresh-faced from the February chill.

'How are you, love?'

'Much better, thank you.'

'You looked proper gorgeous at the ball.'

'Ah, thank you, Joan.'

'I know you don't like me sayin' this, what with the professional relationship you both keep remindin' us all of, *but* … you and the inspector made a lovely picture, waltzing away together like you was born to be partners.'

'Oh, you did, dear!' exclaimed Jim. 'We *all*-thought so. Every single one of us!'

'Well, thank you both,' said Amanda politely. She had to admit to herself how comfortable and natural it had felt, dancing that waltz with the inspector again. Of course, she didn't have to admit that to anyone else, especially her present company.

'Now,' commenced Joan, 'you know why we're here.'

'We'd like our forgetting spell, please,' requested Jim.

'Oh, but first,' insisted Joan, 'I expect you'd like to know about Ryan Ford. Viola tipped me off about him. Thought I was the resourceful type.'

'Oh she is, aren't you, my girl?' agreed Jim, giving her a wink.

'Never you mind about that now, Jim. Let me tell Amanda what she needs to know. So ... naturally, I 'ad an excuse to visit the house, being the post lady an' all. Now it so happens that the one drink Ryan cannot resist —'

'Joan found out from John. Bailey-Farrell, that is,' interjected Jim.

'— is Hobb's Cure Kiwano and Custard Apple Cordial. Ryan had it once in Zimbabwe when he was playing cricket there. Elixir of the Gods, John says 'e calls it. Of course, we couldn't get any quickly. So ... Jim made it!'

'Got the fruit from the Indian greengrocer's down south of here,' Jim elucidated, 'put it in the juicer, added some soda water, and Bob's your uncle.'

'We used an old glass bottle, printed a label and there you were! Knew he wouldn't be able to resist. I put it an envelope, stamped and so on with 'is name and address, made it look like it was from a female fan.'

Amanda was intensely curious to see where this story was going to go.

'First though,' commented Jim, 'my Joanie puts in a little ingredient of her own.' They looked at each other gleefully.

'It so happened,' continued his wife, 'that I 'ad a couple of sleeping pills, Adazypam, that I had left over from when I 'ad my bit o' back trouble. Well, I 'ad to calculate, because it's not like in the films, where you slip someone a Mickey Finn and, the next thing you know, as they're out cold. Takes about an hour and half for them to kick in proper, you know. So I reckoned the fair's main event starting time, and how long for the village to clear.'

'So what time did you deliver it?'

'About quarter past one. John's there, being in on the "surprise", and encourages him to open it. Ryan has a nice big glassful, John and I have a little bit, except mine goes in the cheeseplant — in the ironic colander, hanging in its macramé holder, if you please. I'm not judging. — And it was done. John goes off to the fair a bit drowsy. Oh, e's a lovely lad. If I didn't 'av my Jim 'ere ...! Anyway, there you go, my lovely.'

'Well! That's remarkable. How ingenious of you both!' She reached a hand out to each of them. 'Thank you Joan, Jim, thank you both so very much.'

'Our pleasure. Glad we could do our bit. Now, p'raps you'll do yours for us, love.'

'You really want to forget?' Amanda asked, doubtfully

'We do,' they said in unison.

The spell took time to cast, but it worked quickly, leaving them with only a slightly dazed look.

'Well, thank you both very much for coming to see how I am,' said Amanda. 'As you can see, I'm on the mend.'

'Yes, well, that's good,' replied Joan. 'Er ... has that nice John been over, yet, with some flowers? That Dale, the new florist, said he'd been into the shop and bought some.'

'Yes, he did drop in before the ball. He brought chocolates and grapes too.'

'Hm, well, I do hope as you're not taking that too seriously,' cautioned Jim.

'I wasn't, but why?' asked Amanda.

'Well ...' contributed Joan, portentously, 'I think I can guess what it's all in aid of.'

'Well, good,' Amanda responded, 'because it makes no sense why such a paragon is dancing attendance on me.'

'Ahhh. You haven't seen the article in *Hey There*

Magazine then?'

'No ....'

'I'll drop it into you, love.'

Amanda smiled in anticipation. 'Thank you, Joan. I can't wait.'

'Well, you take care of yourself,' said Joan giving her a hug.

'And thank you, so very much, Jim,' Amanda added, 'for the apple pies you brought.'

'Don't you eat them all at once,' he told her with a grin.

'I won't.'

'Bye, love.'

One by one, or two by two, the Sunken Madley defenders came for their forgetting spells. And still the identity of Viola was unknown to Amanda. Maybe that person would come after the last forgetting spell had been cast, she speculated.

Later, when Claire was heating up pudding in the kitchen, the sound of post falling onto the doormat was heard. Amanda hurried into the hall. There it was: Joan's promised copy of the practically all-photographs *Hey There Magazine*.

From the kitchen, Claire, spooning cream onto steaming slices of apple pie, heard a giggle ... then another ... then laughter breaking out. She hastened in with the tray, smiling at her friend's mirth.

'What? Come on, Ammy, what's the joke?'

'It's all in here. An interview with John Bailey-Farrell. Actual text nestled in amongst the photographs of him and his recent ex-girlfriend, and the one before that.'

'Well?' asked Claire, serving out the pudding.

'The last-but-one romantic engagement was the daughter of some multi-billionaire. Here's a photo of her strutting her diamond-heeled stuff. And the last one was the film starlet ... right?'

'I know.'

'Well, according to this bit here — an interview with John's mother — they were both extremely demanding and above themselves and so his mother told him ... for his next girlfriend he should seek out ... wait for it ... a simple village girl!'

Claire cracked into merriment.

'Oh Ammy, and you couldn't be further from that if you tried! Oh, poor misguided man. You'll have to let him down gently!'

Chapter 52

༄

AN AFTERNOON OUT

Trelawney dropped in to see if Amanda fancied a drive out to Paddington Station, Heathrow and a stop-off along the way. Her 'Uncle Mike' was going to Spain to see his sister for the weekend. It was time for a de-briefing.

At the station, Hogarth climbed into the back passenger sear of Trelawney's car and was greeted warmly.

'Thank you for the ride, friends. Let's save the real chat until we're settled with coffee. Amanda, how are you?'

'Better every day, thank you, Uncle Mike. Tell us what you have planned for your weekend break.'

For the next forty minutes, as they drove west out of London and joined the M4 to Heathrow airport, Hogarth extolled the virtues of Spanish cuisine, in general, and his brother-in-law Harry's, in particular.

'Did I tell you, Amanda, that my sister and her husband produce cookery books?'

'Really? What fun!'

'Indeed. I think you'd like Vera and Harry.'

She turned around in her seat and smiled at Mike.

'I'm sure I would. Do they ever visit the UK?'

'Only occasionally. But you'd be welcome to come out there, you know.'

'But they've never even met me.'

'I've told them about you. I mean it. You have a standing invitation. If you want to recuperate …'

Amanda suddenly thought of it: Spain, warmer climate, delicious food, kind people but ….

Mike was still speaking '… among people who know that you're the W-word and relish that.'

'In that case, … it does sound very attractive.'

'Ask your grandparents and Amelia,' he suggested. 'This is us, Thomas, these services here.'

Trelawney turned off the highway onto the slip road, and into the notorious Heston services. However, it was, at least, anonymous, and they found privacy at a vacant plastic table, with cups of tea, coffee and hot chocolate.

'First things first,' declared Hogarth. 'A match was found, thanks to our friends at Interpol, for the photograph of the pseudo-Melius Honeywell.'

'Oo and who was he actually?' asked Amanda, excitedly.

'He was a mercenary who disappeared at the beginning of the 90s. Trying to discover his true identity has been a challenging task, like peeling away the layers of a giant onion. The best so far has been the name Lucas Peterson, born either in The Balkans or Slough. The Foreign Office favours the latter.'

'What? Slough, up the road from here?'

'Yes, someone in the department described it as "like the Balkans only without the nice scenery and interesting architecture". But I digress. Peterson, as we shall call him, for I doubt it was his real name, was hired to remove the one witness to an assassination that took place at The Grange in the early 1930s'

'Aha! Now we come to it,' Amanda exclaimed.

'During the 1930s, the de Havillandes played host to several notables, including some from overseas, as well as fellow countrymen. Unfortunately, one of them was spying for the Russians. Someone working for British intelligence was ordered to deal with the matter. He had inside knowledge of the house including, as Amanda has told you, Thomas, a space behind a panel in the ballroom with a hidden door. From there, he came out and dropped the chandelier onto the spy. However, as he retired to his hiding place, he caught sight of a little child. Reporting back, it was decided that, given the infancy of the witness, it was unlikely that she either understood or would later recall what she had witnessed, and the matter was filed away.

'So far, so good,' said Amanda.

'However, the British agent later defected, taking his knowledge of the incident with him. Later, he recanted and was brought in, and as he had significant information about the Russians to offer, all was forgiven.'

Mike paused for a sip of coffee and then continued,

'Fast forward, if you will, to many years later. The Russian spy, who had met his end under the chandelier, before passing into the great beyond, had fathered a son and daughter. They and their children have become something of a dynasty in the politics of a certain country. Now, those responsible for the reputation and security of this dynasty, took it upon themselves to attempt to eradicate the one witness to their founder's unfriendly act towards a foreign power. Of course, we are all pals together now, and such a scandal as having been a spy against the Brits would not be in the cause of either the dynasty in question nor international relations. Consequently, Lucas Peterson was tempted out of hiding, having no track record for the past 30 years, and charged with the removal of Miss de Havillande. While, that is, masquerading as the substitute piano tuner.'

'So who got to him first?' asked Trelawney.

'Lucas Peterson had been in hiding for 30 years with good reason. He had made a great many enemies. One, in particular, Mollo Tovarich, had taken a particular hit job by Mr Peterson extremely personally. It came to his ears that the aforementioned Peterson was not, as had been assumed, dead, but very much alive and active on an assignment in Sunken Madley. Thanks to the British agent's defection, Tovarich was able to access the report on The Grange assassination, including the plans of the house, and dispatch his enemy before Peterson could dispatch Miss de Havillande. Of course, the recent incident of the chandelier has brought all of the this to light — if you'll excuse the pun — and, naturally, the British would have warned the power in question that if any harm should, in the future, come to Miss de Havillande, the truth about their political dynasty's forebear will be made public and everyone very uncomfortable,' Hogarth finished with a flourish of the hand.

Amanda almost applauded. 'My word!'

'So, thanks to the efforts of both of you,' Hogarth commended them, 'the matter is now dealt with and at rest. You may close the case, Thomas, with the official story being that the chandelier fell by regrettable accident.'

'So-o-o-o,' Amanda deliberated, 'the little girl was astonished because the door opened in the wall. That was it? Because there was a door where she wasn't expecting one. And a person came out of it?'

'It would be reasonable to assume,' answered Mike.

'Hmm … I suppose so.'

'Thank you, Mike,' said Trelawney. 'Well, I'll wrap things up, then, in Sunken Madley.'

'You'll still be visiting on Saturdays for the classes though. We still don't know what Ryan's role or allegiance is, and we need to find out,' Hogarth added, as a rider.

'Of course. Understood.'

'You may like to know the latest news on the Flamgoynes. The verdict has been returned of Death By Misadventure, in that those who perished appear to have willingly pursued the path of a dangerous storm, thereby subjecting themselves to the risk of lightning strike, and impact with objects struck or displaced by high winds.'

'Good,' said Amanda, relieved.

'Indeed. So, Thomas, tell us how your father got the evidence out of Flamgoyne.'

'I was able to get him to tell me only this much: that he made Pasco a promise. And Pasco let him leave with the goods.'

'Hmm,' replied Hogarth. 'Do you have any idea what the nature of that promise might have been?'

'Not really. He was hardly in a position to grant Pasco amnesty or a bolthole, at that moment. In fact, given the odds, he had every reason to believe that the Flamgoynes, at least some of them, would return .... Why? Have you some idea, of what that promise was, Mike?'

'Possibly. I have spoken with your father, Thomas, and he has given me leave to tell you this much: at present, the Flamgoyne solicitor is going over Lady Flamgoyne's papers, but she does appear to make her wishes clear, in her will, as to the disposal of her estate, in the event of her death. The estate cannot go to anyone not of sound mind, comatose, nor to a vassal, nor to anyone not presenting themselves at the reading of the will.'

'When is that?'

'Tomorrow. Now, given that every Flamgoyne is either deceased, fled or falling into one of the other categories, there is only one viable legatee.'

'Which is?'

'Kytto Trelawney.'

'*What?* My father is to become Lord Flamgoyne? I don't believe it,' insisted Thomas quietly but hotly.

'Of course not, lad. He stated he is Trelawney and will remain so. And as for the title, he would waive it. Claims it's honorary anyway "and a lot of nonsense." He sounded remarkably like you, in fact,' remarked Hogarth with amusement.

Thomas grinned. His friend continued,

'Of course, that would mean that you would be heir to Flamgoyne, just as Amanda here is heir to Cardiubarn Hall.' Hogarth leaned back in his chair, crossed his arms, and commented with a smile he was taking no pains to suppress, 'Now isn't that an entertaining thought, children?'

That drew a chuckle from Amanda and Thomas joined in, then asked,

'What would my father do with the estate? Did he say?'

'He's going to hang fire on any decision until A, the bequest is definite, and B, the Cardiubarn case is solved, and Amanda inherits. He seemed to think you could put your heads together, and come up with a rather nice plan for, at least, some of the land. The other thing he would do, he said, is to keep his promise to Pasco.'

'Ah. To remain in service at Flamgoyne?'

'Better than that: to manage it, not as vassal but as a free man, waged and charged only with that which in good conscious he would do.'

'Do you really believe Pasco would be loyal to my father?'

'The point is that your father believes it.'

'Phew! Well! This *is* news,' said Thomas, leaning more heavily on the table.

'And … Kytto's pronouncement about what he would do if he inherits brings us to the next step for you two.' Amanda and Trelawney looked at Hogarth suspiciously. 'The last piece of the puzzle of the Cardiubarn case. What do we know so far? Come on ….'

'Granny planned to bump them off, literally,' Amanda began, 'by arranging for an icy patch to be on the road. But they were already dead before they went over the cliff, because Gronetta, and probably her son, sent out poison-pen letters, spell-timed to disintegrate in the van and gas them all. That's what happened and why the van spun out of control on the bend and went down onto the rocks.'

'Good,' said Hogarth. 'What we don't know …'

'… is how the Flamgoynes,' Thomas took up the thread, 'knew about the van journey, and arranged for the charmed letters, rather than ordinary ones, to be sent out.'

'In other words,' added Amanda,' what we don't yet know is the identity of the missing link.'

'And finding it is your next task,' Hogarth instructed them. 'The final one that will conclude and finally close this case.'

'Then it will be all over! Everything,' said Amanda with relief. But Hogarth halted her mid-sigh.

'Far from it, my dear. In fact, … everything is just beginning.'

Amanda shook her head in bewilderment, 'I don't understand, Uncle Mike.'

'No need to at the moment. One thing at a time, both of you.'

'*What* is beginning?' Thomas pressed. 'Do you mean that, before, at least the Flamgoynes were concentrated in one place, and now they are scattered, underground, could be anywhere, could emerge at any time?'

'That is certainly part of it. And since you insist on knowing more than I think is helpful to you right now, I will say this much: your *real* work has yet to commence. So make the most of your downtime, a few days at least before you go in search of your missing link.'

'I expect it's in Cornwall,' Amanda speculated confidently. 'It's always entirely about Cornwall.'

Hogarth regarded her keenly and put down the cup that he was about to raise to his lips. He glanced from her to Thomas and back.

'Is *that* what you both think? That it's always been entirely about *Cornwall*?'

Amanda and Thomas looked at one another and then back at Hogarth.

'Yes,' she affirmed.

'Of course,' agreed Thomas.

'Oh no, my dears,' Hogarth responded slowly. 'I thought you both understood. This has never been *entirely* about Cornwall.'

They looked at him, frowning in confusion.

Hogarth shook his head. 'No …. It has always been, even more so, about, … Sunken Madley ….'

Chapter 53

DOUBT, AND A CHANCE FOR THOMAS

Amanda wasn't sure how to broach the subject. After all, Uncle Mike was the inspector's best friend, and she didn't want to sound like, well ... she was calling his integrity into question, because she wasn't. She just wasn't sure how reliable Uncle Mike's information was.

She glanced speculatively at Trelawney's profile, as he drove them back down the M4 towards London. Checking his rear-view mirror, he caught sight of her looking at him.

'Is everything all right, Miss Cadabra?' he asked, sympathetically. 'Are you feeling drained after that?'

'No, well, a little perhaps, but ... I was thinking ... that is, I wanted to ask you something.'

'Anything. Go ahead.'

'Well, what did you make of that story Uncle Mike told us, about the assassin and the Russians, and all that?'

'What do you mean, Miss Cadabra? In what respect?'

'Didn't it all sound rather ... convoluted to you?'

'History, particularly political history, very often is, as I'm sure you know,' Trelawney said mildly.

'Yes,' she agreed slowly. 'Do you think Uncle Mike has been reliably informed?'

'Why would he not be?'

On impulse, she asked him, 'What does your intuition tell you, Inspector, about all that business with the chandelier and the assassinations?'

'My intuition, Miss Cadabra, says to let sleeping dogs lie, make out my report with the official line of an accident, clear out of The Grange and go back, until Saturday, of course, to Cornwall. Where, incidentally, I hope to have dinner with my father and see if he'll tell me more about what happened at Flamgoyne, after I left. If I'm lucky, he'll make me his shepherd's pie.'

He had clearly signalled end-of-subject.

Accepting his decision, she asked, 'Is that your favourite, Inspector?'

'It is. My father makes it especially well.'

* * * * *

No luck was needed, regarding the shepherd's pie. Kytto enjoyed both his son's company and cooking for him.

By the following evening, Trelawney had written his report, removed himself from the small salon, collected his gear from his mother's house and was back in Cornwall, now at the dining table with his father.

'What happened after I left?' he asked, tucking into the luscious minced meat and mashed potatoes, with the cheese crust he relished.

'Pass the salt, please …. Thanks, Thomas. Well, …

Pasco and I sat down. He knew where the family had gone and why. I told him there was a good chance that they would be defeated.'

'Is that what you believed, Dad?'

'It was what I *hoped*. And yes, I did think the village was in with a chance.'

'Based on?'

'Based on Pasco's patent fear. And I knew it was not just of his Flamgoyne mistress and masters, but of what would befall him if they were destroyed.'

'Mike said something about how you got him to hand over the evidence?'

'Yes, I believe, deep down, he's a good man. Oh, I know he's a Flamgoyne, but I believe what your aunt says: no child is born evil. Your Great-uncle Elwen was a good person, and look at Amelia. So I promised him oversight of Flamgoyne, if I should inherit it. I think he'd be loyal to us, and no one knows the house and land better.'

'So *will* you inherit?'

Kyt laughed. 'I was the only one who turned up for the reading of the will! There was the standard proviso about surviving the testator for 30 days, so if I can do that, yes, I'll get it, more's the pity.'

'You don't want it?'

'Oh, the maintenance demands of a place like that! I'd hand it over to The National Trust if the place weren't so poisoned. It's going to take a lot of magical clearing and cleansing. I'm not even sure it could ever be done. Probably, the only cure would be to burn the place to the ground, and rebuild, or let the sheep have the land.'

'You could be right. And as long as Flamgoyne stands, any survivors will surely want it back,' Thomas added.

'Well, that's all for the future. The point is the day was won for Sunken Madley, we got the paper and ink out, and that evidence is with Mike now, I assume. So all's well that ends well.'

'The Wicc'lord must have helped to that end,' said Thomas, thoughtfully.

'I have no doubt. But how is another question. Always from behind the scenes,' responded Kyt.

'So she, or he, will not have been at the defence of the village?'

'Hard to say. They might have been, since everyone would be expecting them *not* to be,' Kyt speculated, getting up to fetch more peas from the kitchen.

'But if it was someone who *wasn't* there ... Dad ... it isn't *you*, is it?'

That drew a laugh from Kyt. 'Son, if it was, would you really expect me to tell you?' With that, his phone rang, 'Excuse me while I answer this ....'

Thomas heard his father's voice in the kitchen, over the sound of dishing the extra vegetables into a bowl.

'Yes .... oh, I'm sorry to hear that .... She's going to be all right? .... I quite understand .... Oh yes, the insurance will cover it ... of course .... You're always welcome ... Yes, wish your wife "get well soon" from me .... Thank you for letting me know .... All the best .... Goodbye.'

Kyt returned to the dining room.

'More peas, son?'

'Please.'

'That was a cancellation. One of the regular guests. The wife had to go into hospital for an appendix op. She's fine, but will need to rest on the ward and at home.'

'Ah,' said Thomas, spooning petits pois onto his plate, 'I expect these things happen.'

'Yes,' he father responded. 'The thing is, son ... the cottage they booked will now be empty tomorrow. ... it's *Marram*.'

Into the silence, Thomas was finally able to drop,

'Ah ... the cottage you said you took me to ... to see the spell-weaver who removed my divination and the memory of ...?'

'That's the one. The one where, I'm confident, ... you will remember.' Thomas was silent. 'It's up to you, son. If you're ready, tomorrow we can go there together.'

Part of him wanted Miss Cadabra's forgetting spell for all the mystical business he'd been involved with in the past few months. But he'd come too far, knew too much: too much about the magical reality that was present in, what he'd so fondly thought of as, 'the real world'. No, there was no going back. The only way forward now was through the past.

Thomas looked up at his father ... and nodded.

Chapter 54

❧

MARRAM

The following day, Kyt drove them to the nearby village of Sandgate. Thomas knew the road. Until he went to university, and even then still in the holidays, he'd been to all of the cottages, helping his father with maintenance. Mrs Polsbarkle, from his father's village, had always seen to the cleaning, hiring whatever seasonal help she needed. However, repairs and improvements were taken care of by the Trelawneys. It was years now, though, since Thomas had been to

Marram. It was named after the grass that held together the sand dunes, just down a gentle slope from the cottage to the beach and the sea.

They got out of the car. The sky was overcast, and the wind from the Channel was fresh. The first thing that was familiar was the sound, the sound of the water and wind singing in a hollow rock, along the shore to the left.

It was a two-bedroom bungalow, with a veranda facing the sea and wooden steps leading from the right-hand end of it, down a slope of grass to the dunes. There was a gap of several yards before the next dwelling, with a row of cottages beyond that rising further up a hill: it felt private. The sound of the gulls and waves filled Thomas's ears, and the scent of the seaweed rose from the tideline below. Even in the worst of weather, this place was beautiful. No wonder the cottage was booked solid. Until today ....

Kyt led the way to the front door, set to the right of a wide window, just as he had led the way on that day; the day he had taken his ten-year-old son to see the spell-weaver, staying there.

Thomas followed him in. The memory swept over him. Clear as the present .... He was back there ... smaller, of course ...with the table and chairs to the left by the front window, the space that went all the way through to the back of the house, the view of the sea through the French windows. The woman ... she sat there, on the other side of the table ... it was covered with a red velvet cloth ... with a gold fringe. It looked warm .... She had ... chestnut hair, with strands of white appearing, and light blue eyes .... She was tall when she stood up to shake his hand and invite him and his father to sit down .... She was ... familiar .... Of course, she was ... she was ... Senara Cadabra.

However, before she spoke, a sound from the other end of the room, near the French windows, called Thomas's attention to a light wooden playpen, quilt-floored, with soft toys scattered about within. And there was the bright face of a fair-haired baby with eyes of azure and a smile of sunshine. She, — and he didn't know why he thought 'she' — was dressed in a yellow babygrow and was looking straight at him, reaching out her little chubby hand.

'Ba!' she said happily. Thomas had never had much interest in infants, but there was something about this child that drew him. He went over and knelt in front of the baby, who was gazing at him, over the top of the low rail of the pen.

353

'Hello,' he said with a friendly smile. And then he saw it. In her eyes. The strangest thing. From deep within the blue irises, it was as though tiny golden specks were surfacing, like the points of light in fireworks or a soup with the smallest ingredients boiling to the top then falling back, vanishing. He blinked. It was gone. He looked more closely but … it was as though he hadn't seen it. The baby grabbed his ear with interest.

'Ah-ba!' He disengaged himself carefully, and turned to the lady who'd sat back down at the table with his father.

'What curious eyes she has. I mean ... they're lovely, ma'am.'

'Tell me, what do you see in them?' asked the lady gently.

'The little brown specks, like fireworks. They were there for only a moment and then disappeared. Does that happen sometimes?'

'Interesting. You have keen sight. I think I see why you are here.'

His father spoke. 'This is Mrs Cadabra, son. Thomas, ma'am.'

'How do you do, Thomas? Ah ….'

A tall, handsome man, with silver amongst in his dark hair, was coming to the table with a tea tray.

'Hello there, Mr Trelawney,' he said, 'Always a pleasure.'

The lady introduced him.

'My husband. This is young Thomas.'

'Hello, sir.'

'Thomas, nice of you to visit us.' He went over to the baby, who reached for him, and picked her up. 'Come on. Let's leave these good people in peace, shall we? And have a little wander on the sand.' With that, they went out.

'Now, Thomas,' said Mrs Cadabra, speaking quietly

and calmly, as she served the tea, 'tell me why you are here.'

'Well, ma'am, I have this thing where I get flashes of things happening in other places, and I can see things in my aunt's crystal balls. I see things all over the place ... like in my tea, and I can do this thing with like ... lines of lights and if they cross then I can see that things are connected .... Things like that ....'

'And ... how does that make you feel, Thomas?' she asked.

'Well, ... when I do them, it feels ... like normal and sort of ... well ... *happy* ... but my mum, just at the thought that I might be able to do this stuff, she gets really ... well, things like that freak her out ... and it's making her *un*happy and ... then ....'

'... and then?'

'There's my family ... well, they're not exactly my family ... except they are. I mean, they're my grandmother's. They can do this stuff, and they want *me* to be able to do it, only my dad said that they mustn't find out that I can, or it's going to be really dangerous for me, so I have to hide it ... and I hate it when I go there, and they're all looking at me and talking about me and wondering if I can, and ... oh ma'am, I just want it to go away! ... And my dad says you can make it go away, so, please, ... will you? Just take it away?'

'Sugar?'

'Er ... one please.'

The lady added a lump and stirred his tea. 'Drink, my dear.' He sipped and felt better.

'This is your wish then?'

'Yes,' he spoke definitely.

'Understand then that I cannot *take it away*, this gift, your divination; I can only *suppress* it. With a spell. And spells wear off. It may not be for years, even decades, but, depending on how long you live, it will, in time, wear off.'

Thomas nodded. 'Now … do you wish to remember that you once could divine?'

Thomas was certain.

'No, ma'am, I want to forget.'

'And to forget that you were ever here and had the spell cast?'

'Yes, ma'am, if you please.'

She looked at his father.

'You wish all of this, too?'

'We've talked about it, Thomas and I, and yes, we do.'

'You are resolved, Thomas?' she asked him seriously.

He nodded again. 'Yes.'

'Very well ….'

She rose and went into one of the bedrooms and returned with a cream coloured candle, matches and a purple corduroy drawstring bag. She sat down and lit the candle. Out of the pouch, she took a smooth oval stone of rainbow colours, a wand, and a bundle of unfamiliar herbs.

'Thomas, look at the flame, concentrate on the flame.' She put the stone in his hand. 'Hold this ….' He heard her crushing the dry leaves in her fingers, releasing a strange aroma, fresh, profoundly pungent green, and then her voice …. He recognised a word here and there … spell-language … Wicc'yeth …. He grew drowsy ….

The vision faded.

He was back in the present. There was his father, watching his face, standing quite still, now smiling and nodding.

'I remember,' said Thomas, still in a daze.

'Yes.'

'Senara Cadabra … of course … it could only have been her … and Perran and the baby … Amanda Cadabra.'

'Amanda Cardiubarn then,' Kyt reminded him.

'I never understood until now what mortal danger I was

in, Dad. How on earth did we manage to keep what I could do a secret?'

'With great difficulty, son.'

'The Flamgoynes, they would have taken me, right?' asked Thomas.

'Of course, and you would have cooperated or disappeared.'

'She saved me. Senara Cadabra saved me ... and she was so ... *kind* .... I never knew until today .... I have to thank her ....'

Chapter 55

༄

I AM VIOLA

Chris Reid came for his forgetting spell.

'Before I cast it,' said Amanda, 'I would like to thank you for your help on the day of the attack. I didn't know you knew any magic. Or your grandmother.'

'She knows some Obi —Myah — the good stuff. It's like Jamaican Wicca. Gran told me to make a talisman of my own. So I collected stuff from the ground and trees, sort of followed my instinct. And then I thought, this is a talisman for the village itself, and it seemed right to put it where I did, on the green. And ...' he added, putting a hand in his pocket, 'I want you to have it. Because, after today, I won't remember what it's for ....'

'Thank you, Chris, but somehow I think you should keep it. Because, although you may not remember why you have it, you'll always feel its power, and, one day, — who knows? — it might be needed again. It's *your* power that is in it. Maybe it will only work for you.'

'You think so?'

'I do,' Amanda affirmed.

'OK.' Chris nodded contentedly.' I'll put it somewhere special.'

'Oh, by the way, thank you for carrying me upstairs. I know I'm no feather!'

He grinned. 'Life isn't always like it is in the movies. Let's say it was a good workout. Anyway, my pleasure. OK, Amanda, I'm ready. Do your stuff!'

* * * * *

Still, there was no hint of Viola. Mrs Uberhausfest and Moffat had come and gone. Now, finally, the Grange ladies had arrived at Amanda's cottage. Tempest, refusing to accept any of the duties of host, was making Churchill very uneasy, simply by dint of staying still. The terrier, in spite of instructions from Cynthia, kept up his barking protests.

'Oh dear!' exclaimed Miss de Havillande. 'I'll take him for a walk in the orchard. That always calms his nerves. I shall return directly.'

As they heard the door close behind Cynthia and Churchill, Miss Armstrong-Witworth said,

'Have you heard from the dear Inspector? We are quite missing him and his colleagues at The Grange.'

'He'll be back on Saturday for the dance class.'

'That's nice.'

'You must be relieved to know that it was accidental,' Amanda remarked.

'I am relieved that that is the … official report,' replied Miss Armstrong-Witworth, then, seeing her young friend's surprise, 'Yes, I know what happened, dear, about the panel and everything.'

'About the assassins and the Russians and the defections and so on?'

'Ah yes ... and you heard that from Michael Hogarth, I expect.'

'You know him?' Amanda was once again astonished.

'Oh, in a life as long as mine, one meets a great many people, my dear.' She smiled and shook her head and tutted. 'He has spun quite a yarn, naughty boy.'

'What do you mean, Gwendolen?'

'Oh, some of it is true. And some of it is not. Tell me what you have worked out. And start from the very beginning. Take your time. I expect Cynthia will be a while. She *will* be back, though. I know that she wants to talk to you. Go on, dear ....'

'Well, in the early 1930s —'

'Let me stop you there. *That* is not the beginning.'

Amanda looked at her. Was it possible that Miss Armstrong-Witworth knew about ...?

'The Frenchman?'

'Yes. It's all right, we know you saw some apparitions in the ballroom, and that you have been back and seen them again. We know that they're there and turn up now and then. Don't worry; we're used to them. So yes, the Frenchman. Let's start there.'

Amanda began afresh.

'In the late 1700s or around 1800, there were *émigrés* in London, from the Terror of the Revolution and then Napoleonic rule? And one was visiting The Grange, and playing the piano when the chandelier rope broke.'

'Yes, *that* is the beginning.'

'But ... apart from the coincidence,' pondered Amanda, '... that it was the same chandelier, falling on a man playing a piano, in the same place, over a century later in the 1930s, then recently ... what is the connection?'

'The connection is through craftwork and economy,'

explained Miss Armstrong-Witworth. 'That is, through people who liked sewing and never threw away any odds and ends that might come in handy, especially nice lengths of gold-coloured cord that could be used for trimming ....'

'They kept the cord, not knowing what it was responsible for? And then, a hundred years later, when someone who knew the house well, really well, wanted to fake an accident ... they used the cord?' Amanda began to see the light. 'Because that had genuinely frayed ... but how ...? Unless ... there was a new cord holding up the chandelier in the 1930s. The assassin cut that new cord and quickly replaced it with the *old* cord before anyone came in .... The stuck door! That bought them a little time ... they unhooked the new cord, hooked on the old, pulled the new off the cleat, wound the old on and slipped back behind the panel.'

'Yes!'

'And that's what the little girl saw. Then,' Amanda continued, now in the swing, 'years later, ... there was a political situation —'

'— No, no, my dear,' Miss Armstrong-Witworth forestalled her. 'All of that is, I am afraid, a complete farrago of nonsense. Oh, the man at the piano in 1932 was, I think, a Russian spy and, yes, he was put out of action by someone working for the British government. And, again, yes, in the manner that you so accurately describe ... but for the rest ... the answer lies much closer to home.'

'What is the link between 1932 and now ...? The little girl ...?'

'That bit is true,' confirmed Miss Armstrong-Witworth.

'If she's still alive and she saw how the murder was done, then .... when *she* wanted to bump off the piano tuner she had a way to do it that would look like an accident ....'

'Good. The next step?'

'The piano tuner really *was* an assassin?' suggested

Amanda. 'Yes, and somehow the little girl, now grown up, knew he was, and decided to get *him* before he got *her*! Miss de Havillande! She doesn't have an alibi. She said she'd left the florist in the garden to come back to the kitchen …. *Miss de Havillande*. And when she was a child, her pet name was "Dolly"! Yes?'

Miss Armstrong-Witworth smiled. 'Not quite. Backtrack to 1932.'

Amanda took a deep breath and tried to visualise the scene as it could have been that day. 'It was just after 6 o'clock, because the man at the piano was in evening dress, which he wouldn't have been any earlier, and there was a child still up, or … children?'

'It was a party, after all,' contributed Miss Armstrong-Witworth.

'Maybe families were staying for the weekend? Maybe there was at least one other child ... a child who, as an adult, came to have links with the Foreign office who would know the identity of assassins ….' Amanda's voice trailed off, as she began to put two and two together. 'Miss Armstrong-Witworth, you told me you were a field agent for the Foreign Office during the Cold War …. Uncle Mike said Lucas Peterson disappeared in the early 90s. That was when the Cold war ended …. Your family and the de Havillandes have always been close …. You …'

Miss Armstrong-Witworth was looking at her with bright eyes.

'Yes,' she encouraged Amanda, 'keep going ….'

'Gwendolen … Gwen-dolly … *Dolly* … of course!'

'So far, so good, dear. You see, I recognised Lucas Peterson from many years ago, from my days in the field. When I was an agent, I am afraid I came to know some rather disreputable people, some of whom were employed in unsavoury tasks. I was there when the explosion happened that we all thought had killed him. In fact, I set it off. Clearly, reports of his death were exaggerated, for there he was, as large as life. And so, when I saw him, oh, at least 30 years older, at the piano in Irma's house, while I was having tea there, I knew him. I was always good with faces and had had training on top of that. I was careful that he didn't get a good look at me.'

'So what did you do next, Gwendolen?' asked Amanda, enthralled.

'I watched whom he watched, where he went and when, and what questions he asked. It may be said that the evidence was circumstantial, but I was sure of his reason for coming to Sunken Madley. I spoke to one of my connections in my former department. I was given leave to exercise my discretion, and I did. He was unfinished business.'

'From your work for MI6?' Amanda asked.

'Indeed. But that was just one side of the coin.'

'And the other?'

'He was hired to do a job.'

'As a piano tuner?'

'That was just his cover.'

'I don't understand.'

'He was here for you, Amanda dear.'

'Me? How come?'

'He was in the employ of a certain Cornish family.'

'C-Cornish? How do you know about …?'

'Because I watch over you, my sweet.'

'Are you …?

'I am Viola.'

Chapter 56

༄

REVELATIONS

Amanda gasped. She was silent, utterly bereft of speech.

'Would you like a glass of water, dear?' asked Miss Armstrong-Witworth solicitously. 'Perhaps it is time for tea.'

'You ... you were the last on my shortlist. The last person I thought ... and then when Uncle Mike was talking about all that political stuff and assassins, I still didn't make the connection, although ... it did stir something in my brain.'

'And you didn't entirely believe his story either, did you?'

'No,' Amanda admitted, 'and I don't think the inspector did either, only he said to let sleeping dogs lie.'

'I didn't know how to warn you without Peterson spotting me, disappearing, and then making an attempt on your life at a later date. All I could do was to make sure that you were kept busy and away from home, so you couldn't have an appointment with him.'

'But I did! I *did* have an appointment! Only then the

piano at Pipkin ...! That was *you*?' Amanda stared at her friend, sitting pale-blue-eyed, sweetly smiling, in a long lavender dress with a Peter Pan collar, and delicate, Michaelmas daisy print scarf.

'It went very much against the grain, if you'll pardon the pun,' Miss Armstrong-Witworth added, 'to disfigure the piano, but needs must.'

'So I had to cancel the tuner,' Amanda acknowledged. 'Until the next day, when the glaziers suddenly found they could do the mirror early.'

'Indeed, they were persuaded by some extra funding.'

'Oh! So then I cancelled the tuner again.'

'Yes ... then Peterson found out you were working at The Grange: big house, lots of empty room, lots of opportunity. And so I had to act.'

'You knew there was a secret passage because, in 1932, when you were three years old, you saw the agent come out of it and go back in?'

'Yes, one of Cynthia's dear kind uncles and aunts, who always looked after Cynthia and her sister, and any other children who were there. One of them, Colonel de Havillande, who, yes, worked for the government, had left, earlier in the day, for London, or so he had said.'

'He was the one you saw coming out of the panel ... when he wasn't supposed to be in the house, and *that* was why you were astonished!' Amanda exclaimed.

'Precisely!'

'So ... over time, you worked out how to open the panel and ...'

'... found the passage to other end,' finished Gwendolen.

'Which is where?' asked Amanda, curiously.

'In the hall cloakroom.'

Amanda frowned in confusion. 'So how come you came from the *kitchen* after the chandelier fell?'

'Once Hillers, in response to you calling for help, had come into the house and moved past the cloakroom, I slipped out through the front door, through the side gate, around to the door of Moffat's quarters and back into his pantry.'

'Aha. That's why Moffat arrived on the scene before you. The stuck door must have been important in buying you time.'

'Yes, but mostly, it was the noises filling the house that would delay any response to the sound of the chandelier falling.'

'You orchestrated them?'

'Yes, I told Hillers that the business with the pigeons was urgent. Of course she had her shotgun with her, as she always brings it, and was only too ready to help out. I told Humpy about the gramophone and made sure there were some records with it of a lively nature. I knew he wouldn't be able to resist. Moffat encouraged Mundly to mow the lawn, Peterson, in his rôle of piano tuner, was adding noise of his own, and the cacophony was bound to irritate poor Churchill.'

'So Moffat was your accomplice?'

'Oh yes, dear, he was more than happy to take part.'

'Really? And he gave you your alibi, of course.'

'Yes, well, of course, we *were* cleaning the silver in his pantry together for while. We kept checking until everyone was where we wanted them to be: Hillers outside, Humpy shut up in the library, you in the small dining room and Cynthia and the florist out in the garden with Mundly, and even John in the small salon. When the coast was clear, I stole along the hall, past all of your doors and into the cloakroom. From there I entered the tunnel, came out of the panel and took care of Peterson.'

'And then, as you say, made your way back and *out* of the cloakroom, as soon as Hillers had gone past in response to my call.'

'Yes, dear.'

'Of course. It all makes perfect sense. And you did all of this to protect me! But, oh, how could I have been so mistaken? You were on my shortlist of Irma, Moffat, Cynthia and you, But I was so sure Viola must be Cynthia. After all, she and Granny —'

'That was how your grandmother and I made sure it looked.'

'Dear Gwendolen ... all this time ....'

'Yes, my sweet Amanda.' She held out her arms and Amanda hugged her. 'I know. I know how you have felt. I knew you were a witch. You are not alone. You have never been alone, however much you have felt it. And eventually, if I am right, then perhaps the time will come when you are going to be very much less alone, if you wish it ....'

'Oh?'

'But never mind about that, for now, my dear. You know who I am and, if there should ever be the need again for the rise of the Home Guard, I will call them forth. However, I strongly doubt the repeat of such an event. In the meantime, I am here. I am your friend. As I was your grandparents' Viola before you, now I am yours.'

'Thank you, Gwendolen. You seem to understand what this means to me. Only ... I should have been able to —'

'No, don't chide yourself for not being able to unravel all of this without a bit of help. You had no way of knowing just how far back my association with The Grange went. And that, not only have the de Havillande and Armstrong-Witworth families always been close, but this is also my house.'

'Yours?' asked Amanda.

'Mrs de Havillande left it to both Cynthia and myself after she inherited from Mr de Havillande. I think, towards the end, she felt she hadn't been quite the loving mother she could have been. Not that she was unkind, but rather absent. She knew how much it would please Cynthia and so ... it is ours jointly. Cynthia's younger sister was always adamant about not wanting to be burdened with any part of looking after "The Old Silo", as she calls it. But, of course, we both agreed absolutely, that, after we've moved on, it should go to Hillers.'

'It's no marvel, then, that you know all about the house! And I did wonder about the panel, but I just thought it would be too much of a coincidence, having the same thing as —'

'No coincidence, my dear. I believe that that was the inspiration for our little hidey-hole, truth-to-tell. Cynthia's great-great-grandfather's watchword was "You never know". And, just in case of need, he had that made. With an entrance or exit, depending on your point of view, in the hall. He made the connecting tunnel through the house himself, with old Jacob the gardener and his brother. They had both been employed and housed by the estate all of their adult lives. They swore they would take the secret to their graves and so they did. The story was that they were laying drains or water pipes.'

'But they were actually building the tunnel?' asked Amanda.

'*And* laying new pipework, to be fair,' adding Miss Armstrong-Witworth practically.

'Oh, how intimately you know The Grange! But no one in the village knows much about *you*, Gwendolen. We don't see you nearly as often as Miss de Havillande.'

'Cynthia has always been more of an outdoor person, striding around with the dogs giving the farmers help when they're short-handed.'

'Miss de Havillande? Farm work?'

'Oh, there's a great deal people do not know about Cynthia. Whereas I, once I retired, was more an indoor person, as I say. I prefer to visit the tenants who are in need of a little indoor help in one way or another. I like to do what I can, even if it's only the washing up.'

'Housework?'

'Sometimes having a tidy home can give people such a lift, when they can't do for themselves. When what you love to do is also what people need – there's magic in that.'

'It's what Granny and Grandpa did,' Amanda said thoughtfully. 'But I don't know about healing herbs or counselling people with their troubles. I actually just like being in my workshop with Tempest,' she admitted, feeling rather inadequate by comparison.

'And don't you mend things for people? Precious, important things that they can't pay you much for?' Gwendolen reminded her.

'If it's a quick job and they can't afford it.'

'Didn't you repair Miss Mittly's father's model galleon? I can't believe *that* was a quick job.'

'Yes, that took me a couple of days, but I was *interested* in that,' Amanda objected. 'Oh, I know I ought to be interested in *people* but —'

'— the Normals confuse you. We all understand. It's quite all right. We love you as you are, my dear. The treasured things that you repair, those are things that mean a great deal. But more importantly: you're *here*. As long as there is someone in the Witch's Cottage, the village feels safe. That, above all, is what you give them, and now you have more than justified that faith in you.'

Amanda smiled. 'I'm glad …. But … if they all … well, feel about me as you say, why do they keep doing that annoying thing?'

'Trying to marry you off?'

'Yes!

Miss Armstrong-Witworth considered, then answered, 'I suppose because everyone else has someone who's always here. Joan and Jim, Cynthia and I, the Patels, the Sharmas, Sylvia and her husband, Alexander and Julian, Esta and Erik —who believe they're just friends — Alex and Sandy, Ruth and Kieran, even Moffat has his sister in Muttring. And you have Claire, but *only* when she's here, and usually she's not. So you see, they would like you to have someone who is around all, or at least, most of the time. Like your grandparents were. Of course, they don't know that they still *are*.'

'You can ...see them?' asked Amanda, astonished.

'But of course,' Miss Armstrong-Witworth replied comfortably.

'How come?'

'Dear Mamma and Pappa were very spiritual people, each in their own way. Dear Grandmamma, even more so. As a result, when I was a child and saw things from other dimensions, as most children do, instead of telling me that I was being silly or naughty for making things up, they allowed me happily to continue to see what I saw, and so I still do. And very important it has been to me. Saved my life more than once.'

'Really?'

'Colleagues used to wonder how I survived so long in so dangerous a job as an agent. Well, that was often how.'

Amanda sat in silence, taking time to try and process the cascade of revelations. Something occurred to her.

'Does Inspector Trelawney know that it was you who ...?' she asked.

'No need to disturb any notions he may have about "sweet little old ladies".'

One thing that neither of them knew was that Trelawney was not quite so naïve. His keen detective work and presence, on the night of the action, were what had secured the arrest of 73-year-old Betty 'blunt instrument' Crockins, during her attempted escape over the roof of the Port Pengrim truncheon factory. He'd got a commendation for that, as well as a bit of insight into the capacity of seniors.

But both Amanda and Gwendolen still had a great deal to learn about the inspector, and so entered the kitchen to make tea, in agreement about keeping the truth, at least for the time being, to themselves.

The doorbell rang.

'Ah, there's Cynthia now.'

Miss de Havillande was, surprisingly, Churchill-less.

'Hello! Met Moffat,' she explained. 'Took Churchie home. Best. Now Amanda … about The Grange … there's going to be a great deal more work to be done. However, we are having three guests, and you must feel free to enlist their help for anything they may be useful for.'

'Really?' In Amanda's experience, strangers just got in the way.

'Yes, Hiller's and Humpy's grand-daughter will be staying and bringing a young lady, a friend from college, and *her* friend, a gentleman, rather older, I gather,' added Miss de Havillande, with the lift of an eyebrow. 'But regarding the restoration, I don't want you to feel you must rush anything at all. However, the success of the St Valentine's Day party has emboldened Moffat, Gwendolen and me to give a Spring Ball. Perhaps for the equinox. What do you think? Can we make some further improvements to the ballroom before then?'

'I'm sure we can ….'

Tempest, curled up on a velvet cushion at the end of the sofa, where Amanda was sitting, had listened, with half an ear, to the conversation that had taken place between his human and Gwendolen. Most of his attention had been devoted to idle thoughts of Natasha, still his object of desire at The Grange. Nevertheless, he had noticed that Natasha's human had omitted to tell *his* human about the journals she had removed from The Grange library shelves, and locked in the desk drawer. It was touching how humans fondly imagined that their little secrets were really secret. Of course, no one would notice the cat, apparently asleep on the library Chesterfield.

His own human, of course, knew better; she understood

that he, her feline owner knew about, and observed, absolutely everything she did. Yes, she was coming along quite nicely. Slowly. But quite nicely.

For a human.

Chapter 57

∽

NAMING THE DAY

'So,' said Vera, as she walked with her brother on the beach, lit by a Spanish sunset, 'our Amanda lives to cast another day.'

'That was close,' Mike remarked.

'Yes, closer than any of us would have wished.'

'Indeed,' agreed Mike. 'I do not see them regrouping any time soon, though.'

'The head has been cut off the snake. Gronetta Flamgoyne is finally laid low, her son and all the rest with her, or unconscious or mazed, yes?

'Correct, and her scions dispersed,' he added.

'Of course, they may never rise again. But I foresee a more likely outcome. So does Harry.'

'Yes, as the spells wear off … we can expect them to pop up. Who knows where or when?'

'Or in what guise.'

Mike smiled. 'But for now ….'

'Yes, let her breathe awhile. She has earned it. I would suggest you get young Thomas to bring her out here for a few days but ....'

'Yes. Premature.' Mike pronounced decidedly.

'Has he told her?' asked his sister.

'What the clans intended for them?

'Yes.'

'No. Why? Do you think he should, Vee?'

'I think, based only on what I know of Amanda through you, that it would make her uncomfortable, make her self-conscious with him. And now that what we have hoped for is closer than it ever was before, I would not wish anything to tip the balance against it.'

They stopped and, for a while, picked the flattest stones they could find and skimmed them into the orange-reflecting waves, laughing at failed attempts and cheering one another's successes, as they had done since they were children. They walked on.

'Mikey ... have you told Amanda or Thomas about you and ...?'

'No, Vee. That is a story for another day entirely.'

'I expect you are right.'

He nudged her, playfully. 'I do like it when my sister says that.'

Vera laughed and linked her arm through his. 'Don't get used to it!'

At last, with the light nearly gone, they turned for home.

'What of Sunken Madley, Mikey? Have its present day inhabitants now atoned for the drowning of the witch, all those centuries ago, that earned the village its damning name?'

'Perhaps. I wonder whose judgement that is to make.'

'And what of its future?'

'There may still be Cardiubarns, as well as Flamgoynes, out there. And now they are all driven underground, where they may turn out to be more dangerous than ever. Who is to say what alliances could be formed? Sunken Madley is now on the map as a powerful force to contend with, for anyone still alive or with the wit to remember what happened on that day.'

'Yes, and a momentous day indeed. A day that we all shall mark henceforth. The 9th February: The Battle for Sunken Madley.'

'No,' replied Mike, 'it was more than a battle. For not only did the villagers find their courage, but the very orchards awoke and took to the air in its defence, so that it now takes its place in the annals of Magical History.'

'Very well, then, brother. The 9th February. Let it be called The Rise of Sunken Madley.'

* * * * *

It was Friday. The work at The Grange — some of which had had to be done without the aid of magic — and the effects of the final spell-bolt, had left Amanda feeling rather weak. Luckily, the healer at the Asthma Centre had a cancellation, and she was able to get a late appointment.

Lying on the couch, a pattern of crystals laid out underneath, the old healer's hands on her shoulders, Amanda felt warmth and comfort travelling through her ... soon she was off ... in the dream state she always enjoyed when she visited him. On the past three occasions, she had visioned crystal caves, flying with beautiful green and blue-winged creatures, looking over the treetops of magnificent forests, from which the dawn mist was rising. But today was different. Today Amanda was back in an unwelcome memory from before she was three years old ....

She saw her little feet treading down stone steps. The

hand holding her own was her great-grandmother's. Down, down, they went ... to a door .... Then she was seeing Cardiubarn Hall over Granny's shoulder, as she was being carried out to the car. There was something she had to tell Granny ... if only she could remember. The great spiked edifice swam before her eyes into a mist that clouded, then resolved into a haze, as she heard the healer's voice calling her back to the room, the present.

As always, Amanda told him what she had seen. He nodded.

'My dear, today I tried very deep healing for your asthma. One thing I did learn. It has no natural cause. It has the feeling of something else. Something ... more ... psychic. Does that sound bizarre to you? I wouldn't want to make you feel uncomfortable.'

'No,' Amanda said at once. 'No ... I understand .... I'm glad you told me. Thank you, anyway. I do feel better ... no aches and pains now. Thank you, Jack.'

That evening, both curious and perturbed, she called in on Aunt Amelia.

'Are you quite restored, sweetie?'

'Much better, thank you,' Amanda assured her.

'What a day that was!' exclaimed Amelia. 'Not knowing until the last minute, and then all of those people coming to help, and the attack, and the orchard spirits. But how well it all ended!'

'Yes. Do you think the Wicc'lord helped?' asked Amanda.

'I should think so, certainly. Let me make some tea. I hope you're not running around and working again already.'

'No, I'm taking it easy, but really I'm much better, and I went to see the healer, which helped. Only he said something. That my asthma wasn't caused by anything natural, but by something ... he used the word "psychic."'

Amelia looked at Amanda in surprise. 'I see. That is strange.'

'I wondered if you'd ask your globe about it.'

'Of course, sweetie.'

Aunt Amelia set the crystal ball upon the round table, and they sat down. She looked into it, turning it every so often.

Amanda looked at her questioningly.

'I am sorry, my dear … all I see is mist … purple mist …I can't tell you any more. It's gone blank. But …' Amelia was quiet, suddenly looking intently into the glass. She murmured,

'Oh, dear, … something is coming your way. Something that really should have been dealt with …. Hmm …. ' She glanced up at Amanda, encouragingly. 'Well, look at what you've survived. I'm sure you'll be equal to …' — Amelia looked back at the ball — '… then again … oh dear ….'

*****

The next day, after the dance class, Trelawney was ushered by Amanda back into the cottage sitting room, for an audience that he had requested with her grandparents. They were having tea and iced buns. Senara looked up as they entered.

'Ah, if it isn't the young inspector. You are positively spoiling us.'

'Good evening, Mr and Mrs Cadabra,' said Thomas.

'Hello there, Inspector,' Perran welcomed him. 'We mean it. It's not often that people from your dimension want a visit.'

Thomas had his doubts that Senara had spoken anything but ironically, but he was here with a purpose. He sat down beside Amanda on the sofa.

'I wanted to thank you, Mrs Cadabra, for what you did for me, for my parents too.'

'You're welcome. I liked your father, and your mother too. And even you, young man. But don't let it go to your head.'

'No, ma'am,' he replied with a smile. 'You certainly had the advantage that day, nearly three years ago, when I came here to see you. I thought it was the first time we were meeting, and all along ....'

'Yes, I did rather enjoy myself that day,' Senara admitted.

'I wish I had known what I do now. I would have thanked you then.'

'Well, you have done so now, and what *I* can do now is to thank *you*. It was your foresight into how Amanda's D.N.A. would, one day, render her eyes, in the presence of magic that was crucial.'

'The brown specks?' asked Thomas.

'Yes, from the age of six, Amanda's eyes have been her tell. The tiny islands of brown in the blue, expand and coalesce when she uses magic. In the presence of your gift of divination, they showed their future selves. Without knowing it, you warned me, young Thomas Trelawney, that Amanda was likely the future witch that the Cardiubarns and Flamgoynes coveted, and that I must save her from them, at all costs. I saved you, and you saved Amanda. That has a nice yin-yang balance about it, wouldn't you say,' Mrs Cadabra added, with a flash of her usual playful humour.

Later, Amanda took Trelawney for a walk in the orchard, leaving Senara and Perran in the sitting room, continuing to enjoy their tea and iced buns. Granny looked at her husband,

'My dear, does Amanda know about ricochet spells?'

'What? How they don't have the same potency as direct spells, you mean?' Perran asked.

'Yes, so they wear off more quickly.'

'Excepting them kill spells. Now *they* don't wear off!' Senara chuckled at that. 'No, I don't think she knows.' said Perran. 'Not unless you told her, love. I didn't consider she'd need to know.'

'Ah.'

'P'raps we should tell her.'

Senara considered. 'Let's not worry her with that just at the moment.'

'No, not just at the moment. She doesn't need to know.'

'Hm …. Not yet.'

Chapter 58

༈

A WALK IN THE ORCHARD

Amanda and Trelawney, strolling amongst the dormant apple trees, were bundled up in coats, scarves and gloves against the February cold.

'You never told me,' she said, 'all about the person whom you met by chance on the road, who spotted the arteries in the surface and suggested a pump that might have kept the puddle full of water.'

'Yes, I've been wanting to ... but what with one thing and another,' he explained.

'Oh, you mean like a battle, infiltration and murder?'

Trelawney grinned.

'How these things do get in the way of communication!'

'Don't they just. Anyway, please do tell me now,' Amanda invited him.

Trelawney related all of the events of that afternoon, upon what was once the old post road to St Austell, right up to the time when the lady drove off.

'You didn't follow her, I suppose?' asked Amanda.

'It didn't seem appropriate.'

'No,' Amanda agreed. 'It's not like you had just cause. She was neither acting suspiciously nor at risk.'

'Quite.'

'But you went back, another day?'

'I did,' Trelawney confirmed. 'As soon as I could.'

'And?'

He shook his head. 'No trace. I asked in all of the obvious places, the gift shops, the tea shops, the post office, the pubs, and down by the shore, but no one remembered seeing her. I had wondered if she was some kind of ... vision or ....'

'Hm, I could be wrong, but I don't think visions carry cameras and travel with macro lenses. Mind you, Granny and Grandpa's eternal teas seem as real as they do. You got right up close to her, didn't you?'

'Yes, when she passed the camera to me to see the magnified image of the photograph.'

'And?'

'Oh yes, I was in no doubt that she was real,' Trelawney said.

Amanda was silent.

'What?' he asked her.

'Perhaps ... she was not ready to be found. Have you thought of that, Inspector?' Trelawney looked at Amanda uncertainly. 'You never know. This lady could just, possibly, turn out, one day, to be important in some way, small or otherwise,' she opined.

'Yes, I wonder about that too.'

'I don't think you will find her. Ask your family about her, though.'

'That I will certainly do.'

Amanda nodded. She gazed at the sky without seeing it. She was getting an Aunt Amelia sort of feeling. That sense of other streams of time and reality. And with it, a strange feeling of serenity. She looked back at Trelawney.

'Remember her,' she said. '… And now … the real reason why I brought you here… oh, but before that. You promised to explain that remark you made, about us owing your grandfather a bottle of the finest rum.'

'Ah, yes,' agreed Trelawney,' so I did. Well, you see, you woke up out your comatose state in response to —'

'— you singing a song. Yes, I remember.'

'It was my grandfather who taught me that song. Granddad Trelawney.'

'What made you sing me that song?'

'Dr Patel said that, when you'd been in that state before, you'd said it was like being in the sea. The Trelawneys have been fishermen for hundreds of years. That is their song. I learned it when I was a young child.'

'A sea shanty?'

'Erm … sort of ….'

'Like *What Shall We Do With the Drunken Sailor*? Only in Cornish?' Amanda hazarded.

'Not precisely.'

'What's it about then?'

'Erm … it's about a fisherman calling someone out of the sea.'

'Someone who'd drowned?'

'No. No, someone living in the sea.'

'What? Like a … a mermaid?'

'Yes.'

'Why was he calling her?'

'Er … he, er … enjoyed her company.'

'Enjoyed … you mean …?' Amanda looked at him. 'It's a love song?'

'Well, er … yes.' He met her eyes, and for a moment they were back at the New Year's Eve Ball at The Sinner's Rue.

At the stroke of midnight, in the strobe-lit darkness, with all of the villagers celebrating around them, for a moment, Thomas had had the urge to kiss her. Amanda had hoped he would. And then, they had both reminded themselves, in no uncertain terms, of their professional relationship. The only difference now is that he knew, and so did she.

Not that it changed *anything*, each of them told themselves sternly. They suddenly both looked away and became in tensely interested in the bare apple trees around them.

Trelawney cleared his throat. 'But the point is,' he said hastily, 'that it seemed appropriate in calling you out of *your* sea. And it was unquestionably effective. Wouldn't you agree, Miss Cadabra?'

'Oh, I would. Erm …yes ….' Amanda was deep in thought, trying to unravel the implications of both his choice of song and its efficacious effects. Not to mention its magical background. 'Well,' she said, at last, finding a light note, 'I do indeed owe your grandfather a bottle of the finest rum I can find.'

'We both do,' replied Trelawney sincerely.' Now, you were going to tell me the real reason for this stroll in this particular place …?'

'Oh yes,' she responded, grateful for the change of subject, 'my friend Hugh, who worked on the Asthma Centre, sent me a homemade present that he told me to take for a walk in the orchard. I'm going to do an experiment now. I'm going to play what I can of the Appel Song — as a thank-you to the Appel spirits who helped save the village on that day — and see what we see. Is that OK?'

Trelawney was surprised that she had an instrument, could play anything on it, and why she thought he might mind. He said politely,

'Of course, go ahead.'

She blew gently across the tops of the pipes to warm up, and then began slowly to play. The air around them seemed to sparkle softly. Gradually ... *they* began to appear: all manner of beautiful creatures of all sizes from miniscule to about three feet high ... but so camouflaged they were not at all obvious. Only one or two glanced up at the humans, with only passing interest, the others being oblivious or occupied. Amanda stopped the music ... and they faded. She looked up at Trelawney with a slight smile, searching his face for a reaction.

Suddenly he spoke.

'No. *No*. This is too much for one day. Talking to ghosts, yes, being convinced that I am seeing *this*: no. I refuse, Miss Cadabra, to believe that you have fairies at the bottom of your garden!'

She broke into a peal of laughter. Thomas could not resist smiling. He shook his head, saying,

'Whatever will you do to me next?'

Chapter 59

NORA'S STORY, AND NEW QUESTIONS

It was a remarkably warm Sunday morning: eleven degrees, a positive heatwave for the time of year, and with little-to-no wind. Amanda prepared a flask of tea, wrapped an oven-warmed pasty in foil, filled a container with chicken for Tempest, and packed up the picnic bag. They set off.

Amanda parked near the library. They got out and prepared to walk the remaining distance to their destination.

'Amanda!'

There was the librarian waving a book and hurrying to intercept them.

'Mrs Pagely, please don't rush.'

'I'm so glad I caught you. You know you were asking for anything on The Grange history, and about any accidents? Well, I knew we had something somewhere. We've long thought the description of one of the houses in this book fitted The Grange. I've marked the page. It's speculation, of course, but I think it might be of interest to you, dear.'

'Thank you, Mrs Pagely, I'll be sure to return it,' Amanda promised.

'It's amazing how things appear and disappear in the basement. But we do have very odd stacks. Jonathan keeps saying he really needs to talk to you about it. But never mind that for now, enjoy your picnic!'

Amanda and Tempest continued along to their favourite spot, up on the ruins of the 1000-year-old priory, with its view over the village, the countryside to the north, east and west, and down the long slow slope into London. It was the best place to think. And she had a lot to contemplate.

She was curious about the book, *Ramblings of a Country House Guest* by Nora Longstaie. Amanda sat down and opened it at Mrs Pagely's marker.

It was in the chapter entitled 'Accidents Do Happen'. Amanda read it aloud to Tempest:

'"*In one house, that I mentioned earlier regarding the summer house that I got to know so well, occurred the most spectacular of all of the mishaps at which I was present, during my houseguest years. I had just come downstairs, when I heard the most almighty crash from the ballroom. At first, I thought the servants had dropped something and, as it was not my house, hesitated to interfere. However, after a minute or two, my scruples, I must admit, were overcome by my curiosity, and I attempted to enter.*

The door was stuck, and it took at least four jolly good shoves with the shoulder to loosen it enough to open the thing. Once I had, I saw the most astounding thing, for the magnificent chandelier had broken loose and fallen onto, not only the rather splendid grand piano but the person who had been playing it. Only his legs were visible sticking out from underneath the glittering mushroom. I cannot think why, in the talkies, females are forever depicted screaming in moments of crisis, for I did nothing of the sort, but rang the bell and called for Flambling. He and some others of the servants arrived along with Josie, my friend and a member of the family, who at once arranged the room to be kept shut and everyone else to be kept away. Josie begged me on no account to mention the occurrence, as it would alarm the other guests and, if the newspapers got hold of the story, no one would ever visit again.

The man under the chandelier was, it seemed, a stranger to all but young Fossy Wallyngton-Smythe, who was known for taking up with simply anyone, even though his father is Minister for Breweries Reform. I agreed that I would say nothing. I saw someone arrive that Josie said was from Special Branch. And that was the last I saw or heard of it. The body must have been removed while we were all having dinner. The ballroom was not used until the following weekend, by which time all was restored, except for some scratches on the parquet. To this day, I have no idea how it all turned out, but I mention it only because that particular stay brought my country-house ramblings to an end. For that weekend I met the man who was to become my *dar*ling husband, *Colonel D'Arcy de Havillande*."

'Ahhh, how romantic! She married Miss de Havillande's uncle! Even though he ... well, never mind that. But how strange that the book had disappeared and that Miss de Havillande knew nothing about it. Or was it? she thought. Was this Gwendolen's hand that had been at work?

Amanda looked up from the book. There was still a sharpness in the air, but, every now and then, came a milder breath that meant that winter was beginning to lose its grip. In only a matter of weeks, the fields would be greening with spring wheat, lambs would be frisking in the pasture, and the trees would bear their young leaves in limes and chartreuse. And there was to be an Equinox Ball, if all went well at The Grange. Sunken Madley held a festival for it, every year that they could be bothered, Amanda reflected affectionately. She looked down at her village with new eyes from when last she had been up here. Now she was seeing the courage, the goodness, the love and, yes, the magic in her neighbours, moving in and out of the cottages, the grand houses, the Corner Shop, The Big Tease, The Sinners Rue, The Snout and Trough, and chatting on the green. And Viola, dear Gwendolen ... somewhere nearby.

Her thoughts turned to The Grange. When Miss de Havillande had finally arrived for her forgetting spell, and she had talked about a lot more work to be done to the house, there was something else she seemed to want to say about it, and, at the same time, *not* say. Who would these three visitors there be? And since she'd have to work around them, what would they be like? Was Ryan's visitor, John, really as nice as he seemed? And Ryan himself, had he been spying for Flamgoynes, after all?

At least Amanda now knew who Viola was. But who was the Wicc'lord? And what was this thing coming that so disquieted Aunt Amelia? What was this psychic cause of her asthma? What did Uncle Mike mean when he said everything had always been all about Sunken Madley?

But one thing at a time. The next step was the last piece of the mystery of the Cardiubarn assassinations by the Flamgoynes ... the missing link, the one who had told the Flamgoynes of the Cardiubarns' van ride. The final fragment that would bring closure, if only to that long past episode in Amanda's strange past.

She picked up Tempest, and they cuddled against each other for warmth. She stood and looked at the horizon. It wasn't so simple this time as looking to the west, as she had always done before. The missing link could be anywhere, anyone. She turned slowly around, her gaze reaching in every direction.

'You're out there ... somewhere. Wherever you are, whoever you are ... I'm going to find you,' said Amanda Cadabra.

THE END

AUTHOR'S NOTE

Thank you for reading *Amanda Cadabra and The Rise of Sunken Madley*. I hope you enjoyed your visit to Sunken Madley both present and past, and your trip to Cornwall.

If the story gave you pleasure, I would love you to tell me your thoughts about your journey through the book. And if you could write a review, that would be of tremendous help. You can post it on the e-store where you bought the book (if you're not sure how to post a review on Amazon, there is a how-to on my website) or on Facebook, Twitter or your social platform of choice. It would mean a great deal to me.

Best of all would be if you dropped me a line at HollyBell@amandacadabra.com so we can connect in person. If there is a character you especially liked or anything you would like more of, please let me know. Amanda Cadabra Book 5 is in the pipeline, and I want to make sure that all of the things that you liked about the first three books make an appearance for you.

For tidbits on the world of Sunken Madley and to keep up with news of the continuing adventures of our heroes Amanda, Tempest, Granny and Grandpa, Trelawney and Hogarth, visit www.amandacadabra.com, where you can also request to enter the VIP Readers Group or sign up for the newsletter to stay in touch and find out about the next sequel. The VIP Readers is a limited numbers group. Members are invited to receive and review an advance copy of the next book. If you are one of that treasured number, thank you for reading, evaluating and giving your precious feedback.

You can also find me on:

Facebook at https://www.facebook.com/Holly-Bell-923956481108549/ (Please come and say hello. It makes my day when a reader does that.)

Twitter at https://twitter.com/holly_b_author

Pinterest https://www.pinterest.co.uk/hollybell2760/
Instagram https://www.instagram.com/hollybellac
Goodreads at https://www.goodreads.com/author/show/18387493.Holly_Bell
and Bookbub at https://www.bookbub.com/profile/holly-bell
See you soon.

ABOUT THE AUTHOR

Cat adorer and chocolate lover, Holly Bell is a photographer, video maker, and student of the Cornish language, when not writing. Whilst being an enthusiastic novel reader, Holly has had a lifetime's experience in writing non-fiction.

Holly devoured all of the Agatha Christie books long before she knew that Miss Marple was the godmother of the Cosy Mystery. Her devotion to JRR Tolkien's Lord of the Rings meant that her first literary creation in this area would have to be a cosy paranormal. If you would like to read an interview with Holly, you can find one here: Flora Meets Independent British Author Holly Bell

Holly lives in the UK and is a mixture of English, Cornish, Welsh and other ingredients. Her favourite animal is called Bobby. He is a black cat. Purely coincidental. Of course.

ACKNOWLEDGEMENTS

Thanks to Flora Gatehouse, for constant support, keen-eyed and intuitive editing and publicity, to Judes Gerstein, my Canadian gem of an advance reader, for noticing issues and offering ideal solutions, to Katherine Otis for her invaluable fine-tooth-combed proof-reading of the manuscript, to Dana,

Mary and other wonderful VIP Readers Group members for their supportive comments and suggestions, and to Katherine DeMoure-Aldrich for round-the-world inspiration and feedback from wherever her travels take her. Thank you to Clifford for another superb suggestion for a car for one of the characters. (The first was for Mrs Uberhausfest, this time it was for Haley.) Thank you to Joe for his loyal support on Facebook. Thanks to Philippa Shallcrass for encouragement and feedback during the writing process.

This book is distinguished by the honour of being able to include a poem written for the story by Cornish Bard Mick Paynter. Thank you, Mick, for your help and kindness when approached by complete stranger lost in Kernewek.

Thanks are also due to the rector of St Mary the Virgin, Monken Hadley whose fund of information helped me to shape the village of 'Sunken Madley', and to Stephen Tatlow, the Director of Music there and the churchwardens for their kind welcome and delight at being fictionalised.

Praise and thanks go out to my new outstandingly talented illustrator Daniel Becerril Ureña (Instagram: danbeu) for his beautiful book cover art.

Also due are thanks to Tanja Slijepčević of Books Go Social for her expert advice and unfailing assistance with spreading the word about both this book and the Amanda Cadabra series.

Thank you, in fact, to all those without whose support this book would not have been possible.

Finally, in whatever dimension they are currently inhabiting, thanks go out to my cat who inspired Tempest, and to my grandfather and brother for Perran and Trelawney. Your magic endures.

ABOUT THE LANGUAGE USED IN THE STORY

Please note that to enhance the reader's experience of Amanda's world, this British-set story, by a British author, uses British English spelling, vocabulary, grammar and usage, and includes local and foreign accents, dialects and a magical language that vary from different versions of English as it is written and spoken in other parts of our wonderful, diverse world.

QUESTIONS FOR READING CLUBS

1. What did you like best about the book?
2. Which character did you like best? Is there one with whom you especially identified?
3. Whom would you like to know more about and why?
4. If you made a movie of the book, whom would you cast and in what parts? Have you chosen any recasting over the first three books in the series? Would you still have the same actress play, Amanda, for example, as you did in Book 1?
5. Did the book remind you of any others you have read, apart from the other books in the series, either in the same or another genre?
6. Did you think the cover fitted the story? If not, how would you redesign it?
7. How unique is this story?
8. Which characters grew and changed over the course of this book, and over the first two books and this one, and which remained the same?
9. What feelings did the book evoke?
10. What place in the book would you most like to visit, and why? Any additional ones to Books 1,2 or 3?

11. Was the setting one that felt familiar or relatable to you? Why or why not? If you read the first three books, how at home did you feel revisiting the locations?
12. What did you think of the continuity between the first book, or Book 3 and this sequel?
13. Was the book the right length? If too long, what would you leave out? If too short, what would you add?
14. How well do you think the title conveyed what the book is about?
15. If you could ask Holly Bell just one question, what would it be?
16. How well do you think the author created the world of the story?
17. Which quotes or scene did you like the best, and why?
18. Was the author just telling an entertaining story or trying as well to communicate any other ideas? If so, what do think they were?
19. Did the book change how you think or feel about any thing, person or place? Did it help you to understand someone or yourself better?
20. What do you think the characters will do after the end of the book? Would you want to read the sequel?

GLOSSARY

As the story is set in an English village, and written by a British author, some spellings or words may be unfamiliar to some readers living in other parts of the English-speaking world. Please find here a list of terms used in the book. If you notice any that are missing, please let me know on hollybell@amandacadabra.com so the can be included in a future edition.

British English	American English
Spelling conventions	
—ise for words like surprise, realise	—ize for words like surprize, realize
—or for words like colour, honour	—our for words like color, honor
—tre for words like centre, theatre	—ter for words like center, theater
Mr Mrs Dr	Mr. Mrs. Dr.
Double consonants for words like traveller, counsellor	
A38, A374	A Road - a main road that is not a highway
A4	8.26" by 11.69"
Annexe	Annex
B6244	B Road - linking lower capacity traffic from residential properties to A roads
Battenberg	Cake made of pink and yellow diagonal squares, wrapped in marzipan
Baulk	Balk
Biscuit	Cookie

Bod	Shortened from of body
Boiler suit	Coveralls
Bonnet	Hood
Boot	Trunk
Car Park	Parking lot
Chicken Tikka Masala	Chicken cooked in yoghurt and spices, served with rice. Britain's unofficial national dish.
Common	Land over which people have traditional rightssuch as grazing animals, walking, collecting wood.
Coupla	Couple of
Corner shop	Small grocery store
Cornish pasty	Disk of puff pastry filled with meat and vegetables then folded and sealed at the edges.
Crumpet	Cake with holes in, served toasted with butter
Cuppa	Cup of tea
Curtains	Drapes
Double cream	Heavy cream, whipping cream

Émigré	French who fled France during The Revolution
Fairy cake	Small round light sponge cake topped with light icing, of a butterfly lid, formed by slicing off the top, dividing it and replacing at angles, like wings
Fridge	Refrigerator
Garden	Yard
Gastropub	Pub that serves high-quality food
Gingernut	Hard (like a nut but not containing any) ginger biscuit
Grey	Gray
Gritter	Salter, sander
Headmaster	Principal
Home Guard	Armed civilians who supported the British Army. Especially held in affection because of the 1960s -70s BBC television series 'Dad's Army'

Jewellery	Jewelry
Lolly	Slang for money
Luvvy	Term of affection
Loos	Restroom
Mac, mackintosh	Waterproof coat
Met, the	The Metropolitan Police Service, policing London
Minibus	Van, minicoach seating 8 - 30 people
Mobile phone	Cell phone
Momentarily	For a moment
M4	M class road - Expressway, Highway
Practise	Practice
Pavement	Sidewalk
Pub	Quiet, family friendly, coffee-shop style bar
Skivvy	Do the menial work of a skivvy - labourer
Scone	Smaller, lighter and fluffier than the US scone, served with cream and jam
Sellotape	Transparent sticky tape
Shepherd's Pie	Minced lamb with mashed potato

	topping
Shortcakes	Crunchy sweet cookie
Solicitor	Lawyer
Tap	Faucet
Tin	Can
Torch	Flashlight
Tyre	Tire
Van	Delivery truck
Victoria sandwich	Sponge cake with jam and cream filling
Whortleberry	Huckleberry

Cornish Accent and Dialect

Awright?	Hello
Dreckly	At some point
Emmet	Tourist
I'llItellywot	I will tell you what
Me 'andsome	Unisex term of endearment
Me luvver	Unisex term of endearment
Piddledowndidda?	Did it pour with torrential rain?
Up North	North of the Tamar River
Wozelike (wozz-ee-laeek)	Always up to something, little rascal
Zackly	Exactly

Cornish

Bian	Baby, small
Pur	Very

Scottish Accent

Ah	I
Auld	old
Canna	Cannot
Din'a	Did not
Dram	Drink
Fer	For
Noo	Now
Wi'	With
Wimmin	women
Ye	You

A NOTE ABOUT ACCENTS AND WICC'YETH

One or two of the villagers have a Cockney accent indicated by the missing 'h' at the beginning of words such as 'hello' becoming ''ello'. There is also a character with a Scottish accent, Cornishmen, a Frenchman, a Welshman and an Australian, with a Swede being quoted. These accents have been rendered as closely as possible using English spelling conventions.

Wicc'yeth, is a magical language peculiar to the world of Amanda Cadabra. If you are curious about the meaning of individual spell words, you will find a glossary at http://amandacadabra.com/wiccyeth/ and Amelia's Glossary with Pronunciation.

THE LAST WORD .... FOR NOW

Thank you once again, dear reader, for allowing me to share Amanda's story with you.

Best wishes,

Holly Bell

http://amandacadabra.com/contact/
http://amandacadabra.com/come-on-in/

Printed in Poland
by Amazon Fulfillment
Poland Sp. z o.o., Wrocław